"We–sh

"Yes, we should."

Loreli had never met such a quiet, yet intense man. He didn't say much, but there was a depth in his eyes that could make a woman drown in them before she even knew the water was rising.

"You don't have to sleep in the barn, Jake."

For a moment he said nothing, then responded, "I know."

Loreli's body reacted with heat. "Then don't," she whispered in a voice as hushed as the darkness. She stood, slowly walked to where he sat, and held out her hand. "Come."

Jake looked up at her and knew he couldn't resist her any longer. He rose to his feet, tossing aside misgivings, attitude, pride, and discipline; he wanted to cleave to her like Adam to Eve. To that purpose he pulled her into his arms and kissed her with all the pent-up emotion he had stored within, then scooping her up into his arms, he carried her into the house.

Other AVON ROMANCES

A GAME OF SCANDAL by Kathryn Smith
HIS SCANDAL by Gayle Callen
LONE ARROW'S PRIDE by Karen Kay
THE MAIDEN WARRIOR by Mary Reed McCall
A NECESSARY HUSBAND by Debra Mullins
THE RAKE: LESSONS IN LOVE by Suzanne Enoch
THE ROSE AND THE SHIELD by Sara Bennett

Coming Soon

ALL MY DESIRE by Margaret Moore
CHEROKEE WARRIORS: THE LOVER by Genell Dellin

And Don't Miss These
ROMANTIC TREASURES
from Avon Books

AN AFFAIR TO REMEMBER by Karen Hawkins
ONE NIGHT OF PASSION by Elizabeth Boyle
TO MARRY AN HEIRESS by Lorraine Heath

ATTENTION: ORGANIZATIONS AND CORPORATIONS
Most Avon Books paperbacks are available at special quantity discounts for bulk purchases for sales promotions, premiums, or fund-raising. For information, please call or write:

Special Markets Department, HarperCollins Publishers, Inc., 10 East 53rd Street, New York, N.Y. 10022–5299.
Telephone: (212) 207–7528. Fax: (212) 207-7222.

BEVERLY JENKINS

A Chance at Love

AVON BOOKS

An Imprint of HarperCollinsPublishers

AVON BOOKS
An Imprint of HarperCollins*Publishers*
10 East 53rd Street
New York, New York 10022-5299

First Avon Books paperback printing: September 2002

Avon Trademark Reg. U.S. Pat. Off. and in Other Countries, Marca Registrada, Hecho en U.S.A.
HarperCollins® is a registered trademark of HarperCollins Publishers Inc.

Printed in the U.S.A.

10 9 8 7 6 5 4 3 2 1

To my mother, Delores—
the best mama a girl could have

Chapter 1

Hanks, Kansas
June 1884

As Loreli Winters stood listening to the farmer bend-ing her ear, she wondered how much longer she would have to endure before she could politely excuse herself and slip away. The farmer's name was Henry Jud-son and he was a handsome brute: all brown eyes and muscles, but she, unlike the other women gathered in the grove behind the small church, had not come here to find a husband. Loreli had traveled to this small Black Kansas colony as a member of a wagon train transporting mail-order brides, but she'd signed on strictly for the adventure, not to be the wife of a Kansas homesteader. Her plans were to stay in town long enough to make sure everything worked out for the friends she'd made on the trip, then strike out West—California maybe. In the meantime, she had this gathering to get through.

1

In preparation for this Friday afternoon event, Loreli had gotten all gussied up, put on her powders and paints, and hoped her flashy blue dress would keep the farmers away. Here, for the first time in a long time, the golden quadroon beauty she'd inherited from her mixed ancestry would not be an advantage. In the billiard dens and smoking cars where she plied her gambling trade, Loreli's looks had won her more hands than she could count, especially when the pigeon spent more time ogling her bosom than his cards. In the past, she'd never hesitated using her face or figure to its best advantage, but not tonight; tonight there'd be no flirting. Loreli's future lay elsewhere. She just hoped the farmers would understand.

Judson, still talking, had three little girls. Although Loreli found the daughters pleasant enough, she had no intentions of taking over the job of raising them. She sensed from their father's conversation that all he was looking for was a replacement for his recently deceased wife.

When Judson began expressing hopes that his new bride would be able to can vegetables as well as his late wife did, Loreli interrupted him with a winning smile. "Mr. Judson, I see someone over there I need to speak with. It's been nice meeting you and your girls."

He opened his mouth to protest, but Loreli had already walked away.

Loreli made her way through the gathering of sixty or so men and women and saw that everywhere she looked folks were mingling and smiling. The celebratory sounds of fiddling and happy voices drifted on the late afternoon air. The brides had picked out their prospective mates before making the trip by using the photographs and portraits provided by the men to the wagon train's organizer,

Grace Atwood. The couples were meeting each other for the first time, and many were already lined up outside the small church waiting to be married.

Loreli threaded her way through the trestle tables set around the church grounds and nodded greetings in response to the familiar smiles beamed her way. The many trials and tribulations that had beset the women on the trek from Chicago seemed to have been forgotten. All the ladies had taken special pains to look their best; their hair was done, their dresses starched and pressed. The men were also decked out, in everything from fancy suspenders and fresh-pressed trousers to shiny new suits.

As Loreli shared congratulatory hugs and small-talk with the women, she asked after Belle, the young woman who shared her wagon, but Belle had already journeyed on with the man she would be marrying. That saddened Loreli because she'd dearly wanted to tell Belle good-bye. Loreli had taken the young woman under her wing during the journey from Chicago, and they'd become very close.

Loreli moved on to congratulate a few of her other friends and noted the interested eyes of some of the men standing nearby. She knew she was hard to miss in the low-cut blue satin dress that left the crowns of her shoulders bare, but because these men were here to marry women who'd become her friends, she didn't give any of the farmers more than a friendly nod in return. Loreli didn't want any misunderstandings.

In reality, though, she secretly wished to be one of the brides. She'd be thirty-five years of age come November, and on her own in life since the age of fourteen. She was tired. Tired of gambling dens, traveling, and having a life that discouraged roots, family, and peace of mind. Deep down inside, parts of herself yearned for the security of a farmhouse, a steady man, and a few kids, but her past life made fulfillment of that yearning impossible. What man wanted a wife whose occupation was gambling? None she'd ever met. Men wanted their women docile and of good character, and in society's eyes, she was neither. She decided she should just go back to her boardinghouse room, lest she be overwhelmed by her mood.

Loreli paused for a few moments to say farewell to Grace Atwood, the woman who'd organized the wagon train, then she headed back to claim the rented buggy she'd driven over in.

Beneath the tree by her buggy stood two little brown-skinned girls. They looked to be seven or eight years of age. Both copper faces were framed by long black plaits that shot out from their heads at a cockeyed angle, as if the person who'd braided them hadn't much experience with the task of doing hair. There were red ribbons tied on the ends, however, and Loreli wondered if the little ones had done the braids themselves. She also noticed that unlike all the other little girls she'd seen at the gathering this evening, these two were not gussied up in starched pinafores and Sunday slippers; they were attired like boys in denim trousers, flannel shirts, and sturdy boots.

At her approach, one of the girls asked politely, "May we speak with you?"

The diction was so adultlike, Loreli was taken aback. Her second jolt came when she realized the two girls were twins, identical, but for an old scar visible on the left side of the nose of the silent one.

"Certainly," Loreli responded, peering down. "What about?"

"Whose mama are you going to be?"

Loreli's perfectly arched brows knitted in puzzlement. "What do you mean?"

"Some of our friends are getting new mamas from the wagon train. Whose mama did you come to be?"

Loreli looked back at the ongoing celebration. She understood now. "I didn't come to be anybody's mama."

The girls passed a happy look between them. The twin who'd been doing all the speaking declared proudly, "Then you can be ours."

Loreli's golden eyes widened. "Excuse me?"

"We need a mama, and since Uncle Jake didn't want to come and pick one out, we decided we'd do it ourselves."

Loreli looked around the glade for this Uncle Jake, or anyone else who might belong to these beautiful but strange youngsters, but she saw only the folks gathered around the church. "Is your Uncle here?"

"No, he's in Lawrence at a convention. He's a Black Republican."

"I see," Loreli said. A voting man. "So, your uncle Jake doesn't know you're here?"

The girl shook her head. "No, Rebecca's watching us. Uncle's supposed to be back today." Then she added, "He's probably going to be real mad when he finds out we snuck off from Rebecca, but we need a mama."

"And he won't pick us out one," the other little girl said.

Loreli hid her smile. Any mama they managed to wrangle would be in trouble indeed. "How far away is home?"

"Not far."

"Then how about I ride back with you? You shouldn't be out in the countryside alone."

The talker twin asked earnestly, "Can my sister ride in

the buggy with you? We came over together on Phoebe, but Dede doesn't like horses very much."

"Of course," she replied, looking down at the shy Dede. Dede was the twin with the small scar on her nose, and now Loreli could tell them apart. "You've told me your sister's name. Now, what's yours?"

"I'm Bebe, it's short for Beatrice," she confessed. "Dede's real name is Deirdre."

"Well, I'm Loreli Winters. Pleased to meet you both."

Both girls offered smiles, and then Dede said, "We're pleased to meet you too."

Loreli looked at the big sorrel they'd ridden over on. Having been raised in Kentucky, Loreli knew good, sound horseflesh when she saw it, and the mare fit that description. Phoebe was a picture of health. Loreli could tell by the shiny coat that the animal received lots of care and love. "You rode that big ol' mare all by yourself?"

Bebe nodded. "Yep."

"I'm very impressed."

"Do you like horses?" Bebe asked.

"Love them."

Bebe smiled. "Then you'll make a perfect mama."

Loreli laughed. "Dede and I will get my buggy. You and Phoebe lead the way."

Loreli drove the black-covered buggy over the flat but rutted road; Bebe and Phoebe galloped alongside. After the long wagon-train ride from Chicago to Kansas, Loreli had grown accustomed to the silence of the land. Unlike the flat barren plains farther west, this portion of the state was green with trees and small rolling hills. She saw a few homesteads way off in the distance, but for the most part the land was open and unfenced as if Mother Nature was throwing wide her arms and offering endless possibilities.

"Is it much farther?" Loreli asked her passenger.

"No, the old riverbed is where we turn off."

Loreli nodded and kept her eyes on her team and the mounted Bebe. The girl's confidence in the saddle reminded Loreli of herself at that age. She too had ridden with her head high, hands sure, and back straight. Her father had called her a female centaur. Loreli thought Bebe could wear that title as well.

As they crested a hill, the panoramic expanse of the plains spread out before the eye like a green and gold blanket.

"Uh-oh," Dede said, peering out into the distance. She leaned out of the buggy and yelled to her sister. "Uncle's coming."

Bebe called back, "I see him."

Dede tugged gently on Loreli's arm. "We'd better stop, Loreli."

Loreli complied, but Dede's worried tone concerned her enough to ask, "He's not going to beat you, is he?"

"No, he'll just fuss. Why *won't* he get us a mama?"

Loreli couldn't answer. She felt better knowing the girls wouldn't come to any physical harm as a result of their escapade, but she questioned why the uncle had left them alone in the first place. Not that Loreli knew anything about raising children. When she was their age, she and her gambler father had been living on the road going from gambling den to whorehouse, looking for the next card game, however, even Loreli knew the twins weren't old enough to care for themselves.

Loreli pulled her small spyglass from her handbag and put it to her eye. Uncle Jake was riding fast, the stallion beneath him moving powerfully. Horse and rider were nearly identical in coloring: a rich mahogany. The horse was from good stock and so was he. Both were hand-somely built. Loreli put the glass away and waited to see how this little drama would play out.

When the uncle roared up, he slid from his horse. He snatched Bebe from the saddle and hugged her as if he'd found gold. Loreli could see the relief and love in his eyes. But when he finally turned the little one loose so she could breathe, he leaned back, looked into her eyes, and said, "You two scared me to death."

Still holding Bebe, he hastened over and grabbed up the smiling Dede. She too was squeezed tightly, then she threw her arms around his neck and hugged him back.

"I should tan both your hides," he threatened.

Loreli knew he wouldn't; it was obvious he loved them too much.

"We went to pick out a mama," Bebe explained spunkily.

Her uncle replied, quietly, "I thought we already dis-cussed this?"

Both girls looked to Loreli. The uncle turned and seemed to notice Loreli for the first time. For a few silent moments, the two adults observed each other.

He nodded distantly. "Hello. Thanks for keeping the girls safe."

"You're welcome."

"I'm Jake Reed."

"Loreli Winters."

"Never seen you before."

"I came in with the wagon train."

"The train with the mail-order women?"

Loreli detected the sarcasm in his tone. "Yes."

His eyes brushed her body in the low-cut blue dress. "Who're you marrying?

Before Loreli could reply, Bebe declared happily, "Nobody."

Dede added, "We want her to be our mama. Isn't she beautiful?"

Loreli, hand on her hip, waited for his reply.

He took a moment to assess her, then finally admitted, "Yes, she is," but then as if the discussion were over, he swung his gaze back to the girls in his arms. "Let's get you two home."

"But you haven't asked her yet!" Bebe protested.

"Asked whom, what?"

"Asked Loreli if she'll be our mama!"

He appeared at a loss. "Girls, I . . ."

Loreli tried to help him off the hook. "Girls, your uncle and I don't even know each other—"

"Aggie's new mama didn't know Aggie's papa when they got married."

Loreli gentled her voice, "But I'm not here to marry up. I'm on my way to California."

Twin sets of eyes saddened. "Oh."

The dejected tones just about broke Loreli's heart.

"See, she can't be your mama," the uncle pointed out gently.

Bebe asked him earnestly, "But when are we going to get one?"

Loreli could see tears of frustration in the child's eyes.

"Bebe—"

"Let me down, Uncle, please."

He obliged. With her back stiff as a pine, Bebe ran and mounted her horse. Before either adult could stop her, she took up Phoebe's reins and kicked the mare into a full gallop.

The uncle yelled, "Bebe! Get back here! Wait for your sister."

But she was gone like the wind.

Loreli could see the tears staining Dede's copper cheeks too.

The uncle looked grim. "Thank you," he told Loreli, as if she were somehow responsible.

Loreli wasn't having it. "Don't you dare blame this on me. You're the one who won't get them a mama."

His dark eyes flashed. Her golden ones flashed back.

"Come on, Dede," he responded shortly.

"I want to ride with Loreli."

He ignored her plea and started back to his big stallion.

"No!" Dede screamed. "I won't ride Fox! Nooo!"

"We're only going a short ways, De. The house isn't far." He tried to put her atop the mount, but she began kicking and screaming. "NOOO!"

Loreli realized this was much more than a tantrum; the girl acted terrified.

Dede's voice pierced the silence, "NOOOO! Don't make me! Don't make meeee."

Loreli couldn't stand it. She leapt from her rig, ran over, and very gently put her hand on his arm. "Please, I'll take her in with me. You lead the way, okay?"

For a few silent moments, he searched her face. Loreli saw pain.

He nodded silently, defeatedly. "Thanks."

Loreli took the trembling, sobbing child in her arms and held her tightly as she carried her back to the carriage.

Dede whispered fiercely, "I don't like horses."

"It's all right, precious. It's all right."

Dede's tears wet Loreli's bare shoulder. "I don't like horses."

"I know, baby. You can ride with me."

While the now mounted Uncle looked on, Loreli put Dede gently atop the buggy seat, then came around and got in. As she picked up the reins and glanced over at the still shaking child, Loreli told her, "We'll have you home in just a moment, pumpkin. Are you going to be okay?"

Dede nodded bravely.

Loreli gave her a soft smile and slapped down the reins to get the horse moving.

Just as the uncle had promised, the sprawling farm-house was only a short distance away. Loreli found the size of the place impressive. There were at least two barns that she could see, and the one and half story wood house stood like a sentinel in the rolling green fields surrounding it. The house had a fine sitting porch and screen-covered windows. Behind the house in a field of knee-high corn stood a set of towering windmills.

Lorlei's attention was caught by a young woman with a worried brown face who stepped out onto the porch. Her severely pulled back hair and plain calico dress marked her as female of the plains. Her dowdy appearance gave the impression that she was older than Loreli guessed her to truly be.

"Oh thank goodness," the woman gushed, sounding relieved. She hastened over to Reed and his mount. "You found them both."

He slid from his horse like a man well acquainted with the move. "Yeah, I did."

Ignoring Loreli, the woman came straight over to Dede and began to scold the child. "You should be ashamed of yourself, scaring everyone like this. I sent your sister to her room to think about what she's done. I suggest you join her."

Dede looked so dejected, Loreli wanted to sock the woman. Instead, Loreli took Dede's cold hand in hers, and said gently, "Let's go see if Bebe's okay."

Dede responded with a downcast nod. When she looked up, Loreli gave her a wink, and Dede returned a watery little smile.

Focusing on Loreli for the first time, the woman asked disdainfully, "And you are?"

"Loreli Winters."

The sour face looking Loreli up and down was so disapproving, Loreli felt compelled to toss back, "The girls want me to be their mama. Isn't that something?"

The woman's eyes went wide.

Satisfied with the woman's reaction, Loreli said to Dede, "Lead the way." Loreli's golden eyes flashed coolly at the uncle for not coming to his niece's defense, then she followed Dede into the house.

Jake felt the sting of the woman's glare, but supposed from where she'd been standing, he'd deserved it.

Loreli, entering the house with Dede, found the interior clean and sparsely furnished. This was a man's place: no rag rugs on the floor, no crocheted doilies tossed around to add a softening touch. One would be hard-pressed to believe two little girls lived here. Loreli wanted to know why, but knew she wouldn't be around long enough to have the question answered.

Holding on to Dede's hand, Loreli let herself be led down a narrow hallway to a closed door. "Is this your room?" Loreli asked.

The solemn child nodded.

Loreli softly knocked and quietly called, "Bebe. It's Loreli. May your sister and I come in?"

The sound of creaking floorboards and footsteps came from inside. The door was opened. A dejected Bebe stood in the portal. "Come in."

She then looked at her sister and said apologetically, "I'm sorry for leaving you, De."

"It's okay."

"Uncle didn't make you ride Fox, did he?"

"He was going to, but Loreli let me ride with her."

Bebe met Loreli's eyes. "Dede doesn't like horses."

"I know. She told me."

"Our mama was killed in a horse accident. Dede was with her."

Loreli now understood. Had she been involved in such a tragedy, she wouldn't want to be around horses either. She squeezed Dede's hand reassuringly. "We're all scared of something, Dede, so it's okay. For me, it's spiders."

Dede asked, "Really?"

"Yep. Can't stand them. They give me the willies." Loreli shook her shoulders in a show of exaggerated revulsion and both girls giggled.

Outside the house, Jake Reed said to Rebecca, "You were hard on the girls, Rebecca."

Rebecca turned his way. "Somebody has to be, Jacob. And what on earth was Dede doing riding with that fancy woman. Where'd she come from?"

"The wagon train."

"She one of those mail-order brides?"

"She came with them, but claims she didn't come to marry anybody."

"Well, I'm glad of that. Can you imagine her married to someone we know? Let's just pray she doesn't stay around here long. Town like ours doesn't need soiled doves."

Jake wasn't really listening. His mind was still on Dede's reaction to being put on the stallion's back. With her screams echoing in his mind, he wondered if she'd ever get over her fear. He was grateful the Winters woman had been there. He doubt he'd ever forget how tenderly she'd comforted Dede. Her tender handling was the kind of caring he wanted Rebecca to show the girls, but she seemed more bent on criticizing and correcting them than showing them kindness.

Rebecca's voice cut into his thoughts. "Did you hear me, Jake?"

He looked down into her scolding brown eyes and confessed, "No, sorry. I was thinking about Dede."

"Were those girls mine, I'd take a strap to them for running off that way. Anything could've happened to them. I sent them into the house this afternoon to read from the Bible. Next I knew they were gone."

Jake realized that this strident, rigid young woman would make a poor mother to his sister's twins. Having lived his life under a parent who did nothing but criticize and berate, Jake did not want the girls to suffer the same fate. "You're right about the dangers, Rebecca, and thanks for looking after them while I was gone, but they're both safe now," then he added, "And I'm not strapping them. They're still trying to adjust to my sister's death. They'll settle down."

"When?"

He shrugged.

"Those girls are willful; they don't mind, and I have to stand over them to make sure their chores are done right. Spare the rod, spoil the child, Jake Reed. A good strapping never hurt anyone."

Her litany of the girls' sins did not sit well with him. They were eight years old, for heaven's sake. "I'm not strapping them, Rebecca. Leave it be."

Her chin tightened as it was wont to do when they butted heads over an issue, particularly issues relating to the twins. Rebecca believed that a woman shouldn't read anything but the Bible, and thought it scandalous that he allowed the girls to read the newspapers and political broadsides that came to him via the mails. She also thought he should *make* Dede get on a horse—tie her to the saddle if necessary to cure her of what Rebecca called "willful tantrums." Jake, knowing why horses set off such a strong reaction in his niece, refused.

Rebecca then said, "Well, how was the meeting?"

Jake sighed with frustration. "A waste." The meeting in Lawrence had not gone well. It had originally been convened to talk frankly about the rising distrust between the White and Black wings of the Republican party. On a national level the Republican party had been slowly but surely distancing itself from its Black constituency, and the issues that affected them. In some areas Republicans were even siding with Redemptionist Democrats to deny the right to vote to the very people who'd helped get the Republicans elected. Black members of the party wanted answers, but the meeting in Lawrence, tense from the opening gavel, had disintegrated into name-calling and threats. Jake had returned home angry and disappointed that nothing had been resolved.

"Papa thinks race shouldn't be involved in politics at all," Rebecca said. "He thinks we should tend our farms and churches and leave the politics to those who know better."

They'd had this discussion many times before. Jake didn't feel like arguing with someone who had no faith in the abilities of her own race. "I should go in and see what the girls are doing."

He went inside.

Rebecca followed.

Loreli and the girls were giggling over things that scared them when Bebe's attention fixed on something by the door. Loreli turned and saw the uncle and the sour-faced woman standing there. "You know," she said, "I didn't get your name."

"Rebecca Appleby."

"Pleased to meet you."

Apparently, Rebecca didn't share the sentiment because she turned away from Loreli and addressed the twins. "Girls, you have chores. Tell Miss Winters good-bye."

Bebe looked resigned, then offered up quietly, "Good-bye, Loreli."

The sadness in the twin set of brown eyes pulled at

Loreli's heartstrings again. She said to them, "It's been nice meeting you."

"We liked meeting you too," Dede responded. Dede looked up into Loreli's face and asked earnestly, "Are you sure you can't be our mama, Loreli?"

Loreli tried not to be moved by the plea in the little one's eyes and voice, but failed. She stroked Dede's hair. "I'm sure, pumpkin."

A tight-lipped Bebe told her sister. "Come on, De. Let's go out to the barn."

Loreli watched their exit with a lump in her throat. She then trained her eyes on Uncle Jake, and told him warningly, "Find those girls a mama."

She gave his sour-faced companion a short dismissive glance, dearly hoping Rebecca wasn't a candidate; faces with that much vinegar had no business being around children. "I'll be heading back now. Nice meeting you both."

The uncle stepped back so she could leave the room. Their eyes met, but she had nothing else to say.

Only after she'd driven out of sight of the house did Loreli let her melancholy have its head. What she wouldn't give to have daughters as fine as those two. Even though she'd only been with them a short while, Loreli liked them both. Remembering Dede's screams filled her heart and made her want to turn around, and go back to give Dede one last hug. The child needed it, Loreli sensed. Getting a mother might help ease her over her fears, as long as the mother wasn't that Appleby woman. Loreli thought back on Bebe too. With the right guidance, Bebe had the potential to grow into a fearless and formidable young woman, full of spunk and determination. Loreli wondered what it might be like to wake up to their smiling faces every day, to share their secrets and watch them grow into women. To have experiences as precious as these would be worth whatever she'd have to give up in return. Not that it would be much. In the last ten years, she'd accumulated enough wealth to live however she pleased, but she had little else. She had no family, no roots, no church. Her faith in God and in herself had been all she'd ever had, even back during the lean times. Like Bebe and Dede, she too had grown up without her mama; and like them, had wanted one desperately. Had Halle Winters lived, she'd be an old woman now. And under her loving guidance, Loreli's life might've been different. She might've learned how to cook and sew instead of how to perform card tricks and the fine art of picking pockets. Maybe she'd even have a husband and a passel of kids by now, instead of memories of every gambling den from Louisville to Atlanta. Being with Bebe and her sister, Dede, made feelings well up inside Loreli she didn't even know she had. She blamed it all on the wagon train. The journey had changed her. Admittedly, she was still her old sassy self, but she'd noticed a new layer forming beneath the cynicism, a layer that seemed to be softening her outlook on life. Lady gamblers seldom rubbed shoulders with *good* women, but the *good* women of the train had taken her in, shown her love, respect, and she now called them friends. The brides had come to Kansas filled with the hope of new possibilities. Some of that thinking must have rubbed off, because Loreli wanted that too, but with such a checkered past, she'd never have the slow, traditional life other women took for granted. She put the twins out of her mind and concentrated on driving.

As he did every night, Jake looked in on the girls before heading off to his own bed. As he listened to their soft breathing and gazed down on their sleeping faces, he thought about his sister, Bonnie. Each small face held remnants of her—the shape of her brow, the curve of her chin. Dede had her sweet nature, Bebe her zest for life. Today's escapade had scared him. Coming home and finding them gone was not an experience he wanted to repeat. He'd been frantic. Although he prided himself on the hold he usually kept on his emotions, not knowing their whereabouts had shattered that control. All he could think about was finding them, and finding them safe. Then to learn they'd gone after a mama—well, he could see that the years ahead weren't going to be easy ones.

Jake was a farmer, and his brief stint at Howard College qualified him as the closest thing the area had to an animal doctor, but he wasn't wealthy by anyone's measure. The corn and hogs he raised brought in money at harvest time, and although his neighbors rarely paid for his medical services in coin, Jake managed to make sure the girls were clothed and fed. All that aside, today proved that they needed more than just food and clothing. Had Bonnie not lost her life in the carriage accident, she'd be the one raising them, but they were now his to look after. He'd initially wanted to blame the girls' sudden quest for a new mother on the organizers that brought in the mail-order women; after all, they were the ones responsible for the hubbub that had been sweeping the colony for the past six weeks. If the twins' friends hadn't been so excited about getting new mothers, today's incident might not have happened. But Jake knew such blame was misplaced. Nothing was that simple. They were girls, and one day would grow into women. They'd be needing guidance along the way, and he didn't know a thing about getting them to that point. He couldn't even take them shopping in town because he knew nothing about buying their clothes, and so rather than ask Rebecca to handle the tasks, he kept them in boots and denims. Neither of the girls seemed to mind, at least so far, but he knew that would change. Soon, their heads would be filled with the yearnings and urges of adolescent girls, and he'd be about as much help to their maturation as a Klansman at a Black Republican rally.

Jake reached down and gently stroked Bebe's brow. Lord knows, he'd already decided to get married just for their sake, but suitable women were hard to find out here. He knew folks in the area were putting money on Rebecca Appleby saddling him. Rebecca had emigrated here ten years ago with her preacher father. She was a decent, churchgoing woman who could cook, sew, and at twenty-five years of age still young enough to bear children of her own, but the fact that the girls didn't care for her or she for them stood as a formidable barrier to asking for her hand. If he married for the sake of the girls, Jake thought it only right that the future Mrs. Jake Reed be a woman they could love, and be loved by in return. Rebecca's preacher daddy had instilled a lot of fire and brimstone in her, and every now and then it raised its righteous head. Like today. Yes, he'd been angry at the girls for disobeying her and leaving the house, but not angry enough to take a strap to them. He didn't know when they'd finally be at peace with Bonnie's death, but the girls seemed to believe that finding a new mother would solve all of their problems. He wasn't naive enough to believe that, but there was nothing wrong with hope.

Chapter 2

⌒⌒◯⌒⌒

When Jake got up Saturday morning, the girls were
gone. Their empty bed filled his insides with the
same stomach-roiling panic he'd had yesterday. Hoping
against hope that they'd just gotten up early, he ran out to
the barns and pens, calling their names. Silence. He stood
in the center of the front yard and yelled across the plains,
but received no reply.

He hurried into the barn to saddle Fox, and found a
piece of paper nailed to the stallion's stall. He snatched it
free and read the childish handwriting.

Dear Uncle,

We will come back when we find a mama.

                                   Beatrice and Deirdre Case

After saddling his horse, a tight-lipped Jake rode hard
towards the rising sun.

His first stop was the Gibson place. Agatha Gibson was Bebe's best friend. Their pa Arthur, was a big-boned man from Tennessee, and the colony's blacksmith. He'd gotten himself a mail-order woman two years ago. Her name was Denise and she seemed a perfect fit for the giant Gibson and his two little girls. Art's first wife, Jeanette, died giving birth to their youngest daughter Charlene.

Jake's hard knocks brought Arthur to the door in his union suit. His large hands were cradling a shotgun, but upon seeing it was Jake on the porch, the big man visibly relaxed.

"Thought it might be trouble," Gibson said, in explanation of the gun. He looked back over his shoulder and called, "It's only Jake, Denise."

Gibson, like some of the other colonists, had come to Kansas as part of the famed Exodus of '79 to escape the bloody Redemption being waged by the South's Democrats. As a result, he was constantly on alert for anyone bent upon harming him, his family, or his rights as a citizen. "What're you doing out this time of morning, Jake? The sun just got up."

"Are the girls here?"

Gibson looked puzzled. "Yeah, my girls are here. They're 'sleep, though."

Jake held on to his patience. "Not your girls, Arthur. Mine. Are they here?"

"Why no. They missing?"

Jake nodded tersely, then gave him a quick account of the twins' quest for a new mother. "This whole bride thing has them on a wild streak."

"Girls need a woman."

"I'm finding that out." Jake ran a frustrated hand over

his short hair. "I'm going into town. If the twins show up here, make them stay put. I'll stop by on my way back."

Arthur nodded. "Sure will. If you need help searching, just come on back and let me know. Hope you find them."

"Thanks. Me too."

Jake mounted Fox and continued the ride to town. As the big stallion ate up the distance, Jake tried to think like an eight-year-old. If he were the girls, where would he go? He was only a few miles from Rebecca's house, but he doubted they'd go there, so it made no sense to stop by to see. He also had no desire to hear Rebecca's, "I told you sos."

At the train station, the driver finally got all Loreli's trunks, valises and hat boxes unloaded from his hack. She tipped him generously for his help, and he departed with a friendly wave.

The train tracks were located about eight miles west of town. The depot was nothing more than a shed but Loreli didn't care as long as she could purchase a ticket. There were about ten people waiting for the train. According to the hand-lettered sign on the depot it was scheduled to arrive within the hour. Loreli, dressed in an emerald green traveling costume and matching hat, spotted a uniformed ticket agent seated behind a table. She headed over to purchase her ticket, and suddenly froze with surprise. In conversation with him were Bebe and Dede. *What are they doing here?* Loreli scanned the area for their uncle or the sour-faced Rebecca Appleby, but saw neither. Leaving her piled-up trunks and hat boxes, Loreli hurried over to get an answer to this early morning mystery.

She heard the agent saying to the girls in exasperated

tones, "I can't sell you a ticket. You don't have any money."

"But—" Bebe began. "We—"

"Mornin' girls."

The twins spun in unison at the sound of Loreli's voice.

The ticket agent asked Loreli with what sounded like relief, "Are these two yours?"

Loreli nodded, her censuring eyes focused on the girls. "I'll take it from here, sir. Thanks."

He rose to his feet, and gushed gratefully, "No, thank you," then he hustled away.

Both girls looked very guilty.

Loreli asked coolly. "What are you two doing here?"

Silence.

Finally Bebe said, "We're going to find a mama."

"Where's your uncle?"

Dede offered meekly, "At home."

"And what do you think he's doing right now?"

Neither girl offered an answer, so Loreli did. "Probably searching the countryside, worried sick."

Twin heads dropped.

"You *should* be ashamed. Now hustle your little selves over to that stack of trunks while I find a hack." She then added a warning, "And ladies, if you disappear on me— pray your uncle finds you before I do."

Loreli waited until they were standing beside her trunks before she strode off to find someone to take them all back to town. The twins needed a mama all right—one with a switch in her hand.

The hack driver who'd initially ferried Loreli to the train depot had been awaiting a return fare, so he was more than happy to take her and the girls back to town. He reloaded her trunks, valises and hat boxes, and after tying the reins of Bebe's mare, Phoebe, to the back of the hack, finally got them underway.

Due to the space taken up by all of Loreli's luggage, Dede had to sit on Loreli's lap. Bebe was squeezed in beside them. Loreli could see the furtive glances the girls kept sending her way when they thought she wasn't looking, but for the first little while Loreli didn't say anything, mainly because she didn't know what to say. How do you relay to two eight-year-olds the anguish they were undoubtedly causing their uncle by running away, but then again, how do you explain to an adult how much a mama means when you don't have one? "You know girls, I grew up without my mama too."

They looked surprised.

Dede asked, "What happened to her?"

"She died in a fire."

There was silence for a moment, then Bebe asked, "How old were you?"

"Three."

"We were seven."

Loreli looked down at them. "You miss your mama a lot, don't you?"

Both girls nodded solemnly, then Bebe added, "We have her picture, and we say hello to her every night in our prayers."

"That's a good thing. I don't have a picture. In fact, I don't even remember what she looked like. I was too young when she died, I guess."

There was silence again, then Loreli said, "Your uncle loves you both very much, and your running away is scaring him to death."

Both girls looked ashamed again, and Loreli told them softly. "I know you're not trying to scare him on purpose, but promise me you'll never do this again. Ever."

Both girls met her eyes.

"Promise me."

Dede was the first to break down, and said quietly, "I promise."

Loreli looked to Bebe. "Be? Promise me."

Bebe audibly sighed her surrender, then offered up grudgingly, "I promise too. We don't want Uncle Jake to be scared."

"Thank you," Loreli said, giving them a hug. She then bestowed a rewarding kiss on each smooth brown brow. "Your uncle shouldn't have to go to sleep every night worrying if you two will be in your beds when the sun comes up," she added gently. "I know it's hard being without your mother, but she's with you in your hearts. Always will be."

Loreli realized that her father had often comforted his own motherless child with the same words. In the end, Loreli had survived and they would too. The fact that their uncle provided a stable home was also in their favor. She'd never had that.

Once they returned to town, Loreli had the driver stop at the sheriff's office. She wanted to see if Jake Reed had reported his nieces missing. He had. In fact, when she and the girls entered, he was inside talking to the sheriff.

Loreli could see the worry drop from Reed's features when he saw the girls. The worry was replaced by sternness. "Where were you?"

Loreli answered. "I found them at the station."

His eyes widened as he scanned their faces "At the train station?"

Bebe nodded. "The agent wouldn't sell us a ticket, though."

Dede explained: "He said we needed some money."

Jake's head dropped and he chuckled in spite of his earlier worry. "Where were you going, girls?"

Loreli cracked. "Without any coin? Nowhere." She could sense the sheriff evaluating her, taking in her expensive traveling costume and feather-tipped hat. She knew from experience that he was trying to determine if she were street woman, confidence woman, or both, so she said to him, "Mornin', Sheriff. Name's Loreli Winters."

He nodded. "Morning, Miss Winters. I'm Sheriff Walter Mack. Thanks for your help." Mack was tall, White, and appeared to be in his late fifties, early sixties.

Jake Reed met her eyes, and Loreli swore he looked no more pleased to see her than he'd been yesterday. "Yes, thank you." He then turned back to his nieces. "You girls have to promise me you'll never do this again."

Dede confessed, "We already promised Loreli."

He looked surprised.

Bebe added, "She said our running away scares you to death."

His lip tightened beneath his mustache. "She's right."

"Loreli's mama got burned up in a fire when she was three," Dede said, "but she doesn't have a picture of her mama like we do."

Loreli, feeling the sympathy in Dede's words, smiled. "And that makes you girls very lucky."

Jake took in the fancy-dressed Miss Winters and had to admit, he hadn't expected that she of all people would understood how the girls must be feeling about losing their mother. Even though she appeared to be of questionable character, he was grateful. "I appreciate you bringing them back."

"Glad I could help."

"Ready to go home?" Jake asked the twins.

They nodded.

First though, both girls gave Loreli a strong hug. Bebe whispered emotionally against Loreli's waist, "I wish you could be our mama."

Loreli, gently holding them both, replied truthfully, "I do too." Loreli knew Jake Reed was watching, but she ignored him. She bent down and looked Bebe and Dede in the eyes. "Now, remember what I said about your mother. Okay?"

The girls nodded.

"And no more running away—you promised. A woman always keeps her word."

They nodded once more.

Loreli stood. The girls looked as sad as she felt.

Jake Reed wondered how she'd been able to establish such a rapport with the twins in so short a time. "All right," he said to them, "let's head home."

The girls offered Loreli a departing wave, then were gone.

After their exit, Loreli turned to leave too, but the sheriff's voice stopped her. "You wanted anywhere, Miss Winters?"

Loreli had been expecting the question. She turned back and drawled saucily, "Sheriff, I'm wanted everywhere— but not by the law. Thanks for asking, though."

He smiled, just as she knew he would. She threw him a wink, then exited back out onto the street.

*　　*　　*

Playing the Good Samaritan had caused Loreli to miss her train, so now she would have to cool her heels until the next train on Friday. The hack driver had waited, so she had him drive her back to the boardinghouse she'd checked out of earlier in the day. On the way she surveyed the town. It was small by anyone's standards: one general store, a milliner's shop, a bank, a livery. A sign on the front of one building read: TAYLOR'S UNDERTAKING— Telegraph and Post Office. She assumed there was also a saloon somewhere, more than likely outside of town, because most communities had at least one nearby. In all, there were about ten buildings connected by a weathered plank walk that kept the citizens from having to slosh through the muddy street when it rained.

Loreli asked the driver. "This town have a name?"

"Yes, ma'am. We call it Hanks."

"Hanks?"

"Yes. It's named that for the soldier who started the town."

"I see." At least she now knew where she was.

The boardinghouse was situated only a short distance from town set among a small group of houses. The proprietor, a gnarled, old brown-skinned woman named Mrs. Boyd, took the paying guest back happily. "You want the same room, Miss Winters?"

"Sure."

"How in the world did you miss the train?"

"Business," was all Loreli would say. She doubted Reed wanted his news spread all over Hanks.

"Well, welcome back. I'll have my son take those trunks and things around to your room."

"Thanks, Mrs. Boyd."

With that bit of business transacted, Loreli went back to the room. By dusk, she was bored. Wondering if she could at least horn in on a card game, she walked down to the sheriff's office.

When he looked up from his desk and saw her, he smiled. "Well, hello there, Miss Winters. What can I do for you?"

"Where can I find a good poker game?"

He went still for a moment. "Poker?"

"Yes, you know, the card game?"

He looked her up and down, then asked, "You're a gambler, then?"

"All my life."

He shook his head with wonder. "Never played cards with a woman before, but I consider myself pretty good."

"Well, that's two for the table. You know anyone else?"

A grin creased his sun-weathered face. "You're serious, aren't you?"

"Yes, sir, I am. Haven't played in so long my hands are starting to itch."

He laughed. "Why'd you come to me?"

"Because lawmen always know where the best games are."

Chuckling, he nodded in agreement. "That we do. That we do. Tell you what. I'm on duty tonight, so we can play here. Give me an hour to rustle up my usual pigeons, and then come on back."

It was Loreli's turn to grin. "You've got a deal."

In an hour Loreli returned dressed in a beautiful indigo gown and smelling good. The sheriff introduced her to his friends: general-store owner, Bert Green; rancher, Howard Burke; and the skeptical-looking banker, Sol Diggs.

Diggs declared, "I don't play with women."

Loreli flashed him a winning smile, "Neither do I."

The rest of the men laughed. Diggs, caught off guard by Loreli's golden charm and beauty, surrendered.

By the end of the third hand, the men knew Loreli was no rube. Her skill with the cards far exceeded their own. She played shrewdly, decisively, and bluffed better than anyone they'd ever sat down with before. Each man sensed she could've wiped the floor with them, but she kept the blood-letting to a minimum.

An hour later, as the men folded and Loreli raked in another pot, the sheriff said, "Loreli, I'm real glad you insisted on playing for pennies."

"Me too," Diggs admitted reluctantly, "otherwise, you'd own my bank by now."

The rotund dark-skinned Bert Green added, "And my store."

They were distracted by the door opening. Loreli, in the midst of raking in her pile of pennies, glanced up to see Jake Reed walk in. When her eyes met his, his registered surprise, then, as he saw the cards, disapproval. Loreli found the judgment irritating. Determined to ignore him from then on, she went back to gathering her coins.

Sheriff Mack asked, "What brings you in, Jake? Those girls aren't gone again, are they?"

Reed shook his head, "No. Came to tell Bert his mare's finally foaled. It's a filly."

Bert Green smiled broadly. "Why, that's good news. The mare doing okay?"

"Just fine. I'll drop my bill by the store in the morning."

"All right." Then Bert asked, "Do you know Miss Loreli?"

"We've met." His eyes were frosty; his tone, no warmer.

Loreli wondered how such a stiff-necked man ever hoped to raise two spirited little girls. "Evenin', Mr. Reed."

He nodded. "Miss Winters."

"You want to sit in a few hands?" Howard Burke asked Jake. "Maybe you can stop her from winning the whole town. She's already won the bank, my ranch, and Bert's store."

"I can't. Rebecca's watching the girls until I get back."

Sol Diggs, the banker, asked, "When are you going to marry that woman, doc? Everyone's waiting, you know. Woman like that will keep you away from all that union nonsense."

Loreli watched Reed's eyes go cold. She wondered what kind of union nonsense the banker had been referring to. She thought Reed was a Black Republican.

Reed's voice mirrored the chill in his eyes. "Any woman I marry will have to put up with my union nonsense, Sol, just as you will before we're done."

The tension in the air rose. Loreli got the impression that Reed and the banker didn't agree on whatever this union issue revolved around.

Sheriff Mack intervened. "Gentlemen, we're here for a friendly game, not political fisticuffs."

Neither man said anything else, but it was clear that their disagreement would continue. In an attempt to defuse the situation, Loreli cut in. "Gentlemen, shall we play another hand, or call it a night?"

Howard Burke pushed his chair back from the table. "I have to get home. Promised my wife I wouldn't be out real late."

The others offered up similar pledges, so the game came to an end. Loreli placed the cards back in her hand-bag and stood. Still ignoring Reed, she said, "Gentlemen, it has been a pleasure. I'll be here until Friday morning. If you get together again, I'll be hurt if I'm not included."

The sheriff cracked humorously, "And our pockets will be hurt if we do, but don't worry. We'll let you know."

"Where are you staying, Miss Winters?" Howard Burke asked.

"With Mrs. Boyd."

"Then I'd be honored if you'd let me escort you back."

Loreli was just about to take him up on the offer when Jake Reed declared, "I'll walk her back, Howard. I'm headed that way."

Loreli found his offer surprising to say the least, but she sensed it had little to do with concerns for her safety.

Burke looked disappointed, but nodded a gentlemanly surrender. "If you insist. No lady should be walking alone at night." Burke turned to the sheriff and added, "No of-fense to how you do your job, Walt."

The sheriff replied, "None taken."

Loreli didn't really want Jake Reed escorting her any-where, but could hardly say that now. It was only a short walk, though. What could happen?

Loreli grabbed her indigo silk shawl and spread it lightly around her bare shoulders. "I'm ready, Mr. Reed."

He opened the door with a politeness she knew he didn't feel. Loreli turned to the other men. "Thanks for a fine evening, gentlemen."

They offered their good-byes, and a moment later, she and Jake Reed were walking together in the silent night. After they'd taken a few steps, he said, "He's married, you know."

"Who?"

"Howard Burke."

"Oh. Is that why you butted in?"

Jake's lips tightened.

"Did you think I was going to lure him into an alley and take his wallet or just throw him to the ground and make him renounce his marriage vows?" She looked over at his granite features. "Never mind. I already know the answer."

Jake wasn't accustomed to being put in his place by such a blunt-talking woman. She was right, however. He had thought she might take advantage of Howard Burke. Burke was a good man, but his weakness for flashy, younger women was well known. "Play cards with men often?"

"All the time," she replied without shame. "It's how I make my living."

He stopped. "You're a gambler?"

Loreli looked into that handsome face and chuckled sarcastically, "No, I'm a minister's wife." She began walking again. "Yes, I'm a gambler, an occupation I'm sure you don't approve of."

"That's not for me to judge," he replied emotionlessly.

Loreli laughed. "Oh, for heaven's sake. Your face twisted up like a child drinking vinegar when you walked in and saw me sitting at that table."

Jake knew she was right. It had bothered him; it still did. "Just had no idea I'd find you there."

"Especially with a deck of cards in my hand."

Jake didn't answer.

Loreli let that go, then took note of all the businesses that had closed down now that night had fallen. "This place shuts down pretty early."

"Saloon's open until midnight."

She refused to be baited. "No thanks. Guess I've forgotten how provincial small towns can be."

"Where were you born?"

"Kentucky."

"Slave or free?"

"Slave." Loreli wasn't ashamed of her past. Like the other three million captives held before the war, she'd had no say in her birth. She glanced his way. "You? Where were you born?"

"Right here in Kansas."

"Slave or free?"

"Free."

That surprised her. "Interesting. Were your parents free too?"

"Mother was. My father was born a slave in Missouri."

"I see. Are they still living?"

"No, my mother passed away during the war. Pa died about ten years ago. What about your parents? The girls said you lost your mother in a fire?"

"Yes."

"What about your father?"

"Died in my arms when I was fourteen."

In the silence that followed, they walked past the milliner's shop and Bert Green's general store. Loreli asked, "The girls doing okay?"

"Yeah."

"How long have they been with you?"

"Little over a year now."

"Must have been quite an adjustment having to take them in."

"It still is, but I'm managing," Jake said.

"What happened to their father?"

Jake shrugged. "He left my sister before the girls were born. Never met him."

"They're very special."

"Yes, they are."

"They love you a lot."

"They mean a lot to me as well."

Loreli was pleased to hear him declare his feelings for his nieces so openly; some men viewed such confessions as unmanly.

By now the short walk to the boardinghouse had been completed. Standing outside its small white gate, Loreli said, "Thanks for the escort."

"You're welcome. You didn't really win the bank and store did you?"

Loreli studied him for a moment, then asked teasingly, "Why? Are you going to make me give them back?"

"This is a small town with small town folks. They're not used to being taken by sharps."

Loreli wondered if he were deliberately trying to offend her. "We were playing for pennies." At his skeptical expression, she added, "It was just a friendly game to pass the time, Mr. Reed. Nothing more. Why on earth would I want to own anything in this poor excuse for a town?" When he didn't answer, she said tightly, "You really need to loosen your stays, Reed, before you injure yourself. Good night."

After closing the door to her room, Loreli tossed her handbag on her bed. She knew she shouldn't let Jake Reed and his judgmental self get under her skin, but he had. If she had a nickel for every time somebody looked down their sanctimonious nose at her, she'd be even wealthier than she was now, but as it stood, she'd learned at a young age to ignore such high-handed folks. Why Jake should be such a thorn was a mystery. Taking off her shawl and hanging it inside the armoire, Loreli began removing the pins from her hair. Maybe Jake's sneering manner affected her more because of the seeds planted in her heart by his twin nieces. Maybe, because she couldn't believe a man that handsome could be so—arrogant, was the word she decided upon. He acted as if being around her fouled his air. She still couldn't get over how he'd bushwhacked Howard Burke's offer to escort her back here. Jake clearly believed she'd been up to no good. In the end, Loreli changed into her nightgown, and decided his attitude didn't much matter; in a few more day, she'd be on her way to California and this backwater would just be another memory.

After tucking the twins into their beds, Jake Reed sat in the parlor's silence and let the day's tension seep out of his bones, or at least tried to. The day had certainly ended a lot calmer than it had begun, even with the difficult birth of Bert's new filly. He could still feel the panic that had grabbed him this morning upon finding the girls gone. How on earth had Loreli Winters gotten them to make that pledge not to run off again? It was quite obvious there was more to her than he initially assumed, a lot more, he mused sarcastically, thinking of the card game he'd found her in tonight. By her flashy clothing and bold ways, he'd initially assumed her to be some type of fancy woman, whore maybe. That she was a gambler threw him a bit; it didn't raise her stature any higher, but at least she didn't work on her back.

He walked out onto the moonlit porch. The path to figuring out the best plan for the girls' future was no clearer than it had been yesterday. Arthur Gibson was right. The twins needed a woman in their lives. When they first arrived, Jake had been unwilling to admit that fact, because he'd arrogantly believed he had the ability to do it alone. Now? He ran his hand over his hair, a signature move of frustration. Glancing up at the stars, he called out softly, "Your baby brother needs help down here, Bonnie girl. Can you see what you can do?"

He sat alone in the dark for a few long moments longer, then went inside and went to bed.

At breakfast on Monday, Jake asked the girls how they'd feel about him marrying Rebecca. In response, the kitchen had been silent for the last two minutes.

Jake finally asked them, "Well? No opinions? Bebe, what do you think?"

Bebe fiddled with the eggs and grits on her plate. She shook her head, indicating she had nothing she wished to say.

He glanced across at Dede. "What about you, De?"

Dede shook her head.

Jake spoke gently. "Come on now, girls. You must be thinking something."

Bebe told him quietly, "You don't really want us to say."

Her soft voice, so filled with sadness, pulled at his heartstrings. Jake responded with the truth. "You're wrong, Be. Because whomever I marry is going to be your mother, and it should be someone you can love."

Bebe met his eyes. "Then we don't want Rebecca as our mama."

Dede added, "She doesn't like us to have fun, or to get dirty."

"Life isn't always about fun, girls," Jake explained.

Bebe replied respectfully, "But sometimes it is, Uncle Jake."

Jake studied her honest little face. She was right of course, and getting dirty was part of that fun. He remembered many a day he and Bonnie had returned home covered with river mud. Amazingly, his Bible-thumping father hadn't minded too much; he'd send his two dirty children to the pump to bathe, and no sin was attached. "Then who would you want me to pick?"

"How about Loreli?" Dede asked hopefully.

Jake sighed. "We've already discussed this, De."

"I know, but you asked me to tell you the truth."

He had, hadn't he? He tried again. "All right, besides Miss Winters, is there anyone else?"

Silence.

Bebe finally declared, "It's all right, Uncle Jake. Dede and I decided we don't want a mama anymore. We'll just grow up without one."

That said, Bebe pushed away from the table. "Come on, De. Let's go feed Suzie."

Jake sighed unhappily.

Dede got up from her chair, but instead of following her twin out the back door, she stopped in front of her uncle and confessed, "Bebe's not telling the truth. We didn't decide. We just don't want anybody for a mama but Loreli. That's all."

He looked into the small brown face that was a true miniature of his sister Bonnie's, and was moved by her honesty. "Thanks, De."

"You're welcome."

A moment later she was gone, and he was left with her words: *"We just don't want anybody for a mama but Loreli. That's all."*

Jake ran his hand over his head. Now what? he wondered. He was honest enough to admit the girls were right about Rebecca. She wouldn't make them a good mother. Her joyless outlook on life would stifle their buoyant spirits. He didn't want to come home after a long night away worrying whether Rebecca had strapped the girls, or had them standing in the corner for being themselves. In addition to the hogs that he raised and the crops that he grew, people in the area came to him all the time seeking help for their sick or injured animals. In trying to help his neighbors it was not uncommon for him to be away for hours on end in that capacity, and in his capacity as a delegate for the Republican party. No, Rebecca wouldn't do, and out of all fairness he needed to tell her that so she could get on with her life. In a way, he was glad he hadn't already asked her to be his wife because had they already been married when the girls first arrived this dilemma would be moot.

Jake stepped outside and found the girls tossing corn to the chickens. Suzie, a big brown hen, ruled the pens with such authority that at mealtime the three younger hens—Babe, Myrtle, and Peg—always let her feed first. The pigs, cows, ducks and other animals gave the old biddy a wide berth as well. They seemed to know that Suzie was as mean as a winter on the plains and would challenge a bull if she got mad enough. Surprisingly, though, she seemed to love the girls. Dede especially. From the moment the girls came to live with Jake, Suzie seemed to sense their troubles and not once had she pecked them, chased them, or treated them as she did everyone else.

As Jake walked over to the pens, he called out to his nieces, "Hey, you two. Do you want to go into town? Maybe get some jawbreakers and some new hair ribbons?"

Their twin faces lit up with joy. "Yes!" they both squealed.

He grinned. "Then go wash your hands, and we'll get going."

As they ran past him to head for the pump, he picked up the pail of corn and tossed a few more handfuls to the hens. Suzie, evidently having had her fill, stood back and let her companions have the feed. Jake, noting her magnanimous gesture, bowed her way. "Thank you, your majesty."

Suzie responded by fixing him with a disdainful black-eyed stare.

Smiling, Jake tossed out a few more hands of corn, then went to hitch up the wagon.

One of the first things Jake learned about the girls when they came to live with him was that they loved to sing, especially on a trip in the wagon. Initially their repertoire had consisted of lullabies and silly children's ditties like "Pop Goes the Weasel," and "Jimmy Crack Corn." Thanks to blacksmith Arthur Gibson, who was also the organist at the church, the twins now sang "Amazing Grace," "Home on the Range," and "Battle Hymn of the Republic."

They were singing that now, on their way into town, their heads thrown back, boisterously belting out the ringing refrain: *"His truth is marching on."* Jake couldn't contain his grin.

When they were done, his heart was full as he looked into their shining, happy eyes. They'd come to mean a lot to him in the short time they'd been his, and if they wanted a mama—he'd get them one, come hell or high water.

Chapter 3

⟨◦◦◦⟩

After breakfast in Mrs. Boyd's small dining room, Loreli, wearing a violet walking dress and a saucy matching that, strolled down the town's main walk— destination, the general store. She was almost out of hand cream. Although she doubted a town of this size would carry the brand she favored, she hoped to find a reasonable substitute.

Loreli received more than a few smiles and tips of the hat from the men she passed, and she smiled right back. She knew she was a good-looking woman, and admittedly enjoyed seeing that reflected in a man's eyes. This being such a small town, she was certain most of the residents knew about her connection to the mail-order brides by now. The men's smiles not withstanding, Loreli doubted their wives would be as welcoming. Local women took an immediate disliking to her. Most seemed threatened not only by her profession, coloring, and clothing but by her bold, independent approach to life. She remembered being run out of a small town outside of Reno by a bunch of Bible-pounding harridans who accused her of planting the seeds of the devil in the minds of the local women. It seemed only the devil would advocate women wanting to vote, a subject that had come up in passing during a card game she'd had with some of the town fathers. Apparently, one of the men had gone home and mentioned the conversation to his wife. By morning, the local correctness society had pounded on the door of her rented room, demanding she leave town. Because Loreli knew she couldn't look to the law for help—sheriffs seldom intervened in such incidents—she packed up and took the next stage.

Now, as she neared the store, she forgot all about those women. Her face brightened on seeing Zora Post, one of her bride friends from the wagon train, coming toward her on the walk.

A gleeful Zora squealed, "Loreli!"

As the two women embraced, the short, brown-skinned Zora said, "I thought you'd already left for California."

"Missed the train. I'll try it again on Friday. How's married life?"

"It's only been two days, but surprisingly well. His name's Cyrus Buxton. He's very nice." She gave a wry, knowing smile. "*Very* nice."

Both women laughed.

Still grinning, Loreli tossed back, "Did anyone get a chance to talk with Belle before she left?" Loreli's young wagon mate had been taken advantage of and impregnated by one of her father's clerical colleagues before the trip to Kansas. Belle had been very afraid that the groom she'd contracted to marry in Hanks would send her back to Chicago once he discovered she was carrying another man's child, but he hadn't.

"She's doing fine, far as I know. She and the husband will be living on a place about fifty miles north of here. I'm going up to help out when the baby comes."

It saddened Loreli to think she might never see her young friend again, but it pleased Loreli to know that Belle had married a man who truly cared.

Loreli could see some of the local people looking on curiously as she and Zora continued to talk. A few women hastily averted their eyes, as if the faces of Loreli and Zora might blind them.

Zora must have noticed the women's action's too. "I've heard there's a bunch of biddies not happy with our arrival here. Calling us hussies for agreeing to marry men we'd never seen."

"Ignore them. I always do."

"Oh, I plan to. A good number of the brides are living within spitting distance of each other—we'll make our own way."

Loreli grinned. "I raised you all well, it seems."

Zora nodded. "That you did, constable. That you did."

During the brides's journey from Chicago, Loreli had been voted the constable. It became her job to settle disputes, preside over meetings, and keep everyone pulling together. She'd even foiled, single-handedly, a group of nasty outlaws intent upon doing the women harm.

Zora then said, "Too bad you won't be around to eat at the restaurant I'm going to open, though."

"A restaurant?"

Zora beamed proudly. "Yep. You know I always

wanted to own one, and now, with my new husband's help, I can."

"That's wonderful," Loreli exclaimed. Zora's pepper pot had kept the brides fed during the month-long trip to Kansas. "Where's the restaurant going to be?"

"Cyrus owns a small plot on the edge of town. We've decided to build it there."

Loreli was impressed by Zora's big plans. "I hope it'll be so successful there'll be people lined up from here to Kansas City wanting to get in. Just be sure to serve those old biddies burnt crow, though."

Zora laughed. For the next few moments they talked about the fates of the other brides, and then it was time to part.

"Listen, I have to get going," Zora said. "Cyrus is waiting for me over at the bank. He's a clerk there."

As the two women shared a farewell embrace, Loreli whispered emotionally, "Take care of yourself, Zora. Tell the others I send my love."

"I sure will, Loreli. You take care as well. And leave those men some of their money once you get to California."

Loreli laughed. "I'll think about it."

As a waving Zora strode off toward the bank, Loreli felt as if a very important part of her life would be left behind when she boarded the train on Friday, and it made her uncharacteristically sad. Shaking off the sudden pang of melancholy, she went into the general store.

She spotted the short, balding Bert Green first off. He was wearing an oil-cloth apron over his shirt and trousers, and was leaning over the counter talking with an older, brown-skinned woman wearing an ugly blue bonnet.

When Green looked up and saw Loreli, his face took on what was for her a familiar expression of panic. Loreli simply shook her head. She'd be willing to bet he hadn't expected to see her in the light of day. In small towns like this, a gambling woman was only one step up from a saloon whore, and it was obvious from his reaction that he didn't want to acknowledge their previous association. Loreli sighed at the unfairness of it all, but since there was nothing to be done about it, she gave him a short, impersonal nod, then took a slow walk around the place to see what he stocked on his shelves.

Stepping around a big wooden pickle barrel, and another barrel holding crackers, she made her way past canned goods, potted meat, dress goods, guns, and feed. In the ladies toiletries section, she found quite a variety of hand creams, but not her brand. He did stock bottles of Lundborg's perfumes, and the sight of her favorite scent, Alpine Violet, made her smile. She carried the perfume and a jar of the hand cream to the counter, where two women were now being waited on by Green. The older woman wearing the ugly bonnet had been joined by another lady, who must have purchased the red-checkered headdress she wore in the same place.

Intending to patiently wait her turn, Loreli stepped in behind them. As she did, the two slowly turned and made a big show of critically eyeing her up and down, from her violet hat to her black high-heeled boots. Their silent disapproval echoed as loud and as clear as the dismissive snort they emitted before turning back to Green.

A bit peeved, Loreli wondered if the two were part of the biddy-contingent denouncing the new brides. From the sour looks on their pursed, prune faces, she'd be willing to bet they were. "And good morning to you too, ladies," Loreli drawled sarcastically. She saw their shoulders stiffen. Evidently they hadn't planned on their rudeness being challenged. Loreli added, "Lovely day, isn't it?"

She heard them fumbling to mumble something appropriate.

Loreli turned her cold golden eyes on Green. He met her gaze nervously, as if worried about being exposed, but Loreli had no such plans. "Is this the correct price?" she asked him, holding up the bottle of perfume for him to see.

He stuttered, "Uh-uh, yes, it is, Miss. Would you like to purchase it?"

"Yes, I would."

"Forty-seven cents, please."

Ignoring the two tight-lipped biddies, Loreli handed over her money for the perfume and the hand cream. Green gave her back the change, which she placed in her handbag. "Thank you," she said.

"You're welcome," he returned, smiling falsely.

Loreli again shook her head at the hypocrisy in the world, then turned to leave. She'd met many Bert Greens in her day, and would probably meet many more before the Lord called her home, but it didn't mean she had to like it.

Her mood immediately brightened at the sight of the twins sauntering into the store.

"Loreli!" they squealed in unison. They ran to her, wrapping their little arms around her waist and clung to her for all they were worth. A laughing Loreli bent to hug them as well. "How are you?"

When Jake Reed walked into the store that's how he found them. Loreli and the girls froze. It was obvious from the tight set of his jaw that he didn't like the picture they presented. His frigid eyes met Loreli's. Still holding the girls, she straightened, intending to give him a good piece of her mind if he said one out-of-line word.

He spoke coolly, "Girls, why don't you have Mr. Green show you his new hair ribbons. I want to speak to Miss Winters outside."

The girls looked up at Loreli with worried eyes, and she reassured them in soft tones, "It's okay. Go see about those ribbons. Your uncle and I need to talk."

The girls turned to go, but not before looking back at their uncle, then again at Loreli.

Mr. Green came out from behind the counter and said kindly, "Come on with me, girls. Just got a new shipment of pretty new ribbons yesterday."

Loreli and Jake faced each other across the floor like gunfighters in the street at high noon. The biddies were openly staring.

Jake gestured to the door. Loreli stepped outside.

Hand on her hip, she waited for him to begin.

"You know the girls are set on you being their mother. You also know you can't be, so why are you teasing them like this? All this hugging and running into you is not helping them."

"They pounced on me like they hadn't seen me in six years," Loreli replied coldly. "What was I supposed to do, cuff them and send them on their way?"

His eyes flashed angrily.

Loreli told him, "Being mad at me is not going to change how those girls feel."

"You can't be their mother."

"Who said I wanted to be?"

The air between them fairly crackled.

He made a visible show of calming himself. "Look," he began—both he and Loreli could see passersby viewing them curiously, but ignored them—"this mother thing is very important to them."

Loreli waited. "And?"

He ran his hands over his hair. "And . . . I don't know what the hell to do about it."

Loreli went silent for a moment. "At least you're being honest with yourself. First time?"

He shot her a quelling look.

She raised her hands in innocence, "Sorry. Man like you doesn't impress me as needing to be honest."

"Why not?"

"You've got life all figured out. Arrogance, is how I believe Mr. Webster's dictionary defines it."

"And you're not?"

"Of course I am. I'm a woman in a man's world. I have to be arrogant. What's your excuse?"

"I'm a Colored man trying to hold on to his land."

Impressed, Loreli searched his eyes. "You're not as thick-headed as I thought, Reed."

"I'll take that as a compliment."

"Please do."

It was his turn to search her eyes. "Is there anything that scares you?"

"Sure. Lots of things."

"Such as?"

Loreli paused. He was arrogant enough to believe he had a right to ask something so private, but she was gutsy enough to tell him the truth. "Dying alone. What scares you?"

"Not raising those girls the way my sister would have wanted them raised."

His honesty made Loreli wonder why he'd revealed such a truth to her, a woman he'd known only a few days. On the other hand, she'd revealed a truth about herself and could find no reason as to why. She did know that they'd just exchanged tiny parts of their souls. As a result, something touched her inside, but she wasn't sure what it was.

When they glanced up, the twins were standing in the store's doorway, watching them. Bebe asked, "Can Loreli have supper with us tonight, Uncle Jake?"

Loreli answered before he could reply, "I can't, pumpkin. I've made other plans." She hadn't really, but Jake was right, she needed to distance herself so the girls would stop wishing on her. She didn't want to analyze how pushing them away made her feel. "So give me a hug. This'll probably be the last time we see each other. I'll be heading off to California on Friday."

Both girls gave Loreli a hug, and she hugged them in return. When they stepped back, she touched each head lovingly, then stuck out her hand to Jake. "Pleasure meeting you."

Her gesture seemed to throw him a bit. There was confusion on his face as he looked first at her outstretched hand and then back up into her sparkling eyes.

Loreli couldn't resist teasing him. "Not accustomed to shaking hands with a woman, Reed?"

His eyes emotionless, he grasped her hand and shook it. "Have a safe trip, Miss Winters."

He gently herded the twins back into the store, leaving Loreli to watch their departure wistfully.

"Uncle Jake, were you mean to Loreli?" Dede asked Jake on the ride back home.

Surprised by Dede's uncharacteristic boldness, he glanced her way and replied, "I don't think so."

As if she needed further explanation, Bebe asked him, "Why can't Loreli be our mama?"

He didn't hesitate. "She's not a proper lady."

"Why not?"

"Well, she's a gambler for one."

Dede asked, "What's a gambler?"

"A person who plays cards for a living. That's not a job a woman should have."

Bebe said, "Our teacher, Mr. Hazel, told Aggie the same thing when she said she wanted to be a doctor. He told her that's not a job a woman's supposed to have. Is that what you mean, Uncle Jake?"

Uncle Jake stammered, "Well no, I mean—I don't know what I mean."

Bebe declared, "Well, Aggie's Auntie Kiss said that that kind of thinking is called prejudice, and that a woman can be anything she wants, 'specially if she's good at it. Is that true, Uncle Jake?"

Jake twisted in his own trap. "I suppose it is prejudice in a way, pumpkin."

Dede looked surprised. "That's what Loreli calls us. Are you going to start calling us that too?"

Jake swallowed hard. Good lord! Where had that come from? Better yet, what was wrong with him? He'd never called the girls by pet names before, ever. He added yet another failing mark to Loreli's slate. "No. I guess I picked it up being around Loreli today."

Smiling, the girls settled back against the seats. They remained silent for the rest of the ride home.

When he stopped the team beside the house, the girls left the wagon without a word. He remembered how his heart had panged upon hearing Bebe's brave declaration that they didn't mind growing up without a mama. Watching them slowly and silently entering the house made the pang return. He was the only one who could give them the thing they wanted most, and he was at his wits end as to how.

After putting the girls to bed, Jake went out to the barn to check on his overnight patients: a sow that had gorged itself on so much of its owner's rhubarb it could barely waddle, and a sheepdog who'd tangled with a wolf and lost badly. Upon finding his guests settled in, he walked back around to the front of the house. It had become his habit to sit on the porch and let the night breeze ease away the worries of the day.

Tonight, however, he was brought up short by the sight of Bebe seated on the edge of the porch in the moonlight. Her brown ankles were visible beneath the hem of her flannel nightgown as she slowly brushed her toes against the grass.

Jake joked gently. "Didn't I put you to bed *hours* ago?"

She looked his way and solemnly nodded. "Yes."

Concerned he stepped up on the porch. "Not feeling well?"

"I feel fine. I came out to pray to mama. Aunt Leslie told me that when mothers go to heaven, God makes them into stars so they can look down at night and make sure their children are having good dreams."

He smiled softly. Leslie had been a friend of his sister's who'd taken the girls in for a short time after Bonnie's death. "Which star is your mother?"

"Dede and I decided it's that big one right there, because it's always in the sky."

She was pointing at the North Star. "You may be right, Be."

"I miss her, Uncle," Bebe said softly.

Her sadness mingled with his own. "We all do."

Bebe confessed, "I asked her to ask God to send us another mama. Dede needs one so much. . . ."

Her honesty cut open Jake's heart. "Yes she does, doesn't she?"

"I don't think she'd be scared all the time if she had another mama."

Bebe turned around to look up at him. Even in the dark Jake could see the plea in her eyes. Dede hadn't adjusted as Bebe had to the death of their mother. Rebecca Appleby kept insisting Jake force Dede to move on with her life and face the fact that her mother was gone, but Jake had no idea how to force an eight-year-old to do that, nor would he feel comfortable doing so. Everyone dealt with grief in their own way. The loss had left Dede fragile in many respects. Her aversion to horses being one. She also had nightmares. He doubted she'd ever get on a horse of her own free will. He hoped time would eventually cure her, but there were no guarantees.

Bebe then asked, "Do you think mama will hear me?"

"I'm sure of it, but now you should head back to bed, Be. It's late."

"Yes, sir."

She got up slowly, then gave him a hug. "G'night."

He bent and kissed the top of her hair. "Good night. See you in the morning."

Alone now, Jake looked up at his sister's star and said, "Well. Bonnie? I'm still waiting."

As if in reply, a shooting star streaked across the sky. Jake's eyes followed it until it burned out of sight.

"Thanks," he said aloud, then to himself, *Now if I only knew what it meant.*

Later, lying in bed, Jake realized he had to make a decision. The girls needed a mother and he needed to find them one as soon as possible, not only for their well-being, but for his future as well. He needed to get back to work. Since their arrival he'd had to cut back not only on his delegate duties but his doctoring as well. An offshoot of his political work were his attempts to organize the area's farmers into a union so as to counteract the heavy-handed tactics of men like the banker Diggs. Thanks to Diggs and his bank policies, most of the farmers in the area were wallowing in debt. Not only did they have exorbitant mortgage payments over their heads, but the large debt was compounded by the additional monies borrowed to buy seed, livestock, and equipment. Jake and a few of the other descendents of Hanks's founders were fortunate enough to own their land, yet they still felt the pinch at harvest when their hogs and crops went up for sale at prices that barely returned a profit. Jake thought that forming an alliance might help. Farmers and fieldworkers all over the South were organizing into similar cooperative groups, then banning together with unions like the Knights of Labor to demand, among other things, fairer prices for their crops, equal pay for workers in the fields, and a reformation of the way the government handled everything from banks to the distribution of silver. Times were hard for everyone trying to make a living from the land and even more taxing for those in the fields in the South. The Knights of Labor and unions like it were vowing to change things and Jake had been quietly doing his part to make sure the farmers in the colony knew about the Knights' beliefs. Since the arrival of the girls, however, he'd been unable to be as active in the effort because he no longer had the ability to just pick up and go. One couldn't leave two eight-year-olds at home alone, no matter how important the call.

But who could be their mother? As he'd noted before, pickings here were slim. Rebecca had been the only reasonable candidate, but he'd ruled her out. Maybe he could travel to Kansas City or St. Louis to see if he could find someone there to marry. In reality though, trying to saddle a woman of good character who would consent to a hasty courtship and an even hastier marriage would be a difficult task. Many women wanted to take their time and be sure their potential mate was a person of good quality. Jake wanted to throw up his hands, but couldn't; the girls needed a mother, and he was the only person who could provide them with one. With that admission came an idea he'd been refusing to consider for the past few days because of its absurdity, but, suppose he asked the gambling woman? Jake questioned whether the situation had become that desperate? The answer came back, yes. He was desperate and the girls, too. Maybe if he could get her to agree to stay with them for say, a year, it would give him time to find a real woman to marry.

He mulled it over some more. If he brought the Winters woman into his household, the gossips would rip him to pieces—but he'd never let the opinions of others color his decisions, and he had no intentions of doing so now. His father had been a minister, had ridden with Captain Montgomery's Jayhawkers during Kansas's bloody campaign for statehood, and fought in the Civil War as a member of the famed First Kansas Colored troops. His father's commitment to justice resulted in Jake growing to adulthood filled with pride and purpose. He'd learned at an early age to do what was right, no matter the sacrifice or consequences, and in this case, the right thing to do for the girls would be to meet with the Winters woman and lay his cards on the table; his own personal feelings about her be damned. Granted he knew nothing at all about her, but the twins had become taken with her and she seemed to have been taken with them as well. Yes, she had a questionable occupation and wore expensive, fancy clothes, but she'd impressed him the day she found the girls at the train station. A less responsible woman wouldn't have bothered to fetch them back to town nor been able to extract their promise to never do such an outrageous thing again. Rebecca hadn't been able to get the twins to promise to buckle their shoes.

Jake's inner debate continued, but in the end, he knew the choice had to be made. The girls needed someone, now. Yes, he'd much rather offer his proposal to a more traditional woman, but since there were none available, Loreli Winters would have to do. Satisfied with his plan, but wary of the results, Jake punched at his pillow to make it more comfortable, closed his eyes, then slept.

* * *

The next morning, Loreli heard a knock on the door. Pulling her ivory wrapper closed, she tied the satin strings and called, "Yes? Who's there?"

"Jake Reed."

Loreli paused for a moment. Jake Reed? What could he be after so early in the morning? "What do you want?"

"I'd like to speak with you."

Loreli opened the door only wide enough for her to see out. She didn't want her attire to give him a case of the vapors.

Hat in his hand, he asked, "May I come in?"

He looked so stern, Loreli wondered if he ever smiled. "Have the girls run off again?"

He shook his head. "They're with Arthur Gibson and his girls."

Loreli stepped back so he could enter. He took a moment to look around the small room, taking in the frilly female attire spilling out of the trunks she was living out of, her paints, powders, and creams on the small vanity table and a brown silk walking-dress lying on the bed, waiting to be donned just as soon as he stated his business and left.

"What can I help you with?" she asked.

Jake could see the outline of her nipples beneath the tightly tied satin wrapper. He moved his eyes to her face. "I want to buy your services."

Loreli raised a finely arched eyebrow. "My services? Can you be more specific?"

"How much will it cost me to buy your services for, say, a year?"

Loreli looked him up and down. "I'm still a bit confused, Reed. When you say services, what are you meaning?"

"I want you to be the girls' mother."

Loreli went still.

In the silence that followed he added, "They need a mother and you're the only one they want."

Loreli spent another silent moment assessing him, then replied, "First of all, you can't afford me. Secondly, why do you think I'd agree?"

"Because you've probably done everything else in life but this, and you seem to care about them."

Loreli thought that true, but . . . "You don't even know me."

"No, I don't."

"What about your neighbors?"

"What about them?"

"The gossip, Reed."

He shrugged. "I'll handle it. Will you agree or not?"

Loreli sensed his inner struggles. He didn't look like a man happy with his decision. "You'd rather be making this pitch to someone else, wouldn't you?"

Jake didn't lie. "Yes."

"But you're choosing me instead?"

He met her eyes. "Yes."

Loreli had to give it to him. He was honest. "Why only a year?"

"It will give me a chance to find a real wife in the meantime."

"A *real* wife," Loreli echoed skeptically.

"Yes."

Loreli chuckled softly. She didn't believe this man's arrogance. "And at the end of this year, then what, I disappear?"

"I don't know. I'm just trying to do what's best now. I'll worry about the future when it comes."

"I see."

"So, how much?" he asked.

"I told you before, you can't afford me."

"Then what do you want?"

"For you to leave, and take your ridiculous proposal with you." Loreli went over to the vanity table. She sat on the small bench, picked up her gold-backed hairbrush and began in on her hair.

He said, "Look—"

She interrupted him quietly, "No—you look. I'm the last person you want raising those girls. I'm a gambling woman, remember? How are you going to explain yourself to your neighbors?"

"I told you, I don't care about them, just the twins."

Loreli scanned his mustached features. "You may not today, but you will eventually. Ever been run out of town, Reed?"

"No."

"I have, numerous times. *Good* folks don't cotton to women like me in their midst. Makes them nervous."

Loreli gave her thick hair a few stiff strokes, then fastened it fashionably low on her neck with a few hair pins. "If we're done here, I'd like to get dressed."

"So, you won't do it?"

"No, because you haven't thought this out clearly, Reed. And even if you had, the answer would still be no."

"Why?"

"Because in a year I might not want to let those girls go, then where would we all be?"

He looked away.

She added, "And besides, how are you going to explain my leaving to them when you finally find this *real* wife? Hell, how are you going to explain it to *her*? I'm a pretty tough act to follow, Reed."

Jake's jaw tightened. "This isn't easy for me, Miss Winters."

Loreli told him truthfully, "I don't deny that. Man like you having to come to a woman like me? Must be damned hard, but—the answer is still no."

"What are you afraid of?"

"Dying alone. I already told you that."

"That isn't what I mean, and you know it."

Loreli stood and faced him. "You want the truth? Well, here it is, Reed. I know less about raising children than you do. I spent my youth in gambling dens, cathouses, and places so foul dogs wouldn't even lie down. Those girls need a mother, not me. What about Rebecca Sourapple?"

His eyes flashed at her pun on Rebecca Appleby's name. "The girls don't care for her."

"I knew those two were smart when I met them. Isn't there anyone else you can ask?"

"The girls don't want anyone else. Just you."

Loreli searched his dark eyes for the lie, but he had one of the best poker faces she'd ever encountered. "Nice try, Reed."

"It's the truth. Bebe told me she and her sister decided that they'd grow up without a mother, but later Dede confessed it was a lie. She said they simply wanted you for their mother and no other."

Loreli did her best to ignore how the words touched her, but found it difficult. "No, Reed."

"Miss Winters—"

"No. Now leave, please, so I can dress."

"Sure."

Holding his hat in his hand, he strode out, closing the door behind him. Afterward, Loreli stood there in the silence for a very long time.

Chapter 4

An angry Jake drove home. Apparently he'd been wrong to think a woman like Loreli would jump at the chance to do something decent with her life. She'd done everything but laugh in his face; at least that's how his male pride remembered it. Didn't she understand how much it had cost him to come to her and ask her what he had? He experienced only a modicum of satisfaction knowing he'd never have to deal with Loreli Winters again because he still had to find someone to love Bonnie's girls.

Loreli spent the day in her room reading a novel she'd borrowed from Mrs. Boyd, trying to forget Jake Reed's early morning visit. It was hard. Every time her mind wandered, he and his words were there offering her a key to a life she'd fantasized about having but knew would never come to pass. Her? A mother? Even in a temporary capacity, what could she possibly teach the twins that would be of any benefit? Yes, she had her own morals and mores, and kept to them as much as she could, but she'd been molded into the woman she was today by events and circumstances that had brought grown men to their knees: hunger, poverty, despair. As a youngster traveling with her father, she'd begged in the streets, taken handouts from the nuns, and run from the authorities more times than she could count, for everything from picking pockets to stealing shoes. As a young woman, she'd gambled in hellholes with men she dared not turn her back on nor win too much from for fear of losing her life. She'd also been beaten, cheated, and robbed.

There'd been good times though. Traveling with her old friend and sometimes paramour, the Black Irishman Trevor Church, to places like Mexico, France, and England, she'd gambled with dukes and lords in palaces and courts too beautiful to describe. She'd made money too. Over the last decade, the nest egg she'd been building had grown large enough to make money on its own, courtesy of the wise investment advice generously offered by the gentlemen bankers and capitalists she'd gambled with along the way. As a result, she wanted for nothing.

In the final analysis, life had laid her low and let her soar high. She'd known gunfighters, and politicians, men of great wealth, and men so desperate they'd bet their daughters' innocence for the chance at one more hand. All of those things and more had made Loreli Winters who she was, but what did any of it have to do with raising two little girls?

By the time evening fell, Loreli's inner debate was still raging. Her inadequacies for such a position were numerous, as were the potential consequences to Reed's reputation. His part in the equation threw her the most: What man in his right mind would propose something like this?

He appeared to be a decent man; a bit straitlaced for her liking, but one of those decent, god-fearing men. Didn't he know the gossips would tear at him like harpies, and that his reputation could be affected, all for bringing a woman like her into his home? Personally, Loreli didn't care about the gossips, she knew she could stand the heat; her skin was tough as hide after all these years. But could he? How thick was his skin? Loreli then realized that she was thinking the matter over now as if she might be considering Reed's offer. Was she? she asked herself. To her surprise, the answer came back yes.

A bit floored, Loreli got up from the chair she'd been sitting in most of the afternoon and walked over to the window of her small room. She looked out at the purples and oranges of the quiet evening sky. Was she really going to say yes? Thinking and doing were two different things, she reminded herself, so she wasn't really sure. She was considering it, however. In a way, Reed was right, she had done a lot of things in life, so why not this? Nothing in California needed her immediate attention, she'd already admitted that. She also readily admitted to being a sucker for someone in need. Granted the twins' plight was far more serious than lending money to someone or nursing a sick friend back to health, but why not stay around and enjoy the girls' company until Reed found this mythical *real* wife? It wasn't as if she had to marry him. More than likely, in a year's time she'd be ready to move on anyway. If she and the twins managed to form a bond, she didn't think Reed would deny her the opportunity to write to them to keep up with how their lives were progressing once he married. If he didn't she'd deal with it when the time came.

Loreli turned her mind back to the dilemma at hand. Her biggest concerns were how the twins would react once she moved in and the inevitable gossiping began. She didn't want them to be subjected to teasing and foul-mouthed slurs because of their new mama's occupation. Children more often than not took cues from their parents, and in a school setting, no matter how large or small the town, children could be quite cruel. The fearless Bebe would probably sock the first one to say anything offensive, but Loreli wasn't sure how the more timid Dede might respond. Also needing consideration was the time limit Reed wanted to impose. How would the girls feel about that? There were many unanswered questions—too many. Yet the longer she debated with herself, the more she kept hearing Reed's words: *They don't want anyone but you.* What if he'd been telling the truth? Loreli didn't know how to answer that either. All she did know was that two little girls craved a mother as badly as she herself had at their age, and that they'd chosen her to fill the role. Their faith in her was as humbling as it was frightening.

The next morning, after a fretful sleep, Loreli washed up, then spent a moment going through the dresses hanging in the armoire. She settled on a navy blue summer-weight gown that had long sleeves, a high collar, and a very conservative neckline. She thought it best to dress conventionally. Reed would probably be spooked enough by her unannounced visit, no sense in making things worse by wearing something more suited to a gambling palace than motherhood. She pinned up her hair, put on a jaunty matching hat, then looked at herself in the mirror. Liking what she saw, she grabbed up her handbag and gloves. First she would talk to the girls, and then to Reed.

While driving the rented hack on the thirty-minute ride to the Reed farm, Loreli thought about what she might say to Bebe and Dede. The first thing she'd have to emphasize was that she would only be staying with them until Reed found himself a wife, and once that became a reality, she'd be moving on. Loreli figured once she set them straight on that, the rest of the discussion would be easy, or so she hoped.

When Loreli pulled up in front of the house, the girls were on the porch reading. The moment they recognized the morning visitor, they exploded off the porch like firecrackers, excitedly yelling her name.

Stepping down out of the carriage, Loreli couldn't hold in her grin. "Good morning, pumpkins."

"I thought we weren't going to see you again!" said Bebe excitedly.

"Guess I was wrong."

Dede's eyes were filled with awe. "That's a beautiful hat, Loreli."

"You like it?"

"Yes."

Loreli reached up and withdrew the hat pins. She handed the little blue hat to Dede. "Would you like to wear it?"

Dede looked so surprised. "May I?"

"Yes, you may."

While the grinning Bebe looked on, Loreli set the hat on Dede's braided head, positioned the pins, then adjusted the small spray of netting that adorned it. Stepping back, Loreli viewed her handiwork with mock solemnity, then asked Bebe, "What do you think?"

"I think she looks real fine."

"I agree."

Dede smiled happily.

Loreli scanned the grounds for some sight of Reed. "Where's your uncle?"

Dede answered, "In the barn working on Mr. Gleason's sow. She ate too much rhubarb."

"I see. Well, let's go find him. I want his permission to talk to you girls about something."

"What?" Bebe asked.

"Oh, this and that. It's nothing bad, if that's what's worrying you."

"Good," Bebe said. Each of the girls took one of Loreli's hands and the three of them headed around the back of the house.

"Were you reading your school lessons back there?"

Bebe said, "Yes, but there's no more school until our teacher, Mr. Hazel, comes back from Leavenworth."

Dede piped up, "His sister is sick."

"Ah. So when's he coming back?"

Both girls shrugged.

Jake came out of the barn intent upon checking on the girls and their lessons, but he stopped short at the sight of them walking in his direction with Loreli Winters. What the hell does she want? he asked himself, even as he was struck by her golden beauty as she laughed at something the girls said. Her blue dress had long lace-trimmed sleeves and a lacy collar that led down to a neckline baring just enough of the tops of her breasts to make a man's eyes want to see more. Quickly pulling his mind away from that thought, he again wondered why she'd come. Yesterday, she'd all but tossed him out on his ear. She'd turned him down once, he didn't need to hear her say no again.

Jake had been so focused on Loreli, he hadn't seen the fancy blue hat on Dede's head. He did now.

Loreli watched Reed's dark eyes sweep Dede's head. She assumed the slight stiffening of his jaw meant he didn't approve. "Good morning, Reed."

His frosty eyes met hers. "Miss Winters. What brings you here?"

"I'd like to talk to the girls, if I may?"

"What about?"

"The proposal you made me yesterday."

He stilled, studying her. "Have you changed your mind?"

Loreli shrugged. "I want to hear what the girls think, first."

Dede asked, "About what, Loreli?"

Loreli looked down at her, and said gently, "Let me talk to your uncle for a moment, okay?"

Dede nodded.

Loreli then asked Reed, "So, may I?"

Because Jake didn't know what she might be up to, he stated bluntly, "They're not pawns in a game, Miss Winters."

"This isn't a game, Reed."

Their eyes held. They assessed each other. After a few silent moments, he nodded his approval. "All right, but I'd like to speak with you afterward."

Loreli had no problem complying with the request. "Sure thing."

He told his nieces, "You girls be good now, hear?"

They replied, "We will."

Loreli and the twins headed back to the house. A concerned Jake watched them until they disappeared from sight.

The inside of the house was cool with the breeze of morning. Short hemmed curtains flapped over screened windows. There was a narrow door in the hallway leading to the girl's room that Loreli hadn't noticed on her initial visit. "What's behind that door?" she asked curiously.

"The attic," Bebe said. "Uncle Jake says grandpa lived up there before he died. We're not allowed up there."

"I see. Well, lead on."

Loreli followed where the girls led and was once again struck by the interior's lack of frills. There were no prints or framed pictures on the walls, no knick-knacks, doilies or fancy lamps. In the sitting room that also served as the dining room was a settee—old, but clean, and in a corner by the far wall, a serviceable wooden table and chairs. That was it. There were no end tables, no china cabinet, or hutches of any kind.

It took her a moment to get settled on the terribly lumpy settee, but she kept her face free of complaints as the girls took spots at her side.

Bebe raised her eyes to Loreli and asked, "What did you want to talk to us about?"

"Well, I suppose I should start at the beginning. Yesterday your uncle stopped by my room and asked me if I wanted to be your mama."

The girls looked stunned. Dede finally gasped, "He did?"

Loreli nodded. "Yes, he did. What do you think of that idea?"

The girls shared a silent glance, then Bebe answered excitedly, "We like that idea very much, Loreli."

Loreli smiled. "I like the idea too, but—"

"But what?" Dede asked in a worried voice.

"I'm only going to stay until he finds a real mama for you girls. Shouldn't take him more than a year, he thinks."

"And then you'd go?" Bebe asked.

Loreli nodded solemnly. "Yes, pumpkin, I would."

Neither girl had much to say after that. The twins shared another look, then Bebe asked Loreli, "Can Dede and I talk by ourselves?"

"Certainly. How about I step out onto the porch? You can come and get me when you're done."

The girls agreed.

Loreli struggled to her feet. As she left, she swore the settee was stuffed with potatoes and that it had left bruises all over her behind.

Out on the porch, Loreli looked out over the blue-skied horizon, at what might very well be her home for the next year or so. There wasn't another house for miles. This could be a lonely, isolated life for a woman accustomed to the fast-paced, hurly-burly, comings and goings of the big cities. There'd be no piano players, loud saloons, or big shops like New York's Bloomingdale Brothers to spend her hard-earned gold in. There were no high-priced hair dressers, well-known dressmakers, or fancy candy stores. She'd have the companionship of the girls and the brides from the wagon train and little else. Living here would be like falling off the face of the earth in many respects; no one from her past would think to track her here unless she told them where to look. Admittedly, she found that to be a blessing of sorts. The straitlaced Reed and his neighbors would undoubtedly be disturbed by the types of people she called friends, not because her friends were unsavory individuals but because of the way they made their living. Her longtime housekeeper, Mrs. Oliver, would undoubtedly faint upon receiving a telegram announcing Loreli's plan. Amused by the thought, Loreli just hoped her old friend recovered enough to be able to gather up *all* the items she would want shipped.

Loreli walked to the edge of the long porch and scanned the cornfields and other crops stretching off in the distance. She took in the barns, the hogs pens, the two milk cows grazing in the field, then smiled at the sight of a line of baby ducks waddling single-file behind a brown, feathered parent. There were chickens scratching about, two sheep dogs pacing about as if on patrol, and two long-necked geese causing a commotion near one of the barns. The geese were repeatedly charging and squawking angrily at a young goat tied to a post. The goat was fending off the charges well. Neither bird wanted to tangle with the goat's horns it seemed, so they settled for fussing and flapping their wings instead.

Loreli couldn't remember being around such a menagerie; she was a city girl—however, once she grew accustomed to the smell of the hogs, and she prayed it would be soon, she didn't think it would be too bad being here.

Her thoughts drifted back to Reed. She was certain she'd thrown him for a loop by showing up this morning and asking to speak with the girls, but he impressed her as a man needing a bit of upheaval and spontaneity in his life, and she felt well qualified for the job.

Loreli spent a few more moments looking over the

house. The roof appeared to need some work as did the planks of the porch beneath her feet. Hastily glancing around to make certain she wasn't being observed, Loreli pulled on the porch columns to test their strength. They didn't budge. It was a well-built place.

It was a warm humid day and Loreli now wished she'd worn a different gown. She could feel her body beginning to perspire as the sun rose higher in the sky. Opening her handbag, she withdrew her small ivory fan. After easing the bodice of her dress a discreet distance away from her skin, she fanned the breach. The effort didn't help much. Heat like this, so early in the day, was not a good sign. If the temperature continued to rise, it would be sweltering by noon.

Still fanning, Loreli turned, then froze at the sight of Jake Reed standing on the ground beside the porch, watching her. *Where had he come from?* She saw his gaze settle on her hand holding her dress open. He appeared to disapprove of the way she was attempting to cool herself, so an irritated Loreli stopped fanning and confronted him: *"What?"*

"Nothing."

"You have that look on your face again, Reed."

"What look?"

"The one you had the night I played cards with the sheriff. I suppose *good* women don't fan themselves?"

He didn't respond, thus raising her pique even higher, but remembering the girls, Loreli kept her voice low as she told him, "All I was doing was fanning myself."

"Wearing a lighter-colored gown might help."

Loreli held on to her patience. "Thank you, doc. I'll be certain to remember that for the future."

"Where are the girls?" he asked.

"Inside deciding whether they want me or not."

"Did you tell them I'd be looking for a real wife in the meantime?"

"I did."

Loreli had a question. "You didn't tell them about coming to see me yesterday. Why?"

"I didn't want their hopes dashed if you said no."

Loreli understood his reasoning. In spite of Loreli's problems with him, she still couldn't get over what a fine specimen of a man Reed was. Chocolate brown skin; dark, nearly black eyes. The jaw was strong, and the lips full beneath a provocative moustache. He stood just over six foot tall, and the shoulders in the faded blue shirt were broad. In reality though, she thought such handsomeness a waste; a man as irritating as he had no business resembling a dark-skinned sculpture by Michelangelo.

As if he'd read her mind, he asked tightly, "Something you wish to say, Miss Winters?"

Loreli shook her head. "Nope."

The twins appeared on the porch, thus ending further conversation. Loreli turned away from him to ask the girls, "So, what have you decided?"

"We want you to stay, Loreli," Bebe replied.

Loreli's smile met theirs. "Even if it's just for a year?"

"Even if it's just for a year," Bebe echoed, then added, "a year's a long time when you're eight, Loreli."

The honesty in the little brown face made Loreli's heart swell with sweet emotion.

Dede then looked up at her uncle and asked earnestly, "May Bebe and I be in the wedding like Aggie and her sister were when her pa got married?"

The question stunned Loreli. She stared down at Dede, then over at Reed. *Wedding? Nobody said anything about getting hitched!*

Before Loreli could reply, Reed said to Dede. "Of course you can be."

Loreli fought hard to keep the surprise from her face.

"How about you two go back to your lessons?" Reed said to the girls. "Miss Winters and I have some talking to do."

The happy girls nodded, then giggling with glee, hurried off.

Once they were out of earshot, Loreli whispered fiercely, "You didn't say anything about marrying up!"

"How else are you going to be their mother?"

"By just moving in."

"Maybe where you come from, but not here."

Yesterday, Loreli had accused Reed of not having thought his proposal through fully; apparently she hadn't either. "I don't need your name to do this, Reed."

He folded his arms across the braces on his chest and said easily, "Yes, you do. Had you not been so quick to show me the door yesterday, I could've explained this then."

Loreli ignored his attempts to make this her own fault. "I thought you weren't concerned about the gossip."

"Directed at myself, no, but at the girls, yes."

Loreli realized his worries mirrored her own, but marry—*him*? Every inch of her body knew this wouldn't work; she'd only wind up snatching him off his high horse and then stepping aside so she wouldn't break his fall. Her word had been given, however, and as she told the girls, a woman always keeps her word. *Good lord!*

"Problems?" he asked, and she swore he was smiling behind those unreadable eyes.

"Frankly, yes. I'm no wife, Reed."

"And I'm no husband, so we're equal in that respect."

"Then why not do this my way? Hire me as a governess or something."

"No," he said, his voice quiet but final. "We'll marry next Saturday. If you want one of the other women to stand up with you, let them know. I'll contact the preacher."

"You always this bossy?"

He didn't flinch. "If you don't want to do this, then there's your buggy."

Loreli studied him. "Had I not given my word, the buggy and I would be gone, so don't tempt me."

"That means a lot to you, doesn't it—giving your word?"

Loreli paused a moment to think about her answer, then replied, "Yes, it does. Your word and how you treat folks are the only things you're judged by where I come from."

"That's good to know."

"Why?"

"Because that's how my sister would've wanted her girls to approach life."

Loreli was a bit taken aback by what sounded like praise. "Are you giving me a compliment, Reed?"

"I think so."

She smiled. "Well, thanks, but back to this wedding."

"Yes?"

"Is this supposed to be a love match?"

The question seemed to catch him off guard because he stared at her. "I'm not sure what you mean."

Loreli sighed. She was glad he wasn't a train robber. His lack of planning would land him and his gang right in jail. "Reed, if you and I are going to be getting married all of a sudden, your neighbors will be expecting us to act as if we're in love."

He stared.

Loreli threw up her hands. "You really haven't planned this out, have you?"

When he met her eyes, his mustached lips were tight. "Apparently not."

She chuckled and shook her head. He had the face and temperament of a god, but the sow in his barn could've thought this out in more detail. "Well, the other choice is, they can see us at each other's throats—which, personally, I have no problem with, but it won't go a long way in squashing the gossip."

His jaw tightened even more.

Loreli raised her palms in a show of innocence. "You're the one all fired up about having a wedding."

Jake wondered when and how he'd lost control here. One minute he'd been in charge and laying down the law. Now he felt as if he'd just laid down in front of a train. Love match? With her? Without a doubt, Loreli Winters was one of the most beautiful women he'd ever seen, but she made her living playing cards, for heaven's sake. Men like him didn't have love matches with gambling queens!

Loreli had no trouble reading his thoughts. For the first time since meeting him, she could see the emotions plainly on his face. He was appalled by the thought of having to pretend to be her love. Not that she expected anything different, but deep down inside her feelings were hurt. She shrugged it off. Over the years she'd become quite adept at burying the effects of the sleights sent her way by the decent church-going folks of the world.

Not bothering to mask the coolness in her voice, she asked him, "So, how do you propose we act instead?"

Jake knew he had no alternative, so he replied. "No, you're right. It will be expected."

Loreli wanted to ask him how he expected to troll for a new wife while still married to his old one, but decided to save that query for another day. She could only shake her head at his naiveté.

Hoping to cover his earlier misstep, Jake said, "I don't expect this to be easy, Miss Winters, but we can at least be civil for the girls' sake."

"I'll have no problem. You might, though."

"Why?"

"Because you're accustomed to giving orders, and I'm not accustomed to taking them."

He didn't seem to appreciate her candor, but Loreli didn't plan on surrendering even an inch of herself to this arrogant man, handsome or not. "I'm assuming you want me to move in here with you and the girls?"

"Yes, but after the ceremony."

Loreli had no problem with that. "Then I'll head back to town. I need to make arrangements to have some of my things shipped here from back East. Where will I sleep?"

Their eyes met.

"My room." he told her. "I'll bed down in the barn."

"The barn?" she echoed skeptically.

"Yes, the barn. That a problem?"

"No, Reed."

"Anything else need discussing?"

She shook her head. "Not that I can think of, no."

"Then I need to get back to work."

Without another word, he turned and walked back toward the barn.

Loreli watched his departure with both hands on her hips. This plan of his was destined to blow up in his face. She didn't know how, where, or when it would occur, but she hoped to be downwind when it did.

Putting the maddening Jake Reed out of her mind, Loreli went back into the house to find the girls.

Seated on a bench behind the barn, Jake pondered a future that included one Loreli Winters, soon to be Mrs. Loreli Reed. How in the world did he plan to integrate such a flamboyant woman into their lives? She was right, he hadn't thought this out fully. It never crossed his mind that there would be the expectations she'd described, mainly because his plans were to turn the raising of the girls over to her and then go back to his own life. In his eagerness to get this situation settled, he hadn't thought past that or about any of the rest. He just wanted to get the girls settled in and reclaim his life. When the twins first arrived he'd refused to make a choice between seeing to their needs and to his own, and so tried to do both. Rebecca, the Gibson family, and a few other trusted acquaintances had been called upon to keep the girls when he had to be away overnight for doctor calls, political meetings, and the like, but after the fifth or sixth time, he'd been unwilling to impose upon them anymore and so sent out the word that farmers who lived more than a day's ride away would either have to transport their sick animals to the Reed place or find help elsewhere. There'd also been political rallies he'd wanted to attend around the state, and he toyed with the idea of taking the girls along, but knew they wouldn't

be interested in listening to day-long speeches on anything. Trying to make a living and keeping track of one's
personal goals while trying to raise two grieving little
girls had to be the hardest thing he'd ever done in his life.
But when the Winters woman arrived this morning and
hinted she might say yes to his proposal, he'd secretly
wanted to jump for joy.

Yes, she was a very controversial choice; and no, he
wasn't sure how it would all work out, but at this point he
didn't much care. The twins adored her and she them. She
could see to their raising and he could go back to making
a living so he could provide for them all. Rumor had it that
a small brouhaha was brewing between the area's older
women and the mail-order brides. Taking the Winters
woman as his wife would place the Reed household
squarely in the center of the "hussy contingent", as he'd
heard the new women were being called. Jake planned to
be too busy to be a part of such divisiveness. He knew the
wedding wouldn't deflect all the talk, but it was better
than having folks brand Winters his mistress, or worse, his
whore.

Inside the house, Loreli took a slow stroll around, looking at the walls, windows, and evaluating the rooms'
empty spaces. The curious but silent twins walked at her
side.

Bebe finally asked, "What're we doing, Loreli?"

"Trying to decide where we're going to put the paintings when they arrive."

"What paintings?" Dede asked.

"The ones I'm having shipped from back East to put on
all these bare walls."

The girls shared a stunned look. "You have paintings?"

Loreli gave Dede a smile. "Yep, I do. Lots."

It was Bebe's turn. "What else do you have?"

"Settees, tables, china cabinets, drapes, tableware, beds, dressers, you name it."

Dede gushed, "I'll bet you're richer than Mr. Diggs."

"Mr. Diggs, the banker?"

The girls nodded yes.

Loreli shrugged, "Maybe."

Loreli decided if she was going to live here, it would have to be in a style she was accustomed to. She'd seen closets furnished better than this place. She wondered why this fine old house had next to nothing inside. Was it because Reed hadn't been able to afford any? She had many questions, but decided it didn't much matter why the place was so empty; her things were coming. It might take a month to get everything shipped out, but she didn't mind the wait. "Now, let's go see your room."

Bebe asked, "Are we going to get pictures too?"

"If you'd like."

Their answering grins were so wide with happiness, Loreli couldn't contain her chuckles.

Their room was as sparsely appointed as the rest of the house. The one bed the girls shared and the small dresser against the wall were the only furnishings. Atop the dresser was a hairbrush and comb and a picture in a small tarnished silver frame.

Loreli picked it up and looked at the young woman posed so seriously. "Is this your mama?"

Both girls nodded.

"What's her name?" Loreli asked.

"Bonnie," Bebe replied.

"She's beautiful," Loreli told them. And she was. The resemblance between Bonnie and the twins was striking. Loreli could see Bonnie's eyes and the shape of her mouth reflected in the faces of her daughters. She could also see the facial similarities between this woman and her brother, Jake. Loreli looked into the woman's eyes and saw an intelligence and a kindness that spoke to her soul.

Loreli set the picture down gently. The girls were watching. "You both favor her very much. Well, while I'm here, I'm going to do my best to make her proud of all of us. Okay?"

The girls smiled.

Loreli hugged them both against her side, and prayed that Bonnie's spirit would guide her, so she wouldn't mess this up. "Now, how about we go shopping?"

Their eyes went wide as saucers.

Loreli asked, "Ever been *shopping* before?"

Dede answered in a voice shot through with awe. "No."

"Then it's time you learned how. Let's go find your uncle."

"Shopping?" Jake asked after she and the girls came into the barn to inform him of their plans. "Where?"

"In town," Loreli replied. "The girls could use a few things."

Jake looked down at the girls standing by her side and said, "Bebe, how about you and your sister go back to the house and wait for Miss Winters. She and I need to talk for a moment."

The girls appeared uncertain, but did as they were told.

Once the two adults were alone, Jake said bluntly, "I don't have money for shopping trips, Miss Winters."

"I don't need your money."

His eyes flashed.

"Whatever I purchase, I plan to pay for out of my own purse, so don't worry." She then asked, "Is there a reputable seamstress in town?"

"Why?"

"Because if you're set on marrying up, the girls will need something to wear that isn't made from denim."

Jake met her fearless eyes. He took the shot personally.

As if reading his mind, Loreli cracked, "No offense intended, but at a wedding, they should look like little girls."

"Millie Tate's the town seamstress. Her shop's next to the bank."

"Thanks. I'll have them back before dark." She headed toward the door.

Jake knew he owed her a thanks for agreeing to take on the girls, though he hadn't expressed it. "Miss Winters?"

She stopped and looked back.

"Thanks for agreeing."

Loreli remembered the disdainful look he'd had on his face when they were talking a bit ago and said, "Thank the girls. They're the only reason I'm here, but you're welcome."

He met her cool eyes.

"I'll see you later," she said, and left him alone in the barn.

Chapter 5

With the twins skipping happily by her side, Loreli stopped first at Sol Diggs's bank. She needed to establish an account in Hanks so she could transfer money from her account in Philadelphia. Like most buildings in small backwater towns, the interior of the bank was airless, hot and gloomy. The faint light coming in through the fancy front window did its best to knock back the shadows but had a hard time. Were it not for the oil lamps and the opened door, one wouldn't be able to see at all. Loreli walked over to the lone teller's window. The young man standing behind it nodded politely, then said, "May I help you, Miss Winters?"

Surprise played over Loreli's face. "You know me?"

He nodded. "Yes, ma'am, I do. I'm married to your friend Zora Post."

"Ah, then you must be Cyrus Buxton."

He grinned, showing off a beautiful smile. Cyrus was what the race called "red-boned." He had red hair, reddish brown skin, sherry-colored eyes, and enough freckles to share with everyone in town. Loreli guessed him to be in his mid-thirties. "How's Zora doing?" she asked.

"Fine, just fine. She's up in Lawrence today. She tell you about the restaurant?"

"Yes, she did, and I'm very impressed."

"She's a take-charge woman, my Zora. I like that."

Loreli liked him as well for being so supportive of Zora's dream.

Cyrus then looked over his cage at the girls standing at her side. "Hello, Bebe and Dede. How're you girls today? Did the doc come into town with you?"

Bebe, as always, spoke for them both. "Hello, Mr. Buxton. We're doing well. No, Uncle is at home."

Buxton then turned his attention to Loreli. "So, what may I help you with today, Miss Winters?"

In response, Loreli turned and looked down at Dede and said, "De, tell Mr. Buxton why we're here." They'd practiced what she was supposed to say on the way into town.

Holding tightly onto Loreli's hand, Dede replied in a very soft voice, "We're here to move some money."

With a smile, Loreli excused herself from Buxton, then leaned down to speak quietly with Dede while Bebe looked on. "You have to say it louder, pumpkin. Men don't hear women sometimes if you don't speak up, especially when it involves money. Now, Mr. Buxton doesn't seem like that type, but let's practice with him just the same. Okay?"

Dede smiled a bit more confidently and told Mr. Buxton in a slightly louder voice, "We've come to move some money, sir."

Buxton grinned. "Oh really? From where?"

It was Bebe's turn, "Philadelphia, sir."

He looked to Loreli. "Philadelphia?"

Loreli was in the process of digging in her handbag for her bank documents. "Yep, I want my bank there to transfer some of my money here. Can you do that for us?"

"How much?" Buxton asked.

Loreli took a pen from the well on the counter in front of his window and wrote down the amount. She handed the paper to the clerk.

He read the number and his eyes widened.

"Is that a problem?" Loreli asked.

He cleared his throat and croaked, "Uh, no. It's just— this is a lot of money. I—I have to get Mr. Diggs. Can you wait right here?"

Loreli nodded. "Sure can."

He hurried away and disappeared into a door behind him.

Loreli told the girls, "Well, I guess we'll have a seat."

The three of them walked over to one of the benches by the window. They'd just gotten settled when Sol Diggs came out. His pomaded gray hair, tailored suit, and healthy girth branded him a prosperous man.

"Miss Winters," he cooed, walking toward her. "It's a pleasure to see you again. You haven't won any more parts of town since I saw you last, have you?"

Loreli smiled. "No, I haven't." It pleased her that Diggs, unlike store owner Bert Green, had no problem acknowledging their past acquaintance.

Diggs turned to the twins, "Hello, girls."

They nodded.

Diggs said to Loreli, "Buxton here says you want to do a little business?

"Yes, if I may."

"Of course. The sum is a bit more than we're accustomed to handling, but I see no problems."

Loreli knew very little about Diggs and even less about how he ran his business, so she felt compelled to ask, "My money will be safe here, won't it, Mr. Diggs?"

He smiled. "Why, Miss Winters, I'm offended."

"I'm only asking because the last time a bank owner tried to take advantage of me, the judge, who happened to be a good friend, took everything the bank owner possessed and turned it over to me as compensation. Even confiscated the poor man's shoes."

Diggs blanched and stammered, "Really?"

"Yes, he did, but I won't have to worry about that here."

"Oh, no," Diggs promised quickly. "Your money will be as safe as my own."

"Good. So, are there documents that need my signature?"

Loreli guessed her story about the judge must've made Diggs nervous because he snapped at Buxton, "Get the lady some slips, Cyrus. We don't want to keep a new customer waiting."

Buxton, already prepared, handed the forms to his boss. The immediacy of the action caught Diggs so by surprise, he dropped the papers and they went fluttering to the floor. Both men bent hastily to retrieve them only to wind up soundly bumping heads in a scene so comical the girls giggled.

Diggs's hand went to his ringing skull. He paid no attention to Buxton's attempts to make amends and gritted out, "Get back to your window, Buxton, I'd like to be alive when the day ends!"

Buxton left holding his own head. Loreli fought to keep from laughing out loud.

The distressed Diggs then said, "My apologies, the man's cursed. Mayhem follows him like a cat, been like that all his life. Hope his new missus knows. If you'll sign these papers we can get you on your way, Miss Winters."

Still chuckling, Loreli and the girls went over to one of the raised tables so Loreli could write. As she filled out all the information on the bank's slips, she explained to the twins what she was doing. She wasn't sure the girls understood it all, but she didn't fret. As long as they understood a woman could have her own money and transact her own business without the benefit of a man's help, approval, or interference, they would have learned their lesson for the day.

After receiving Mr. Diggs's assurances that her money would be resting in her new account in his bank no later than the day after tomorrow, Loreli and the twins headed toward the door. They were almost bowled over by a White man who came barreling into the bank. He was tall, thin, and dressed in shabby farmer's clothes. Upon seeing Diggs, the man shouted angrily as he waved a document in his hand, "Damn you, Diggs! What's this supposed to mean?"

Diggs replied coolly, "You know what it means, Peterson. Your farm reverts to the bank on Monday."

The man looked stunned and angry. "You foreclosed on me?"

Loreli moved the girls closer to her side to keep them safe.

Diggs replied sharply, "I warned you back in December that come June your note would be due, and June is here."

"How could you do this? You know how hard I've been working. Give me until the harvest at least. I've got a good crop of corn growing."

"No. I've been carrying you for two years. I have bills to pay too."

Peterson barked disdainfully, "Bills for what—more fancy suits and carriages! You're just punishing me because you think I'm organizing for the Knights."

Diggs puffed up like an adder. "The Knights be damned. This has nothing to do with that. You owe me money, Peterson, and I'm tired of waiting."

Peterson sneered. "You're offal, Diggs. I got five kids. How am I supposed to take care of them? Where are we supposed to live?"

"That's not my concern. Now, leave before I send for the sheriff. You're frightening my customers."

Peterson turned and eyed Loreli and the girls for a second, then swung back to Diggs. "You'll pay for this, Diggs—one way or another. You'll pay."

Peterson stormed out.

Loreli met Diggs's eyes, and he said, "Sorry you and the girls had to witness that."

"Does he really have five children?" asked Loreli.

Diggs paused for a moment to assess her face, then offered. "Yes."

"How much does he owe?"

"Suffice it to say, more than I'm willing to carry any longer."

"How much?"

He kept his face blank. "As an officer of the bank, I'm not at liberty to divulge such private information." Then he smiled and asked, "Is there anything else I can do for you, Miss Winters?"

Loreli swore he looked like a shark who'd just finished a big, fine meal. "No, Mr. Diggs. The girls and I will be going."

Holding the twins' small hands, Loreli led them back out into the sunshine.

"That was Carrie's and Jimmy's pa, Loreli," Bebe told her.

"Are they friends of yours?"

"Carrie is. Jimmy likes to put crickets down girls' collars."

Loreli smiled.

Dede asked, "Why won't Mr. Diggs let them live in their house anymore, Loreli?"

"I guess their pa hasn't paid back some money he borrowed from the bank."

"Well, I think that's mean."

Loreli had to agree. Whatever his beef with the bank, Peterson still had five children to provide for, and Diggs hadn't seemed sympathetic in the least. Loreli understood that banks were in business to turn a profit, and although she had no idea how much Diggs had helped the Petersons in the past, she thought surely the bank could've held off until the man harvested his crops. Was he really being punished for being a member of the Knights of Labor? Loreli didn't know much about the inner workings of the group, however, she was aware that the Knights let members of the race join their ranks, and that they advocated equal rights and pay for women.

Bebe said, "If I was rich, I'd give Carrie's pa all the money he needed."

Hearing the genuine tone in Bebe's voice, Loreli asked her, "Would you?"

"Yes."

"I would too," her sister declared proudly. "I like Carrie."

Loreli decided she liked Carrie as well, if only because the twins did. The girls had already proven to be good judges of people; after all, they'd known better than to call Rebecca Appleby a friend.

"When I grow up," Dede said, "I'm going to be rich so nobody can tell me not to live in my house."

Loreli thought that a logical goal. She'd been poor and she'd been rich. Rich was better.

Next stop, the seamstress shop, owned by Mildred Tate. A bell on top of the door tinkled out their entrance. The tiny shop was filled with fabrics, dress forms, and notions. As Loreli and the twins stood a moment taking it all in, a woman who looked to be in her late twenties came hurrying out of the back. She had short, sparse hair, a tall, birdlike body, and her brown face was as long as and homely as a mule's. She smiled upon seeing the twins but stopped dead in her tracks at the sight of Loreli. "Hello, girls," she said, then asked warily, "Who's this with you?"

Bebe declared proudly, "This is Loreli, Miss Millie. She's going to be our new mama."

The woman's eyes widened with surprise, then her lips tightened. "Hello," she offered stiffly to Loreli, looking her up and down. "You came in with those mail-order brides, didn't you?"

Loreli sensed the woman's distaste. "Yes. Name's Winters, and you are?"

"Mildred Tate. Rebecca Appleby and I have been best friends since childhood."

"Well, now," Loreli cracked, "isn't that something?" So this was a friend of Rebecca's.

"Yes, it is, isn't it," Millie shot back coolly. "So, you and Jake are getting married?"

Loreli assessed Mildred Tate and remembered the banker Diggs saying everyone in town was waiting on Rebecca to saddle Reed. "Looks that way."

"When?" the woman demanded sharply.

Loreli thought Mildred Tate not only rude but nosy as well. Even so, Loreli refused to let this mule-faced Millie rile her into acting rude in return, at least not in front of the girls. "A week from Saturday. We're here because the girls need dresses."

"Oh, really?" the woman replied sarcastically. "And you came to me?"

Loreli held on to her patience. "I'm told you're the best seamstress in town."

The mule smiled smugly. "I am the *only* seamstress in town."

Loreli wanted to shake the snide smile off the hussy's face. *Not in front of the girls,* she reminded herself. "So, can you have them ready by the day of the wedding?"

"I could."

Loreli was liking the woman less and less. "May we see some patterns, then?"

Mule-faced Millie all but stomped over to a stool, returned with a *Godey's Lady's Book* and practically threw it onto the table by Loreli. "See if you like anything in there."

That did it. Loreli looked down at the girls who were staring at Mule-face Mille as if she might be dangerous. "Girls, I think we're going to find somebody else to make your dresses."

"Good luck," the seamstress threw back in superior-sounding tones.

The girls were watching her warily as Loreli took them by the hand and escorted them to the door. "Good day, Miss Tate," Loreli said.

Once outside, Loreli turned back and saw Mildred Tate malevolently watching their departure. *What a nice woman*, Loreli thought sarcastically.

As they crossed the street, Dede asked "Loreli, why was Miss Millie being so mean?"

"I think it's because she's a good friend of Rebecca's, pumpkin, and was probably hoping Rebecca would be your new mama."

Bebe made an ugly face. "Ugh, we didn't want Rebecca to be our mama, did we, De?"

"Nope. She won't even let us get dirty. Will you let us get dirty, Loreli?"

A chuckling Loreli looked down and said, "Dirty as you want, just as long as you take a bath before you climb into bed."

Loreli squeezed the twin small hands affectionately, and the girls smiled contentedly in response.

Their next stop was Green's General Store. Loreli wanted to see the fabrics he had for sale. If Mildred Tate didn't want the job of making dresses for the girls, Loreli would buy the fabric and find someone else who would, even if she had to postpone the wedding.

The store was filled with customers looking at this and buying that. When Loreli and the girls entered, many of the customers nodded her way and smiled at the twins. Loreli wondered if they'd be so friendly once word of her upcoming nuptials made the rounds.

Bert Green was waiting on a lady at the counter. When he looked up and saw Loreli, his face immediately filled with panic, but upon noticing the girls, he appeared to relax. Loreli reminded herself to never play cards with him again.

Ignoring him for now, she and the girls found the fabrics over in the dry-goods section of the store. There wasn't much to choose from unless you wanted denim, calico, or stiff, serviceable cottons. None of which were right for wedding dresses.

Bebe picked up a catalog and began to look at the pictures inside. "What about these dresses, Loreli?"

Loreli took a look over Bebe's shoulder. "Let me see the front of the book, Be."

Loreli smiled at the familiar picture on the cover. It was a Bloomingdale Brothers catalog. The New York City–based establishment carried everything from bridal gowns to roller skates. She was sure to find dresses for them now. Of course it would take a while to get the dresses shipped. She wondered if Reed would mind putting off the wedding for a few weeks. Delaying the ceremony might also give her time to change his mind about marrying her, but then again, the girls had their hearts set on being members of the wedding party. Loreli knew she wouldn't be able to bear the sadness on their faces if the plans were changed, so she was stuck whether she liked it or not.

Catalog in hand, Loreli went to the counter. Behind it Bert Green was stacking cans of Mr. Campbell's Pork and Beans.

"Mr. Green?"

When he looked up and saw it was her, he glanced around nervously before responding, "Uh, yes."

"May I take this and return it later?"

He nodded hastily. "Sure, sure."

"Thanks. Come on girls. How about some lunch? Hungry?"

They grinned.

After eating a small lunch in the dining room of Mrs. Boyd's boardinghouse, Loreli and the girls went up to her room to change her clothing. It was far too warm for the dress she had on. She stood behind the screen and put on a simple blue blouse and a darker blue skirt. Then, after slipping her feet into a comfortable pair of small-heeled boots, and using the hook to do up the buttons, she and the girls took their catalog and headed behind the boarding house to a bench that sat beneath a large tree.

They spent over an hour going through the catalog. After borrowing a measuring tape from Mrs. Boyd, Loreli measured the girls in accordance with the catalog instructions and wrote down the numbers on a piece of paper. She listed the ordering number for dresses, underwear, and shoes, then added nightgowns, Nottingham lace curtains and the poles needed to hang them. Thinking about the winter to come, she picked out a few small carpets for the floors; and to keep the carpets clean, she ordered a

Grand Rapids carpet sweeper that rolled on four wheels. The girls were speechless as the list grew longer and longer. Because of Loreli's generosity, they would now have Sunday hats, gloves, and velvet slippers, and everything else little girls needed.

The fascinated girls skimmed through more pages and Loreli wrote down the numbers of a few additional items she thought they and the household would need. She even added a few items for their uncle, then said, "All right, our last order of business is to find the page with the roller skates."

"Roller skates!" Bebe repeated with wide eyes. She shared a happy smile with her sister, then began to tear through the pages. They found them on page 145. The skates were made from japanned iron and polished beechwood with oak-tanned, black grain leather straps and patent buckles. Loreli ordered one pair of skates for each of the girls and a pair for herself.

It was now late afternoon and the sky was darkening as if a storm were on the horizon. "I should get you girls home before it rains."

"We could stay here with you," Bebe offered with a sly little smile.

Loreli laughed, "Oh, no. I don't want your uncle mad at me."

Dede asked, "Are you and uncle going to kiss?"

For a moment, a confused Loreli tried to figure out what Dede meant. "Kiss? When?"

"Once you get married. Aggie says her papa and her new mama kiss all the time when they think nobody's looking."

Loreli chuckled. "I don't know. How about you ask

your uncle when we get back?" Loreli couldn't wait to see his face.

Dede nodded as if that were a good idea, and with the question settled for the moment, they returned the catalog to the store. Since the undertaker's place served as both the post office and the telegraph office, they stopped there to send their order back East, then headed to the Reed place in Loreli's rented buggy.

When they drove up to the house, the air outside was fragrant with the smells of chicken frying. Loreli's mouth began to water.

"Uncle Jake's got supper ready," De announced.

Surprised by that, Loreli asked, "Your uncle cooks?"

Bebe glanced Loreli's way as if the question was a silly one. "Sure. He cooks dinner, breakfast, and lunch for us, everyday."

Dede added, "He cooks good too."

"Oh, really?" An intriguing bit of information. She had no idea he was domesticated. Interesting.

The girls jumped down from the buggy and an eager Bebe told her sister, "Come on. We have to tell Uncle Jake about all the things Loreli got us." And off they ran, leaving Loreli to escort herself in.

Inside the house, she found the apron-clad Jake Reed in the kitchen taking the last pieces of chicken out of the skillet on the stove. The girls were excitedly relating the details of their trip into town. Loreli was certain he couldn't understand a word they were saying because they were both talking so fast, and trying to talk over each other.

"Hold on," he said laughing. "You're going too fast." Only then did he see Loreli standing in the doorway. He paused, then nodded. "Miss Winters."

"Reed."

"Sounds like you three had quite the time?"

"We did," she replied.

"Girls, show Miss Winters where to wash up. Supper's ready. You can finish telling me about the trip while we eat."

Loreli met his eyes. Was this an invitation for her to stay?

Dede must have read the expression on Loreli's face. "You are going to stay and eat with us, aren't you, Loreli?"

Loreli couldn't say no to such a face, and besides, she'd had a grand time with the twins today and didn't want it to end, at least not yet. "Yes, I'm staying. That chicken smells so good an army couldn't drag me out of here."

Dede giggled as she and Bebe led Loreli out the kitchen door to the pump near the back porch. Loreli felt Reed's eyes on her back every step of the way.

When they got to the table, the fat golden pieces of steaming bird were piled on a chipped blue platter. Accompanying the chicken were green beans with cut up potatoes, corn, and cornbread. As everyone took their places, Loreli looked out over the scene and felt a contentment so ideal it scared her; she could learn to like this family living, but she reminded herself that her role here would only be a temporary one. Soon as Reed found a woman he deemed more suitable, she'd be out on her ear. This was just pretend.

Reed's voice broke into her thoughts. "Let's bow our heads."

After everyone quieted, he recited a short grace, thanking the Lord for the food. Then plates were filled with the supper's samplings and the girls launched into an exuberant retelling of the day's big shopping trip.

Bebe told her uncle, "We bought hats and shoes . . ."

Dede added, "And dresses, and a carpet for our floor."

He stared at Loreli. "Carpets?"

She shrugged. "Floors get cold in the winter."

His face tightened a bit. "What else did you buy?"

Loreli got the impression he wasn't as enthusiastic about the purchases as the girls.

Bebe said, "We got capes and hairbrushes. Hair curlers, gloves . . ."

Dede gushed, "We even got to move some money."

Jake found that confusing, but before he could ask what she meant, Dede said, "But do you know what was the best, uncle?"

"No, De," he said smiling in spite of himself. "What was the best?"

"The roller skates. We got roller skates!"

He looked across the table at Loreli as if she were responsible for buying the girls liquor. "That's real nice, De. Real nice."

He then asked Loreli, "No elephants?"

Not liking the dig, she shook her head, "No. Maybe next time."

As they continued the meal, the girls kept up a steady chatter about the day and their plans for their booty when it arrived. The adults viewed each other with an increasing coolness. For the life of her, Loreli couldn't figure out why he was acting so put out, but since she knew he'd inform her soon enough, she did her best to ignore him and his mood.

When the meal was done, the girls cleared the table and started washing the dishes out by the pump near the back porch. Loreli and Reed stepped out onto the front porch to talk.

Loreli decided not to allow him the first shot. "So, what sin have I committed this time?"

"Did you have to buy so much?"

"I didn't buy frivolously, Reed. Everything I purchased the girls needed."

"Curtains?"

"The house needs those."

"We have curtains."

"I know, that's why I ordered new ones. Not sure they'll fit, though. I didn't have the window measurements."

He ran his hand across his hair. "And what is this about moving money?"

"I'm having some of my money transferred to the bank here. I just talked the girls through what I was doing. They need to know about such things."

"That's what husbands are for."

She folded her arms across her chest and asked challengingly, "Oh, really?"

"Yes, really," he responded.

"And suppose they have no husband? Should they find some random man on the street and ask him to handle their finances?"

He looked real uncomfortable in response to that. Loreli had him, and they both knew it.

He came back with, "But did you have to buy so much? Once you're gone I don't want them thinking I'm going to continue spoiling them this way."

She sighed. "Reed, look. I purchased necessities only. There were no silk sheets or crystal goblets, just basic little-girl needs. Underwear, stockings, shoes."

"Expensive, I'll bet."

"No, not really."

The wind picked up all of a sudden and a boom of thunder shook the surroundings. They both looked up at the darkening sky. "Storm's coming," Reed said. "We'll have to finish this later."

"There's nothing to finish. The things are bought, they'll be here early next month."

His expression made her think he wanted to argue further, but all that he said was, "I have to put the animals in the barn. You may as well stay the night. You might not make it trying to beat this storm back to town."

Loreli wondered if he were really concerned for her safety or the safety of the marriage agreement they'd made. "You know, Reed, something happens to me and you're free to find that real wife."

He groused back, "I can't afford the one I'm getting."

As fat rain drops began to fall from the sky, he took off at a run for the barns. Smiling and shaking her head, Loreli stood and watched the storm roll in, then headed in to find the twins.

He came back into the house a short while later soaked to the skin. It was now pouring. The heavy rain continued for the next two hours. Eventually Loreli took out a deck of cards and taught the girls to play solitaire. Their uncle sat by one of the lamps reading an animal-husbandry journal, and keeping an eye on the interactions between the twins and Loreli Winters.

It was then that Dede looked up at him and asked, "Uncle Jake, are you and Loreli going to kiss?"

He looked so dumbstruck, Loreli had to drop her head so he wouldn't see her grin. When she'd composed herself, she looked up into his dark eyes and said, "She asked me the same question. Since I couldn't rightfully answer, I told her she should ask you."

The sharp look he shot Loreli's way made her chuckle inside. Her expression revealed no clue to her thoughts.

Gently, he told his niece, "De, that's not something girls your age should be concerned about. Okay?"

She dropped her eyes, and nodded. "I'm sorry, Uncle Jake."

"No sorry needed. It's adult business, is all."

Loreli wanted to yell "Coward!" but she didn't. Instead she smiled at Dede and was quite amazed when De flashed a devilish little smile right back. *Well, I'll be. Maybe Deirdre Case isn't such a wallflower after all*.

An hour or so later, it was time for the girls to go to bed. After they put on their thin flannel nightgowns, they gave Loreli a hug and a kiss good-night. They repeated the ritual with their uncle, who then said, "I'll be in in a moment to hear your prayers."

As the twins headed into their room, Loreli thought about the unfurnished space the girls shared, and a question she'd been brooding on all day. "If it's none of my business just say so, but why is there so little furniture here?"

"My father sold everything when my mother died."

"Why?"

"To atone for his sins. He viewed her death as his personal punishment from God."

That was certainly not the answer she'd been expecting. "He was a preacher?"

"Yes. He had this house built for her." Jake didn't want to talk about his father because of the harsh memories still haunting his soul.

"What sins did he think he had to atone for?"

"Pride, arrogance, and adultery."

Loreli asked very carefully, "He wasn't faithful to your mother?"

"No."

"But why sell everything?"

"In one of the gospels of the New Testament, Jesus tells folks to rid themselves of all their possessions, and my father took the words to heart."

"So, he sold everything?" Loreli asked.

"Everything. Beds, tables, chairs, sideboards. After her death, Bonnie and I grew up with only the things you see inside."

"But don't you think her girls should have more?"

"To be honest, I haven't really thought about it, one way or the other?"

"They're children, Reed. Don't you think you should?"

He began to pace. Finally he said, "I won't have you disrupting our lives this way."

"Disruption keeps you from being stagnant, Reed."

"Oh, now you're calling me stagnant?!"

She smiled. "If the shoe fits . . ."

His handsome face went stony. "I have to see to the girls."

"I'll be right here."

He stormed off. Outside the thunder boomed in concert.

Before knocking on the girls' closed door, Jake drew in a deep breath to calm himself. He knocked.

Bebe's small voice chimed happily, "Come in."

They were in bed. Bebe at the head, Dede at the foot. For the first time Jake attempted to see the room with fresh eyes. He realized the Winters woman was correct. There were no frills or other items associated with girls their age. He remembered the doll his sister dreamt of having when they were growing up but never received because his father thought toys a waste both economically and emotionally. Jake realized he'd been unwittingly subjecting the girls to the same kind of joyless life.

Dede's concerned voice brought him back. "Uncle, are you all right?"

He smiled softly. "Yep. I was just thinking is all." To change the subject he said, "Sounds like you two had a fine day with Miss Winters."

Bebe responded with a big smile. "Oh, yes, uncle. She's so nice. She took us to the bank and we helped her move some money."

"You did?" he asked in a wonder-filled voice. "Did you actually get to carry it?"

They laughed, and Dede said, "No. It's going to come by wire. We just got to talk to Mr. Buxton and tell him what Loreli wanted."

Bebe said proudly, "She let me write the date on the slip."

"And I got to write in the name of our town."

"My, my. I'm very impressed."

Bebe said, "She said we needed to learn that a woman can take care of her own finances without a man's help, approval, or . . ." She paused, searching for the word.

"Interference," Dede provided, proud that she'd remembered something her sister hadn't. Dede then added sagely, "Loreli's very smart, Uncle Jake."

"Much smarter than mean old Miss Millie," Bebe said.

Jake was confused. "What happened with Miss Millie? Is she going to sew your dresses for the wedding?"

"She threw a book at Loreli, so we had to leave."

"What?"

"Miss Millie didn't like Loreli because she thought you were going to marry Miss Rebecca. That's what Loreli said."

Jake went still. "How did Miss Millie find out about the wedding?"

Bebe confessed softly, "I told her Loreli was going to be our new mama. Was it a secret, Uncle?"

"No, it wasn't a secret." And it certainly wasn't one now. More than likely Millie Tate had closed her shop immediately after the girls left and ran to tell Rebecca all she knew.

Bebe looked worried. "I wasn't suppose to tell. Was I?"

He came over and stroked her head reassuringly, "You didn't do anything wrong. Not a thing."

He then leaned down and kissed her on the forehead. "Go to sleep now. I'll see you in the morning. Miss Winters is going to spend the night because of the storm." He walked to the foot of the bed and gave Dede a kiss on the forehead as well. "Sleep tight," he told her affectionately.

"Don't let the bed bugs bite," they chimed.

He grinned, turned down the lamp, and left them to their dreams.

Chapter 6

When Jake returned to the front room, the Winters woman was nowhere to be seen.

"I'm out on the porch," she called. "The rain's stopped."

Jake opened the screen door and stepped out. The moon cast a bright light over the night. The air was fresh with the smell of rain. Loreli turned back to look at him and even in the dark he was moved by the faint scents of her cologne and how much of a woman she was. To a plain-living man like himself she was as exotic as a sapphire in a pile of coal. She sparkled, glowed, and seemed intent upon turning his world upside down. Stagnant, she'd called him. Admittedly he didn't like change and upheaval, at least not in his private life, but that didn't make him stagnant, did it?

"The girls heading to sleep?" she asked.

"Yes. They told me about the visit with Millie Tate."

"Not a very nice woman."

"De said she threw a book at you?"

She chuckled. "Not actually, but it certainly seemed that way. She said she was a good friend of your Rebecca."

"She's not '*my* Rebecca.' "

"Well, apparently some folks see it differently. When are you going to tell Rebecca about . . . us, this?"

"Tomorrow, first thing," Reed replied.

"She's probably going to be angry. I know I would be if I thought a man was courting me and he turned around and married someone else."

Jake didn't expect tomorrow to go well. "The girls don't like her."

"I know." Loreli looked out over the moonlit night and said quietly, "Well, I hope it won't be too painful for her."

"For her?"

She turned back so she could see him. "Yes, her. You're not going to be the one with the broken heart, Reed, she is."

He didn't want to think about it. The confrontation with Rebecca would come soon enough. A short silence filled the air.

"I've decided to close the discussion we were having about all the things I bought. I'm not going to argue with you on such a beautiful night." The storm had swept away the heat and humidity and replaced it with a cool, skin-brushing breeze. "I love it when it rains."

"Why?"

"Oh, when I was about the twins' age, my pa and I were in Kentucky somewhere and we were walking to the next town. We'd just gotten run out of the last one, and it was hot, dusty, and humid. Seemed like we'd walked for miles. I was hungry, my clothes were filthy and sticking to my skin, and then it started to rain. I never felt anything so good as that water in my life. I was so happy I started to dance right there in the muddy road, and my pa laughed and laughed. Rain always makes me think of that day and of him."

Jake felt her smile touch him in the same places that the twins' smiles did. That filled him with alarm. Surely he couldn't be developing feelings for this impossible woman? "Why were you two run out of town?"

"Pa made a bet he couldn't cover. The men he owed wanted to string him up right then and there, but they didn't."

"What stopped them?"

"My pa being who he was."

She must've sensed his puzzlement because she explained further. "My pa was Hamilton Beauregard Winters, the only son of Horace Beauregard Winters, one of the wealthiest slave-owners in the state of Kentucky."

"Your pa was White?"

"Yep, and he had the audacity to fall in love with my mother and be wealthy enough to live with her openly during a time that should have gotten them both killed. But because my pa was a Winters, folks left them alone."

"How did his father feel about that?" Jake asked.

"Disinherited pa the day my parents set up housekeeping. Pa didn't care. Back then he had more than enough money to take care of us."

"Then how did you wind up living such a hard life?"

She quieted and Jake wasn't sure she planned to answer until she said, "After my mother died, he couldn't bear to stay in the same place, so we drifted around. He ran his thoroughbreds in races for a few years, but eventually had to sell them to cover gambling debts, and after that, he drank or gambled away everything else he owned. He died when I was fourteen, but his grief over losing my mother killed him long before."

The story made Jake view her differently. He could no longer see her as just another gambling queen. It was apparent from her voice that she'd known pain and heartache. "He must've loved her very much."

"He did, and continued to do so until the day he died."

A silence settled over them again, letting the soft, chirping sounds of the night rise to their ears. He realized he wanted to know more about this fascinating woman, then hastily pulled his mind away from those thoughts. He didn't need to know any more than he did now. "You can sleep in my room tonight. I'll bunk in the barn."

"Thanks. I'll head back first thing in the morning. I need to wire a friend. I can take the girls with me if you're really going to talk to Rebecca."

"I am, so taking them with you would be appreciated."

"I don't mind in the least." She then turned to glance at him. "See, we can be civil."

He met her eyes in the moonlit dark. "I suppose we can."

Jake could sense the currents building between them, and fought to keep them from muddling his mind. "I put clean sheets on the bed when I changed my wet clothes. You can turn in anytime you like."

"Thanks," she said sincerely.

"Good night, Miss Winters."

"It's no sin to call me by my given name, you know."

Jake felt the eddying currents rise higher.

She told him, "Repeat after me—Loreli."

He smiled faintly, then said quietly, "Loreli."

Saying her name for the first time affected them both, but neither made mention of it.

For a moment there was silence, then he said, "Now, your turn, say, Jake."

Loreli responded quietly, "Jake."

Jake's heart skipped a beat and blood rushed to his loins. Pushing himself to remain unmoved, he replied, "Good night."

He stepped off the porch and took a few steps toward the barn, only to have her call out. "Jake?"

He turned back. Telling himself that her standing in the moonlight was not the most beautiful thing he'd seen in all the world, he asked, "Yes?"

"You're a great cook."

He couldn't stop his chuckle. "Thanks," he told her. Their eyes were locked and Jake stood there for a moment caught by her beauty. The longer he stood there, the harder it became to move. Finally, shaking himself free of her spell, he resumed his walk to the barn.

Later, Loreli lay on a too-hard bed, looking up into the dark and thinking back on Jake Reed. Hearing him say her name had triggered a wanting inside herself that was as surprising as it was disturbing. She wasn't even sure she liked him, but something in the way he'd said her name . . . Loreli might have chalked up her reaction as imaginary were she unfamiliar with the concept of wanting a man. She wasn't. She'd been celibate by choice for almost two years, and so far it hadn't been a problem, but being with him tonight seemed to emphasize just how long the two years had been.

As women sometimes do following such an admission, Loreli wondered what kind of lover he'd be. Fast, slow? Was he the kind of man who'd place his lady's pleasure above his own or one of those who saw women only as vessels for a man's needs?

She decided it didn't matter one way or the other, because she and Reed would never be lovers, so she turned over and closed her eyes. She drifted off to sleep hearing him softly calling her name.

Thursday morning, Jake waited until Loreli and the girls had driven to town before mounting up to ride over to Rebecca's.

After answering his knock upon the door, she stepped onto the porch. Her greeting was cool. "Good morning, Jake."

He took off his hat. "Rebecca."

"What brings you out so early? The girls need watching?"

He shook his head. "I came to tell you—well—I'm getting married a week from Saturday."

She tightened visibly. "What?"

"Rebecca—I'm sorry."

"So the rumors are true? It's that Winters woman, isn't it?"

"Yes."

She searched his eyes, then asked bluntly, "Why her and not me?"

He fiddled with his hat for a moment, trying to come up with a lie, then chose to go with the truth. "The girls."

"The girls," she stated skeptically. "You let two eight-year-olds decide your future?"

"It's their future too, Rebecca."

"I know they don't like me, but to let them influence you this way? The woman's a gambler, for heaven's sake, Jake. What will people say?"

"Whatever they like, as long as they don't say it to the girls."

She shook her head in disbelief. "Pa said you'd never marry me. I kept telling him he was wrong—that you'd come to your senses—but you've lost your mind completely."

He didn't argue with her. He wanted her to get it all out, because once she did he didn't plan to discuss the issue with her ever again. "I apologize for hurting you, but it wouldn't've worked out, you and me."

"Why, because those girls didn't like being around someone who believed children should be seen and not heard?"

"Yes, and neither did I," he added pointedly.

His frankness caught her by surprise. She recovered quickly. "Then you're right. Your tossing me over for a whore confirms you aren't the man for me."

"She isn't a whore."

"How do you know? You met her a few days ago, she could be anything."

He didn't argue. "Are we done here?"

"Apparently, we are."

Jake knew she was angry with him, but there was no cure for her distress short of making her his wife, and he wasn't going to do that. "I'll be heading back now, Rebecca. Again, I'm sorry for causing you pain."

"Good-bye, Jake."

That said, she went back inside the house.

Jake remounted Fox, and rode away.

It was midafternoon before Loreli and the girls returned. They found Jake seated on the porch in one of the old cane chairs. He looked grim, but his countenance brightened when he saw the girls.

"Hello, Uncle," his nieces called as they ran up onto the porch.

He kissed each girl and asked, "You ladies get all of your business taken care of?"

Loreli followed the girls up the steps and pulled off her soft leather driving gloves. "Sure did. Wired my housekeeper in Philadelphia about having some of my belongings shipped here—"

"Can we go play?" Bebe asked. "Loreli bought us some new jacks."

"Sure, go ahead," Jake told her with a smile.

The girls disappeared around the back of the house, leaving Loreli and Jake alone.

"Housekeeper?" Jake asked querulously.

"Yes. Her name's Olivia Oliver. . . . How'd *your* morning go?"

He offered a brief shrug. "It's done."

Loreli's stare caught his eyes when he looked up. "So, you talked to her?"

"Yes."

Loreli doubted he'd unburden himself to her, but she made the offer anyway. "If you want to talk—"

"I don't."

She shrugged. "Suit yourself."

For a moment silence came between them, then he said, "You were right about the girls needing all the things you purchased."

Loreli was surprised, to say the least. "What brought this on?"

"I looked at it from their point of view."

"I see."

"Rebecca accused me of having lost my mind for looking at life through their eyes. Told me I shouldn't let eight-year-olds decide my future."

"And what did you tell her?"

"That that was why I couldn't marry her."

Good answer, Loreli said to herself.

As if talking to himself, he continued, "Thought I'd be able to look past the things about Rebecca I didn't care for, and that she'd change once she got to know the girls better, but . . ."

Their eyes met.

"I'm sorry," Loreli replied genuinely.

"Don't be because truthfully, I'm not." Then he added earnestly, "Maybe I have lost my mind in choosing you, and maybe I didn't plan this out real well, but the girls seem happier than they've been since coming to live with me. That means a lot."

"Yes, it does," she agreed.

Then as if he'd revealed too much of himself and his feelings, he changed the subject. "Are you staying for supper?"

Loreli suddenly wanted to know more about the man he kept hidden beneath the marble façade, but doubted the two of them would ever grow close enough for her to do so. "Am I invited?"

"Yes."

"Then I guess I'm staying."

After supper, Loreli helped the girls with the dishes, then, while they ran off to finish their game of jacks, she went to find Reed. He was out by the barns repairing a busted slat in one of the animal pens. His sleeves were rolled up, revealing the dark hard muscles of his arms. From his handsome mustached face to his chiseled physique he was gloriously made. When she neared, he stopped hammering and looked up.

Gloriously made, she echoed inwardly. Composing herself, she said, "I'm heading back to town. Thanks for supper."

He straightened to his full height, "You're welcome." He paused for a moment, then asked, "Can you cook?"

"Not a lick."

He stared.

Loreli shrugged. "It's the truth. No sense in lying about it. I can't cook beans."

"Why not?"

"No reason to learn, I guess."

"All women cook."

"Says who?" she asked, crossing her arms.

He left that alone. "Do you sew?"

"Nope."

"Can?"

"As in vegetables and fruit?"

"Yes."

"No," she answered, as if he'd asked her something ridiculous.

He threw up his hands.

Loreli told him. "Look, Reed, you knew I wasn't a conventional woman when you met me. Why are you surprised that I'm not all of a sudden?"

"I don't know, maybe I was hoping you had some domestic in you."

"Domestics clean houses. I buy them."

He shook his head and she swore she saw him smile, but there was no trace of it when he asked, "Are you coming back tomorrow?"

"I don't want to wear out my welcome."

"I wouldn't worry about that. The girls will never complain."

"What about you?" It was a loaded question and Loreli knew it.

He bent and pulled the broken slat free. "It's the girls you're here for, not me." He paused and straightened, then dusted off his gloved hands on the legs of his denims. "This'll be a marriage in name only, remember?"

Loreli met his eyes, then asked boldly, "No marriage bed?"

He shook his head, saying, "No."

"We're adults, Reed, anything is possible."

"That isn't."

"Why not?"

"Because it just isn't." He picked up the replacement slat and began to hammer the ends into the gap left by the broken one.

Loreli watched him hammer for a few moments. Feeling more frustrated than she wanted to admit, she asked him, "Is this your way of ending the conversation?"

"You're a smart lady, Miss Winters."

"I thought you were going to call me Loreli?"

"I'll see you tomorrow." That said he went back to hammering.

Simmering, Loreli gave him a chance to say more, but when he seemed bent on ignoring her presence, she spun on her heels and walked away.

As Jake watched her storm off, the man in him appreciated the righteous sway of her sassy hips. He agreed with her—anything *was* possible, but their sharing a bed was out of the question; a man as simple and as inexperienced as he had no business in a bedroom with a woman made from sapphires. After being around her for the past few days, he was convinced that her claims of not being a whore were true; however, he was equally convinced that she knew her way around a boudoir a whole lot better than he did, and therein lay the problem.

That night, as Loreli lay in her bed at the boarding-house, she and her slightly bruised ego decided that something had to be wrong with Reed to dismiss her so out of hand. Didn't he know she'd been called one of the most beautiful women anywhere, and that she was supposed to be the one doing the turning down, not him? Jake Reed apparently had no idea that men flocked to her side wherever she went, or that on those very rare occasions when she did say yes, there were no commitments or ties? Loreli could never remember being faced with a man who appeared to have no interest in her at all. It wasn't natural, or at least that's what her ego maintained. Maybe it was a religious issue, she mused, or maybe something was wrong with him, her ego added again. The last thing she wanted to admit was that there might be something wrong with her, but that's the impression he left her with. Did he still believe she made her living by working on her back?

Loreli had no answers, and as she drifted off to sleep, the questions continued to swirl.

Before turning in for the night, Jake went to check on the girls. As he watched them sleeping so innocently, he knew that marrying Rebecca would not have been in their best interest. Yes, they would have grown up to be god-fearing and polite, but he wanted them to be that and more. The world was expanding. Times were changing, and women of all races were beginning to do more than cook, clean, and sew. They were now doctors, heading up newspapers, running businesses. They were working in factories and making everything from shoes to clocks, and wanting to be paid the same as men. *Domestics clean houses. I buy them*! Loreli had said. That's what he wanted his sister's girls to have, that kind of confidence and spunk. Of course he didn't want them to grow up and become poker players; he preferred they marry and have a family, but Loreli was right again—what if they didn't find husbands or even want one? In that case they would have to make their own way in the world, and he wanted them prepared. He was the only family they had, and once he died and passed on, they'd have only each other to rely on. No, Loreli Winters might make him a laughingstock when word got out that he was marrying her, but he didn't care. As he'd noted earlier, the twins seemed happier, and that meant more to him than anyone would ever know.

Content with himself and his decisions, he tiptoed out of the room and closed the door softly behind him.

* * *

In town the next morning, Loreli went to the bank to see if her money had been successfully transferred. Inside, she saw the smiling Cyrus Buxton, and to her surprise, three of her friends from the wagon train: Gertrude "Trudy" Berry, Fanny Ricks, and Ruby O'Neal.

After sharing hugs with everyone, Fanny, the youngest, said to Loreli, "We thought you were goin' to California?"

"Nope, still here. Probably be here for another year or so."

The three friends appeared puzzled. Trudy, who'd left her life as a washerwoman to become a mail-order bride, asked, "A year?"

Loreli nodded. "Are you three in a hurry?"

None were.

"Let me check with Cyrus about something, then let's find a place where we can sit and talk. I have a doozy of a story to share."

They all nodded and waited for her to conduct her business.

Loreli's quick discussion with Cyrus Buxton confirmed that her funds had been wired from her bank on Thursday, and that everything involving the transfer had gone smoothly. Her own flush account brought to mind the dire straits faced by the farmer Peterson. She'd been moved by his plea for the well-being of his five children. She made a note to speak to Reed about the family when she saw him later. Maybe there was a way for her to help Bebe and Dede's friend Carrie. Loreli thanked Cyrus, then exited with her friends.

Since Fanny lived in town, the four women went to her house. Fanny's new husband, Ben Leslie, was a Pullman porter. According to Fanny he'd left this morning and would be gone for twenty-one days. The women made themselves comfortable on the house's side porch, and there, seated in the early morning shade, shared glasses of lemonade and swapped stories of their new lives.

Loreli asked Fanny, "So, how's life with your new husband?"

The happy look on Fanny's young face told all. "Just wonderful. I miss him already. Loreli, he's the first man I've ever known besides my father who thinks it all right for a woman to be smart."

Loreli was pleased. Fanny, an Oberlin graduate, had signed on to the wagon train because, according to her, the men she knew back home in Illinois thought her too intelligent to marry. Loreli was glad Fanny's new husband appreciated his young wife's strong mind. Too bad he had to leave so soon after the wedding.

Trudy and Ruby also related good news. The men they'd married appeared to be fine individuals as well. Loreli knew some of the wagon-train women must be unhappy with the men they'd chosen as husbands, but she was glad that the women she'd grown closest to weren't counted in that group. Trudy was married to a man named Samuel Taylor. He was a farmer and the local undertaker. He and Trudy lived on a farm west of town. Ruby, a former schoolteacher, was happy with her pick as well. Her husband, a farmer named Vernon Parker, had an empty barn on his property that Ruby planned to turn into a school.

A bit confused by Ruby's plans, Loreli asked, "Isn't there a school here already?"

"There is," the statuesque Ruby replied, "but according

to the girls—oh, did I tell you my Vernon has two daughters, twelve and eleven?"

"No," Loreli replied, smiling with surprised delight. "Do you three get along?"

"No cat fights yet. They're studying me and I'm studying them."

Everyone smiled.

Ruby continued. "I guess his first wife left him and the girls to go live somewhere else. Vernon said she didn't like the life here. Too slow. Anyway, the girls say the teacher, Mr. Hazel, doesn't believe in teaching females—"

"What!" the women shouted in unison.

"That's the most ignorant nonsense I've heard in some time," short dark-skinned Trudy declared.

The others nodded with vigorous agreement.

Ruby said, "I agree, so I'm going to teach my girls myself. If there are any other girls who wish to attend my classes, they're welcome. I'm going to call it the Ruby Parker School of Progressive Education for Women."

"Good for you," said Fanny. "Count me in if you need teaching help, Ruby. My certificate from Oberlin allows me to teach, and I'm real good with little girls."

Ruby grinned. "Why thanks, Fanny. Oh, those old biddies around here will have a fit if I open up a school that has *two* teachers."

Everyone laughed because they'd all had negative encounters with the town's clan of established women. Granted, the brides greatly outnumbered the old guard, but the old guard were accustomed to being the only women around and didn't care to share their pedestals with a bunch of mail-order interlopers.

Trudy said, "I had a group of them hiss at me when I was coming out of the general store yesterday. I had to remember my manners. Good thing Sam was with me."

Loreli added, "Well, I'm sure the heat's going to rise once my news gets around."

"What news?" Fanny asked.

"Well, girls, I'm getting married next Saturday."

Shocked silence came over the porch.

Trudy's eyes were wide. "To whom?"

"Jake Reed."

Ruby, equally as wide-eyed, gushed, "The doctor? He came out to the farm a couple days ago. Loreli, he's gorgeous. Vernon said all the eligible women around here have been after him for years!"

"Well, I may let them have him." Loreli told them the story of her initial encounter with the twins and what had come about as a result. She also gave them the rundown on the limits Reed wanted to impose on this marriage of convenience.

"And you're going to marry him?" Trudy asked.

Loreli shrugged. "Yep. Crazy isn't it?"

Ruby disagreed. "I don't know, Loreli, the girls sound mighty needy to me, and you'd be good for them, but how's the uncle going to find this so-called new wife with you around?"

Loreli shrugged again. "No idea, but he seems to think it's possible."

Fanny confessed, "I certainly wouldn't want to follow you, Loreli. No woman with any sense would."

"Well, that's not my concern. I'm doing this for the twins. Wait until you meet them. They are such sweethearts."

Trudy had a doubt-filled look on her face.

"What's wrong, Tru? Don't you think I can be a mama?"

Trudy said, "It's not that. I think you'll make a hell of a mama, Loreli, but I just can't see you married to a man who had a fit simply because you were playing cards with the sheriff."

Loreli thought that a good point. "The way I live my life is an ongoing point of contention, it's true, but he's really sticking his neck out for those girls, and I respect that. Besides, who knows what might happen in a year's time. Maybe he'll mellow a bit."

"Suppose you fall in love with him?" Trudy asked in a serious tone.

Loreli raised an eyebrow. "Bite your tongue."

"That's something to consider, Loreli," Ruby added sagely.

Loreli disagreed. "No, it isn't. He's already said we aren't going to share a bed."

Fanny's mouth dropped in astonishment.

Loreli chuckled. "Close your mouth, Fan, before something flies in."

Fanny finally found her voice, "No marriage bed? Is something wrong with him, Loreli?"

"There can't be," Ruby answered first. "The Lord would not make a man that good looking for no reason. Girls, wait until you see him. He's tall, dark, has a mustache, and that form—"

"Ruby!" Loreli told her laughing.

They all laughed.

Fanny said, "Well, Loreli, you know I'm a romantic at heart, and if I were you, I'd watch my step. When Cupid shoots his arrows, he doesn't always care what you want."

Loreli rolled her eyes. "I'll keep that in mind."

"But suppose you do fall in love with him, Loreli?" Trudy asked. "Then what?"

"There is no *what*, Trudy, because it isn't going to happen. In a year I'm pulling up stakes, and I'll be gone."

Her friends looked skeptical but let the subject drop for now.

"Okay," Ruby announced, "now that that's settled, let's plan Loreli's wedding."

Loreli began to protest, but her friends, like Cupid, didn't care what she wanted. They went right ahead and made plans.

After leaving her friends, Loreli went back to the bank. She knew the twins were anxiously awaiting her arrival out at the Reed place, but she had one more bit of business to take care of.

Cyrus greeted her return with puzzlement. "Did you forget something, Miss Winters?"

"In a way, yes, Cyrus. I'd like to speak with Mr. Diggs, if I might."

"He's in with his wife, right now. Would you care to take a seat while I tell him you're here?"

"I'd love to," Loreli said.

So Loreli sat on the bench, and Cyrus went to alert Mr. Diggs.

A few moments later, a very well-dressed woman came sweeping out of Diggs's office, saying, "And don't forget, I'm having the club members over this afternoon. It might be nice if you came by and put in an appearance."

Sol Diggs came out behind her, responding tightly, "I

have a meeting this afternoon. Maybe next month."

"You've been saying that since last December, Solomon. If you don't wish to come, just say so."

"I don't wish to come."

She sniffed huffily, then started walking in Loreli's direction, toward the bank's front door.

Loreli judged Mrs. Diggs to be in her late thirties. She had soft brown skin and was dressed in a mauve walking gown far too expensive for a backwater like this. Her hair was up, her hat fashionable, and when her eyes met Loreli's, they were cool as February.

Diggs appeared more enthusiastic. "Ah, Miss Winters, I hope I haven't kept you waiting for very long?"

"No more than a minute or so."

Sol made the introductions. "Vicki, I want you to meet Miss Loreli Winters. Miss Winters, my wife, Victoria."

The woman's manner didn't warm up one bit. She nodded tightly. "Miss Winters."

"Mrs. Diggs."

Victoria asked in a haughty voice, "You're one of the wagon-train women, aren't you?"

"I am."

Victoria Diggs looked Loreli up and down, then, as if Loreli had taken up enough of her time, pointedly turned back to her husband. "Do try and make the club meeting, Solomon. As town leaders, we have appearances to maintain." With that said, she swept from the room as if she were Queen Victoria.

Loreli, a bit stunned, stood there in the silence for a moment, then raised an eyebrow Diggs's way.

"Sorry about that, Miss Winters," he stated with irritation. "She's from Philadelphia, and she's never forgiven me for moving her out here."

"No apology necessary," Loreli replied, although she sarcastically wondered when moving from Philadelphia had become an excuse for rude behavior.

Diggs asked then, "So, what can I do for you today, Miss Winters?"

"I'd like to buy Mr. Peterson's mortgage."

As if he hadn't heard her, Diggs bent forward and asked, "Excuse me?"

"Mr. Peterson's mortgage—I'd like to purchase it."

He eyed her suspiciously. "Why?"

"Because I do. I heard you talking with him yesterday, and since I own a bit of real estate back East—thought I'd see what I can pick up while I'm here. I'll give you your asking price, plus an ample commission for the bank."

He scrutinized her silently for a moment. "Is that why you wanted to know how much he owed?"

A poker-faced Loreli lied, "Yes."

He smiled, and his eyes glinted greedily. "Well, let's go into my office."

He called to Cyrus, "Make certain we're not disturbed."

A bit less than an hour later, Loreli Winters affixed her signature in all the necessary places on the bank's documents and purchased Mr. Peterson's mortgage for two-hundred and fifty dollars. To a struggling farmer it was a substantial sum of money, but not for Loreli—she'd won and sometimes lost that much in one night on a single turn of a card or toss of the dice. For her this was an investment in the future of a family with five children. Just because she'd grown up without a roof over her head didn't mean other children had to, at least not as long as she had the ability to keep it from happening.

Mr. Diggs smiled as Loreli handed the papers over. He then handed her the deed, saying, "All yours now. I enjoy doing business with a woman who knows her mind, and has the funds to back it up."

Loreli hoped her smile didn't appear too false. "And I enjoy doing business with you." She stood. "I should be going. Thanks very much for your help." She folded the deed and placed it in her handbag.

He escorted her to his office door, then opened it. "Have a nice day, Miss Winters."

"You do the same."

Her work now done, Loreli drove out to the Reed place. Putting the Petersons out of her mind for now, she wondered what Reed would say once he learned that the small wedding he'd planned had been replaced by a slightly more elaborate affair. Probably throw a fit, she mused, but her wagon-train sisters were determined to make the wedding day a special occasion, and there seemed to be no getting around it, or out of it.

Chapter 7

〰〰〰

When Loreli arrived at the house, the girls came tearing off the porch.

"We didn't think you were coming!" Bebe yelled happily. She and her sister waited by the carriage for Loreli to step down, then they hugged her in turn.

Loreli thought their hugs balm for the soul. "How are you two? I'm sorry if I worried you. I ran into some friends and we got to talking—"

The sight of Jake on the porch made her stop. She straightened and faced him. Remembrances of their last encounter put a chilliness in her greeting. "Afternoon, Reed."

He nodded. "Miss Winters."

Jake thought no woman had the right to be so beautiful. She was dressed all in green today. From that feathered hat to the form-fitting jacket and matching fancy skirt, she was the closest he'd ever seen to perfection. "The girls were worried."

"I know. I spent the morning with some friends from the wagon train. We lost track of the time."

Dede asked, "Are your friends mamas now too?"

"Some of them are, yes. One even has two daughters."

"Just like you," Bebe pointed out proudly.

Loreli grinned down. "Yep. Just like me."

She could feel Reed's eyes, but she didn't look his way.

Jake stood silently watching while Loreli and the girls chatted about her friends. His mind went back to the conversation they'd had yesterday. He'd never been around a woman confident enough in herself to know that if something sparked between them, anything might be possible. The way he was raised, such forwardness branded a woman as scandalous, and *good* men knew to avoid them at all cost, at least publicly. He took in her clothing, her golden skin and that winning smile, and swore he wasn't affected by her, but knew it was a lie. Being around her made him feel as if he'd been placed under a spell—how else to explain his having picked her for the girls? If it was a spell, he needed an antidote quickly, before he embarrassed himself by taking her up on her offer and entering an arena he had scant experience in. Jake knew the ins and outs of human anatomy, but she'd obviously had lovers in the past. He didn't want to be compared and then found lacking. His declaring there'd be no sharing of a marriage bed had to do with pride, and Jake had always had more than his share.

Loreli looked up at Reed and asked, "How far away is the Peterson place?"

Jake's face mirrored his confusion. "Matt Peterson?" he asked.

She shrugged her ignorance. "I don't know his given

name, but the girls told me his daughter Carrie is a friend of theirs."

Jake nodded. "That's Matt. He lives about five miles east of here. Why?"

"I'd like to speak with him about something."

Bebe entered the conversation and said to her uncle, "Mr. Diggs told Carrie's pa they couldn't live in their house anymore."

Dede piped up, "I told Loreli when I get big, I'm going to be rich. Then nobody can tell me I can't live in my house."

Confused, Jake said, "Girls, how about you go inside and finish your lessons? I want to speak with Miss Winters."

The girls looked at Loreli as if she might countermand their uncle's request and let them stay by her side, but she asked, "Did you hear your uncle?"

They dropped their heads and went into the house.

Smiling at their retreat, Loreli then turned her attention back to Reed.

"What do you want to talk to Matt about?" Reed asked.

"His mortgage from the bank."

Jake became suspicious. "Why?"

"Banker Diggs foreclosed on Peterson's farm. He and his family have to be out by Monday." She then described the encounter she and the girls witnessed between Peterson and Diggs.

When she was done, Jake ran his hand over his head in both anger and frustration. "He could've given him until the harvest."

"That was my thinking too, but he wouldn't. In fact, he seemed right pleased with himself."

"Diggs is a snake, always has been. Matt's worked hard to get a profit out of that land. Another year or two and he might've made it." He then asked, "So why do you want to talk to Matt?"

"Because I purchased his mortgage from the bank."

He looked stunned. "What?'

Loreli explained, "I now own the mortgage to his place."

"Why on earth did you do that?"

"Because the man has five children, Reed."

"But . . ."

Jake had so many questions he didn't know what to ask first.

She chuckled. "Close your mouth, Reed, and tell me how to get to his place."

"What are you going to do with his note?"

She looked at him as if it were a silly question. "Turn it over to him, of course. What did you think I planned to do?"

The speechless Jake had no idea. He stared at her with wonder-filled eyes. "You're going to just give it to him?"

"Sure, why not? I don't need a farm—wouldn't know the first thing about running it." She shrugged as if that were explanation enough.

Jake found her even more astonishing. Just when he thought he had her pegged, she pulled the rug from beneath his feet and sent him sprawling. "Matt has a lot of pride. It might take some doing to get him to accept your charity."

"The man has five children. Pride won't feed them."

Jake shook his head at her blunt reply. "You're right, of course, but pride's all a man has sometimes."

"True, but you can't eat it or make love to it, so . . ."

Jake wondered if that last part had been aimed at him personally.

"So, are you going to direct me there or not?" she asked.

He nodded. "I'll drive you."

"That's not necessary."

"I know."

Jake studied her for a long moment. "You always go around stirring up trouble?"

Loreli wasn't sure if he were teasing or simply being his usual critical self, so she placed a hand on her hip and tossed back, "Yes. Can't you tell?"

Jake, enjoying her sassy stance, replied, "I can."

Loreli smiled. "You think Diggs is going to give me trouble over this?"

Jake ran his eyes over her mouth and wondered how it might be to kiss her. "Yep. He wants Matt off that place for more than owing money."

Loreli eyed him. "Explain."

"Diggs doesn't want the farmers around here to organize."

"Organize as what?"

"A union."

Loreli had heard about hod carriers, dock workers, and the like forming trade unions, but farmers? "Why would farmers need a union?"

"To set fair crop prices among other things. The Digges of the world shouldn't be allowed to make their living off the misery of others."

"Are you leading this union organizing?"

"Around here, I am."

"Could the girls be in danger from this?"

"I would hope not, but organizers have been killed in some places."

Loreli realized he was a lot more involved in politics than she'd first thought.

"Well, sometime soon, I'll need to hear more on this, so I'll know what I might be in for."

He thought that only fair. "How about later this evening?"

"Good."

For a moment there was silence. Jake knew Loreli wouldn't let the girls come to any harm, not without a fight. He also knew it wouldn't be long before the male in him roared past the tight controls he'd placed on his emotions, before he sought her out, consequences be damned. The shape of her mouth teased him, the curves of her body filled him with need. Bringing himself back under control, he directed Loreli: "You get the girls, I'll get the buggy."

As he headed off, Loreli watched him and wondered what he planned to do about the heat rising between them, and more importantly, when? She then reminded herself that she'd known the man less than a week, and therefore needed to stop thinking like a cathouse trollop. Besides, there seemed to be no reason to rush things with him. In spite of yesterday's no-marriage bed declaration, the desire burning in his eyes just now had been real. It meant one thing: the marble archangel was developing cracks.

Moments later they piled into the wagon. Jake and Loreli sat up front while the girls sat on large hay bales in the bed. As always, the twins sang, this time, the "Battle Hymn of the Republic." They were singing with such relish and fervor, a laughing Loreli had tears in her eyes. Their singing of the *Glory, Glory Hallelujah!* refrain was slaying her the most. The girls were throwing back their heads like two little coyote pups and belting out the words with such enthusiasm, and in voices so sweetly bad, Loreli thought she might hurt herself. She turned around so she could see them as they sang their way to the final notes. *"His truth is marching onnnnn!"*

When they were done, she said genuinely, "You two can sing for me anytime."

Their responding grins made Loreli melt inside. Turning back to Jake, she asked, "Don't you think that was some fine singing?"

"Real fine singing," he agreed.

For the rest of the ride, Loreli did nothing but relish how good she felt. Her problems with Reed not withstanding, she enjoyed being a part of this family, at least so far. Reality dictated that sooner or later she and the twins were going to disagree over something or the other, and when it became time to issue some discipline, they'd probably place Lorlei's name on their witch list right beside old Rebecca Sourapple, but for now happiness reigned and Loreli was content.

As the wagon approached the Petersons' farm and Loreli got her first look at the small, listing sod house, she sensed hopelessness, poverty and despair. Like other such homesteads on the plains, the dwelling had been made from stacked, thick cuts of sod mortared together with mud. Soddies, they were called—damp when it rained; drafty when the winter winds blew. The roof was nothing more than a thin sheet of plywood with a layer of sod on top. There was one rough sawed window cut into the left front wall to let in light. The house sat flush with the ground so there was no porch or steps. Loreli could only imagine how cramped it must be inside with five growing children and how dark and gloomy. Soddies were very flammable during the hot dry months of the summer, so great care had to be exercised with candles and lamps.

Loreli glanced at the twins. The pall that hung over the place seemed to have affected them as well. They'd quieted when Jake turned the buggy toward the house, and were now sitting and watching silently.

"How long have the Petersons lived here?" Loreli asked Jake.

"Almost three years."

Loreli could see a large patch of corn growing emerald green under the afternoon sun. "Corn's growing."

Jake nodded. "Looks like a good strong crop. He had a real hard time getting the ground ready that first year. He had no animals to plow with, and no one to help him plant but his wife, Susan—his children were too young. I brought over an ox and offered to lend him a hand, but he turned me down flat. Proud man, real proud."

Loreli hoped she wouldn't have to argue with this proud man about taking the mortgage from her. Even a blind badger could see he needed help. As her father used to say, what some men called pride, other folks called simple stubbornness.

Jake brought the wagon to a stop, and a few moments later, a man Loreli now knew to be Matt Peterson came out from behind the house. He raised a hand to shade his blue eyes from the late afternoon sun. "Afternoon, Jake. Hi, girls. Who's that with you?"

The girls hopped out, then Jake came around to help Loreli down.

"Want you to meet Loreli Winters," Jake told him.

Loreli stepped to the ground. "Afternoon, Mr. Peterson."

"Ma'am."

Peterson studied her for a moment as if trying to place her face. "You were in the bank."

"Yes, I was."

"Sorry you had to see that," he said.

"No apology needed. You were speaking your mind."

"Diggs is a thief."

Out of the house stepped a tired-faced young woman dressed in a well-patched brown calico farm dress. She had light brown hair and a curly-haired toddler on her hip. Beside her stood two little girls who couldn't be more than four and five; an older girl, Loreli guessed to be Carrie, and an older boy, the cricket-carrying Jimmy. Upon seeing Jake, however, the woman's tired face broke into a smile, letting Loreli see traces of her former beauty.

"How are you, Jake?"

"Fine, Susan. And you?"

She hefted the toddler to a better position. "I'm doing well."

Matt Peterson said to Loreli, "Miss Winters, this is my wife, Susan. Sue, this is Loreli Winters."

The woman nodded a greeting. "Pleased to meet you."

"Same here," Loreli replied. "What's the baby's name?"

"Nathan, after Matt's pa."

Loreli reached over and ran a gentle finger down his

smooth, chubby cheek. "How are you, precious?" she
cooed.

Susan introduced the other children. The entire family
was painfully thin.

"Want to see our new scarecrow?" Jimmy asked the
twins.

Their brown eyes widened excitedly. "May we?" Dede
and Bebe asked their uncle.

"Go right ahead."

The children ran off. Susan set the toddler on his feet,
but kept a sharp eye on him as he waddled around on his
unsteady little legs.

Peterson asked Jake, "I suppose you heard about Diggs
foreclosing on us?"

Jake nodded. "I did."

"Granger, Doyle, and Sears all got notices too."

Jake replied grimly, "It's the organizing."

"I know."

Diggs, in cahoots with some of the area's big grain processors, didn't want the farmers to speak with one voice.
The banker and his moneyed friends wanted things to remain just the way they were, under their control. If the
farmers banded together, making the processors have to
bid for the crops, control would be in the hands of the
farmers and things would change. Diggs hoped that by cut-
ting the feet out from under intelligent and forthright men
like Peterson, other men would think twice about becoming involved. "So what're your plans?" Jake asked him.

"If I didn't have Sue and the children, I'd make the
sheriff put me off this land," Peterson stated flatly. "But I
can't risk my family being harmed."

Susan said, "Diggs hasn't given us a lot of time to decide what to do. We don't have much money, so I suppose we'll have to stay with my sister up in Lawrence for a spell. After that?" She shrugged.

Loreli's lips tightened. She couldn't wait to play poker with Diggs again. Maybe she'd get the chance to teach him a little about foreclosure. She filed the thought away for later, then said to the Petersons, "Suppose there was a way you could stay? Would you?"

Peterson eyed her suspiciously.

Susan looked from her husband's face to Loreli's before asking her, "What would we have to do?"

Loreli fished in her handbag, then withdrew a folded document. "Just take this."

The woman took the paper but promptly passed it to her husband. He hesitated for a moment to study Loreli, then took the paper from his wife. Unfolding it, he slowly read the wording. His lips tightened. "What is this?"

"Your mortgage."

"I can see that, but why's your name on it?"

"Because I now own this land."

He swung angry eyes to Jake. "What the hell does she mean?"

Loreli declared instead, "Talk to me, Mr. Peterson. That's my name on the paper—not his."

Peterson looked at her as if she'd just announced she was the Queen of England. "You're a pretty uppity woman, woman."

She raised her chin, put one hand on her hip and tossed back, "Yes, I am. Now, do you want to talk about staying on this land or not?"

His wife put a gentling hand on his. "Matt, at least listen to what Miss Winters has to say. Remember, she said she might have a way to help us."

He looked down into his wife's pleading eyes, but his own were clearly angry as they met Loreli's. "Let's hear it."

"My plan is to give you this land free and clear."

Peterson tried to hide his astonishment, but failed. "Why?"

"Because the twins and Carrie are friends."

In the silence that followed, an amazed Peterson turned to Jake for explanation.

Jake shrugged. "It's what she wants to do."

Peterson looked as if he wanted to ask her a dozen questions, but could only manage one. "Who are you?"

Loreli smiled. "Loreli Winters. I'm a gambler by trade, but next week I'm going to be Jake's wife."

Peterson's eyes widened. "What?"

Jake said, "Yep." And he felt no shame in supporting her claim. Her wanting to help Matt and his family filled Jake with more pride than he'd ever imagined. She was one remarkable woman.

Susan asked Loreli, "Are you really going to give us the deed?"

Loreli saw the hope and joy waiting to spring to life in Susan's brown eyes, and replied gently, "I wouldn't tease you about something so serious."

Susan's happy tears spilled down her cheeks. She brought her hands to her mouth in wonder.

Peterson's jaw tightened. "Thank you, but we don't take charity."

Loreli looked at him as if he were a candidate for an asylum.

Susan stiffened. She stared at her husband with what appeared to be disbelief, then dropped her head resignedly. She said quietly, "It was nice of you to pay us a visit, Miss Loreli. I—I have to get back to my darning. Good-bye, Jake."

Susan scooped up the baby and hastened into the house.

Her husband watched her exit with an obvious pain in his eyes, but Loreli wanted to take a buggy whip to one Matt Peterson. She glanced at Reed. His face was tight and showed no emotion.

Peterson locked gazes with Loreli but directed his words at Reed. "Take her home, Jake. I don't need handouts." He shoved the paper back at her.

Loreli snatched it free, and snapped, "No, what you need is someone to take a stick to your stubborn head."

Jake made a move as if to intervene, but the flash in Loreli's golden eyes froze him in midstep.

Loreli added coldly, "Pride is fine, Mr. Peterson, but it won't mean a damn thing to your five hungry children."

He flinched, then snapped coldly, "Jake—get her out of here."

A sneering Loreli threw back, "Don't bother, I'm leaving."

And she stormed back to the wagon.

Loreli was still simmering when Jake halted the wagon in front of his house. She hadn't said a word during the ride back. The twins, having never seen this side of their new mama before, were watching her warily as they hopped down from the bed to the ground.

Noticing their concerned faces, Loreli said, "I'll be better in a little while. I just need time to cool off."

"We saw Carrie's mama crying," Dede said softly.

Loreli nodded sadly. "I know, pumpkin, but I'm sure she'll be okay."

The girls nodded, then ran off to play.

In the silence that followed, Jake said quietly, "Your plan didn't go very well."

"No, it didn't," she agreed.

"You shouldn't have pushed him that way."

"I should have pushed him off a cliff."

In spite of the serious moment, he chuckled softly. "You do have a way with words."

"Peterson didn't seem to think so."

"You tried. Like I said, Matt's a proud man."

Loreli snarled. "Pride's not going to feed those children. Did you see how sad his wife looked when he turned down the deed?"

"I did."

"Well, call it pride if you like, but I think it's stupidity."

"You can't judge what drives a man."

Loreli looked his way. His eyes met hers and he said, "You can't."

His words held a wisdom that cut through her anger. She surrendered. "You're right, I suppose. I only met the man an hour ago, and I don't know anything about him, but I did meet his children. Why uproot them when it isn't necessary and start all over again somewhere else? He's just going to place himself under the same kind of debt and spend the rest of his life trying to repay it."

"I agree, but you did your best. If he won't accept your help, there's nothing you can do."

Loreli was slumped back against the seat. Her beautiful face mirrored her frustration.

Jake sensed her essence slowly weaving its way into his being. He thought back on the way she'd stood up to Matt Peterson. She'd been just as fearless as Jake initially imagined her to be, if not more. A man with her by his side would never have to worry about facing obstacles. Life had honed her fine as a blade. He looked over at her tight face and said easily. "I'm going in to prepare some supper. You coming?"

She sighed. "I guess so."

Jake met her eyes. "You did more than most folks would have."

She nodded. "Not that it made much difference, but thanks."

He made four of them some sandwiches out of the last pieces of a smoked ham he'd been given by a farmer for curing sick sheep, then added some dried apples and peaches. It wasn't fancy but it was nutritious, much better than the corn bread and pot likker the Peterson children and other children of struggling families were routinely given because that's all there was to eat. He hoped Matt would come to his senses, because Loreli was right, children couldn't eat pride.

Putting aside thoughts of Matt's family and their troubles for now, Jake went out to the back porch to call the twins and Loreli. He stopped and stared speechless at the sight of Loreli jumping rope. The girls were twirling and chanting a sing-song rhyme while a laughing Loreli was in the center jumping to her heart's content. The light of happiness in the girls' eyes shone even from a distance. Shaking his head at her unpredictability, he feasted his eyes on the small patch of golden ankle above her short-heeled green boots made visible by her held aside green skirt. She'd removed her jacket for the play and the white, high-neck blouse she had on beneath looked to be made of the softest material he'd ever set eyes upon. Her breasts bounced a bit in tandem with her jumping. Feeling himself becoming aroused, Jake quickly swung his eyes back to the girls' happy faces, hoping it would calm him down. It didn't. "Come eat, ladies!"

Bebe called back across the field, "Loreli's jumping to a hundred. She's on ninety-six!"

"Okay," he yelled, smiling. "Come on in when she's done." Shaking his head again, Jake went back into the house.

A bit later, as they sat on the front porch with their plates, Jake asked Loreli, "Well, did you make it to one hundred?"

Loreli responded proudly, "I did indeed. Probably wouldn't have if I hadn't been on that wagon train. Mr. Blake, the wagon master, really made us work."

Dede asked, "Did you jump rope?"

Loreli chuckled. "No, pumpkin, but he made us do a bunch of things that turned us into real strong women."

"Like what?" Bebe asked.

"Well, we had to pitch our own tents, fix our own wagon wheels when they broke, drive the mules and horses."

Dede asked with wide eyes, "All by yourself?"

Loreli nodded. "Yep, there were only two men on the train, so the ladies had to do everything."

Bebe said, "I've never fixed a wagon wheel before."

Dede added, "Me neither."

"Well, how about I teach you sometime this summer?"

Their eyes lit up. "Will you?"

"Sure."

They looked to their uncle. "Can we?"

He smiled, "Sure, why not?" He had no idea how learning to fix a wagon wheel might help them in the future, but he saw no harm in it.

After everyone had eaten, Jake said, "There are a few hours of light left, so how about we go over to the old Fisher place and see if the fish are biting."

The girls' eyes widened with glee.

"Now?" Bebe asked.

"After the dishes are done."

Bebe looked dejected. "Oh."

Her sister looked disappointed as well.

Loreli laughed, "How about I help? Three of us can do it faster than two. In fact, I'll wash and you two dry."

The smiles returned.

Less than an hour later, they were back in the jostling wagon, heading up the rutted road. The girls were singing, "Home on the Range." Loreli had never heard the tune before, but she got a big kick out of her twin coyote pups singing in their sweet, off-key voices, *"Hoooome home on the raaaannnge—where the deer and the antelope plaaayy . . ."*

When the last note faded into the silence, Loreli applauded enthusiastically. "Where in the world did you learn that lovely song?"

Bebe replied, "Everybody in Kansas knows that song, Loreli."

"Oh, really?"

Jake said, "It was written by two men from Smith County. Doc Brewster Higley did the words, and his friend Dan Kelley came up with the music."

Loreli replied, "Well, they did a real good job."

Loreli looked toward the setting sun. It was as fiery red as she'd ever seen it. "Where's this old Fisher place and why is it called that?"

Jake said, "The Fishers came here from Tennessee with the first wave of Exodus folks back in '78. Like most of the 'dusters, they didn't bring enough supplies or provisions, so after two years they abandoned the place and moved back East. There's a little creek out back."

The Fisher house, once a fairly wide soddy, had fallen in on itself. The thick verdant plains grass surrounding the place didn't look as if it had ever seen a plow. As soon as the wagon stopped, the girls, poles and buckets in hand, jumped down from the bed and took off running toward the back of the place.

Jake came around to help Loreli down. He'd done this before, but for some reason, when he closed his hand over hers, a sweet flame rose slowly and licked gently at the foundation of the gates he'd built around his self-control, heating them, bending them, searing open the locks. And as he looked at her, his eyes said what his voice could not: he wanted her.

Loreli felt the heat too, in his hands, in his eyes. Were she not certain the girls would come back and interrupt, she was equally certain she and this gorgeous man would be doing something totally unrelated to catching fish.

Bebe called out, "Are you coming, Loreli? We already found some worms!"

"Be right there," Loreli called back without leaving his eyes.

"Okay!" Bebe ran off.

The moment was over, but the awakening of their

senses remained. He reached up and swung her down, slowly. When Loreli's feet touched the ground, she hardly noticed—his hands on her waist, though, were hot, strong.

The air was charged. They could both feel it. "We—should get going," she said softly.

"Yes, we should."

Loreli had never met such a quiet yet intense man. He didn't say much but there was a depth in his eyes that could make a woman drown in them before she even knew the water was rising.

He was still holding her by the waist, so she said, "You have to turn me loose, Jake."

He shook himself as if he'd been in a trance. "I guess I do, don't I? Sorry."

"No apology needed." In reality Loreli wanted him to hold more than her waist, but he removed his hands, and together they went to find the girls.

They didn't catch any fish, but they had a fine time. The girls sang, hunted for more worms, and got all muddy playing on the creek bank. Jake spent most of his time watching Loreli, and she spent her time watching him. While the girls played, the eyes of the adults questioned, assessed each other, silently circling like partners in a slow dance.

Soon, however, it was time to head back. Both girls were covered with creek mud, so the first order of business upon arriving home was the heating of water for baths.

Later, after the squeaky-clean twins were snug in their bed, Loreli was seated on the porch watching the stars come out. Jake was seated on one of the cane chairs behind her. They were both very aware of each other.

Loreli said, "I really hadn't planned on staying here tonight, so thanks for putting me up yet again."

"It's late, you may as well stay."

Loreli had intended to return to town, but the more time she spent around the twins and this simple life, the longer she wanted to stay. She should've gone back to the boardinghouse because the hem of her skirt and slips were a mess after all that mud, but she'd been having so much fun, dusk had fallen before she knew it. "I just don't like putting you out of your bed."

"Don't worry about me. The barn's fine."

She turned to look back at him sitting quiet as a shadow, then said, "You don't have to sleep in the barn, Jake."

For a moment he said nothing, then responded, "I know."

Loreli's body reacted with heat. "Then don't," she whispered in a voice as hushed as the darkness. She stood and slowly walked over to where he sat. She held out her hand. "Come."

Jake looked up at her and knew he couldn't resist her any longer. He rose to his feet, tossing aside misgivings, attitudes, pride, and discipline; he wanted to cleave to her like Adam to Eve. To that purpose he pulled her into his arms and kissed her with all the pent-up emotions he had stored within, then scooping her up into his arms, he carried her into the house.

He set her down on his hard bed and immediately began to shuck out of his braces and his trousers. She hastily undid the buttons of her jacket, then tossed the garment aside. Nude from the waist down, Jake joined her on the narrow bed. The power of his kisses melted her back and down, and she groaned as he pushed her dress up to her thighs and boldly stripped away her satin drawers. He eased her legs apart, filled her—and she sighed with joy. Three strokes later, he shuddered and was done. He withdrew from her and left the bed. His breathing filled the silence of the room.

Loreli was so stunned, she couldn't move. *That was it?* For all intents and purposes, she was still fully clothed, for heaven's sake! *This can't be happening,* she told herself.

Watching her just lie there in the dark brought all of Jake's misgivings to the fore. He knew that she found him lacking. "What's the matter?" he asked grimly.

Loreli lied. "Nothing." She sat up. Grabbing her drawers, she stood and said, "I'm going out to the pump—back in a few minutes."

But she didn't come back. After making use of the water, she walked around to the porch and took a seat instead. *Good lord.* She tried to let the night's silence soothe her, but it only helped a little. She'd seen jack rabbits make love longer. She thought back to what her friend Ruby had said about the lord not making a man as handsome as Jake useless in bed. Well, Ruby didn't know what the hell she'd been talking about; Jake Reed was as handy in bed as a fish was with a deck of cards. Going into this pretend marriage Loreli knew that he was a simple farmer. She also knew he wasn't worldly, but she had not expected this! She ran her hands over her eyes. *Good lord!*

Behind her, she heard him step out of the door and onto the porch. She stilled.

In reality, Jake's pride didn't want to confront the hows and whys of whatever she might be feeling. He'd been raised to believe that only a man's needs mattered in the marital bed, and he wanted to cling to that position because he didn't know any other position to take, and because it was safe. However, Loreli had been chopping down his views on a lot of things lately, and turning formerly safe positions into kindling. "I want to know what's wrong with you," he told her.

"Nothing."

"If I can ask, you can answer."

Loreli didn't like being chastised by him, probably never would, but she had to admit he was correct. If he was brave enough to drop that marble pride of his and ask what he had, she owed him at least an honest answer. A less concerned man would already be asleep by now, not caring what might be wrong.

So she turned back and asked in a serious voice, "Are you sure?"

Jake steeled himself. "Yes."

She went silent for a moment in order to form the right words. "Well—how do I say this? What we did back there can be a lot more fun when both people get to play, Jake."

He looked out over the night and tried not to be offended by her explanation or moved by her use of his given name. He failed. "And that means?"

"It means, it started out just fine, but then you seemed to forget I was there with you."

"But, women aren't—"

"What? Supposed to enjoy it. A man told you that, right?"

His face hardened. "Look, everything I've been taught, everything I learned—"

"Is wrong," she stated flatly. "Dead wrong. And if you say anything about how *good* women are supposed to behave in the bedroom, as opposed to women like me, I will sock you, I swear."

He shook his head. *Lord, she had fire.* "Okay, for the sake of argument, let's say I am wrong. What would you have me know?"

"That women have needs too. I'm a very passionate woman, Jake Reed, and whether you know it or not, or like it or not, you seem to be a passionate man. Take the time to enjoy the scenery next time. Play with a few buttons, ruffle a few feathers. Let me do the same."

His pride raised its head again. "Now you're going to give me lessons?"

"Only if you'll take them," she tossed back bluntly.

They assessed each other for a long, silent moment, then he said, "I'll see you in the morning."

He walked by her and off the porch, then strode toward the barn.

As he disappeared into the night, Loreli threw up her hands in frustration. She wanted to punch the porch column, but knew she'd only injure herself, so she settled for a short vivid curse instead.

On the ground behind the barn, Jake lay on his pallet looking up at the night sky. He supposed Loreli had gone on to bed by now, but his memories of their disastrous encounter wouldn't allow him to sleep. He'd been right about being unable to satisfy her; he felt like a fool. Having to stand there and listen to her tell him what he already knew about his inadequacies as a lover had not been easy. Jake was thirty-seven-years old and he'd never had a prolonged relationship with a *real* woman before. There'd been the prostitute his father had taken him to visit when Jake turned sixteen, and a few years later, the randy wife of one of his college classmates. Since then, when the need became necessary he'd drive over to Lawrence to visit a woman whose only concern was the monetary exchange at the end. He was the son of a preacher, a quasi doctor. Before meeting Loreli, his physical needs, though as strong and sharp as any normal man's, hadn't been all-consuming.

Her arguments to the contrary, Jake knew only what he'd read and been taught: women did not enjoy the act—they weren't biologically equipped to experience any pleasure from physical stimulus, and those few women who did were either freaks of nature or mentally depraved. So what was the truth? Loreli certainly believed in her version, but she didn't impress him as being a freak of nature or depraved. She'd said the game was more fun when two people were involved, and the pictures those thoughts conjured in his mind made his manhood swell and thicken once more. He swore at his body's undisciplined reaction.

Frustrated he turned over on his pallet. Now he wanted to know just what she'd meant about this "fun," even as he told himself he'd never fall victim to her softness again. His body, remembering how hot and tight she'd felt sheathing him, laughed at that lie. Determined not to think about her, Jake punched his pillow and turned over, but more than an hour passed before he finally drifted off to sleep.

Lying in his bed, Loreli decided that her first order of business would be to replace this bed. It was hard, unyielding, and would always remind her of the debacle that had taken place atop its sheets. It was hardly big enough for one, let alone two, and it would have to be much larger if she were to act on the other decision she'd made. Loreli had had two choices confronting her: she could either resign herself to be in this pretend marriage and endure his poor lovemaking, or do something to remedy the situation. She'd chosen the latter.

He was a passionate man; she knew that. His kisses had left her breathless, and what little she'd felt of his touch had been thrilling, so he wasn't a cold fish. However, he needed instruction, and the idea of playing teacher to his student made her feel deliciously scandalous indeed. How would he react if she did offer to give him the lessons he'd taunted her about on the porch? His reactions aside, when she was done tutoring him, he'd know exactly what every woman wanted her man to know about the art of bringing her pleasure. Just the thought made Loreli want to immediately seek him out and begin now, but common sense told her to hold off. Firstly, she knew she'd have to be subtle. She'd also have to respect his manly pride and not make him think less of himself. Jake was a big strong man, and she wanted him to show her that strength in every way, but didn't want him to feel diminished in his own eyes when they were done. Loreli had never consciously set out to seduce a man, yet she had no qualms where this one was concerned. One, he deserved it on more than a few levels and two, she always did like an adventure. She jokingly also told herself that she owed it to whomever this *real* wife turned out to be to show him the way. Although Loreli hardly qualified as a courtesan, she did know what her body enjoyed, and by the time she was ready to pull up stakes, he would know too. Tonight had not been one of the better experiences of Loreli's female life, but with time, patience, and a bit of womanly wile, the future could be ripe with passionate possibility.

Happy with her kernel of a plan, a contented Loreli turned over and went right to sleep.

Chapter 8

The next morning, Loreli awakened to the smell of bacon frying. She made use of the water in the hand-basin and put on the mud-stained clothes she'd removed the night before. Once dressed, she coiled up her hair, then went out to face the day.

"Good morning," she cheerily called as she entered the parlor.

The twins were already seated at the old table. "Good morning, Loreli," they replied, smiling.

When Jake came in from the kitchen carrying a bowl of scrambled eggs and a platter of bacon, he looked her way and mumbled around his mustache, "Morning."

"Morning," she said in return. "Everything smells wonderful, Jake."

He set the bowl and platter on the table. "Have a seat if you want to eat while it's hot." He then disappeared into the kitchen.

Wondering why he was acting so put out when she

was the one left high and dry last night, she turned back to find the girls staring her in the face. They were watching her so intently, she felt compelled to ask, What's wrong?"

"Uncle's grumpy this morning," Bebe said. "Is he mad at us?"

Loreli made a show of thinking. "Let's see? Did you girls go out and rob a bank last night?"

Dede's eyes widened. "No."

"Good. Did you sneak over to Rebecca's and tip over her privy?"

The girls giggled. "No."

"Ah, I've got it now—horse rustling. There's a report of two little brown twins, wearing pigtails and masks, terrorizing the countryside. That you two?"

The girls laughed louder. "No, Loreli, we're not rustlers."

"Then, I guess your uncle's not mad at you because those are the only things I can think of that would make him mad at you."

The ever-wise Dede said, "Then is he mad at you?"

Loreli turned and looked at the beautiful child. "In a way, but I think I know how to fix it."

Bebe threw in her two cents. "I think De's right. You and uncle should kiss. Aggie says her pa and her new mama always do that when they get mad at each other."

"Do they?"

"Yep, and she says after they get done kissing, they act real happy and jump up and down on the bed because she can hear the bedsprings squeaking."

Loreli doubled over with laughter. She gave each girl a fat kiss on the cheek. "Thanks so much for picking me to be your mama. I wouldn't have missed this for the world. You two make this so much fun."

They grinned up at her. "You're welcome."

Loreli wiped at the tears of mirth in her eyes. "Now, no talk about kissing when your uncle comes back, okay? If there's any kissing talk to be done, I'll handle it."

Grumpy Uncle Jake came back to the table carrying a jam pot and a plate with sliced bread. It took all Loreli had to compose herself, but she did. He sat, said grace to bless the food, then placed a helping of eggs and bacon on the girls' plates. He avoided Loreli's eyes, but it made her no never mind because she had a plan, and she reminded herself with a smile, she had the twins.

The sound of knocking at the front door interrupted them in midmeal. Jake got to his feet and went to see who would be calling on such an early Saturday morning. It turned out to be Matt Peterson.

Jake held the door open so he could come in. "Morning, Matt."

"Morning, Jake. Is Miss Loreli here?"

Jake observed him closely, "Yes. Why?"

"Like to talk to her if I might."

Jake hoped Peterson hadn't come over to rile Loreli some more.

Matt must have read Jake's mind, because he said, "I didn't come to cause any trouble. Just to talk."

Jake was glad to hear it. "I'll get her."

Leaving Matt standing by the door, Jake walked back into the dining room and said, "Loreli, Matt Peterson's here. He wants to speak with you."

Loreli asked coolly, "What about?"

"Not sure."

Sighing, she put her napkin down on the table. "You girls finish eating, I'll be right back."

They nodded and watched her go.

Loreli met Peterson's blue eyes and reminded herself to keep hold of her temper. If the man chose to be stubborn, it wasn't her problem to bear. That was his poor tired wife's task. "Good morning, Mr. Peterson."

"Morning, Miss Loreli." He then paused for a moment as if searching for the right way to begin what he'd come to say. "Yesterday—I wasn't very respectful, and I turned you down because of my pride."

She waited.

"Like you said, pride is fine, but it won't feed my family. Me and Susan got into a big argument after you left."

Loreli found that news distressing. "I didn't want that to happen, believe me."

"I know, but—well, to make this short, she's leaving me and taking the children with her if I don't come back with your deed."

Loreli felt surprised, but kept it from her face. Susan hadn't impressed her as having the inner strength to issue such a serious threat, let alone carry it through. "Wait right here and I'll get it."

She hastened to the parlor for her handbag. She returned with the document and handed it to him. "You must love her very much."

"More than my pride."

He looked down at the deed. "You're certain you want to do this?"

"Positively. You own the place, but if Diggs asks, I'm

renting it to you for one dollar a year. Later on, I'll have a barrister friend draw up a deed transfer so that everything will be legal and binding."

He nodded. "Thanks."

"You're welcome."

"Don't know how I'll ever be able to repay you."

"Just work your land and raise your children. That's payment enough."

Peterson looked over at Jake. "You've got you one fine woman here."

Jake observed the remarkable Loreli Winters. "I'm finding that out."

Loreli's eyes met his. She wondered if he were being sincere or if it was just an act for Peterson's sake.

Peterson's voice interrupted her thoughts. "Well, I should be heading back. Thanks again, Miss Loreli, and my apologies for yesterday."

"None needed. Tell Susan I said hello, and don't forget, you're all invited to the wedding."

"We'll be there. Bye, Jake. Take care of her. Men around here find out how fine she is, you may have to fight to keep her."

Jake looked at Loreli. "I'm not worried. Once they find out she doesn't take orders, they'll send her right back."

Loreli put her hand on her hips in mock offense.

Jake then said to Peterson, "Come by tomorrow evening if you can. I'm having some of the men over to talk about organizing."

"Sounds good." Matt gave Loreli one last look of gratitude, nodded her way, then departed.

In the silence that followed his exit, Jake told her, "That was a good thing you just did."

"It was easy."

He paused for a moment to take in her lovely face and seductive golden eyes. He could still hear the sighs of pleasure she'd voiced the night before when he filled her flesh with his own. The memory affected him now just as much as the reality had then. Would he be able to make her purr like that again? Lord knew he wanted to. One taste of her hadn't been nearly enough, he honestly admitted, even though she probably would never let him near her again.

"Penny for your thoughts," Loreli said.

Jake shook himself free. "Just thinking about Matt Peterson."

Loreli doubted the passion she'd seen in his eyes had anything to do with Matt Peterson, but she didn't challenge him. "Will you have some time today to tell me about the farmer's union? We didn't get around to it last night."

His jaw tightened.

"Forget about what happened last night. I have."

"That's easy enough for you," he said.

"No it isn't, believe me."

He searched her eyes. "It was that bad for you?"

"Some of it, yes. Some of it no. It was a little too fast to tell."

His eyes went cold.

"Oh, don't get mad. That was a joke, nothing more."

He leaned down then and kissed her with such slow authority she thought she might melt.

"That slow enough?" he whispered as he drew away.

Loreli swore she saw stars. "Why, Jake Reed, I do believe you've mastered your first lesson."

His mustache twitched. "Audacious woman. What number is taking you across my knee?"

"Number two if you like," she replied saucily.

The sensual force of her words seared him to his core. "Lord," he whispered, shaking his head with wonder, "what's a man like me supposed to do with a brazen woman like you?"

"Anything he wants—within reason, of course."

Then, throwing him a sly wink, Loreli went back to finish her meal with the girls.

As she walked away, Jake was mesmerized by the tempting sway of her hips beneath the green skirt. Her playful innuendos had left him hard as a beam. He was beginning to understand the basics of this two-player game she wanted him to learn, and although he didn't want to admit it, he was more than beginning to enjoy it.

After breakfast, Loreli helped the girls with the dishes. While they worked, Bebe asked, "Do you think a girl should be allowed to ride in The Circle?"

Loreli glanced at her.

"What's The Circle?"

"It's a horse race."

"Tell me about it."

"Well, after harvest there's a fair, and part of the fair is the Circle. Uncle took us to it last year."

"Why is it called the Circle, is it held in a ring?"

"No, you race in a big circle around town."

"I see. Are children allowed to enter?" Loreli asked.

"Yes, but there weren't any girls last time."

Loreli washed another plate. "Is there a rule that says girls can't?"

Bebe shrugged. "I'm not sure."

Dede looked up at Loreli. "Tell her no, Loreli."

Loreli studied Dede. The little face, framed by lopsided braids, appeared distressed. Loreli set Dede's reaction aside for a moment and turned her attention back to Bebe. "Is this a lead-in for permission to ride in this Circle?"

Bebe shrugged. "I guess so."

Dede tugged on Loreli's sleeve. "She's going to get hurt and die just like mama."

Bebe leaned in angrily. "Stop saying that. I'm not going to die!"

"Yes, you are!"

"No, I'm not! You're the only *baby* who's scared of horses!"

Loreli didn't want to hear another word. "Beatrice Case, apologize to your sister, right now."

Bebe's eyes were flashing and her lip was poked out. "I'm sorry," she mumbled.

Loreli cocked a hand against her ear, and said firmly, "I can't hear you, Beatrice."

Bebe looked up at Loreli, then told Dede in a louder voice, "I'm sorry."

Dede just stood there with her arms crossed over her chest.

Loreli shook her head. She'd fooled herself into believing the twins got along all the time, but now knew how ridiculous that thinking had been. Children living together were bound to bump heads. *Well, I guess the honeymoon's over*, she thought.

Loreli said to Bebe. "I don't ever want to hear you making fun of your sister that way again. Do you hear me?"

"Yes."

"Good. Now. Have you talked to your uncle about riding?"

"No."

"Well, don't you think you should?"

Bebe stared at the floor.

"He's going to say no."

"He may not."

"I thought I could just ask you," Bebe said sullenly.

"You can, but your uncle has the last word."

"Why?"

"Because he's your uncle."

"But—"

"Ask him, Bebe. Then if he says no, we'll go from there."

"I hope he says no," Dede snapped.

"Shut up!" Bebe yelled.

Loreli shook her head. "How about we talk about something else?"

Both girls looked sullen now.

"Okay, then how about you get to the rest of your chores?"

They hung their heads. "Okay."

And off they went, but they didn't walk side by side as they usually did.

Loreli went back into the house and found Jake seated at the table going over his accounts.

"The girls are fighting," she told him.

"You sound surprised," he said without looking up.

"I suppose I am. I thought they got along real well."

"They do, but not always. What's it about this time?"

"Bebe wants to ride in something called the Circle?"

That got his attention. "She does?"

Loreli nodded. "She thinks you're going to tell her no, though."

"She's right. She'll only get hurt."

"You sound like Dede. She's afraid her sister will get hurt and die, but I think Be rides very well for her age."

"Yes, she does, but girls don't race in the Circle."

"Why not?"

He went back to his ledger. "They just don't."

"Is it illegal, or in the rules . . ."

He looked up at her. "Well, no, but—"

"Do other children ride?"

"Boys, yes. Girls, no."

Jake could tell by the flash in her eyes that she was raring up for a fight over this issue. "Leave it alone, Loreli."

She looked at him with the most innocent of faces. "Leave what alone?"

"The trouble you're getting ready to stir up."

"If she wants to ride, she should be able to."

"She's going to get hurt."

"Why, because she's a girl?"

He sighed. "Look, it's a very rough-and-tumble race. Anything might happen."

"Yep, your niece might actually win the damn thing."

Jake closed his eyes and prayed for strength. "No."

"Jake—"

"No."

Loreli sighed this time. "Okay, I'll leave it alone."

"As if I believe that."

"No?" she asked playfully, sidling closer to his chair.

"Not for a minute."

Their eyes held. Loreli was enjoying both the banter and him.

Jake could feel his body's natural reaction to the warmth of her nearness. "I'm supposed to be working on these bills."

"I'm not stopping you . . ."

Jake's eyes brushed her sweet mouth. "No, but you are distracting me."

"Me?" she asked. "I didn't think anything could distract you."

Loreli swore she saw a smile peep out from under the mustache, but it disappeared so quickly she decided it must have been her imagination.

"Go away, and let me work."

"How am I going to seduce you if you won't even look at me?"

Jake began coughing. In a strangled voice he asked, "Seduce me?"

"Yes, Jake, but not until we replace that bed of yours. It's hardly big enough for one, let alone two."

His coughing fit worsened.

"Would you like some water?" she asked with mock concern.

Jake met her knowing temptress eyes and shook his head.

"Okay, well, I'll let you get back to your accounts."

When she walked out, he was still coughing. *That ought to give him something to think about!* Loreli thought, smiling.

Alone now, Jake finally pulled himself together. *Seduce me!* He'd never heard such an outrageous boast from a woman before in his life. How was he supposed to respond? The logical parts of himself assumed she was just teasing, just pulling his leg, but the man in him wasn't so sure. At his age, Jake Reed could feel his staid, simple life spinning out of control like a runaway top. The twins' arrival had been the first adjustment he'd had to make, and now a cyclone named Loreli Winters had swept into his world, blowing around his beliefs, ripping away his views like the roof off an old barn, and buffeting him with winds so sensually strong he found it hard to breathe. She'd called him stagnant. Well, at least stagnant was ordered. This woman was not, and Jake had no idea what to expect next.

Putting aside thoughts of Cyclone Loreli and how aroused he continued to be by her brazen ways, Jake went back to his books but found his mind drifting to Matt Peterson. The revelation that Susan had threatened to leave her husband over his refusal to accept Loreli's gift had been a surprise to Jake; Matt too, by the looks of him. Jake had never known Susan Peterson to challenge her husband on anything, let alone issue him ultimatums. Jake thought back in an effort to remember if Loreli had had a chance to speak to Susan privately during yesterday's visit. He was positive that she'd been at his side the whole time, so he couldn't lay Susan's sudden show of backbone at Loreli's door. Firing up a woman as downtrodden as Susan would've been right up Cyclone Loreli's alley.

The outrageous declaration she'd made a moment ago filled his mind. He knew there were women who routinely seduced men, though he had no personal knowledge of such ladies. He always assumed women like that were whores. Jezebels, as his father used to call them. Women bent on seduction were not fresh-skinned, beautiful women who smelled of violets or wore fancy dresses and even fancier hats. Jezebels didn't care about children. They most certainly didn't skip rope or buy deeds for destitute farmers. What kind of woman was this? Cyclone was an appropriate metaphor for her, he decided, and as the winds around their relationship gathered speed, Jake didn't know whether to run for the cellar or stand and let the storm's full force carry him away.

He tried to go back to the accounts, but realized that working on the ledgers would take more concentration than he could muster at the moment. He closed the book, set the pen aside, and went outside to see what his ladies were doing.

Out back, he saw Loreli hitching her horse to the carriage she'd driven over in. As she went about the task, she appeared to be instructing the girls on the procedure. Both of his nieces were peering and pointing and Loreli was responding to their questions patiently. He enjoyed the scene. Rebecca would never have offered the girls such lessons, mainly because Rebecca had never hitched or saddled a horse in her life. In her world, his world, women left such chores to their menfolk. Apparently, Loreli had not been reared in such a world, and if she had, life had changed her views. She was as independent as any man, and confident enough for two. The girls could have worse models, he told himself. Much worse. They could have been Rebeccas. That might have seemed fine before Loreli came into their lives, but now Jake sensed just how limiting such a traditional life might have been. He wanted the twins to have the best life possible, and now, thanks to Loreli, they were learning that it was possible to achieve their goals, and as she'd so succinctly declared, *without a man's approval, permission, or interference.* From where he stood, women doing for themselves was a radical idea, almost as radical as farmers banding together in a union, but he liked it, and silently thanked Bonnie's spirit for placing Loreli in their lives.

When Loreli was done hitching the horse to the buggy, she let Bebe drive the short distance to the back porch. Loreli and Dede sat on the seat beside her. Loreli kept one eye on the driving and the other on the critical face of Dede.

"Why're you letting her drive?" Dede asked.

"Because everybody has to learn sometime."

"I don't want to learn."

Loreli said assuringly, "That's okay, pumpkin, but you may change your mind once you're older." She could see that Dede didn't agree, but Loreli didn't press the child any further.

Bebe was concentrating very hard on keeping the slow-moving horse in the direction she wanted him to go. When she pulled back on the reins to halt the carriage beside the porch, she excitedly called out, "I did it, Uncle! Did you see me?"

"Sure did, Be. That was some mighty fine driving."

"So can I ride in the Circle at the fair?"

The question caught Jake off guard. "Well—"

Before he could say, no, Bebe rushed into a plea. "Loreli will help me practice if I ask her—I know she will. She knows a whole lot about racing horses, she told me so."

Jake looked at Loreli.

"It's up to you, Jake, but truthfully, I rode in races at her age. I didn't win many, but my pa let me ride."

Bebe said, "Please, Uncle. I won't let the lessons interfere with my lessons or my chores. I promise."

He studied her, then Loreli.

Dede was slumped back against the seat. "She's just going to die."

"I'm not going to die!" Bebe said firmly. "If I don't race, how am I going to make Anthony eat crow?" she asked Dede.

To Loreli, this issue suddenly sounded like more than just the opportunity to compete. "Who's Anthony?"

Bebe said, "Mr. Diggs's son. He's a fat toad."

Loreli was so surprised by this statement she chuckled. "Excuse me? A fat toad?"

"The fattest," Dede said. "And always saying, 'Girls ain't worth nothin'!"

"Oh, really?" Loreli responded. "And this is why you want to get in the race, Bebe?"

She nodded.

Loreli looked up at Jake.

And all Jake could think was, *Oh, lord. Here we go.* Jake knew that Loreli would take Anthony's wrong-headed thinking as a personal affront and decide to train Bebe for the race whether Jake agreed or not. In reality, Bebe didn't stand a chance at winning. Anthony had beaten all the young riders for the past two years, but Jake understood Bebe's desire to shut the boy up. Anthony Diggs was a bully, and used his family's wealth and position to lord it over all the other children. Maybe getting beat by an eight-year-old girl would teach the ten-year-old

Diggs boy not only some manners but humility as well. The way things stood now, Anthony had neither.

Jake came to his decision; in reality, the only one he could make. "Okay, Bebe, you can ride, and Loreli can help you get ready. Harvest is still a couple of months off, so there's plenty of time."

Bebe jumped out of the carriage and ran over to her uncle. She gave him the biggest hug an eight-year-old could muster. "Thank you, Uncle. Thank you."

Holding her tight, he kissed the top of her head. "You're welcome."

She then walked back over to the carriage and looked at her despondent twin. "De, I'm sorry I poked fun at you this morning. I didn't mean it."

"I know."

"I'm not going to die. I promise."

Dede still didn't look convinced. "Okay."

"You can help me practice, if you want?"

Loreli knew then and there how much the girls loved each other.

Dede eyed her sister and asked, "What can I do?"

"I don't know." Bebe looked to Loreli. "What can she do?"

Loreli put an arm around Dede's thin shoulders and hugged her gently. "You can be my assistant, how about that?"

Dede asked her, "What's an assistant do?"

Loreli thought for a moment. "Well, you can do the counting to see how fast she and Phoebe can ride around the house, and you can make sure she gets to practice on time. Being the assistant is a very important job."

Dede asked Bebe. "You really want me to help?"

"Yes."

Dede smiled. "Then I want to be Loreli's assistant."

Bebe grinned and got back behind the reins, and drove slowly around to the front of the house. Walking beside the buggy, a thoughtful Jake was again pleased that Loreli had come into their lives. She seemed to have an intuitive way of handling the girls that came from her heart. For Dede to decide she wanted to help was a big step in light of how she felt about horses. Maybe being a party to this would help her master her fears. He was just about to ask Loreli if she was taking the girls with her to town when he spied Rebecca's old buggy coming up the road. He wondered what she wanted.

"Company?" Loreli asked, not recognizing the carriage.

Dede look out at the buggy. "Nope. It's just Rebecca."

"Oh," Loreli said. "Are you girls going to ride to town with me or stay here with your uncle? I need a bath and to change my clothes."

"May we go?" Dede asked him.

Jake absently nodded as Rebecca's carriage reached the house.

"Well, run and wash your face and hands, and we'll go," Loreli told the girls.

They didn't have to be told twice. Racing off, they disappeared around the back of the house.

Jake walked over to the carriage and gave Rebecca a hand down from the buggy. "Rebecca."

"Jake." Her cool eyes swept Loreli, but Rebecca didn't offer a greeting.

Loreli knew how disappointed and angry Rebecca

must be at being set aside by Jake, but Loreli didn't think it a reason to be rude. "Afternoon, Rebecca."

Rebecca met Loreli's steady gaze, then grudgingly replied, "Afternoon."

Jake was admittedly uncomfortable in the middle of this situation, but his decision was made. He was not going to marry Rebecca. "What brings you over?" he asked.

"I came to get the girls. It's Saturday."

Loreli could see the twins standing by the side of the house just out of sight. They were shaking their heads.

As if sensing them nearby, Rebecca asked, "Are they ready?"

Before Jake could offer an answer, Loreli said, "For what? The girls and I are on our way to town. Do you need them for something else?"

"Today's Saturday, the day I do their hair."

"Ah, I see," Loreli responded.

The girls were really shaking their heads now.

"Well, since I'm here," Loreli told Rebecca, "I'll be taking on that chore from now on."

Rebecca's anger was plain to see. In a huff she turned to Jake. "Is that true?"

"She's going to be my wife, Rebecca, so yes, it's true. But I do want to thank you for all your help in the past."

"I see."

Loreli didn't believe Rebecca *saw* at all, otherwise the woman wouldn't have driven over here to begin with. Loreli wondered if he'd ever kissed Rebecca the way he'd kissed her. Had they ever made love? Remembering her own disastrous bedroom encounter, Loreli tended to doubt it.

Rebecca then asked Jake, "Are you attending church in the morning, Jake?"

"I always do."

Rebecca gave Loreli a pointed look and declared smugly, "You probably don't attend church, though, do you?"

Loreli decided that one day, real soon, she and Rebecca were going to have a nice long talk, preferably in private, because with the girls looking on, Loreli couldn't tell her what she wanted to. "What denomination is the church?"

"Baptist. My father's the pastor."

"Well, I was raised Catholic, but I don't think the Lord minds where you praise Him as long as you do."

Rebecca's eyes widened. "Catholic?"

"Yes, you know, the religion with the Pope?"

Rebecca looked stunned.

The young Loreli had once attended a school run by nuns in New Orleans for about six days only to have her father pull up stakes and head them elsewhere. She hadn't been in the school long enough to learn much about the religion or what it represented, but the sisters of the order had been especially kind, so since then, Loreli always claimed Catholicism as her spiritual base. "Are there many Catholics here?"

"No."

"I see."

Rebecca seemed to realize she was in over her head in this conversation. She turned away from Loreli and said to Jake, "Well, if she's going to do their hair, I guess I rode over here for nothing."

Jake responded, "I'm sorry, Rebecca."

"So am I."

Rebecca gave Loreli one last contemptuous look, then walked back to the buggy.

Jake hastened over to give her a hand up. She accepted the help with a tight face. Once she was seated behind the reins, she looked down at Jake. "You're making a big mistake marrying that one, Jake. Hope you can live with your choice."

His lips tightened beneath the mustache. "I think I can, Rebecca."

Rebecca snapped the buggy whip angrily over the horse's back and turned the buggy back to the road. Only after it seemed certain that she was gone for good did the twins come out of hiding and show themselves.

Loreli asked, "Are you ladies ready?"

"Now we are," Dede said cryptically.

Loreli could see the mask Jake had lowered over his features. Did he regret not asking Rebecca to be his wife? Loreli couldn't imagine him viewing the situation that way, but who knew. Maybe he wanted to change his mind. "Regrets?" she asked him.

He turned her way and shook his head. "No. None. I'll see you all when you get back. Girls, be good."

"We will, Uncle," Bebe offered reassuringly.

Dede waved. "Bye, Uncle."

"Bye, De. Have a good time."

He and Loreli shared a look, then he nodded a goodbye.

The girls hopped in the buggy and Loreli headed toward town. On the way, the girls sang: "The Flying Trapeze," "Oh, Susannah," and "Listen to the Mockingbird." Their little voices warmed Loreli's heart and soul.

Loreli drove to the boardinghouse and parked the rig

out front. Loreli let Bebe tie the leads to the post to keep the horse from wandering away, then all three ladies skipped up the walk to the house.

They were met at the door by the landlady, Mrs. Boyd. She stepped outside and stood in front of the entrance like a guard. "I see you've finally come back," the old woman declared frigidly.

Loreli replied warily, "Yes, I have. May the girls and I go in?"

"No."

"No?"

"No. I don't want your kind here."

Loreli surveyed the woman for a moment, then turned and said quietly to the twins, "Girls, how about you wait for me in the buggy? Okay?"

Eyeing Mrs. Boyd, they nodded and went back down the walk. Once Loreli saw that they'd climbed aboard, she directed her attention to the cross-armed Mrs. Boyd and asked tartly, "Now, you were saying?"

"I said, I don't want your kind here. Our colony was nice and calm until you wagon-train hussies came to town. Taking our men—"

Loreli chuckled, but there was no humor in her eyes. "Mrs. Boyd, because I was raised to be respectful of my elders, I'm going to ignore you. If you want me out, just say so, and I'll move my things someplace else."

"I want you out, and there ain't another place in town that'll take the likes of you. I already made certain of that!"

Loreli's lips tightened. She was determined to remain calm; the girls were watching. "Then let me retrieve my belongings and I'll be out of your hair."

The old bat stepped aside. "Ten minutes."

Loreli was so angry that she didn't even look at the woman as she entered.

Upstairs, a muttering Loreli packed her things. She was furious but not surprised by Mrs. Boyd's actions mainly because it was just the kind of reaction Loreli had been expecting once word got around about her upcoming marriage. The next few weeks were going to be challenging, she conceded, and before it was over more than a little fur was going to fly around here. She and the brides had driven cross-country in a wagon train, endured heat, axle breakings, and swarms of biting insects. No one was going to be intimidated by a bunch of old bats bent on making life hell.

Loreli walked over to the armoire and took down her small cache of gowns. Having been thrown out of places before, she rarely removed all of her belongings from her trunks when she was on the road. Being able to beat a hasty retreat was necessary at times, so she'd learned to fill her trunks quickly. Today, though, she took her time. She didn't give a flying fig about the landlady or her ultimatums, but Loreli did keep in mind the twins waiting outside.

After making two trips back and forth, Loreli managed to get all of her trunks and hatboxes in the buggy. The girls were squeezed in tightly but didn't complain.

As Loreli took her seat behind the reins, Dede asked, "Are you coming to live with us now?"

"Looks that way, pumpkin."

"Why is Mrs. Boyd so mad at you, Loreli?"

"Mrs. Boyd wanted Uncle to marry Rebecca too, didn't she Loreli?" Bebe answered.

"You may be right, Be, but she's not only mad at me—she's mad at all of my friends for coming here."

"Why?"

"Some people don't like strangers."

"But your friends came to be mamas," Bebe protested. "Mamas aren't strangers."

Loreli smiled softly at Bebe's innocent logic. "Maybe someone should tell Mrs. Boyd that."

Chapter 9

By the time Loreli and the girls returned it was late afternoon. Jake met them on the porch, and was surprised by all the items crammed into the buggy. "Welcome back. What's all that?" he asked.

"My things," Loreli explained as she and the girls stepped down to the ground. Loreli pulled off her gloves.

"What things?"

"My belongings. Mrs. Boyd no longer wanted me as a boarder, so I've decided to move in. All this going back and forth to town is making me dizzy anyway."

Jake was puzzled. "What do you mean she didn't want you as a boarder?"

"She asked that I leave."

He stared.

Loreli told him, "I don't know why you look so surprised. This is only the beginning, I'm sure."

Bebe asked, "Beginning of what?"

"A bunch of adults acting like children, that's all," Loreli told her.

"Oh," Bebe replied, then she asked her uncle, "aren't you glad Loreli's going to live with us?"

Loreli waited.

Jake met her eyes. With the girls staring at him so expectantly, he knew a negative answer wouldn't sit well. "Yes, I am."

Loreli noted his hesitancy, but kept that to herself.

"Can Bebe and I help take in your things?" Dede asked Loreli.

"Sure. Grab some of the hatboxes, and I'll get the trunks."

Jake came off the porch. "I'll help too."

So for the next few minutes, Loreli's belongings were moved from the buggy to the house. Initially everything was placed in the sparsely furnished parlor.

Dede asked her uncle, "Is Loreli going to move upstairs into grandpa's room?"

Jake's lips tightened beneath his mustache.

Loreli remembered one of the girls mentioning that their grandfather lived in the attic room before he died. Ignoring what appeared to be the beginnings of a protest by Reed, she told the twins, "Let's see if it'll do."

They led her to the door, and Dede said, "It's always locked, Loreli. Uncle has the key."

Loreli turned to ask Jake for the key, but found him right behind her. His face was grim. He put the key in, turned it, and the door opened on a stairway filled with cobwebs and dust. It was quite apparent no one had been up the stairs in a long time. Wiping away the cobwebs, Loreli and the girls climbed up and into a shadowy, nearly airless room. Loreli swept away more of the cobwebs guarding the entrance and looked around. She sensed Jake behind her. "This was your father's room?"

"Yes."

It was difficult to see the room's true dimensions due to the boarded-up windows, but it appeared to be more than large enough for Loreli to turn it into her own. The ceiling sloped in response to the house's roof, yet was high enough to accommodate Jake's height, so there was no danger of Loreli hitting her head. "I'll take it," she declared.

Even though there was little light to see by, Loreli had no problems seeing Jake's terse face.

"The roof leaks," he told her.

"We'll get it fixed."

"It's probably infested with insects."

"We'll clean them out." Loreli observed him for a moment. "If there's a reason I shouldn't move up here, you should tell me."

He shook his head. "There's no reason."

Loreli sensed he wasn't telling her the truth, but she didn't press. "Then as soon as we find a roofer, I'll start cleaning this place up. How long has it been closed up?"

"Since my father died."

"Do you know someone we could hire to fix the roof?"

"I can do it."

"Are you certain?"

"Yes. I just need to buy new shingles."

"Okay, then our first order of business will be to get the roof repaired and take down the wood on the windows so we can let in some light and see what else needs doing."

Now that the room had been given a bit of air through the door, the mildew could be smelled.

"It stinks in here," Bebe said.

Loreli smiled. "Yes it does, but we'll fix that too."

So after giving the dark place one more glance around, they all trooped back downstairs. The girls went out to play, leaving Loreli and Jake alone in the parlor.

"How badly does the roof leak?" Loreli asked him.

"Enough to soak the floor when it rains."

The mask had fallen over his features again, letting her know something was bothering him, but she knew he'd not reveal his feelings willingly. Deciding to let him wrestle with his demons alone, Loreli stated, "Well, I still haven't had a chance to wash up, so is it okay if I use your room to take a bath?" She was still dressed in the muddy clothes she'd had on yesterday. Her plan to clean herself up while in town this morning had been ambushed by Mrs. Boyd's eviction.

"Sure, I'll get some water heating."

"Thanks." She glanced at him, then asked, "Did you and your father get along well?"

"No."

And he left her for the kitchen.

The tub he dragged into the room was the same hip tub the girls bathed in. It was only large enough to stand in, and so ancient the white enamel paint had chipped off in some places. Loreli would've given gold for the chance to leisurely loll around in something big enough to sit and stretch out in, but since this was the only tub available, she'd have to make do.

He brought in the first caldron of heated water and poured as much of it into the tub as the vessel would hold.

Loreli had already removed her jacket. "Thanks."

"You're welcome. Will you need more?"

Loreli walked over to see how much water was left in the caldron. "Nope. This should be enough."

She began undoing the buttons on her blouse. "I shouldn't be long."

Jake found himself watching her well-manicured hands freeing her buttons. When she began in on the tiny buttons on her cuffs, he looked back up at her face and found her watching him. Boldly holding his eyes, she eased the tail of the blouse free from the waistband of her skirt, then removed the blouse and tossed it onto the old chair near his bed.

Jake subconsciously blinked, and blood roared through his veins. Her camisole was lace-edged and feminine and the soft tops of her breasts tempted him so badly his hands ached with the need to stroke her skin. Her hands went to the button at the back of her skirt to undo it, and the skirt whispered to the floor to pool at her feet. Clad in her camisole, pink satin drawers, garters, stockings, and boots, she stepped out of the skirt and let him feast his eyes on her long firm legs, the curves of her hips, and the bare expanse of her neck and arms. "More?" she asked softly.

Jake drew in a steadying breath. He wanted to leave the room, lord knows he was supposed to, but his feet seemed to have grown roots.

Loreli, her own desires rising, said, "I'll take that to mean yes."

And in response, she slowly drew off the camisole. The thin chemise that remained was made from a thin, clingy fabric that revealed the shape of her breasts, the tight buds of her nipples, and the sweet curve of her waist. Without a moment's hesitation, she slowly drew it off also.

Jake was on fire. The sight of her breasts moving gently with her motions made him instantaneously hard. He wanted to ease her back onto the bed and fill her with his need, but his hastiness last time had resulted in disaster. He didn't want that. Finally finding his voice, he asked, "Is this part of your plan to seduce me?"

Wearing nothing but her drawers, garters, and shoes, her eyes sultry in the shadowy room, she asked, "Is it working?"

He closed his eyes on the rush of heat that filled him. "Yes."

She walked toward him, slowly, purposefully, then stopped close enough for him to touch.

He looked down into her eyes and couldn't hide his smile. "You are such a fast woman," he whispered.

She gave him a small smile in response, then reaching out, picked up his hand and slowly moved his palm over the passion-hard tips of her breast. "Remember those buttons I said you should play with . . . ?"

The tight bud burned Jake's skin. He felt fire licking through his blood. Knowing he had to touch her or cease breathing, he slid one long finger under the soft curve, then traced a path back up to her mouth. Leaning down, he kissed her, gently at first, learning her, inviting her, then fueled by all that made him man and her woman, he gathered her roughly into his arms and kissed her fully and possessively. He moved his hands over her breasts, then down the silken golden skin of her back. He lowered his mouth to her nipples and swore he'd been given paradise. Her soft moans of response floated over the silence. Now that he knew how she wished for him to proceed, he blazed his own trail. He cupped her breasts and brought the sandy brown points to his lips, and pleasured each until she arched her back for more.

"Slow enough for you?" he rasped out.

Loreli's lips parted, but the sound of pounding on the closed door startled them both.

"Uncle! Loreli! Bebe's cheating! She missed her threesies in jacks and she keeps throwing over!"

Jake kissed Loreli's mouth for another moment or two, then raised his head and yelled out, "Tell Be I said give you a turn!"

"Okay!"

They heard footsteps running away.

Holding each other's eyes, they said nothing for a moment, then Loreli reached up and caressed his strong jaw. "You should probably go check on them."

He nodded. "I will, but your bathwater is probably cold by now. Do you want me to heat more?"

"No need. I'll make do."

Neither of them was really concerned with such mundane matters; their bodies were still aroused and their hands wanted to further touch and explore.

"You're not making it easy for me to leave by standing there like that," he told her.

"No?" she asked, her face a study in sultry innocence.

He ran his eyes over the provocative picture she made standing before him, so beautifully undressed. "No." He reached down and picked up her skirt. He pressed it gently against her breasts, then he picked up her hand and placed it against the skirt to hold it in place. "Now, get washed up."

She said with a mock pout, "Yes, Jake."

He chuckled. "Fast, fast, *fast* woman."

Jake headed to the door. His manhood was hard and thickened by his desire, but he knew if he didn't leave now, he never would. He'd tasted sapphires, and he wanted more. He turned back to look at her and damned if she didn't look just as fetching covered by the skirt as she had bare. "No more seducing until the wedding night, Loreli."

That caught her by surprise. "Why?"

"Because, regardless of the pretense of this marriage, we're going to be man and wife and that should mean something."

"Sounds like the son of a preacher talking."

He nodded. "It is. As much as I've enjoyed these last few minutes. I do respect you, Loreli, and this is how I choose to show it."

"And suppose I don't want to wait?"

"Get washed up," he said softly.

"Jake—"

"I'll see you when you're done."

And then he was gone.

Loreli wanted to curse, throw something, anything, but in the end she smiled. *Lord, what a man.*

After washing up, Loreli stepped into clean underwear, put on a fresh camisole and donned a brown shirtwaist and matching skirt. She stuck her bare feet into a pair of soft flat-soled slippers, then, after braiding her hair into a long plait and circling it low on her neck, she looked down at herself to gauge her appearance. Making a note to order a mirror for this room the next time she went into town, Loreli left to search out her family.

She found the girls sitting on the back porch. They were facing each other and playing a hand game that in-volved the alternate clapping of their hands against each other's. The exchange of handclaps was done in rhythm with an old slave ditty called "Sangaree," a song Loreli knew from her own childhood, so she lent her voice to the game.

> *If I live*
> *Sangaree*
> *Don't get killed*
> *Sangaree*
> *I'm goin' back*
> *Sangaree*
> *Jacksonville*
> *Sangaree*
> *Oh Babe*
> *Sangaree*
> *Oh Babe*
> *Sangaree*

The song continued and the girls incorporated a few verses that were new to Loreli, but as they clapped their way to the chorus again, Loreli joined in, singing: *"Oh, Babe—Sangaree. Oh, Babe—Sangaree."*

When the game ended, Loreli's smile matched the girls'. She looked around. "Where's your uncle?"

"He's out in the cornfield looking at the corn," Dede answered.

"I see."

Before Loreli could ponder what he might really be doing out there all alone, Bebe asked, "Are you really going to do our hair today, Loreli?"

Loreli remembered Rebecca's visit. "Do you want me to?"

"Yes," Dede said. "My head's itching."

"Well, let's go get some soap and oil and get started."

Dede was first. Seated on the porch, Loreli spread a towel over the lap of her brown skirt to keep it from being stained. Dede positioned herself between Loreli's legs, and Loreli went to work. With Bebe looking on, Loreli quickly undid Dede's slightly cockeyed braids. As the strands untwisted and the long hair came free, a foul smell rose up with such force Loreli quickly drew back. "De, what is that smell? You two tangle with a skunk this morning?"

Bebe said tightly, "No, it's the oil."

Loreli bent and smelled the top of Dede's head. "That's hair oil smelling like that? What's your uncle put in it, bear grease?"

"It's not Uncle. It's Rebecca."

"Rebecca?"

"Yes. Uncle tries to do our hair, but he isn't very good at it," Bebe explained.

Dede picked up the story. "So Rebecca does it every other Saturday and she puts the oil in it. She says it helps hair grow."

Grow what? Flies? Loreli thought. "Well, Rebecca doesn't have to do your hair anymore. You heard your uncle say so."

Dede turned her face up so she could see Loreli, then asked, "And we won't have to use her oil?"

"Nope."

"Good." A pleased Dede turned back around.

After unbraiding both heads, Loreli and the twins went to the pump.

Loreli let them use bars of her fancy scented soaps to

wash away the grime and Rebecca's grease. Soon they smelled heavenly. The twins took turns having their freshly washed hair oiled and braided by their new mama. When both heads were done, the girls happily patted their new dos and smiled.

Loreli wiped her hands on the towel across her lap, then stood. She couldn't help but be moved by their smiling, gleaming faces. She'd parted their hair neatly down the front, so as to showcase the twin French braids that ended with brand-new, multicolored ribbons. Both girls had a fairly good grade of hair and just needed someone to teach them how best to care for it. The slop Rebecca called hair oil had done nothing but weigh down their tresses with a thick layer of sticky, stinky grease. Loreli's oil, made of lemon and orange, bergamot and vanilla had given their hair shine and vitality.

Jake was in the cornfield ostensibly to gauge the health of his crop, but in reality he was trying to will himself back to calm. His blood was still humming from the short heated encounter in his bedroom, and his manhood was thick and throbbing with desire. He wanted more of her; there was no denying that, and therein lay the problem. He wasn't supposed to be wanting her this way. Remembering the softness of her skin and the way her nipples burned against his hands only heightened the memories and increased his need. She'd warned him early on that finding a woman to replace her wouldn't be easy and he now understood what she'd meant. Where in the world would he find someone as vibrant, as brave and as outrageous as Loreli? Even though he'd only touched her twice, he knew without a doubt that any woman he did find would have to be as spirited as she seemed in the bedroom, yet he couldn't imagine a *real* wife displaying or dispensing such passion.

Jake continued his walk through the chest-high wall of corn, pausing to search through some of the stalks for worms and other pests. The few he found he tossed to the ground and crushed under his boot. If only his wanting of Loreli could be eradicated so easily, he thought. He'd began their relationship by vowing to keep her at arm's length, comfortable with the knowledge that he wouldn't be attracted to her. But now, less than a week later, all he could think about was cupping her breasts, kissing them, and hearing her sighs. Things weren't supposed to work out this way, he groused inwardly; he was supposed to be in control of the situation, not hard as gun metal and twice as hot.

Admittedly Jake was both, and his noble pledge to refrain from all further intimate activity until the wedding night would be kept. Yet after kissing her lips and feeling her warm skin beneath his hands, the wedding suddenly felt years away.

Jake walked back up to the house and found the girls admiring their reflections in an ivory and gold hand-held mirror, which he assumed belonged to Loreli. The change in their appearance made him pause. Gone were the thick unkempt braids that were so tangled near the roots he could barely draw a comb through.

"Do you like our hair, Uncle?" Dede asked excitedly.

He ran his eyes approvingly over their neatly done braids. Their faces were bright and clean. "I sure do. Looking mighty pretty, Miss Dede. You too, Miss Be."

Bebe grinned and told him, "Loreli said we don't have to use Rebecca's old stink oil on our heads anymore."

He drawled. "Good. It'll probably cut down on the flies in the house."

The girls giggled and Loreli looked at him as if she'd never met him before. Reed making jokes!

He must've seen her face because he asked her, "What's wrong?"

"That was funny, Reed."

"Yes, it was."

"You have a sense of humor."

"That so surprising?"

She searched his mustached face. "I'm not sure."

He eyed her. "You may find me full of surprises before it's all said and done."

Loreli cocked her head. "Oh, really?"

He turned to find the girls watching them intently. "Yes?" he asked them.

Both shook their heads. "Nothing."

"How about you take the mirror back inside and we can unpack my trunks," Loreli told them.

The girls did as instructed, leaving Jake and Loreli alone on the porch.

"Were you serious about the wedding night?" she asked.

"Yes."

She turned back and studied him for a moment before admitting, "Never met a man like you before, Jake Reed."

"Good," he told her softly.

She chuckled. "Good?"

"Yes."

"Why?"

"Because you'll remember me."

Loreli went still. She searched his face. She would remember him, and a jumble of emotions filled her at that moment; emotions she couldn't name because she'd never experienced them before. Was she falling in love with this man? Lord, she hoped not because there was no future in it. That the question had been raised was disturbing, though. The last thing Loreli needed was to find herself pining after a man determined to replace her as soon as opportunity allowed. No, she wasn't falling in love with him; she couldn't allow it.

Jake, still waiting for her response, wondered what she might be thinking. She made her living keeping her face free of expression, and she was doing that now. "What's the matter?"

Loreli shook herself free. "Nothing. I-I'm going in to help the girls."

As she went inside, Jake wondered if it was his imagination or had she really retreated. It certainly seemed that way. But what had he said wrong this time? He sighed and went to feed the hogs.

With the help of the twins, Loreli unpacked her many trunks and hatboxes. Most of the items had been stored away since she'd left Chicago with the wagon train just over a month ago. To her dismay, some of her gowns had gotten wet during the trip and were now covered with mold and mildew. They were unsalvageable. Others however, though creased and wrinkled, just needed airing and a good ironing. These she had the girls take outside into the sunshine and drape over the porch rail. While they were outside, she lined up her hats and shoes along the walls of the parlor. The room now resembled a department store back East, Loreli mused.

In the course of the work, the girls tried on everything of hers that they could: hats, gloves, jewelry. They opened up little cosmetic pots and smelled her perfumes. She put tiny spots of rouge on their cheeks and little dabs of scent behind their ears. "You're both too young for all of this, but we're just playing," Loreli told them.

Grins creased their twin brown faces.

Jake came in and his silent looming presence made Loreli and the girls look up. He scanned the clothes set about the room before settling his attention on the lightly painted faces of the girls. "Supper's almost ready. Go wash your faces and hands."

Hearing his disapproval, they nodded sadly. "Yes, Uncle."

After they were gone, Loreli drawled, "You certainly know how to ruin a party."

"They're too young to be all painted up."

"Which is what I told them when I put it on. We were just having a little fun. Goodness, do you have to view everything so seriously?"

Tight-lipped, he looked away.

Loreli told him bluntly, "I won't have you constantly looking over my shoulder or second-guessing me. Either you let me be the mother I think I can be, or get someone else."

Jake had already pondered that impossibility.

"You're going to have to trust me, otherwise this won't work," Loreli added.

He met her eyes. "I agree."

Loreli had been expecting more of a fight. "Why are you surrendering so easily?"

He chuckled. "You'd rather argue?"

"No, not really, but—"

"You made your point. I do have to trust you. Forgive me if I overreacted."

Loreli asked very seriously, "Who are you, and what have you done with the real Jake Reed?"

He shook his head and grinned. "Uppity woman."

"The uppitiest you're ever going to meet."

"No doubt in my mind about that."

"Well, since this uppity woman is blessed with a man in her life who can cook, what's for dinner?"

"You over my knee if you don't behave yourself."

She shot him a saucy look, "Really?"

Jake was filled with the urge to kiss that sassy mouth of hers, but he'd made a pledge not to touch her again until their wedding night.

"Having a little trouble with that vow you made?" she tossed out.

He raised an eyebrow. "Oh, now, you read minds too?"

"Yes."

"Then you know I meant what I said."

"No one need know you broke your pledge," Loreli offered.

"I will, so stop tempting me."

"I like tempting you. Never been around a man with real morals before. Takes some getting used to."

Their eyes met and held.

He told her solemnly, "I realize I'm not as worldly as some of the men you might have known before. I'm just a Kansas farmer—probably bore you to tears before the year's out, but I'll protect you and respect you to the best of my ability."

Loreli was very moved by his simple declaration. "That's all a woman can ask of any man, Jake."

"Then let's go eat."

She nodded and they went inside the house.

Chapter 10

When it was time for the girls to go to bed that evening, Loreli found an old pair of cotton stockings amongst her belongings and fashioned them into nightcaps for the girls. The lightweight caps would keep their hair from being mussed while they slept.

The twins beamed upon receiving this new gift. "Aggie sleeps in a stocking cap too," Bebe said.

Loreli grinned. "Does she?"

Bebe nodded like a horse. "So does her sister, Charlene."

Jake wondered how something as simple as a stocking cap could bring two little girls such joy. He supposed that was why God made mothers, to take care of things like that. "Okay you two, let's hear your prayers."

"Now that Loreli's living with us, can she hear our prayers too?" Dede asked him.

He looked at Loreli.

Honored by the request, Loreli said, "I'd like that very much."

The girls were already kneeling beside the bed.

Dede went first. "Dear God: Thank you for my sister, and Uncle, and Loreli. Thank you for Emily's new kittens. And for Suzie, and Pal and Rabbit . . ."

Loreli had no idea who these folks were, but kept silent.

"Please say hello to our Mama," Dede continued. "Tell her we love her and we miss her, and thank her for sending us Loreli. Amen."

Loreli felt emotion fill her heart and throat.

"Dear God," Bebe began. "Thank you for my sister, my uncle Jake, and for Loreli. Please bless all the sick animals, and Aggie, and her sister Charlene, and Carrie. Tell Mama we're being good and that I'm glad she sent us Loreli too. Amen."

Loreli had never been privy to anything like this, and except for her wagon mate, Belle, it had been a long time since anyone had sent prayers up to heaven on her behalf. She wanted to cry.

The girls were now scooting under the thin blanket, and Jake bent down and kissed them on the forehead. "Good night," he whispered.

He stepped aside. Loreli bent to bestow her kisses as well. "Good night, pumpkins. Sweet dreams."

"Good night, Loreli."

"See you two in the morning," Jake said.

"Good night, Uncle."

He blew out the lamp, and he and Loreli tiptoed out, then they stepped onto the porch. The sun was dying in a blaze of vivid reds and oranges.

"Never had anyone pray for me that way before," Loreli said.

"Children's prayers are very special."

"I'm finding that out. Do you listen to their prayers every night?"

Jake nodded. "Didn't your father listen to your prayers before you went to sleep?"

"No, my daddy lost his religion when my mother died. He said he never had much use for God after that. I prayed sometimes anyway, even went to church with the sisters a couple of times."

He wondered if she realized that he could hear the pain in her voice. Did it mean she was dropping her guard? "Well, my father heard our prayers whether we wanted him to or not, but I promised myself that when I grew up I wouldn't force my children to pray the way my father forced us."

"Explain," Loreli prompted.

"He told us what to pray for."

"I don't understand."

Jake sighed.

"The only thing my sister and I were allowed to pray for was the redemption of our souls."

"I see."

"He wouldn't have stood for the girls praying for the animals or their friends. Redemption was all you were supposed to ask for.

"Are you really Catholic?"

Loreli chuckled. "If you can become a Catholic after only six days, I am." She then explained her short stint with the nuns in New Orleans. "Just wanted to give Rebecca something else to chew on."

"Well, she took the bait."

"That she did. How long has her father been a preacher here?"

"Five years or so. He took over after old Reverend Pease died."

"How many churches does this place have?"

"One."

"So I should expect some hostility tomorrow?"

"I wouldn't doubt it."

"Won't be anything new for me. Those old biddies can hiss at me as loud as they want, but I will call them out if they start in on the girls."

Jake smiled at the fight in her tone. "Let's just wait and see how it goes before you start strapping on weapons."

"I'm warning you, Jake. I won't put up with any shenanigans from Rebecca or her friends."

"I don't expect you to."

"Good."

He eyed her with a mixture of humor and wonder. "Have you been this fearless all of your life?"

"No, but after my daddy died, it was either learn to be fearless or spend the rest of my life on my knees. I chose to stand and fight."

"Must've been hard being on your own."

She thought back and said quietly, "Harder than anyone will ever know."

Jake wanted to ask her to explain but he didn't feel comfortable delving into something that sounded so personal. If she had the desire to share her life's journey with him, he knew she would in her own time.

Loreli didn't want to discuss her past, mainly because she wasn't certain how he might respond, so she changed the subject. "Tell me about this union business."

Jake sensed she wanted to talk about something else so he didn't question her change in topics. "It's a national movement that's trying to bring workers, farmer, and trade unionists together to form one voice."

"The Knights of Labor?"

"They're involved, but there are also farmers' alliances and grangers in the ranks too. Ideally, we could become strong enough to form a pretty powerful third political party, and that's been discussed as well."

"A third political party?"

"Sure. We can't look to the Democrats for relief. Their main concerns are disenfranchising us as quickly as possible, and restoring the Confederacy. The Republicans may as well be Democrats for all the good they're doing the race these days. So why not form a third party to carry forward the issues of the workers and the poor?"

Loreli admittedly paid very little attention to politics, but even she knew that the Republicans were no longer supporting the rights and issues of the race, and that the nation's Black newspapers were howling with outrage over the lack of commitment by the party of Lincoln.

"With all this industrialization going on and the factories being built," Jake said, "people are being paid less for working more. Skilled workers like shoemakers are being replaced by machines that can make hundreds of shoes a day, and run by people who are rendered mindless by the sheer repetition of their jobs. If we can get all of the factory workers and farmers and the trade unionists to unite, we could get the mortgage mess cleaned up, demand that folks be paid what they're worth, and make sure the money they are paid is worth something."

"Sounds pretty grandiose."

Jake shook his head.

"I don't think so. This country owes it to the farmers to make sure we stay afloat. After all, the nation's getting bigger every day and folks have to be fed, but the way it stands now, all of the tariffs and taxes seemed designed to break us, not build us up."

"I can't see the bankers and capitalists wanting to change things."

"Of course not. They're getting fat. They don't want to have to tighten their belts just so children won't have to work in their mines fourteen and fifteen hours a day, or so that the thousands of women working in the garment factories can make more than a few pennies a week in wages. No, the rich want to preserve the status quo and they're doing everything in their power to stop us. Some organizers have been killed."

Loreli found that disquieting, "You said that before."

"Yes."

"Have you been threatened?"

"Not so far."

"Do you think you may be?" she asked.

"Anything's possible."

"Well, I'm an excellent shot."

He gave her just the ghost of a smile. "I figured that."

"Well, let's hope Rebecca and her friends figure that out before church tomorrow. I'd hate to have to give them a demonstration."

Humor lit his eyes. "Let's hope that won't be necessary."

As the sun disappeared below the horizon, dusk rolled in. Loreli stared at the view. "What was it like growing up here?"

"Not bad, though it wasn't called Bloody Kansas for nothing."

"What do you mean?" she asked.

"Lots of fighting between Free Staters and the Missouri border gangs who wanted the territory to be proslavery. Blood was shed on both sides before it was all decided."

"Wasn't John Brown from Kansas?"

"He was born elsewhere, but Kansas became his home. He and my father were good friends. They were both Old Testament men—all hellfire and brimstone, and an eye for an eye." Jake paused for a moment as the memories flooded his mind. "Mr. Brown had the coldest blue eyes I've ever seen on a man—had ten children too."

Loreli didn't know that.

"I remember him and pa sitting on this very porch, planning and plotting their holy war against slavery—and in their minds it *was* a holy war. Even though my father claimed to be a man of the cloth, both he and Brown helped the Jayhawkers—"

"What's a Jayhawker?" Loreli interrupted.

"Members of a guerrilla band of Kansas Free Staters commanded by Captain James Montgomery."

"I've never heard of a jayhawk. Is there really a bird by that name?"

"Supposedly. A jayhawk is an Irish bird that hunts smaller birds and shakes them to death the way mousers do rats, but the Kansas Jayhawks hunted proslavers."

"And your father knew these men?"

Jake nodded. "Yes, he even rode with Captain Montgomery for a while, as did Mr. Brown."

"It sounds odd to hear you refer to him as Mister

Brown. I'm so accustomed to hearing him called by his full name."

"I was what, nine, ten years old when I first met him? Being a youngster, I had to address him that way."

"Makes sense, but never thought I'd be standing on the same porch that he once stood on."

"Wanting to eradicate slavery made him fearless, but my mother swore he was unbalanced," Jake said.

"Why?"

"She called him a zealot, and sometimes zealots do things that god-fearing folks wouldn't."

"Such as?"

"Back in 1856, proslavery Missourians sacked and burned Lawrence. Many of the citizens were murdered. Mr. Brown was living over near Pottawatomie Creek at the time, and when he heard what had been done in Lawrence, he became so enraged and so filled with vengeance he kidnapped five of his proslavery neighbors."

"Were these neighbors involved in the Lawrence fight?"

"No."

"What did Brown do after he kidnapped them?"

"He and his sons killed them. Split their heads open with broadswords."

Loreli was surprised. "My. So that's what you meant by an eye for an eye."

"Yes."

Loreli had never heard that story before, but figured that since slavery was unbalanced, it seemed only fitting to pit a man like John Brown against it. "What was your mother like?"

"Timid but loving. She didn't want anything out of life but to go to church and raise her family. She thought her dream had come true when she married my father. He was a simple preacher, and she was proud that he was a Jayhawker and an abolitionist, but finding out he was an adulterer turned the marriage into a nightmare and broke her heart."

"When did she die?"

"During the last year of the war. My father was away fighting for the Union at the time."

Loreli's voice softened. "My daddy died that same year. September 20, 1865." She would never forget the date nor the horror that befell her in the hours immediately following his death. She changed the subject again. "How long have you been doctoring animals?"

"Most of my life. Started with an eaglet I found when I was about ten. I went to Howard College, hoping to learn enough to get a certificate, but I quit after three months and came home."

Loreli was surprised. "Why? You're certainly smart enough to have done well."

"Thanks, but I missed the land. Missed the sunrises and the sunsets. Back East was too noisy and crowded. I'm a country boy—all that rushing around wasn't for me. So, I left Washington and came home."

"Was your father angry?" Loreli asked.

"Of course, but I didn't care. Didn't care about anything he had to say back then."

"Why not?"

"I blamed him for my mother's death. Bonnie did too. He never treated her right. Left her home for days, sometimes weeks at a time. When he wasn't off Jayhawking, he was out saving sinners or coveting his neighbor's wife. She begged him not to join Lincoln's war back in '62. I remember the argument they had the night before he left again in '64. She told him then she wasn't well and didn't want to be apart from him, but he told her fighting slavery was more important than any mortal's health. He left her and us the next morning."

"How old were you?"

"Just turned seventeen. I wanted to fight. I'd already signed my name, but he made me stay and take care of my mother and Bonnie. He said it was a fight for men, not boys."

"Maybe he just wanted to protect you," Loreli offered.

"Maybe he just wanted to leave his family to see what was on the other side. He never seemed happy at home."

"Well, I've had restless feet all of my life too, I can't fault him for that."

"But you don't have a family and two children. You didn't leave in the middle of planting season and assume your children and wife would somehow survive without a means of support."

"But it was the fight against slavery, Jake. Everyone left families behind."

"I know, but I could have gone in his place. He didn't have to go."

She heard the underlying bitterness in his tone. "Did the two of you ever reconcile before his death?"

"No, after my mother died, he saw the devil in everything and everywhere, mostly in himself. He spent the last years of his life in that room upstairs on his knees in the dark, begging God to forgive his sins. He rarely bathed, ate just enough to stay alive, and berated me for trying to keep the farm going. Wanted me on my knees praying for his soul instead of planting."

Loreli now understood some of the reasons behind Jake Reed's stoic exterior. In the face of such difficult family circumstances, she would have been forced to view life stoically as well. She also understood why he'd been so grim when showing her his father's attic room. "If you don't want me to open that room again, I'll understand."

"No, it's time for light up there. It's been closed off long enough. Maybe it'll help me get rid of a few ghosts of my own."

Loreli was touched by his readiness to share his past. "You've told me a lot about yourself this evening."

"I hadn't planned on it, so how about you return the favor?"

She turned and looked at him in the shadows. "You want to know something about me now?"

"I think it's only fair."

"Okay, how about this? The fire that killed my mother was set by men hired by my father's mother?"

"What?"

"Yes. They came to the house one night while my father and grandfather were away on business." She looked out over the darkness and continued, "I guess my grandmother had a conscience of sorts because the men took me out of the house first. I don't remember if my mother put up a fight or not, I was too young to remember, but my pa always said I got my spirit from her, so I imagine she did fight them, but it didn't matter. They took me, tied her up and nailed the doors and windows shut."

Loreli's voice was barely above a whisper, "Can you imagine being tied up and unable to free yourself while someone is nailing you in. She must have been terrified. They poured kerosene around the outside and set it on fire."

Jake was appalled. "What did they do with you?"

"Gave me to my grandmother who in turn, sold me to a friend of hers in the next county. My father didn't tell me this story until I was ten or so. Said I wasn't old enough to know the truth before then."

"How did he find you?"

"At first, she told him I too had been burned to death, but when he couldn't find my body in the ashes and rubble, he confronted her. She eventually told him what she'd done with me, and he immediately came to claim me."

"But why did she do such an awful thing?"

"She hated my mother, I suppose. He was her only child and he broke her heart by marrying a slave woman, but once my father found me, we never returned to his parents' home."

Loreli then said, "Second story. My father was killed in a card game. Stabbed to death by two thugs. Later that night, before I could find somebody to bury him, those same men came back, dragged me behind the boarding-house where my daddy and I had been staying and took what innocence I had left."

Jake whispered, "My lord."

"Yep. So, although Rebecca and her kind might not believe it, I've been very, very particular about who I invite into my bed since then."

Jake didn't know what to say or feel.

She asked him emotionlessly, "Are we even, now, you and I?"

He still found it hard to speak. "Were the men caught?"

She shrugged. "Sheriff didn't care about a mulatto and her troubles. One of the whores from the saloon took me in, patched me up. A few weeks later, I took off north. Eventually wound up in Philadelphia."

"How'd you feed yourself?"

"Playing cards, throwing dice, pitching pennies. My daddy was one of the best gamblers in the south and he taught me well."

The night's silence rose between them for a moment, then Loreli said, "I vowed to never be that kind of victim again, and I haven't. No matter what it took, Loreli has always been in control of Loreli."

Jake heard the mix of anger, defiance, and pride in her voice. He wanted to somehow go back in time, find the men and punish them until they hurt as much as she'd been hurt. Jake knew about rape, but blessedly no one in his acquaintance had ever been subjected to such an outrage. He could only guess at how long it must take a woman to get over such a horrendous experience, or if she ever did at all. "Are the memories still there?"

"They're always there. I don't think it's something you forget. The harshness dulls after awhile, but it never goes away."

Jake knew then and there that he would hurt anyone who called her whore in the future.

"I don't know if I'm supposed to tell you this, but I will because it's part of the story too."

"Okay."

"Well, later in my life I met a wonderful man who helped me heal some of the scars. He taught me that a man and woman coming together didn't have to be a nasty, painful, or degrading act; it could be beautiful, loving, even fun. He helped me learn that a man could touch a woman with wonder, desire—passion."

Loreli looked over at Jake and said, "I'm not trying to upset you, Jake."

"I understand. Did you love this man?"

Loreli replied truthfully, "I did, but loving him was like trying to love the wind. He's even more restless than I am."

"So is he still in your life?" Jake steeled himself for the answer. For reasons he refused to examine, Jake didn't want to learn that this mystery man was awaiting her in California.

"Haven't seen him in years. Last I heard, he was in Cuba somewhere on a sugar plantation."

"Working?"

She chuckled. "Owns the place more than likely. Trevor Church never did an honest day's work in his life, far as I know."

Jake turned the odd-sounding name over in his mind, and realized he didn't know one man of color with the name Trevor.

"Where's he from?"

"Ireland. His mother was an Irish noblewoman—his father, a Black British seaman."

"That's unusual."

"Not really, according to Trevor. Britain's Black seamen have fathered children all over the empire just as their White comrades have done. In fact, he swears mulatto children like him are the true reason the term Black Irish came to be."

Jake didn't know anything about Black Irishmen or even White Irishmen, if the truth be told. What he did know was that he was suddenly jealous of the man's place in Loreli's life, even though Jake knew he had no right to be. How had he gone from barely tolerating this woman to being jealous of the people in her past in less than a week? Once again he could only wonder if he were under some kind of exotic spell. He'd never had a woman affect him this way, but then, he'd never met a woman like Loreli.

Because of the lengthy silence, Loreli felt compelled to say, "You are angry, aren't you?"

"No, I'm not. I'm just thinking what a remarkable woman you are."

She studied him for a moment. "Are you being serious, or sarcastic?"

"Serious, Loreli. Very much so."

"Compliments?"

"Yes, and don't act so surprised. I've given you a few before now."

"You're right, you have, but—"

"But what?" Jake asked.

"I didn't know how you'd react to hearing about Trevor, is all."

Silence reigned for a moment, then he said, "No man enjoys hearing about the accomplishments of another man, especially in relation to the woman he's about to marry."

"But we aren't marrying for each other. We're doing this for the girls."

"True, but I'm still a man, Loreli."

Her heart pinged. "So, you are upset?"

"No, I'm not."

"I think you are."

He shook his head. "I'm not."

"Then let's change the subject."

"Fine."

"You are upset."

Jake's lip tightened. "I thought we were changing the subject?"

"You're probably never going to meet Trevor, you know."

"Loreli?"

"Sorry. So, what shall we talk about? Politics is always a safe subject. You're a Republican, am I correct?"

"I was for the last election, but if the Populists can gather enough support I may vote for them this time."

"Who are the Populists?"

"That third party I told you about earlier."

"Oh."

Loreli sensed he was still out of sorts about Trevor, and she didn't really care to discuss politics. "Your turn."

"For what?"

"To pick a topic of discussion."

"I think I'm going to head to bed. Church in the morning."

"I see." She scanned his shadowy outline in an attempt to guess his real mood. She got nothing. "Good night, then."

"Good night."

He walked off the porch and headed toward the barn.

As she watched him fade into the darkness, she wanted to yell at him, *You are upset!* But she kept it to herself.

* * *

Loreli awakened Sunday morning in Jake's hard-as-a-rock bed, and swore she had bruises all over her body. Dragging herself over to the basin, she rinsed her teeth, then washed her face.

The girls, still in pajamas and house coats, were already at the table awaiting breakfast when she arrived. Even though it was early, the temperature was high, hinting at the hot day ahead.

"Morning, Loreli," the twins called cheerily.

"Morning, girls."

Jake came out of the kitchen and set a platter of bacon and eggs on the table, then took his seat. "Good morning," he said to her.

"Morning," she replied. He had his mask on, so she assumed he was still out of sorts about last night.

Dede said, "You look sleepy, Loreli."

Loreli put the cotton napkin across her lap. "I am. Your uncle's bed turns into a rock pile every night. How on earth do you sleep on that thing?" she asked him.

"Feels fine to me."

"Guess it helps to be made of stone, Reed."

He shot her a quelling look. "Bow your heads so I can say the grace."

So they did.

Once he was done, the eggs and bacon were dished out, and everyone started in on their meal.

In an effort to draw him out, Loreli asked, "What time do you usually leave for church?"

"Service starts at ten, so we head over around nine."

It was now seven. "Okay."

At eight-thirty, Loreli, wearing a sun yellow walking suit and a big feathery hat, had both girls ready for final

inspection. Their faces were clean and their hair neatly
braided. They'd donned clean shirts and denims, and
their dusty little boots had been buffed and shined with an
old rag.

Loreli beamed down at them approvingly and said,
"Ladies, I think we're ready to go to church. Shall we?"

They grinned and raced out the door.

Loreli picked up her yellow parasol and yelled after
them, "No running in the house!" She didn't really mean
it, but she knew that's what a mama was supposed to say.

Outside she was pleased to see Jake all gussied up as
well. The faded farm clothes he usually wore had been replaced by a bright white shirt and a pair of black, well-
fitting trousers. The braces were black with silver fittings.
A string tie hung from beneath his shirt collar, and he had
on what she guessed to be his Sunday hat. Dressed up he
was even more handsome.

As she and the twins joined him beside the wagon, he
said, "Girls, you look real nice."

They smiled and climbed into the bed.

"You look nice this morning too, Loreli," Jake said. In
reality he thought she was dazzling. Every eye in the
church would be turned her way.

"So do you."

"Thanks." Jake handed her up, and tried not to be affected by her warm, soft palm in his, but failed. The heat
rushed up his arm and into his blood. He wasn't supposed
to be thinking about a woman's flesh on Sunday morning,
but with her around he seemed incapable of doing anything else.

Grim, he climbed up behind the reins and set the team
in motion.

During the ride, the girls occupied themselves with looking for funny-shaped clouds in the blue sky overhead. Dede found a rabbit, and her sister pointed out a dragonfly. While they went on with the game, Loreli said quietly to Jake, "You're mighty tight-lipped this morning."

"I'm fine."

Loreli knew that if she disputed his claim an argument would break out, so she didn't press. "How many people usually come to Sunday service?"

"Forty-five, fifty folks, on average."

Loreli was impressed. "That's quite a few, wouldn't you say?"

"Yes. Sometimes twice that many show up at Christmas time."

They were having this nonsensical conversation to keep from talking about what really stood between them, and they both knew it. Loreli refused to broach the subject again because he'd already rebuffed her efforts once, and Jake didn't want to bring up his reaction to her story last night because he still hadn't come to grips with his jealousy. So instead, they sat silently and watched the fields roll by.

As he drove, Jake realized this would be his first public outing with Loreli Winters, and he could already hear the whispers and speculation their arrival would spawn. By now everyone in the colony knew he was marrying her; some would think him insane, and others, like Rebecca's friends, would probably be outraged. He didn't feel the need to explain himself, however, nor would he run and hide. If gossip followed him the rest of his life, so be it. The girls' needs outweighed everything else.

He glanced over at Loreli. *Lord, what a beautiful woman.*

Her nearness, coupled with the faint but heady scents of her fine perfume, was enough to tempt a saint. He wondered if she knew that hot blood flooded his loins every time he looked at her.

Loreli glanced at Jake and all she saw was a man behind a mask that she wanted to shake until he told her the truth about what was bothering him. She understood why a man would be offended by his lady love carrying on about another man, but she wasn't Jake's lady love. Yes, they were physically attracted to each other—that had already been proven—but that's as far as their connection went. Loreli wasn't naive enough to believe there could be more; this was only a temporary arrangement. He was the one who'd made it clear that he would be looking for another woman to fill her role, so why get so upset about Trevor? If she didn't know better, she'd think he was jealous. A bit surprised by that thought, she looked over at him curiously. "Jake Reed, are you jealous?"

"Of what?"

"Quit dancing around, you know what I'm asking."

"And if I am?"

She scanned his distant features. That was not the response she'd expected. "I don't know," she said honestly. His answer had floored her.

"Then you shouldn't ask questions with answers you can't handle."

He remained silent for the rest of the ride, and Loreli did too.

To Loreli's surprise, the Hanks Baptist Church was the same church that hosted the celebration for the mail-order brides and their new grooms. It was here that she'd met the twins. Had it really been such a short while ago? she asked herself. So much had happened since then. It certainly was the same church. As Jake brought the team to a halt in the area reserved for vehicles, Loreli smiled at the sight of familiar faces. She saw Fanny and Trudy and a few of the other brides and their new families. Many of her friends waved and called to her excitedly. She waved and responded just as exuberantly. They seemed as happy to see her as she was to see them.

Jake helped her down, and she hurried off to receive hugs and give out a few of her own. In reality, the women had parted company about a week ago, but for many, including Loreli, it seemed like months.

Introductions were made. In all, thirteen brides had settled nearby and eight of them were attending the church service this morning, including Fanny, Ruby, Trudy and Zora. Loreli was glad they'd come.

Rebecca and her three friends didn't seem to share Loreli's sentiment, however. Loreli could see them standing by the church's door. Their faces were decidedly critical as they took in the happy reunions. All four women were dressed in black. They resembled disapproving crows.

As the church bell sounded, the people gathered around the grove began to move toward the church and head inside. Loreli, walking with Jake, took the girls' hands and joined the procession.

The brides and their new families sat on one side of the small whitewashed church. The old guard smugly chose seats on the other. Sol Diggs and his well-dressed wife came in and took seats in the front pew. With them was a stout boy. When the twins cut their eyes at his entrance, Loreli guessed he must be the notorious Anthony Diggs.

Loreli's gaze strayed to store owner Bert Green, seated behind the Diggses. Beside Green sat a beanpole of a woman, Loreli assumed to be his wife. Near the front of the church, Loreli spied her other poker partner, Howard Burke. She wondered if the painted-up young woman at his side was his daughter or his wife.

A short balding man in a flowing red and black robe appeared at the front of the church, and when he cleared his throat all the congregation's whispering and visiting ceased. "Good morning," he said in a rich, rolling voice that filled the small space.

The congregation responded in kind, and the man in the robe smiled. He looked out over the gathering and said, "For all of the new people here this morning, welcome. I'm Pastor Dexter Appleby. I hope you will avail yourselves of this house of the Lord, and feel free to worship with us every Sunday."

Loreli thought Pastor Appleby sounded much more charitable than his daughter.

Appleby said, "We're going to start our service this morning as we always do, with a hymn from the voice of our own resident angel, Sister Victoria Diggs."

She stood and bowed regally. A very large man in a well-fitting suit stood and walked over to a corner of the church. He pulled aside a black tarp to reveal the organ beneath. The wood on it was cracked and warped, but a church with an organ was a church to be reckoned with. The first few notes the man played were so clear and pure, Loreli's mouth dropped. In spite of its battered looks, the organ was in perfect tune. Too bad the same couldn't be said for Victoria Diggs. Her first notes were as sour as month-old eggs, and the ones that followed were no better. Loreli looked over at Jake to gauge his reaction, but he wouldn't look back. She turned to Fanny, only to find her bent over, pretending to cough into a handkerchief in order to conceal her real reaction.

Everywhere Loreli looked, the people on her side of the church were either coughing into handkerchiefs or staring at Victoria Diggs as if she possessed two heads. The woman's singing was atrocious. The twins sounded like the great Black songstress Elizabeth Greenfield in comparison. Who in the world told this poor woman she could sing? Loreli wanted to know. She'd heard bullfrogs carry a better tune!

To the brides' distress, Mrs. Diggs sang two more verses. The man on the piano sounded as if he might be a skilled musician, but Victoria's terrible voice made a true determination impossible. Finally, she sat down, and had the nerve to appear pleased by her awful performance. Loreli looked over at the biddies' side of the church; they seemed unaffected by the horrendous singing. Loreli didn't understand this at all. Not at all.

A smiling Pastor Appleby stepped up to the pulpit. "Ah, Sister Diggs, just knowing I'm going to hear your voice makes it a blessing to wake up every Sunday morning."

Loreli wondered if the man had been drinking. She glanced up at Jake, but again he ignored her.

Pastor Appleby sent the children off to Sunday school, which was conducted outside on the trestle tables. The two teachers, Rebecca being one, led the way.

Once the silence resettled, Appleby began to preach. His subject: The Perfect Wife. "The perfect wife, first and foremost, is a Christian," he told the congregation. He then called everyone's attention to the Bible, Proverbs, chapter 31, verses ten to thirty-one. Then he read the thirtieth verse: *"Favor is deceitful, and beauty is in vain, but a woman that feareth the Lord, she shall be praised."*

In the way that preachers often do, Appleby asked his flock, "Does it matter if the woman is beautiful?"

"No!" came the reply from the old guard of the church.

"Does it matter if her skin is golden and her dresses fine?!"

"No!"

Loreli stiffened. Surely he wasn't referring to her. She looked over at Zora who raised a questioning eyebrow in response.

Appleby went on, "What matters, according to the Bible, is if she can seeketh wool and flax, and worketh willingly with her hands. Does it say anything about wearing fancy hats or shoes?"

"No!"

He looked out over the congregation and his voice took on a serious tone. "There are new elements in our midst that may make our ladies question their roles—elements that bring influences from places filled with vice, and reek of unclean places."

Loreli's jaw tightened.

"Don't be taken in," Appleby warned. "The Bible says a woman should maketh fine linen and look well to the welfare of her household. It says nothing about founding restaurants or opening schools. A woman's role is to rise while it is still night, and give meat to her household."

So now it's Zora's and Ruby's turn, Loreli thought sarcastically. She had no doubts: the man had been drinking.

Upon hearing the pastor's words, the folks on the other side of the church were now looking even more smug, and making a point of turning to gauge the reaction of the newcomers. Loreli wanted to react by standing up and telling off Pastor Appleby, but this was a house of worship, and she didn't wish to embarrass Jake or the twins. So Loreli and her friends had to sit there and listen while the pastor dragged them over the coals. He talked about Jezebels and harlots, strumpets and whores. It was the most unchristian Christian gathering Loreli had ever had the misfortune to attend. She and her friends were angry, as were their men.

Jake wanted to snatch Dexter Appleby by his sanctimonious collar and toss him in a pig trough. No man of the cloth had the right to be so judgmental. Appleby was mad because of Jake's decision not to marry Rebecca, and was taking it out on the reputations of Loreli and her friends. Jake had hoped to avoid being in the middle of this cat fight, but it didn't appear as if he would be able to. Appleby had tarred all the new women, and the results were that no one on Jake's side of the church was feeling the least bit charitable when Appleby left the pulpit.

Loreli couldn't believe Victoria Diggs was standing to sing another hymn, but she was. Once again the pure notes of the organ were buried beneath Queen Vicki's awful voice.

Blessedly, the service ended a few prayers later. Loreli and the brides couldn't leave the church fast enough.

Outside, none of the brides bothered to stand in the pastor's receiving line; they were too angry. Most gave Loreli a hug and a promise to help her with the wedding, then headed straight home. Loreli looked up into Jake's tight face and asked, "Is Appleby always so *charming*?"

"I didn't like it any better than you did."

"Well, good. I thought it was just my imagination."

"It wasn't."

"Man like that doesn't belong in the pulpit," Loreli drawled. "He belongs in the congregation with the rest of us sinners."

Zora and Cyrus walked over. Zora huffed. "There is no way I'm going to call that nasty little man my pastor. If there isn't another church to attend around here, I'll start one myself! I'll see you in a few days to help with the wedding, Loreli. Nice meeting you, Jake." Zora then turned to the upset Cyrus and said, "Let's go home, honey. If I stay here another moment, I may sock Appleby."

Cyrus took his spirited wife by the arm and escorted her over to his buggy.

Jake and Loreli, like the other parents, were waiting for the children to be dismissed. Sunday school was still in session at the trestle table. In the meantime, the last of the congregation filed out of the church, and those who found the service inspiring waited in line for their turn to talk with Appleby. Loreli wanted to sock him, too!

Jake saw some men he needed to speak with about the union meetings, so he excused himself from Loreli for a moment to seek them out. While she stood there, members of the old guard walked by and flashed her triumphant smiles.

Millie Tate, the seamstress, breezed over to Loreli and asked haughtily, "Did you find someone to make those dresses?"

Loreli didn't believe in being a hypocrite, not even on Sunday. "Why do you care?"

Millie appeared taken aback. "Well, I was just being neighborly. It *is* Sunday."

"Go away, before I smite thee with my strumpet's staff," Loreli told her, showing her the parasol.

Millie's eyes widened and she hurried off.

Loreli smiled smugly.

The Sunday school was finally dismissed, and the twins came running to Loreli's side. They had with them two little dark-eyed girls who favored each other enough to be twins as well.

Bebe made the introductions. "Loreli, this is Aggie Gibson and this is her younger sister, Charlene Gibson. This is Loreli, she's going to be our new mama."

"Hello, ma'am," Aggie and Charlene said shyly. Both girls were nearly as fair-skinned as Loreli, and were dressed in starched calico dresses and dark stockings.

"Hello, girls. I'm glad to finally meet you. The twins talk about you two all the time."

Charlene said, "You're awfully pretty, Miss Loreli."

"Why, thank you, Charlene."

"Did your parents come to church with you?" Loreli asked. She dearly hoped their parents weren't members of the biddy crowd; she didn't want the girls' friendships to be affected by this nonsense.

Aggie offered a reply, "Our papa did. He's over there talking to Mr. Reed."

Loreli looked in the direction the girl indicated and saw Jake in conversation with the big man who'd played the church's organ. "Is that your papa?"

"Yes," Charlene said proudly.

"Their papa plays the organ," Dede said.

"And he plays very well," Loreli added.

Jake and the papa of the Gibson girls walked over to

join them. Jake made the introductions. "Loreli Winters. Arthur Gibson."

Gibson was even bigger up close. He had a receding hairline and shoulders wide enough to block out the sun. Loreli stuck out her hand as she always did; and although he appeared a bit surprised by the gesture, he took her hand in his and shook it in greeting.

Loreli said, "I'm pleased to meet you, Mr. Gibson. Your girls are lovely."

"Thanks. Pleased to meet you as well."

Loreli was accustomed to being stared at by men, so she paid Gibson no mind when he couldn't seem to take his eyes off of her.

"I hear you and Jake are marrying," Gibson said.

Loreli looked at Jake and kindly said, "Yes, we are. I do hope you and your family will join us for the wedding."

"Wouldn't miss it for the world. I'm sure my wife would be willing to lend a hand with the fixings if you need help."

"That's a very kind offer. The girls and I will drive over next week so I can introduce myself."

"She'd like that." He was still staring, but trying not to.

Jake asked, "How about we stop over on our way home instead? That way Loreli can meet Denise, and you and I can talk about some things."

The girls began jumping with glee.

Jake looked to Loreli. "Do you mind?"

"Oh, no. I'd like that in fact." Arthur Gibson seemed so friendly, Loreli could only surmise that he and his wife were not members of the old guard.

"Then let's head over to the wagon," Jake said.

Bebe asked, "Uncle, may De and I ride with Mr. Gibson?"

A smiling Art said, "I don't mind, if you don't, Jake."

The girls were looking so eager, Jake nodded. "Go ahead. Mind your manners, though."

"We will!" they promised.

The four young friends raced off to see who would reach the Gibson wagon first.

Chapter 11

The two wagons pulled out of the church grove. Jake handled the reins while Loreli sat on the seat beside him. The day had turned as hot as the early morning had hinted it would be. Even though Loreli's parasol kept off the sun, it did nothing to reduce the effects of the heat. She was broiling in her clothes and still simmering inside from Appleby's raging sermon. "I won't be going back to that church."

"I understand."

"I know I'm a sinner. I don't need it thrown in my face."

"The girls and I will still go, though."

"I don't think the girls should be around that pious little insect either, but that's your decision."

"They enjoy the Sunday school."

Loreli couldn't argue with that, so she didn't. "What is Gibson's wife like?"

"Nice—bossy."

"I like her already."

He chuckled softly, "The two of you should get along fine."

There was humor lighting his dark eyes. Loreli decided she liked seeing him smile. "I didn't mean to upset you last night."

For a moment there was only silence, then he responded quietly, "I know."

"Just thought the story might help you understand why I am the way I am," Loreli confessed further.

"And I appreciated it. It can't be easy to talk about." Jake thought back on all she'd suffered at the hands of those men, and how alone she must have felt facing life on her own. "You didn't do or say anything wrong last night. The problem is my own."

"Is it something you wish to talk about?"

He shook his head. "No." And Jake didn't. In a year's time she would be moving on; that was a given. A man like him had no business thinking she'd stay. Gambling queens did not hitch themselves to hog farmers, at least not permanently.

Loreli searched his face but couldn't see behind the mask. "Are you sure?"

"Yes."

"Okay." In order to lift the mood, she changed the subject. "Tell me about the Gibsons."

"He and I have been friends for many years now. He lost his first wife after Charlene was born. Then about a year and a half ago, he got himself a mail-order woman."

That surprised her. "This is the wife he has now?"

"Yep. Denise answered an ad Art ran in a newspaper back East. They started writing back and forth. A few months later, she came out on the train. She's from Cleveland, I believe."

Loreli had only been to Cleveland once, for a high-stakes poker game. The other players had been city officials, a Catholic priest, and members of an acting troupe in town to do a performance of "Uncle Tom's Cabin." She'd done well that night.

Jake went on. "He and Denise got along so well, all the unmarried men around wanted wives too."

"And that's when they sent for my friends?"

"Yes."

"So are you going to tell Arthur the truth about why we're getting married?"

"Haven't decided."

"Don't you think you should? I'll need to know how to act."

They were turning off the main road and down a thin gravel track that led to a long squat farmhouse. Surrounding the house were fields of chest-high green and yellow cornstalks. The familiar scent of hogs permeated the air.

"Can you pretend as if this is a real love match?" Jake asked.

She searched his face. "If that's what you want me to do."

"I do." He slid his eyes over her lightly painted mouth and felt his manhood thicken with life. "Denise has been after me about finding a wife. Arthur may be able to handle the truth, but I'm not real certain about Denise."

There was no time for further discussion as the wagons reached the house. Standing on the porch steps, shading her eyes against the fierce sun, was a tall, big-boned woman dressed in a brown day dress. Denise was a beautiful, brown skin giantess. Her husband, Arthur, rivaled a titan in size. Loreli thought them a perfect match.

Denise called, "How do, Jake? Who's that with you?"

"Denise, this is Loreli."

Arthur Gibson and the girls piled out of his wagon, and Jake came around to help Loreli down from his. He placed his hands on her waist and slowly swung her off the wagon. The heat of their bodies mingled.

"I like it when you do that," she said in a voice only he could hear.

His mustache twitched with amusement. "Behave yourself, we're with company."

"Just playing my role," she replied softly.

The girls ran inside so that Aggie and Charlene could change out of their dresses. Loreli and Jake stepped up onto the porch.

Denise, who hadn't taken her eyes off of Loreli since the moment Jake drove up, immediately came over and stuck out her hand. "Denise Gibson."

Loreli liked her already. "Loreli Winters. Pleased to meet you."

Denise scanned Loreli for a silent moment before turning to Jake. "Now I see why those old hens in town are flapping and squawking. She's a beauty, Jake."

Loreli looked his way to see how he would respond. Because he seemed at a loss for words, Denise drawled, "Jake, you're supposed to say, 'Yes, Denise, she is . . .'"

"He'll do better," Denise promised Loreli. "He just needs a few lessons. Spending so much time with livestock and cold fish like Rebecca Appleby, it's a wonder he knows how to speak at all."

Jake shook his head with amusement. Loreli chuckled. A smiling Arthur Gibson cautioned his wife, "Now, Denise—"

"It's the truth," Denise replied. She gestured to the four chairs on the porch. "Have a seat. I have some lemonade inside. Do you want a glass?"

Everyone did. Jake and Loreli took seats side by side. Denise returned promptly carrying a tray topped with the glasses of lemonade. Once everyone chose a glass, Denise set the tray down on the porch, then took the vacant chair next to her husband.

Loreli took a sip and found the drink refreshing after the drive in the hot sun.

"Rumors say you came out with the mail-order brides," Denise said to Loreli.

Loreli nodded. "I did. Came mainly for the adventure. Had no plans on marrying at all, until I met Jake." She turned to him, looked up into his handsome brown face, and confessed, "Never thought I'd fall in love with a man at first sight."

Jake knew she was just acting, but his body didn't care. The desire in her eyes looked so real, he reached out and stroked her cheek.

The moment was interrupted by the girls coming outside. The Gibson daughters had changed into shirts and denims.

"We're going to show Charlene and Aggie our new jacks," Bebe said.

"Okay," Loreli told them, wondering how she'd ever be able to leave them when the time came to dissolve this so-called marriage.

After the girls went charging off, Denise said, "Those twins are good girls. Glad Jake finally found someone to love them."

Loreli had no idea her feelings for the girls showed so plainly, but she basked in the unexpected compliment. "They make it real easy."

"When's the wedding?" Arthur asked.

"Saturday afternoon," Jake replied. "Just a small gathering. Nothing fancy."

Denise brought her hands together in a show of glee. "This is so wonderful. I've been praying for Jake for a long time. I knew Rebecca wasn't the one. You're his blessing, Loreli."

In response, Loreli turned to Jake and said softly, "He's been my blessing too."

Jake felt like a barn about to catch fire. She was handling this play far better than he. In an attempt to extricate himself from the spell of her tawny eyes, he stammered, "Uh-uh, Art, how's the stallion?"

"You two can talk about that horse any time," Denise scolded. "I want to hear about the wedding."

Loreli could have kissed her. "She's right, Jake. So tell her."

The faint, sweet notes of Loreli's perfume were threatening to overwhelm him. Trying not to inhale too deeply, he shrugged and said, "Nothing to tell."

Loreli sensed their game was unsettling him. Enjoying it, however, she countered playfully, devilishly, "Sure there is. My friends from the wagon train are handling the decorations and the food. There's going to be a fiddler and a piano."

Jake stared at her as if she'd just declared the President had been invited. He wanted to shout his disbelief, but remembered he was supposed to be acting as if he were in love with this impossible woman. "I didn't know you and the ladies were doing so much," he managed to say calmly.

Loreli leaned over, and lovingly hooked her arm in his. "I'm sorry, I thought I told you." They both knew she hadn't. Continuing her subtle assault, Loreli smoothly threaded her fingers into his. "We ironed out all the details when I met them in town on Friday."

Loreli liked the size and feel of his large hands. The dark fingers were long and the nails cut short.

Jake fought to keep himself unmoved by the warmth of her soft fingers, but she was entirely too close to mount any kind of defense. He knew she was acting this way because he'd asked her to, but she was also trying to get a rise out of him, and she'd certainly done that. He shifted imperceptibly on the seat to accommodate his body's response to her stimulating nearness.

While Denise and Arthur looked on knowingly, Jake leaned over and whispered in her ear, "Are you enjoying yourself?"

Aware that the Gibsons were watching, Loreli smiled up at him and said softly, "As a matter of fact, I am. Are you?"

Jake was about to respond when Arthur said, "All right you two, close the curtains. There are children about."

Loreli dropped her head as if embarrassed. "Sorry."

"Never apologize for being in love," Denise said. "Art and I sure don't. Do we, darlin'?"

Laughing, he replied, "Not a bit."

"Please, say you'll stay for supper?" urged Denise. "There's plenty."

Jake looked over at Loreli. "Well?"

Pleased with the offer and the camaraderie, she replied, "I'd like to stay, but it's up to you."

He turned back to Denise and declared, "We'll stay."

Because folks often lived miles from the nearest neighbor, visits, especially with good friends, were special.

The meal consisted of grilled chicken, collards, squash, and the best yeast rolls Loreli had had since leaving Chicago. "Denise, everything is wonderful."

Denise grinned. "Thanks. What's your specialty?"

"Poker."

For a moment, Denise cocked her head Loreli's way, and then she laughed. "I meant cooking."

"I know that's what you meant. I can't cook. Jake thinks it's a sin, but I'll make up for it in other ways . . ."

Seeing the sly promise in her eyes, Jake shook his head at her outrageousness and told her, *"Eat."*

It was early evening by the time the Reed family was ready to head home. While Jake brought the wagon around, Denise demanded and received a parting hug from Loreli.

"You take care of yourself, now," Denise said.

Loreli had a feeling she and Denise were going to become good friends before it was all said and done. "You do the same. I've had a nice time."

Jake drove up in the wagon. The girls got in the bed, and Loreli told Denise and Arthur, "I know I'll see you both soon."

"Count on it," Denise replied.

So with a wave to the Gibsons and their daughters, Loreli climbed aboard. The twins called good-byes to Charlene and Aggie while Jake headed the wagon back out to the road.

Once they were underway, Loreli leaned over to him and asked, "How'd I do?"

He nodded and said, "You did fine."

She smiled. "Good. Had you going there for a bit, though, I'll bet?"

He smiled. "Behave."

A contented Loreli sat back against the wagon seat and listened to the girls sing "Amazing Grace."

The men Jake had asked to attend the union meeting began arriving at the Reed barn around eight o'clock that same evening. There were six in all, including Arthur Gibson and Matt Peterson, who was the last to arrive.

Jake started the discussion. "Do we want to organize?"

Art spoke up. "I think we should."

Matt Peterson said, "You all know where I stand. The faster we do this, the better off we'll all be."

Jake agreed, but a few of the men weren't so sure. One man, fifty-five-year-old Paul Fletcher said, "There's only six of us. What difference can so few make?"

"It only takes one man to change the world," Jake pointed out.

Jake hadn't wanted Fletcher to be involved. The overweight Fletcher and his wife, Wanda, were good friends with Sol and Victoria Diggs, and Jake was certain Diggs would know everything that had gone on in the meeting by the time the cock crowed in the morning. However,

Fletcher was one of the largest landowners, and his throwing in with them was almost necessary if they were to succeed.

Fletcher said, "Well, I don't think we should rock the boat. Look what happened to Doyle, Granger, and Sears. I hear the bank foreclosed on them."

"All the more reason to band together," Matt Peterson said. "Maybe Diggs wouldn't have foreclosed had he known we were behind them."

Jake said, "Matt's right. We might also have been able to call on the Knights for support."

"Have we heard anything more from the Knights, Jake?" Arthur Gibson asked.

"Not since the meeting I had with their man last month. He was supposed to come down here and talk with us, but so far, nothing."

One of the men in the back, Wayne Young, asked, "Is it true the Knights aren't segregating, and that men of the race can expect to be officers as well?"

"As far as I know. According to their man, there are thousands of us in their ranks, and all are given full membership."

It was well understood that for any of the unions and farm associations to amass the clout needed to challenge the nation's capitalists, incorporating the thousands of Black workers into the fold was a necessity. Yet, many of the organizations were unable to set aside their prejudices and were relegating the men of the race to separate entities formed within the larger body. So far, the Knights continued to agitate for a colorblind labor movement, but Jake was a realist. In the face of the steady disenfranchisement of the race being perpetrated at all levels of American society, it was anyone's guess as to how long the Knights would remain prejudice free.

"Well, I say we pool our corn crops this year and let the big owners bid," Jake said then.

Paul Fletcher pointed out sagely, "Some men up near Topeka tried that tactic and failed."

"Only because they didn't stick together," Arthur countered. "Some withheld part of their crops and made side deals. It undercut the others, and the whole alliance fell apart."

"That won't happen here," Matt Peterson declared.

Fletcher groused, "How do you know?"

"Because we're all honest men, Paul," Jake said.

The big-jowled Fletcher didn't look convinced. Jake wondered how long it would be before Fletcher went his own way. Jake didn't see him sticking it out, for many reasons. The least being, the man was afraid.

Art said, "Well, Jake, I say we form an alliance and see what happens. If we don't get what we want—well, at least we will have tried. It isn't as if we're getting rich doing it this way."

The rest of the men agreed. At least everyone but Fletcher, who said, "I need to think about this some more. You all are relatively young men, I'm not. If I'm going to take this risk, I have to be sure it's right."

Jake's jaw tightened, but he said evenly, "Take some time, then. We'll need your decision by midweek."

Fifty-year-old Brass Barber owned a farm almost as large as Fletcher's. Until this point in the meeting, the black-skinned, gray-haired Brass had been content to keep his own counsel, as was his way, and had not offered any comment. He did now. "Paul," he told Fletcher pointedly, "if you decide not to go with us, I expect you to keep everything you've heard here tonight to yourself."

Fletcher squirmed under Barber's direct eyes. "Of course, I will."

No one believed him for a minute.

Jake said, "All right, then. How about we meet again next Sunday?"

Art cleared his throat to get Jake's attention.

A puzzled Jake asked, "What?"

"You're getting married on Saturday, remember?"

Suddenly remembering that to be true, Jake dropped his head with amused embarrassment.

As the men laughed, and those unaware of Jake's upcoming nuptials offered congratulations, Art added, "I don't think Loreli's gonna want us hanging around."

Jake grinned. "You're right, Art. Thanks. How about we meet in two weeks, then?"

Everyone thought that a better plan.

"Meeting adjourned," Jake then declared.

Paul Fletcher practically ran from the barn. The others shook their heads.

After his departure, Jake told the rest of the men, "I'd hoped tonight's meeting would help us determine which of our members were weak and which strong."

Matt Peterson cracked, "Guess you got your answer."

Jake nodded. "I did, so since we all know Paul's not going to join us, I can now tell you the truth. Sometime around mid-August, a man from the Knights of Labor will be coming down to initiate us."

You could hear a pin drop as the five men stiffened with surprise. They all turned Jake's way and stared.

Jake confessed, "I lied about not having been contacted earlier because I wasn't sure where everyone stood."

Barber chuckled and shook his head knowingly. "You always were the cleverest one around, even as a boy."

Jake had known Brass Barber most of his life. He accepted the compliment with a smile. "Thanks."

"So, what do we have to do to prepare?" Art asked.

"I'll let you know when we meet again in two weeks."

Wayne Young said, "I hear they have a secret ceremony. That true?"

Jake didn't reply.

The men noted Jake's stance and Barber quipped, "Jake's always been a sphinx when need be too."

The men laughed. They gave their good-nights and headed for their wagons. Art was the last to leave. He and Jake stood outside the barn, watching the late evening settle in.

"Fletcher's going to run right to Diggs," Art said knowingly.

"He won't have much to tell, other than the news that we're pooling our crops."

Art thought about it a moment. "I suppose you're right. We didn't make any ironclad plans or discuss any strategies."

"Correct. So Fletcher knows nothing."

Art smiled. "You're always thinking, Jake. Guess that's why you're our leader."

Jake looked toward the house and saw Loreli and the girls set off for a stroll. Loreli had changed out of that stunning yellow dress and into a plain brown skirt and blouse.

Art turned to see what had drawn Jake's attention, then smiled. "That's some woman, Jake. How'd you manage to land her?"

"I didn't. The girls did."

He then told Arthur the story. All of it.

When Jake was done with the telling, Art could only stare, then upon finding his voice said, "And she agreed to marry you?"

"Yep, and in the meantime, I'll look for somebody else."

"Why not ask her to stay? You two seem to get along."

"No."

"Why not?"

"Look at her, Art. Do you think a woman like that is going to want to spend the rest of her life smelling hogs?"

Art sighed his surrender. "You do have a point."

"Even if I could convince her to stay, she wouldn't be happy. She's a city woman. She can't even cook, for heaven's sake."

"She's beautiful, though."

"No denying that," Jake agreed, his tone admiring. "Will you stand up with me at the wedding?"

"Sure." Art then peered over at his old friend Jake, and as men often do, asked, "Well, have you and her—"

Jake didn't even look at him. "Shut up, Art. That's none of your business."

Art showed his palms in surrender. "Sorry. Just curious."

Jake turned to him finally and his mustache lifted with amusement. "Go home. Denise is probably waiting."

Art tossed back, "Nothing like having your own personal, willing woman waiting, Jake. You should try it."

Jake chuckled. "Go home, you ox."

Art headed toward his wagon and waved good-bye.

After hearing the girls' prayers and kissing them good-night, Loreli and Jake stepped out onto the porch. The sun was going down, and Loreli was once again transfixed by its fiery red beauty. "I love your sunsets, Jake."

Jake thought the beauty of the sunset pale in comparison to the fiery sapphire woman standing on his porch.

"How'd your meeting go?"

"Not bad. I think we lost one person tonight, though."

"Is that good or bad?" she asked.

"Good probably. He's a friend of Diggs."

"Ah," she voiced, then directed her attention back to the sunset.

Jake ran his eyes over the slope of her shoulders and down the curves of her waist and hips. His vow to stay away from her until the wedding night rose up to taunt him mightily. He wanted to touch her so badly, his heart was pounding, his hands ached. Remembering Art's comments about willing, waiting women taunted him also. Jake had to dig deep into his will not to go to her side, but in the end, desire won out. He walked up behind her, and after lightly placing his hands on her shoulders, slowly stroked her arms up and down. Leaning toward her, he fervently brushed his lips across the back of her neck, whispering, "I have to touch you . . ."

Loreli melted back against his hard frame as naturally as if they'd been doing this their entire lives. The hands moving ever so slowly over her arms were hot, gentle. She turned her head so their eyes could meet, then asked sultrily, playfully, "Have we been introduced?"

His lips against her ear, his hands still savoring the soft, warm flesh of her arms, Jake breathed, "I believe we have. I'm the one taking the lessons . . ."

Loreli's amusement mingled with her rising reaction to his hands and lips. She husked out, "I remember you now."

"Good, wouldn't want you to forget me."

She turned to face him and her golden eyes were suddenly serious. "There's no chance of that."

Her answer pleased him, and he reached out and ran his finger down her silken cheek. "I'm glad."

Entranced, Jake slowly moved his finger to trace her parted lips. He wanted this woman so very much. "I'm not supposed to be doing this, am I?"

Her reply was a whisper, "No."

He bent down and kissed her so passionately and thoroughly, Loreli melted right there on the spot.

Her desire rising, eyes closed, Loreli purred, "You must be trying to get promoted."

"And, go to the head of the class . . ." Jake's manhood, aroused and ready, demanded he do something about the passionate ache she caused, but he'd made a vow. "But not tonight. Tonight, I have to say—good night, Loreli."

Loreli tried to think of something that might make him stay. She didn't want him to go. "Sit and talk with me a while. You don't have to run off."

Even as Jake yearned to pull her into his arms, he knew he had to leave her. "If I stay, we won't be talking."

She studied him, then said seriously, "I'm willing."

"I know, but a man should stand by his words."

Loreli wanted to make love until the sun rose, and he did too; she could see it in his dark eyes, feel it in his touch, and hear it in the timbre of his voice. However, he seemed to be ruled by something more noble than lust, and she had to respect him for that reason. "Then go on to bed. I won't tempt you."

"Just looking at you tempts me," he confessed, taking in her face and form. Jake thought about the men in her past. Had they too been as bewitched by all that she was? He quickly set aside thoughts of the others; he didn't want their ghosts looming over the short time he'd have with her. He bent to touch his lips to hers. "Good night," he whispered.

Loreli reached up and stroked her finger against his firm jaw. "Good night."

And he was gone.

That night, as darkness fell over the land, Loreli slept with such peace and contentment, she didn't even notice the rock-hard bed.

The next morning, after breakfast, Jake rode off to check on the health of Bert Green's new foal while Loreli and the girls stayed behind; today was Monday, and Monday was washday.

Dede, watching Loreli fill the big caldrons with water from the pump, asked, "But why is Monday always wash day, Loreli? Uncle Jake never washed on Mondays."

Loreli shrugged. "Well, your Uncle Jake's not a woman, and in the woman's rule book, Monday is always the day you wash." Loreli was glad she had a vivid imagination. Coming up with answers to the dozens of questions the girls seemed to have every day often took honesty, ingenuity, and in some cases, downright guile. Of course there was no official woman's rule book, but women had rules just the same, and the girls needed to know they existed even if the book was an imaginary one.

While the water heated on the big grate in the pit behind the house, the girls took Loreli to meet all the animals. Bebe pointed to a big brown hen, who at their approach raised her head to eye Loreli sharply. "That's Suzie. She's the boss hen."

Dede added, "She even bosses Uncle Jake."

Loreli eyed the hen. The hen continued to fix Loreli with her stare. "She looks pretty mean."

"She is, but not to us," Bebe said easily.

They then pointed out the other three hens: Babe, Peg and Myrtle.

"That's Mr. Cook up on the roof of the barn."

Loreli looked up and saw a rooster seated on the roof. "What's he doing up there?"

"Suzie doesn't like him, so he stays up there so she won't peck him."

Loreli looked back at Suzie, who was still eyeing Loreli malevolently. Loreli made a point to stay out of Suzie's way. "Why is the rooster's name Mr. Cook?"

"That's who Uncle Jake got him from."

"Ah, I see," Loreli said.

They passed the large and smelly hog pens with its fat, slow-moving hogs.

Bebe informed them, "Some of the hogs are mean, 'specially when there's piglets. Uncle won't let us come here when there's piglets."

A wary Loreli asked, "Are there piglets now?"

"Nope."

Loreli thought that good news. Some of the hogs were as big around as a large tree trunk. She certainly wouldn't want to have a confrontation with them. If the smell didn't kill you, the solid weight of one falling on you would.

The girls showed her the ducks and their downy ducklings. She met Emily the sleek, gray mouser, and her brood of new kittens. The girls then took her to greet the two dogs that Loreli had previously seen prowling the property like lawmen. Bebe knelt beside one dog whose black wolf-like appearance made Loreli a bit nervous. Bebe rubbed him lovingly, and the dog turned his head and dragged his large tongue across her face. She squealed with delight. She hastily wiped her hands across her face. Dede giggled.

Bebe said to Loreli, "This is Pal. His mama was a wolf, but she died in a trap. Uncle found Pal and brought him home."

"Curl up your fingers, Loreli, and let him sniff your hand," Dede then told Loreli. "That way he'll know you live here."

A bit apprehensive because the black dog was so big, Loreli came forward anyway and held out her hand. The dog ran his nose over her balled fist, then looked up at her.

Dede commanded gently, "Say hi, Pal."

The dog barked. Loreli laughed and reached down to pet him. She could feel the strong muscles beneath his black coat. "Hello, Pal."

Loreli and the girls spent a few moments with the fierce-looking Pal, then it was time to meet the sheepdog, Rabbit. The gray in his coat and the age in his eyes made Loreli believe Rabbit was much older than Pal. Mimicking the same actions she'd used to introduce herself to Pal, Loreli let Rabbit sniff her hand. While the dog took in her scent and the girls stroked him, Loreli asked, "Why is he called Rabbit?"

The kneeling Bebe hugged the dog close. "It's because he's scared of rabbits."

A surprised Loreli had never heard of such a thing.

Bebe said, "Uncle Jake has had Rabbit a long time."

Dede stroked the old dog's back. "Uncle Jake said the man who owned Rabbit was going to shoot Rabbit because Rabbit was scared of everything, but Uncle Jake took him home."

Loreli thought Uncle Jake had a very kind and generous heart. "So, is Rabbit scared of everything around here too?"

"Pretty much. He's even scared of his own shadow, but we love him anyway."

Loreli stroked the old back one final time, then she and the girls moved on. Loreli could see the goat kid tied to a corner of the horse paddock. The first time she'd noticed the animal had been on a previous visit. At that time the young goat was being harassed by a pair of geese. Today there were no geese to be seen. "Why's that goat over there by himself."

Dede corrected her. "It's a she. Her name's Elvira."

"She sick?"

"No," Bebe said. "She bites. Mrs. Mitchell, her owner, says that dumb old goat will bite anything and anyone."

Loreli chuckled. "Really?"

Bebe nodded. "Yep. After she tried to bite me and De, Uncle Jake tied her up over there."

"Does your uncle or Mrs. Mitchell know why Elvira likes to bite?"

"Elvira thinks she's a dog," Dede said sagely.

Loreli's shoulders shook with humor. "A dog!"

"Yep. That's what Mrs. Mitchell said."

"What'd your uncle say?"

"The same thing," Bebe replied.

An amused Loreli shook her head. A sheepdog scared of his own shadow, and a goat named Elvira who thought she was a dog. Jake Reed had quite a menagerie.

When they all walked back across the yard to where the caldrons of water were heating, the water was hot, so they began the day's big chore.

Washing was hot, grueling work, especially on such a humid day. Loreli, wearing an old tan blouse and dark flowing skirt was wet from her breasts to her thighs, mostly from the washboard and the wringer, but also from sweat. Her life, and more recently, the rigors of the wagon train had taught her not to be ashamed to do a hard day's work, or be ashamed of her own perspiration. And washing was just that—hard work. Whether it was the flesh-stinging, skin-chaffing lye water the clothes were washed in, or the struggle hanging sheets and other large items on the clothesline, it wasn't easy.

By midafternoon, they were done. Hot, wet, and sticky, she and the girls looked over the lines of clothes drying in the sun, and Loreli felt a real sense of accomplishment. She knew it was only wash to the girls; she'd even had to fuss at them a few times in order to keep them on task, but for her, the new mama, washday represented her first real task. She was proud it had been done well. "Thanks for your help, girls."

Bebe groused, "Are we going to have to do this every Monday?"

Loreli told her plainly, "Yes." Then she asked the twins, "You've never helped with the wash before?"

"No."

Dede chimed in, "Sometimes. Rebecca did our wash. She said we only got in the way."

Knowing the girls a bit better now, Loreli wondered if they had made themselves unwanted on purpose. At eight years old, Loreli knew she wouldn't have wanted to be toiling over a wooden scrubboard, wrist-deep in hot water that burned her hands. Children were children and they didn't like to work, at least not for a long span of time; however, Loreli planned on having them assist her every Monday. A bit of hard work never harmed anyone, least of all two healthy eight-year-old girls.

Chapter 12

Bert Green's new foal, Sunshine, appeared to be thriving. Its dark coat was sleek and shiny, and although the filly's spindly legs looked as delicate as twigs as it ran back and forth around its mother, the foal was healthy and strong.

Jake folded up his bag and stood. Bert Green was in town running his store, so his wife, Belinda, stood watching from a spot outside the paddock. "Sunshine okay?" Belinda asked as Jake left the paddock and slid the bolt on the wooden gate.

"She's doing just fine."

Belinda and Bert had been married for fifteen years. She was as thin and tall as her husband was short and round. Smiling, she said to him, "Don't know what folks 'round here would do without you, Jake."

"Just helping out my neighbors. That's all."

"Well, we do appreciate it."

Jake didn't care to acknowledge the effect his physique

247

and face seemed to have on some women, but ladies like Belinda Green always made a point of reminding him by shamelessly flirting with him at every opportunity. Today she had a light in her eyes she probably hadn't shown her husband in years, if ever.

Her voice throaty, she asked, "Would you like some coffee? Got some fresh on the stove, inside."

Jake ignored the emphasis she'd placed on the word *inside*. "No thanks. I have a few more stops to make this morning."

Jake began walking back to where he tied up Fox. The sooner he got away from Belinda the better.

Belinda fell in beside him. Her long legs beneath her pink and brown calico dress easily matched his own. "What's this I hear about you marrying up?"

Jake untied Fox. "Saturday." He hitched himself up onto the stallion's saddle.

Belinda looked up. "Lot of women around here disappointed at that news, Jake Reed."

"Don't know why," he replied. "Most of the women around here are already married. Those that aren't, we don't suit."

"Well, when the gambler woman breaks your heart and you need a soft shoulder, I'm here."

Jake ignored that too. Bringing Fox around, Jake rode away from Belinda Green.

On his way back home, Jake stopped in to check on: a sick lamb, a dog accidentally shot by his drunken owner who mistook the domesticated canine for a wolf, a sow that wouldn't eat, and a mule with an infected hoof. Jake treated them all to the best of his ability, and in exchange received: a jug of apple cider, two wild turkeys, and a grouse. Very few of the farmers had cash to spare, so they paid him with whatever they could, however they could. Jake graciously accepted it all as payment in full.

As Jake approached the road that led to his farm, he saw a heavy laden caravan of wagons up ahead. There were three of them, and whatever they were hauling in the beds lay hidden beneath tightly corded tarps.

Curious, Jake gently urged Fox into a faster pace in order to see where the wagons might be headed.

To his surprise, Brass Barber was driving one of the wagons. Commanding the other two were Brass's son, William, and Brass's widowed daughter, Nora. No Nonsense Nora, as she was known, had taken over the running of her husband's small freight-hauling company after he died unexpectedly a few months back. Outside of Loreli, Nora was probably the prettiest woman in the county.

When Jake caught up to the wagons, a smiling Brass halted his team. "Afternoon, Jake."

"Brass."

Jake then turned to the other drivers. "Hey, Will. Nora."

Nora, never known for her tact, asked, "Is it true you're marrying a gambling queen?"

"Yes, I am."

Nora laughed. "Well, she'll probably be a whole lot more fun than any of these local crows, so congratulations. Can't wait to meet her."

Jake and Nora had grown up together, and she'd also been one of Bonnie's best friends. Nora might have been one of the women he considered marrying had he not looked upon her as a younger sister. Their sibling-like relationship excluded her as a candidate, that and the fact that she could handle a sling shot like the biblical David.

William, five years younger than Nora, added, "Yes, congratulations, Jake. That bride of yours must be a pretty good gambler, because she owns a lot of stuff. We're hauling all of this to your place."

Jake viewed the wagons with confusion and alarm. "My place?"

Brass chuckled at the look on Jake's face. "Yep. All of this is hers. Came in on the train this morning."

Jake continued to eye the tarp-covered wagons with amazement. "She said *some* of her things were going to be shipped."

"Well, son, the word *some* can mean different things to different people. In this case she should have said *many* things."

Nora, smiling at Jake's stunned face, added, "There's so much here, we thought we were going to need four wagons, but we managed to load it all into three."

"My lord," Jake whispered. The house wasn't large enough to hold all this. "What could she have been thinking?"

Brass slapped the reins down on the backs of the team to get them moving again. "Don't know, but there's a piano in the wagon Will's driving."

"A *piano*!"

Will said, "Yep, a piano. Guess you'll have music at the wedding."

Nora, driving her team as efficiently as the men, laughed. "I really can't wait to meet her."

Jake couldn't either.

When the wagons drove up, Loreli paid them little mind. It was the tersely set face of Jake as he rode up on Fox that drew her attention. She wondered what was wrong. Loreli put down her lemonade and stood on the steps. The girls, who'd thought a glass of lemonade more than adequate pay for helping with the wash, had their attentions fixed on the wagons.

"What do you think is in them, De?" Bebe asked.

The always sage Dede responded, "Whatever it is, it's a whole lot more than our roller skates."

Jake dismounted. He stalked to the porch and said to Loreli, "We need to talk."

"What's in all those wagons?" Bebe asked.

"Loreli," Jake gritted out.

But before she could respond, Brass Barber eased himself off the wagon seat and down to the ground. He looked up at Loreli on the porch and said, "You Miss Loreli Winters?"

"I am."

"Well, I'm Brass Barber. This here's my daughter, Nora, and my son, Will."

"Pleased to meet you all," Loreli replied.

Nora called out, "How do, Loreli. Hi, girls."

The twins grinned and called back, "Hi, Miss Nora. Are our roller skates in there?"

"Not that I remember seeing, but there's a whole mess of other things."

Loreli brightened. "Are those my things from Philadelphia?"

Brass said, "Yes, ma'am."

Loreli flew off the porch. She asked excitedly, "Is there a bathtub? Oh, please tell me Olivia sent it like I asked her to."

Nora's shoulders shook with humor. "Now, that I did see. Got it on this wagon here, as a matter of fact."

Loreli declared, "Then by all means, let's get yours un-loaded first. Lord, I can't wait to take a real bath!"

The girls came down and stood by her side. "Can we help?"

Loreli hugged them both to her damp, sticky side. "Of course, and when we're done, we are going to have the best bath any girl has ever had."

Their eyes grew bright as diamonds.

On the porch, Jake tried to banish his bad mood but failed. As Loreli and the others went to work on the cords holding down the tarps, Brass stepped up onto the porch and looked into Jake's eyes.

The older man smiled and offered wisely, "Son, women are a race unto themselves, and they have different needs than we men. If you're marrying up, you need to re-member that."

Jake heard him, but it didn't mellow his mood. "You'd think she was furnishing a castle."

"But she's happy. Look at her. That is a gorgeous woman, Jake. Why be mad at something that fine, and I've seen that bathtub. It's big enough for two."

That said, Brass went down to help with the unloading. Jake, humorously shaking his head at Brass's parting words, followed suit.

Waiting beneath the tarps were, among other things, upholstered chairs with embroidered backs and finely curved legs, dining china, flatware and a hutch to put them in. The girls carried in lamps, and then hatboxes, while Nora and Loreli hauled in trunks and the drawers to the two chifforobes. The men somehow managed to get the piano inside. Next came Loreli's massive bedframe and its accompanying headboard. Brass likened the procedure to trying to thread hogs through the eye of a needle.

Jake's mood had lightened but he still had trouble handling what he saw as Loreli's excessive amount of possessions. Having been raised on a Kansas farm under an austere, Bible-thumping daddy, he'd never had many material things; even now, a man full grown, Jake lived modestly. He grabbed hold of another fancy-legged chair from Will's wagon and headed for the porch. *How much money does this woman have?* his mind kept asking. It took him a moment to find a place to set the chair because by now, the parlor was so filled with goods, it resembled a big department store back East. Furniture, dishes, clothes. One would think England's queen was coming to visit. The only thing missing were servants, and knowing Loreli, Jake wouldn't be surprised if there weren't a butler or a chambermaid hiding under the tarps as well.

In the midst of the hubbub, his eyes met hers. He was certain she could see his discontent because he didn't try and hide it.

Loreli didn't need to be a carnival mind reader to sense Jake's disapproval, but she didn't care. If she was going to live in this backwater, she would at least be comfortable; and if her possessions somehow offended his small-town sensibilities, then he could register his protest by continuing to sleep on that board he called a bed, and by refusing to use her big luxurious bathtub. She shot him a look, then went back outside to help with the ongoing task of emptying the wagons. If he wanted to fight, she'd oblige him, but not until after she had her bath.

In all, it took the men, women, and children over an hour to empty the three wagons, and when they were done, they were all weary but pleased.

After the Barbers left with the bank draft for their services, and Loreli's deepest thanks, she and the twins stood in the middle of the packed parlor and just looked around at all that was there.

Dede asked in a soft, awed voice, "Where are we going to put all of this, Loreli?"

Jake, stepping over an ottoman and squeezing by the chifforrobes, drawled, "My question too."

Loreli heard the censuring tone in his voice and so tossed back, "We'll just build a bigger house. How's that for a solution?"

The girls eyes widened with glee.

"She's just fooling, girls," Jake clipped out. "We are not building a bigger house."

The twins looked deflated.

"I'm sorry, girls," Loreli apologized. "I was just fooling, but I wasn't fooling about that bath, so who wants to be first?"

They began jumping up and down in an attempt to be the first picked. To aid in the decision, Loreli fished a coin out of the pocket of her skirt. "Heads or tails?"

They chose and she flipped the coin into the air. When it landed in her open palm, she showed it to the girls. Tails. Dede would be first.

Loreli had instructed the Barbers to take the tub around to the back and set it on the ground near the back porch, and when she and the girls stepped outside, that's exactly where it was. The girls dragged the twin caldrons to the pump, and while Loreli pumped the water, the girls investigated the tub.

Bebe confessed. "I don't think I've ever had a bath in a tub *this* big, Loreli, at least that I can remember."

"Well, you will tonight, and it's going to be heavenly. Oh, do me a favor and take those rugs out of it. My house-keeper, Olivia, put them in to protect the tub's finish." Loreli went back to pumping. The quiet over by the tub caught her attention and she looked over to find the twins standing speechless. Each held a long box wrapped in pretty foil paper. "What's that?" she asked.

"They have our names on them, Loreli."

Loreli left the pump. Jake stepped outside at that moment.

Dede held up her box. "Look what we got, Uncle Jake."

Loreli surveyed the box in Bebe's hands and upon see-ing Olivia's familiar script, Loreli smiled. "You're right, they are for you. Go ahead and open them."

Having been given permission, the twins tore into the paper. The boxes were opened carefully, however, and the dress that each girl found inside made them speechless once again.

"Oh, Loreli . . ." Bebe whispered in an awestruck voice.

The dresses were fancy enough to wear to the wedding. Both were a soft blue velvet, but the trims and styles were different enough so that the girls would look like distinct individuals.

Dede held hers up for inspection, and as her eyes wan-dered over the lace-edged cuffs and the little rosebuds around the neck, she said, "This is the most beautiful dress in the whole world."

Loreli looked up at Jake a moment and saw in his eyes that he was moved by the twins' show of happiness.

Bebe asked, "May we wear these to the wedding, Un-cle Jake?"

"Of course," he said softly. His eyes met Loreli's again, and held. Her generosity when coupled with the delight showed by the twins effectively negated his bad mood. As Barber said, Who can be mad at a woman so fine? Jake certainly couldn't, at least not for very long. He finally said to Loreli in a tone he hoped conveyed his sincerity, "Thank you."

She bowed elaborately. "You're very welcome."

They were distracted when Bebe gushed, "De! Look?!"

In the bottom of each box, and hidden beneath the paper holding the dresses were two pairs of white stockings and a pair of fancy young-lady slippers. They were black and each shoe had a tiny rhinestone on the front.

"When did you order these, Loreli?" Dede asked.

"Well, I wired your sizes to my housekeeper and told her you two needed dresses for the wedding and it looks as if she came through for us. I wasn't certain the dresses from Bloomingdale's would arrive in time."

Bebe said, "I wish she was here, so I could give her a big kiss."

Loreli laughed. "Me too, Be. She did us real proud, didn't she?"

"I want to give her two kisses," Dede said.

The girls very carefully boxed up their beautiful treasures, then took them to their room.

While Jake and Loreli were alone, he said to her, "You made them very happy."

"They deserve it. Every little girl should have a pretty dress and fancy new slippers. I never did, which probably accounts for why I own so many dresses now."

"Not to mention all the furniture, the china, the chairs and the rest. You can't even turn around in the parlor."

"It won't look that way once we get everything in its place, I promise."

Jake planned to keep her to that. "But why on earth do we need a piano? I assume you play?"

She waved him off. "No."

"No?" He stared, amazed, "Then why own one?"

"Because everybody back East does. Maybe Art Gibson can give the girls lessons on it."

Jake chuckled and shook his head. What a woman. He supposed the twins would benefit from having the instrument in the house, but—she left him speechless.

He eyed her and asked, "So do you have any idea who's going to put together that giant bed of yours?"

Loreli replied with flirting eyes, "Nope, but you'd better come up with someone because our wedding night's less than a week away . . ." She threw him a bold wink and went inside to check on the girls.

Jake laughed out loud at that one.

Getting into the mood of the occasion, Jake pumped the water and set it to heating while Loreli and the girls dug through the jungle of furnishings and clothing in the parlor in a search for toiletries. It took them almost twenty minutes of moving things, opening one crate, then another. Finally they chanced upon a small crate lying beneath the piano. It was filled to the lid with scented soaps and bath salts.

Bebe gasped. "I've never seen this much soap in my life!"

Loreli freed a few bars from their wrappers. "A woman can never have too many soaps," she drawled.

They giggled.

She offered them a sniff of the scented bars in her

hands; Bebe picked the bayberry and Dede, the violet.

Dede explained her choice of the violet. "It smells just like Loreli."

Loreli leaned over and gave her a kiss on the forehead, then one to her sister. "Thanks for inviting me to be your mama," she voiced sincerely.

They grinned and replied as one, "You're welcome."

Loreli opted not to take her bath until after the girls were put to bed; she didn't want to be interrupted or disturbed. Her desires were to stretch out in a tub filled to the brim with hot water and salts, and sit and soak. So after prayers were heard and good-night kisses were given, Jake filled the caldrons for her and set them atop the grate in the pit to heat. Then he wandered over to the pens to check on the animals for the last time that evening. Loreli took down the dry laundry, folded it, and set the baskets inside. So much had happened since the morning, washday seemed like another day entirely. When Jake returned, she was seated on the porch. The weariness in her face was plain.

Jake told her quietly, "You look exhausted."

"I'll be better after I soak in the tub. I can't believe it's really here. Remind me to wire Olivia a raise in pay, first thing in the morning."

He smiled. "Who's Olivia?"

"One of my housekeepers. I told you about her. She keeps house at my place in Philadelphia."

"*One* of your housekeepers?"

Loreli yawned tiredly. "Yes, I have three."

Jake stiffened. "Three?"

"Yes. One in Philadelphia, Denver, and Boston."

"Why so many?"

She shrugged, "I move around a lot, and when I get tired of being restless, I want to go to a place I can call my own—a place that has *my* bathtub, *my* bed linens, *my* cook."

"A cook?"

Leaning her tired self against the porch post, she told him. "Sure, one for each house. In fact, I'm going to find one for here as soon as I get the chance."

"We don't need a cook."

"Sure we do, but I'm too tired to argue about it now. Let's do it tomorrow."

Amusement tinted his tone. "Okay. We'll argue tomorrow."

"Good. How's that water coming?"

Warmed by the pleasure of her company, Jake walked over to the pit to check.

It took the water another thirty minutes to heat, but once it was ready, Jake poured both caldrons into the pearl gray tub. The scent of the violet bath salts rose up to tempt his nose like tendrils of fragrant smoke, and just the thought of her being nude in the tub made his desire rise. Trying to stay distant, he went off to pump more water and set it on the grate just in case she needed more.

Loreli waited until the tub was filled before she began in on the buttons of her blouse. She couldn't wait to slip her naked self into the warm quiet embrace of the water, and let it soak away the day's sweat and tension.

Remembering what happened the last time he'd watched her undress, Jake planned on beating a hasty retreat. "I'll be on the front porch, if you need anything."

To his male dismay, she said, "I left a couple of bath sheets on that stack of chairs in the parlor. Meant to bring them out with me. Can you get them, please?"

By now the blouse was gaping wide, showing off the thin yellow camisole beneath. Seemingly ignorant of his plight, she undid the button on the back of her skirt and less than a breath later it dropped and pooled at her feet. Jake took one look at the long golden legs encased in opaque white stockings and the rose-petal garters anchoring them on her thighs, and his manhood swelled. He hastened into the house.

Loreli watched his retreat knowingly.

He was gone only for a few moments, but apparently Loreli had had ample time to get undressed and ease herself into the tub because that's where he found her. Eyes closed, she was stretched out in the water with her head cushioned on a small pillow. This first look at her wearing nothing but the shadows of dusk and the evening breeze dazzled him so much his steps slowed. "Where do you want this?" he said quietly, holding out the towel.

"Just put it on the edge of the porch," she said, then opened her eyes and sat up, smiling. The water stirred, lapping at her golden breasts with their puckered brown tips.

Clearing his throat, Jake forced his eyes away from the tempting twin sights and walked over to the spot she'd indicated. He placed the bath sheets near the pile of her discarded clothing. He took in a deep, calming breath. It didn't help. "I'll be out front."

Loreli sensed the struggle he was having with himself, and inwardly she smiled sympathetically. "Before you leave, hand me that soap there, please?"

Jake looked down at his feet and saw a bar of green soap lying near her clothing. As he bent to retrieve it, his hands were shaking so badly he wanted to curse. Willing himself to take in another series of deep breaths, he gathered himself, then slowly approached the tub.

When she took the soap from his offered hand, her voice was as soft as Eve's. "Thanks."

The tone of that one word resonated through Jake like the peals of a bell. Her beautiful body teased the man in him mightily, and the desire to stroke her damp breasts and then slowly brush his lips across the nipples grew stronger with each passing moment. In reality, all he need do was extend his hand and paradise would be his, but taking such an action would negate the vow he'd made to himself, and to her. "Am I a fool for insisting we wait?"

Loreli studied him. She knew what he was referring to. "Maybe, but I never had a man save me like a fancy dessert before. It's pretty flattering when you think about it."

Amused by her response, he said, "Plain-speaking Loreli Winters."

"Well, it's the truth. I know and you know too that if I really wanted to push you off the fence, all I'd have to do is stand, and this discussion, your vow, none of that would matter."

The light in his eyes told her she was right.

"But I'm not going to push you because you're a man of principle, Jake Reed, and I've only met a few men who can wear that hat." She searched the planes of his face and offered seriously, "Men like you are rare as manna from heaven . . ." *What would it be like to stay with him for the rest of my life?* She quickly shook off the illogical musing and became herself again. *You're going to be replaced, remember!* "Now, granted, I've been hot as a stove since the first time you touched me."

He barked a laugh, saying, "Loreli!"

"It's the truth," she tossed back shamelessly. "And Lord knows, if I don't get some relief soon, I'm going to explode."

He chuckled. "What kind of relief?"

"The relief a woman gets when a man and woman play the two-backed beast. Providing its done correctly, of course." She looked at him oddly for a moment, then cracked, "I thought you went to medical school?"

He grinned, "Sassy woman, hush up and explain what you mean."

"You really don't know?"

He threw up his hands, "Loreli. My daddy took me to visit a whore when I was sixteen because he said I needed to know how to work my plow and—"

She giggled, "He called it a plow?"

Jake's eyes glittered with irritation. "Yes."

Trying to keep the smile from her face, Loreli said, "I'm sorry. Go on."

"No. Never mind."

"Oh, stop looking so wounded and finish the telling," she teased softly. "I've just never heard it called a *plow* before."

He looked into that beautiful face, and again knew he'd never be able to stay mad at her for long. "All right, but behave."

She raised a hand. "Promise."

"Okay. After the whore, the next time was with a woman at Howard."

"And none of these women took the time to teach you about 'relief'?"

He shook his head. "Didn't know I needed to be taught."

For the first time since the conversation began, Jake realized he was discussing sex with Loreli. They'd had a similarly frank talk the night after their first, and yes, disastrous coming together in his bed, but in the world of a Kansas farmer, this was not something men did with women. Male friends, yes; women, no. Jake wasn't uncomfortable talking with her, though, he realized. Her sassy openness and her unwillingness to judge him made it easy to talk.

"What about afterward—surely once you were grown?" Loreli asked gently.

"No, the women I've visited off and on charge by the quarter-hour."

Loreli searched his eyes. "I see. Well, when a man spills his seed, that's his relief, but a woman's relief isn't that obvious."

"What do you mean?"

"Our relief happens inside. For me, the end is like throwing myself into a waterfall, but right now because of all this touching and kissing we've been doing, I'm sort of stuck on top. I really want to take the plunge, but—I'll wait until the wedding night."

"Do our bodies have to be joined for you to get relief?"

"Nope, but I'll wait until the wedding night."

"But I don't want you to," he told her plainly.

Silence.

He added quietly, "Especially if it's causing you distress."

Loreli didn't know what to make of his offer. "Jake—"

"Tell me what to do . . ."

She studied him for a long moment, then said, "You're probably in distress too. What about your relief?"

"We aren't talking about me." Jake knew she was right, though, he'd been aching hard for days. To deflect her concern, he bent down and ran a light teasing finger slowly over her breast. When her eyes closed, he stroked the damp flesh round and round, and then lazily up and down before tracing a whisper of a circle around the nipple. She arched, and he paid the same slow tribute to the other breast, tracing its nipple with just enough pressure to make her groan throatily.

He knelt beside the tub and kissed her parted lips, tasting their softness until her mouth rose to meet his in passionate welcome. All the while his hands kept up their play on her breasts, and Loreli arched for more.

He murmured against her lips, "Show me what to do."

Loreli let herself feed on being kissed by him and kissing him in return before sliding his hand down her body and gently guiding it underwater to the treasure between her parted thighs. "Touch me here," she whispered.

As he followed her instructions and his warm hand in the warm water began to explore, caress, and slide possessively across her yearning flesh, her legs parted wantonly. Loreli couldn't hold her responses at bay; she'd been celibate for two years. This man had been teasing her body for nearly a week; and when he brazenly began to circle the key to her soul, then eased a bold finger inside, an orgasm powerful enough to satisfy three women rose up and shook her until she screamed his name across the miles.

Filling his eyes with this beautiful outrageous woman, Jake kept his hand still until she quieted.

Slightly panting, and still throbbing, Loreli felt his hand leave her, and she dropped back against the back of the tub, declaring softly, "Lord, that was wonderful."

He grinned. "Was it?"

"Oh, yes."

"Relief?"

She sighed with the glory of what he'd done. "Blessed relief. I can make it to the wedding now."

She looked at him and searched his eyes. "What about you and your relief? I can help," she offered boldly.

"Holding you in my hands and watching you on your waterfall gave me all the help I needed, thank you very much." And it had. He'd need to bathe too, once she was done, and he felt no shame. No man could've stayed unmoved by the heated moments they'd just shared.

She smiled. "Okay, but next time, it'll be your turn."

He shook his head, "Are you always so scandalous?"

"Not usually, must be the company."

He threw back his head and laughed. "Well, this company is leaving. You want more hot water? That in there has to be cool by now."

Loreli splashed it a bit. It had cooled. "Is there any left?"

"Should be by now."

"Then I'd like that very much. When I'm done, you can take your turn in here."

"Sounds good."

After Jake added more hot water to her tepid bath, he set the caldron back on the fire and left her alone to bathe.

*   *   *

The naked Jake stepped into the tub and sighed with pleasure at the feel of the hot water. He sank in up to his lower chest, his legs out. As he tested the tub's dimensions with his long hairy legs, Jake found Brass Barber's estimate to be correct. There was enough space inside to hold two people. Jake picked up his soap and one of the fancy washrags she had given him to use and began to soap himself. He wondered what it might be like to have Loreli in here with him. After tonight's interlude, he'd never see this tub as just a tub again. He'd never seen a woman take such pleasure before. The women he'd visited in the past had shown just enough enthusiasm to make an inexperienced man like himself believe he was doing the deed well, but he knew better now. Women were like finely tuned motors; if one primed the gears and settings with the appropriate amount of precision, she'd sing. The memories of her in his hand made his member rise and his blood rush all over again. *Damn, she was sweet*. He wanted to touch her that way again, so he could watch her arch and hear her cry out his name. Jake had never had a woman reward him that way before, and as he washed, he smiled. He couldn't wait for the wedding night.

Once Jake had cleaned up and put on fresh clothing, he went in to help Loreli move around the items in their "department store." It was pitch-black outside, and were it not for the small lamp atop the piano, it would be just as dark inside. As it was, the parlor was filled with dark spaces and wavering shadows. They tried to lay her large feather mattress flat on the floor. Working in the poor light, it took a while to clear a space wide enough to accommodate its size, but once they did, they set it in place, and Loreli belly-flopped on it like a happy child. "My bed," she proclaimed, "my bed."

Jake smiled at her antics and admired the view she presented. She was dressed in a pearl pink wrapper that was belted around her waist. The tight draw threw into relief the prominent curve of her tempting behind. "Did you find your bedding?"

She turned over and looked up at him. He was bathed in shadows but she could see his glittering eyes. "I did."

Jake could see that the wrapper had loosened from her play. The panels had opened showing off the lacy border of the long pewter nightgown she had on beneath. The tops of her breasts rose temptingly above the vee-cut bodice.

As the silence rose and the shadows flickered, their gazes remained locked. Both knew what they wanted. He gazed down at her spread like an angel on the soft, bare mattress and became aroused by the knowledge that, once again, all he need do was reach out and paradise would be his.

Without a word, Jake took a seat on the edge of the mattress, then leaning over her kissed her slowly, husking out, "I can't get enough of you . . ."

And he couldn't; whether it was her mouth, her throat, or the feel of his hands on her silken skin, Jake wanted to spend eternity just like this.

As the kisses deepened, their passionate breathing floated in the shadows. Lying beside her now, Jake teased the lace border of the pewter gown over her nipples and thrilled at the way her body arched. The soft sound she made in response to his loving thrilled him even more—so much so that he dragged the bodice down and reacquainted himself with the hard jewels of her breast. He dallied, lingered, and savored the knowledge that he was the one setting off the fever in her blood. Needing no more guidance or tutoring, he ran his palm fervently up and down her gowned thigh, kissing her mouth, the smooth line of her jaw, then slid the fabric up her hip so he could savor the bareness hidden beneath. Fueled by the memories of their earlier interlude, Jake touched her, coaxing her to reveal the treasure he'd so delicately opened before, and she parted her thighs willingly, wantonly, letting him explore and learn.

Loreli could feel the waterfall rising, could feel herself straining beneath his bold touches. Once again, he had her hot as a stove; playing her, circling her, causing her legs to part even more and her hips to rise. Just when she knew she could not take any more, the spasms of completion rocked her again, and she cried out hoarsely.

When all was silent once again, a smiling Jake Reed bent down to kiss her good night. He covered her up with a fancy quilt nearby, then blew out the lamp and left her to seek his own bed.

Chapter 13

The next morning, while Jake was out feeding the hogs, a knock sounded at the front door. Loreli, in the midst of unpacking, called out, "Be there in a minute."

The girls, who were seated on the floor removing china plates from a large crate, set aside their chore to go to the door with Loreli. Moving around was not easy, however. A mountain of items had to be stepped over, moved aside, or squeezed past in order to get through the room. The knocking came again, sounding impatient this time, so Loreli yelled out, "I said, I'm coming!"

Her efforts to hurry resulted in her bumping into the edge of a crate upon which sat a large oriental vase. The collision sent the red and gold urn rocking precariously on its circular base, but Loreli steadied it, then headed to the door. "Sorry, I—"

She stopped. Standing on the porch was Sol Diggs, and he appeared to be furious.

Loreli said coolly, "Good morning, Mr. Diggs, can I—"

"The sheriff and I went out to evict Matt Peterson yesterday, and do you know what Peterson showed me?" he snarled.

"A renter's deed?"

"How dare you go behind my back—"

Loreli remembered that the twins were standing at her side. "Girls, why don't you go finish unpacking? Mr. Diggs and I need to talk."

"Yes, Loreli," Bebe said, her eyes on Diggs. "Come on, De."

Loreli, not intimidated at all by Diggs, stepped out onto the porch. As she did, his eyes widened fearfully and he stepped back. Loreli supposed he hadn't expected her to face up to him. In his world, when he bellowed, folks probably quivered; well, Loreli was not from his world. "You were saying?"

He took a moment to puff himself up again. "I sold you that deed in good faith."

"And after you did, how I choose to exercise *my* ownership is none of your business."

"You knew I wanted him off that land."

"Yes, I did, but the deed is mine now. You'll have to find someone else to lord it over."

"I'll get you for this, see if I don't," Diggs growled.

"Oh, now you're threatening me, Mr. Diggs?"

"If the shoe fits."

Loreli tossed back with bitter glee. "When I'm done with you, you snake, you won't have any shoes! Now get off my porch."

He glared at her, then stomped back to his carriage.

An angry Loreli watched the banker drive away. When she turned back to go inside, Jake was standing in the door. He cracked, "You do have a way with words."

"He threatened me, Jake," she declared incredulously.

"I heard him."

"Do you think I should let the sheriff know."

Jake shrugged. "Maybe, but I don't think Sol's danger-ous. Just greedy. One thing I regret, though."

"What?"

"That I wasn't there to see Diggs's face when Matt Pe-terson showed him that deed."

Loreli chuckled. "Me too."

Silence fell between them. This was the first private moment they'd managed to share since the day began. His memory kept going back to the previous night's sensual encounter, and hers did too.

He asked her softly, "Am I promoted?"

She tossed back, "Front of the class."

His mustache lifted. "Glad I improved so fast."

"So am I."

Bebe suddenly appeared next to her uncle. "All the plates are out of the crate," she told Loreli through the screen. "Can we place them in the hutch?"

Loreli beamed down at her. "Yes, you may."

Bebe rushed off to give her sister the good news.

Jake opened the door and Loreli stepped inside. She stopped in the entranceway and stood less than a breath away. He bent down and kissed her gently, whispering, "Good morning."

Loreli was so dazzled by the unexpected greeting that when it ended, it took her a moment to recover enough to say, "Good morning to you, too."

They spent the rest of the morning unpacking the re-maining crates and attempting to bring order to the chaos.

Chairs were set about. The piano was placed and then draped with its embroidered maroon cover. A set of end tables were positioned; the red oriental urn sat atop one, while the other table supported a large, fancy lamp. Everything that could be placed was, and any item that couldn't be was moved to the barn to be stored. When they were done, the once bare house now looked like a home. The only things missing were the paintings she'd wired Olivia about and specifically asked be shipped. They hadn't been found in any of the crates, so Loreli assumed they'd arrive in a shipment of their own.

After a luncheon of sandwiches and cold water, Loreli and the girls moved on to their next task: preparing the old attic room for occupancy. Tying a rag around her hair and grabbing a broom, she and the girls ventured up the narrow stairs. Jake went to fetch a crowbar and some window screening and joined them a few moments later.

First order of business was to take down the wood covering the window so light and fresh air could flow in. Jake tackled that. A few minutes later, the deed was done and sunshine filled the room. The breeze lifted decades-old dust and everyone began to sneeze and cough.

"Girls, how about you head downstairs for a moment until Loreli and I get some of this dust swept up?" Jake said.

Neither twin complained a bit about being asked to leave.

Once the girls were gone, Loreli, wearing a handkerchief tied over her nose and mouth, began to sweep. She stiffened at the sight of large spiders skittering ahead of her broom. Spiders were one of the few things in life she couldn't abide, but Jake wouldn't let her squash them. "They eat mosquitoes, among other things, Loreli."

"They can eat watermelon for all I care. I want them gone."

He chuckled. "Just hold on a moment."

He called down the steps for Dede.

She and Bebe ran up to see what he wanted.

When they appeared, he asked Dede, "Can you catch some of these spiders for Loreli, and put them outside?"

"Sure, Uncle Jake, let me get my jars."

The twins ran off, and a surprised Loreli said to Jake, "She catches spiders?"

"Among other things. She's fearless when it comes to bugs."

"Dede?"

"Yep."

And sure enough, after sending everyone else from the room, Dede spent the next hour catching spiders, crickets, and long, wiggly centipedes. She came back downstairs triumphantly showing off her canning jars filled with insects. She'd put the spiders in one jar and the crickets and the like in the other.

Loreli looked at the collection of bugs. "Dede, I'm real impressed."

"I like bugs, Loreli. Bugs can't kill you like horses can." With that said, she went outside to release her captives into the grass.

Loreli turned to Bebe. "Your sister's pretty handy to have around."

Bebe smiled. "Yep."

Jake used nails to affix the screening to the open window. Glass would have to be ordered. For now the screening would allow air and light in but would keep Dede's bug friends outside where they belonged.

Loreli had Jake haul up some water, then she went to work scrubbing down the walls and floor. The lye in the water burned the skin but her hands were already reddened from Monday's washing, so she ignored the stinging and kept to the task. By midafternoon, she was a mess. Her hair had sprays of dust and cobwebs sticking to it, her dress was filthy and wet in spots, and her face was streaked with dirt. The knowledge that she'd be able to soak in a real tub at the end of the day made the work less distasteful, but no easier.

It was early evening before Loreli declared the room clean enough to move in, but she wanted the walls and floor to dry first. She stood and looked around. The space seemed much larger now that it had been cleaned. She walked over and peered out of the screened opening that served as the window. The room could use another window, but Loreli settled for what she had. Outside she could see the cornfields and the windmills. She wondered what it might be like to wake up here with the sun streaming in. Would Jake move in with her after the wedding or would he continue to sleep on that hard excuse for a bed? Speaking of which, she made a mental note to ask him if he'd come up with a solution for getting her headboard and frame inside the house. It was still under a tarp on the front porch. All in all, Loreli was pleased with the work accomplished today, and the only thing she wanted was to sit her tired self down.

It was not to be, however. As she and the twins and Jake

sat on the porch relaxing, a carriage turned onto the long drive.

"I wonder what Reverend Appleby wants?" Bebe asked.

Loreli viewed the buggy. "Is that who that is?"

Jake stood and looked down the drive. "Yep, sure is."

Loreli had no desire to see the town's religious leader; he'd already proven he had little Christian charity. Her first thought was to go inside the house and make herself scarce until he accomplished whatever he'd come here to do, but she didn't. Hiding or running away was not in her nature.

Jake, not sure what Rebecca's father might be after, sent the girls in the house to play. When the man pulled up to the porch and stepped out of his carriage, Jake walked down to greet him, "Evenin', Reverend. What brings you here?"

"Jacob," he returned tersely. "I've come to speak with you."

Up close, Appleby was a very short man with a sour, pocked-marked face who walked with his chest puffed out and his arms swinging as if he were tall and important. His disapproving eyes swept over Loreli. She met the gaze without a flinch. He issued a snort of disapproval and turned back to Jake. Loreli snarled inwardly.

"I expected better of you, Jacob," the reverend said.

Jake had no plans to let Dexter Appleby grill him like a grouse. "What do you mean?"

The reverend cast a withering eye Loreli's way. "She's what I mean."

Loreli stood up. "Sir, if you have something to say to me, I suggest you say it."

"Harlot!" he spat.

Loreli saw Jake tense with anger, but Loreli didn't need a champion. She simply folded her arms casually across her chest, and drawled, "My, what a Christian thing to say. I'm sure you'll have no trouble getting into the pearly gates."

His whole body puffed up with outrage, reminding her of Diggs. "I demand that you release this man from whatever pledge he's given you."

Loreli responded with mock confusion. "Why?"

"Because he belongs to another."

"And whom might that be?"

"My daughter, Rebecca."

"Ah, I see. How is Rebecca?" Loreli asked him. Her golden eyes flashed her mood.

"Harlot!" he hissed again.

A weary Loreli had had enough. Out of respect for Jake and his relationship with this man, Loreli did not give Appleby the tongue thrashing he so righteously deserved. Instead she walked to the door, then told him, "Sir, I've been insulted by men much taller than you, so I'll see you around." She went inside.

When Loreli disappeared, Jake's voice was harsh as he addressed his pastor. "That wasn't necessary. Your beef is with me. Not her."

Appleby didn't seem to hear. "How could you set aside a good, God-fearing woman like my Rebecca for trash like that?"

Jake's voice was soft but deadly clear. "She isn't trash, so keep your slurs to yourself."

"You've made my daughter a laughingstock and you want me to respect that whore?"

Jake snatched him up by his shirt. "That so-called whore is the woman I'm marrying. One more word out of you and I'll toss you in the nearest hog trough."

Appleby stared as if he'd never met this version of Jake before. "How dare you assault a man of the cloth! You need prayer, Jake Reed. This woman has set the devil loose within you. Fall on your knees with me. Please. Let the spirit cleanse you of—"

Jake tossed him aside. "Go home, Reverend."

Then not trusting himself to be near Appleby any longer, Jake walked off the porch and headed toward the barns and pens.

Behind him he heard Appleby's strident voice calling, "Save yourself, Jacob. Save yourself!"

Jake kept walking.

Jake surreptitiously watched Loreli for the rest of the evening. If Appleby's slurs had touched her, the results were not evident in her golden eyes. As she went about helping the girls get ready for bed she had only smiles for them and for him. A less formidable woman might have crumbled beneath Appleby's verbal assaults, but she'd batted him away like the gnat he was, and paid him scant attention. Or at least it seemed that way. Jake could only guess how many times a woman such as herself had been met with crudeness by men like Appleby, yet she'd had enough respect not to give Rebecca's father both barrels. *Harlot?* Jake wanted to throttle the little hypocrite; everyone in town knew the reverend and Veronica Diggs were sneaking around, everyone except Rebecca and Sol Diggs. For the Reverend Appleby to act so offended by Loreli's presence while his own dirty laundry was blow-

ing up and down the streets made Jake even more glad he
hadn't married Rebecca.

After the girls were tucked in, Loreli and Jake stepped
out onto the porch. Loreli sat on one of the old cane chairs.
The water for this night's much desired bath was heating
out back. Jake stood on the edge of the porch looking out
at the night. He was so silent for so long, Loreli finally
said, "Penny for your thoughts."

"Rebecca's pa didn't have to be so nasty."

Loreli cracked sarcastically, "It's his job to confront
sinners like me."

"No, it isn't."

"Just think, that man could've been your father-in-law."

Jake shuddered. "What a mistake that would've been."
Then he asked quietly, "Did his words hurt you?"

"And if they had?" she asked, more defensively than
she'd intended.

"It was just a question, no need to snap."

Loreli was instantly contrite. "Sorry. The answer is yes.
It always hurts. I've just learned to bury it, that's all."

He wished it weren't so dark so he could see her eyes to
determine whether she was being flippant or serious. It
was hard to tell the difference at times. "I'm putting folks
on notice that I'm not tolerating you being slurred."

She smiled a bit. "Thanks, but it isn't necessary. I can
look after myself."

"You shouldn't have to. That's your husband's job."

Loreli raised an eyebrow. "My husband?"

"Yes. Whether it's in name only or not, I'm responsible
for you."

Loreli eyed him in the dark. "That's a nice thing to say,

but the only person responsible for Loreli is Loreli. That way no one gets hurt or disappointed."

"Spoken like an independent woman."

"Sarcasm?"

He shrugged in the dark. "Maybe. You've never had ties to anyone."

"A few, but I never relied on them for my peace of mind or safety."

"Why not?"

"I've been on my own too long, Jake. Seen too much despair and heartbreak. You rely only on yourself. If you don't have ties, you don't get hurt."

"What about your tie to the girls. Is that real?"

She couldn't lie. "Very real. I fell in love with them the moment I met them. It'll be real hard letting them go." And it would be. In the short time she'd been their mama, she'd come to care deeply for them.

"And what about your ties to me?"

Loreli didn't want to answer that, at least not truthfully. "We knew going into this that it would only be temporary, so whatever we share for however long this lasts is to be enjoyed, then we move on . . ." *So what if I think I'm in love with him*?

Jake turned his attention back to the night. "I see."

An invisible wall seemed to drop between them, and it gave her pause. She asked, "You're still going to be looking for a *real* wife, right?"

"Yes." It was the only reply Jake could give. He certainly couldn't tell her that he loved her and wanted no other. The admission was startling. When had she captured his heart so completely? He knew it would serve no purpose to declare his feelings aloud. If he did, Jake was sure she'd fall off the porch laughing; gambling queens did not fall in love with small-town hog farmers.

"Good," Loreli answered, with more confidence than she felt. "I don't want any misunderstandings about what's going on here." To herself, however, she asked, who would ever believe she, Loreli Winters, would fall head over heels for a hog farmer? Everyone who knew her would wonder if she'd lost her mind. In a way she had. Jake Reed was decent and good. How could she not fall in love with a man who was kind to children and animals? There was no future in loving him though. They were from different worlds and she was no more willing to give up her way of life than he was willing to give up his.

"I think the water's probably hot now," Loreli said. "I'm going to take my bath."

He didn't offer to join her and that was all right; she needed to put some distance between them. She needed to think about some things, and she couldn't do that if he was near. "I'll see you in the morning?"

"Yep. Good night.

"Good night, Jake."

In the tub in the dark, Loreli swatted at the insects buzzing around her ears and shoulders. She thought distancing herself from Jake and her feelings for him a necessary thing. He wasn't going to love her back, so the sooner she was able to rid herself of her attraction to him, the better off she'd be.

Once Jake was alone, he wanted to kick himself for having asked her such a loaded question. What had he expected her to say? Of course there would be no ties. He'd set that in stone when she agreed to do this. Surely he didn't believe that what they'd shared last night would alter that agreement? Yet he had. He had feelings for her that seemed to be burning him up inside. Never in his life had a woman affected him so profoundly, and his hope that he'd affected her as well was illogical. He was dumb as a post for thinking she might return his feelings, and even dumber for having fallen in love with her in the first place.

The next day, Jake noted the slight coolness in Loreli's manner. She was no less loving toward the girls but seemed to be avoiding him and his eyes. He attributed her distance to the question he'd asked the night before and wanted to kick himself again for not keeping it to himself.

On Thursday, Loreli's bride friends rode over to help with the wedding fixings. Jake stayed out of the way. Later, he rode into town to talk with the sheriff.

When he entered the office, Walt Mack looked up and said, "Afternoon Jake, what brings you here?"

"Need to know if you'll read the words for my wedding?"

Mack smiled. "Sure. Be honored. Heard you and Miss Loreli were tying the knot. That's a lot more woman than country boys like us are used to. You sure you can handle her?"

The words were said in jest, and that's how Jake took them. "I think I'm up to the task."

"Well, good. Nothing like confidence. What time shall I come around?"

"The wedding's going to be at five."

"Then I'll come around four o'clock. Wear my best suit too."

Jake smiled. "Good. Oh, Diggs was out at my place

yesterday. He threatened Loreli. She wanted me to let you know."

"Mad as he was, I'm surprised he didn't confront her sooner. You should've seen his face when Peterson showed him that deed. I thought Sol was going to pop every button on his vest. Cursed her something awful on the ride back here. Did you tell Miss Loreli Sol's not dangerous, just greedy?"

Jake chuckled. "I did, but I just wanted to let you know in case something happens. I'm more worried about his safety than hers, to tell you the truth."

Mack nodded knowingly. "I wouldn't want to cross her. Any woman who can play poker the way she can is not a lady to take lightly. Maybe Diggs'll remember that the next time he sees her. He's not invited to the wedding, I take it?"

"Not as far as I know. It's supposed to be a small affair."

"Well, weddings sometimes take on a life all their own, so keep your powder dry."

An amused Jake said, "Sure will."

The sheriff looked at Jake. "Need to talk to you about something else."

"What?"

"Knights of Labor."

"What about them?"

"Diggs is telling folks that you're bringing them in to start trouble."

"The only folks causing trouble are greedy capitalists like Diggs and his pals. If farmers were treated fairly, there'd be no need for groups like the Knights."

"Well, just wanted to let you know what I'm hearing."

"Thanks, Walt."

"You're welcome. My daddy farmed when I was a boy, and we lost the land and everything on it when the mortgage came due, so I know what men like Peterson and the others are facing. Just don't cause any trouble, Jake. My sympathies may be with you, but I was elected to keep the peace and I plan on doing that."

"You don't have to worry. We won't be breaking any laws."

"Good. Then I'll see you on Saturday."

"Thanks, Walt. See you then."

With that small chore out of the way, Jake rode home.

The brides were gone when Jake returned. In fact, there was no one in the house, so he stepped out onto the back porch. He saw Dede over by Rabbit, but he didn't see Bebe or Loreli anywhere.

Dede was attempting to tie a fat gold ribbon around Rabbit's neck, but the dog kept twisting and turning away. When Jake walked up, his obviously frustrated niece said, "Hello, Uncle Jake. Loreli said I can tie this around Rabbit so he can look pretty for the wedding, but he won't stand still. Do you think it's because he's a boy dog?"

Jake hid his smile. "Could be. Maybe Rabbit would rather just look like himself."

"But everybody's supposed to dress up."

Jake shrugged. "Sometimes animals don't know about people rules, De."

She gave in. "Okay. Suzie didn't want to wear a ribbon either."

Jake had no trouble believing that. "Where's Loreli and your sister?"

"Loreli's giving Bebe a riding lesson. They'll be right back."

And all of sudden they came barreling out from behind the barn at a speed that widened Jake's eyes. Loreli was holding the reins and Bebe was seated behind her, Bebe's arms fastened tightly around Loreli's waist. Jake knew Phoebe could run, but he never knew the big mare could run so fast. The horse and its riders streaked by them, racing across the open fields.

Dede watched them silently. "Phoebe's going real fast isn't she, Uncle Jake?"

"Yes, she is. How many times have they come through here?"

"Three. Loreli said they'd race four times, then she's going to show Be how to cool Phoebe off so she won't get sick from running so fast."

Jake thought that made perfect sense. Racing the animal that way and then not tending to her afterward would only make the horse ill down the road. It pleased him that Loreli was giving Bebe the responsibility of looking after the animal's care as well as helping Bebe prepare for the Circle race.

"Are you mad at Loreli?" Dede asked.

Jake searched her eyes. "No."

"Then how come you don't smile at her anymore?"

The honesty in her face made Jake look away. "I don't know, De."

"Well, I think you should kiss and make up."

He chuckled. Out of the mouths of babes. He couldn't tell her that kissing is how this all got started in the first place. Instead, he assured her, "Loreli and I will be smiling again before you know it."

"Good. I like it when you smile and she smiles back."

"You do?"

"Yes, Uncle Jake. You didn't smile a lot before she came."

He shook his head in response to this wise eight-year-old. "Are you enjoying having Loreli here with us?"

"Oh, yes, very much. Are you?"

He didn't lie. "Yes, I am."

"I hope you can't find us another mama, and she has to stay forever."

Jake didn't respond to that. "Well, I'm going out to the barn and put Fox in for the evening."

"Okay, Uncle Jake. Rabbit and I'll wait for Loreli and Be to get back."

"I'll come wait with you soon as I'm done with Fox."

She nodded and hugged Rabbit.

That evening, Jake took the bed and frame upstairs into Loreli's room and put it together. Last night the mattress had rested on the floor, but now it lay atop her big bed. The fancy purple quilt made it look very inviting, and Jake had to stop himself from wondering how it might feel to sleep in the bed with her by his side. There were a couple of chairs, a writing desk by the window, and one of the chifforobes stood gleaming against a wall. Atop it were all of her lotions, creams, and perfumes. His gaze took in the curtain she'd hung over the window, and the soft light given off by the lamps. He realized she'd transformed the place from the dark and joyless space his father had known into a woman's boudoir. There wasn't anything left of the old room to remind him of his father but everything to remind Jake of the sensual new owner.

Loreli watched him scan around. "Do you like it?"

He met her eyes. "It looks real fine, Loreli."

"Loreli said we can help her paint in here later this summer," Bebe said.

Jake smiled.

"Loreli said we can come up and visit her anytime," Dede added.

Jake wondered if he'd be extended the same courtesy. "You and the ladies couldn't figure out how to get that headboard in the house either?"

This was the closest they'd been to each other in the last few days, and both could feel the heat arching between them in spite of the walls they'd been attempting to erect. Jake wanted to touch her cheek to see if it was as soft as it had been the last time he'd caressed it, and Loreli longed to be enfolded within his strong, tender embrace.

In the end, though, they all trooped back downstairs, leaving the moment behind.

The day of the wedding dawned bright and full of promise. The brides began arriving around ten that morning, bringing with them food, decorations, tableware, china, and lots of excitement. Wilma Deets had been a hairdresser before coming to Kansas to be a bride, and she'd volunteered to turn her talents on the twins. While she took the girls to the back porch to get started, the rest of the day's preparations began in earnest.

Loreli was up in her boudoir, sequestered until the wedding. She'd never liked sitting around, but Fanny had been assigned to keep her company, and to keep Loreli away from the goings on downstairs, so passing the time wasn't as bad as it could have been.

Loreli asked Fanny, "How's your husband?"

"I miss him so. He writes, though. I've gotten letters nearly everyday."

"He's a Pullman porter, right?" Loreli confirmed.

"Yes, but from what he's written in his letters, it may not be for much longer."

"Why, is he unhappy working for Mr. Pullman?"

"Extremely. Some of the working conditions aren't to his liking. For example, did you know that the porters have to smile, or risk being replaced?"

"No."

"Some of the passengers know this, however, and taunt the men just to see if the porters will continue to smile. My husband has been cuffed and kicked by folks intent upon seeing how far they can go before he loses his temper, but he can't lose his temper, so he takes the abuse without a word. Some give him a nice tip for being forced to endure their mean-spirited shenanigans—as if that makes it all better."

"Have the porters complained?"

"Oh, of course, but nothing is done about it. My husband and others want to form a union but know they'll be dismissed if they do."

They talked some more about Fanny's Traveling Man, as the Pullman porters were often known, then other things. For Loreli the time seemed to be crawling by.

Downstairs, Jake, tired of being told that he couldn't see Loreli until the wedding, and being bossed around by women he barely knew, sought refuge in his room. They fed him lunch, however, which raised their positions in his eyes, but they wouldn't let him walk around lest he see Loreli on her way to her bath or having her hair done, or lord knew what else. He wanted to shout that he'd already

seen quite a bit of his bride to be, but didn't. It wouldn't
help. He just prayed Art would show up soon so he could
have someone to commiserate with who gave a damn.

By four the guests began arriving. Loreli couldn't ver-
ify this, however, because she was still confined to her
room. She was dressed at least, and in an hour, she'd be
Mrs. Jake Reed. Even though the marriage wouldn't be a
permanent one, she had butterflies in her stomach just the
same.

When Jake was finally allowed out of his room, he and
Art Gibson, his best man, were led out to the back of the
house where all the guests were waiting. The black-vested
suit Jake was wearing was the only one he owned. It was
clean, however, as was the white shirt he had on beneath.
In spite of his disagreements with his late father, Jake paid
tribute to his memory by wearing his father's cufflinks;
and Art would be reading from the Bible left behind by
Jake's mother, the only possession of hers Jake had.

The women had transformed the backyard into an out-
door chapel, complete with a flowered bower for the bride
and groom to stand beneath. Beside it stood Sheriff Walter
Mack. Where the women had gotten all the chairs was a
mystery to Jake, as was where all the people in the chairs
had come from. This had been billed as a small affair, but
in looking around, he saw half the town had chosen to attend whether they'd been invited or not. Even Rebecca
was in attendance. She was seated beside Millie Tate, and
both were dressed in mourning black. Jake turned away.
The piano was near the bower, positioned on a large
square of plywood. Jake couldn't but wonder how the
brides had managed to get it outside. Loreli had bragged
about how inventive the women had become as a result of

the wagon train. After seeing all that they'd accomplished here today, Jake agreed that they were remarkable indeed.

At five o'clock sharp, a young woman took her seat at the piano and began to play. It was plain that she'd been classically trained; the notes of the sonata rose on the air with a grace and beauty small-town folks rarely get to hear. Everyone listened raptly as the woman, another one of the brides, played on.

Then she stopped and began the sweet familiar notes of "Amazing Grace." In response, the twins came out of the back door. Side by side, they stepped down the stairs and began a slow walk to the bower. Their pretty dresses and proud faces earned smiles from the guests and touched a cord inside Jake that made his eyes sting.

When they reached him, Jake leaned down and gave them each a kiss on the forehead. "You both look mighty fine."

"Mighty fine," Art echoed.

The girls grinned and turned to the porch to await Loreli's arrival.

She appeared moments later wearing a blue gown so beautiful that all the guests stared in awe. Low cut and sleek, it had a pleated underskirt and an overskirt that swept across and softly draped at the side. The sleeves were three-quarter length and ended in two small bows. Her matching three-quarter-length gloves fit smoothly beneath the gown's sleeves. The rich silk dress rustled as she walked down the stairs. With a bouquet of summer flowers in her hands, Loreli made her way past the assembled guests and up to the bower, where Jake and the others waited.

Loreli knew this was pretend but it didn't feel that way;

it felt real. Her heart was beating so fast, and she never remembered being this nervous before, ever. The faces of
the guests were little more than blurs. The only person she
could see clearly was Jake.

When she reached his side, she smiled down at the
twins and then over at Art. Jake was instructed by the
sheriff to take Loreli's hand, and once he did, the reading
of the words began. As he came to the part in the ceremony where anyone with a beef against the wedding was
allowed to stand and state their displeasure, Loreli waited
for him to continue. Usually the pause generated nothing
more than a few titters from the guests. Not today.

Today someone actually got up and said, "Loreli, what
the hell are you doing?"

The familiar voice made her spin with dismay. Filled
with shock, she stared into the smiling green eyes of the
Black Irishman, Trevor Church! *What is he doing here?*
Had she been a heroine in a dime novel, Loreli Winters
would have fainted, right then and there.

Chapter 14

"**W**hat are *you* doing here?" Loreli snapped at Trevor.

The guests were buzzing like a beehive hit by a stick, and it didn't take much imagination to know gossip surrounding this event would occupy folks for weeks. As if he were unaware of the drama he was creating, the smiling Trevor responded by saying, "You look lovely, lass."

"Save the blarney, Trev, and answer me," she gritted harshly, suddenly remembering just how angry she'd been at him in Mexico City three years ago.

"Just came to see what possible reason you could have for marrying a hog farmer?"

Loreli didn't dare look at Jake. She could feel the tightness in his body. She wanted to shoot Trevor for embarrassing Jake this way.

Trevor was one of the handsomest men any of the ladies in attendance had ever seen. As he made his way from the back, they took in his smooth golden skin, his black curly hair, and his clover green eyes. His brown vested suit fit his trim muscular body well. He was tall too, his height rivaling Jake's. Loreli didn't care about any of that; she just wanted an explanation.

Loreli finally looked into Jake's face. His jaw was tight and throbbing, his eyes on Trevor. When Jake's gaze left Trevor and slid to Loreli, the coldness she saw chilled her like a November wind.

"I've no idea what he wants," she told him truly.

"No?" Jake's voice was as cold as his stare. "You didn't wire him to come and rescue you from the hog farmer?"

Not liking his sarcasm, she answered truthfully. "No."

By now, Trevor had joined the wedding party under the bower. Instead of responding to Loreli's demand for an explanation, he turned a winning smile on the twins, and said, "My, what lovely young ladies. Trevor Church. At your service." He bowed elaborately before the girls.

They giggled.

"Trevor!" Loreli snarled.

He straightened. Eyeing Jake contemptuously, the Irishman made a show of sniffing the air before he drawled, "Is that a hog I smell, or the groom?"

The guests gasped.

Jake smiled with eyes void of amusement. The fist he exploded in Trevor's face was void of amusement, too, and sent the Irishman sprawling. Blood poured from his lordly nose. On the ground now, Trevor looked at the blood staining his fingers. A brittle light of amusement filled his face. "So, the hog farmer has spunk." Wiping at his nose, Trevor slowly rose to his feet. His eyes were focused cobra-like on Jake. "You want to fight for her?" he asked.

"Nope, she's already mine. I just want to fight you."

Loreli couldn't believe her ears. "This is supposed to be a wedding, not a prize fight!" she told them angrily.

Paying her no mind, they began circling each other. Guests started leaving their chairs, jockeying for a good view.

"Did you hear me?" Loreli snapped.

Apparently not. In fact, Art Gibson came up behind her, and after lifting her from her feet, carried her kicking and yelling away from the combatants. As he set her down, the males in attendance hooted and howled. "Stay here," Art commanded.

Loreli looked at him and uttered plainly, "I'm not your wife, so get the hell out of my way."

Art was so flabbergasted he did just that, but by the time Loreli stormed back to the bower, it was too late; the fight was on.

The twins along with the other children and the rest of the female guests, including Denise Gibson and Susan Peterson, took refuge on the porch. The men on the other hand were ringing the action like spectators at a cock fight, urging Jake on, and cheering as each punch fell. For Loreli, getting through the male throng wasn't easy, but after planting some well-placed elbows and kicking some shins, a path was opened. Now, able to see, she stared wide-eyed at the sight of the two men dancing around like boxers. Jake had blood pouring from a spot over his eye, and Trevor's lips were fat and split. Before she could yell at them, Trevor launched himself at Jake and they began wrestling like Greeks, toppling the bower and knocking over the tables holding the food and plates. The male crowd roared like Romans.

Loreli spotted the sheriff standing beside Brass Barber and Matt Peterson. Hoping they could stop the fight, she pushed and shoved men aside in an effort to reach them.

"Make them stop!" she shouted at the sheriff.

The sheriff, whose attention was on the battle, yelled back over the noisy crowd, "I can't, Miss Loreli."

"Why not?"

"It's a matter of honor."

"But you're a peace officer!"

"But he's a man first," Brass yelled over another loud roar.

"Your friend insulted Jake and he has to pay," Matt Peterson added.

Loreli had never heard anything so harebrained in all her life, but realizing they'd be no help, she frantically looked around for someone or some way to put an end to this madness. That's when she spotted Elvira tied up by the corral. Forcing her way out of the crowd again, Loreli hurried over to the goat. As she approached, Elvira eyed her malevolently, but Loreli snapped, "Bite me and I swear I'll turn you into jerky!"

The goat seemed to take the threat seriously and stood patiently while Loreli undid the rope. Loreli then dragged the goat by the scruff of the neck over to the circle of cheering spectators. Smiling smugly, she slapped the goat sharply across its rump and turned her loose all in one motion. "Get 'em, Elvira!"

Elvira charged into the crowd.

All hell broke loose. Elvira Goat-Dog began butting and biting whatever she came in contact with: buttocks, thighs, flailing arms. Men screamed like little children in their efforts to escape the horned, black-and-white terror.

Those men Elvira couldn't bite right off, she chased; those she chased and caught up to, she bit. It took the goat less than two minutes to send the men running for their lives, leaving only the two combatants on the scene.

By now, Jake and Trevor were so tired, they could barely raise their hands to throw the next fist. So wild and off target were their blows, they looked as if they had been magically slowed down. Their faces were battered and bruised, and their once clean clothes sported blood, grass, and dirt. Loreli was furious with the both of them. This was supposed to be her wedding, dammit, and they'd ruined it. Yes, it was a wedding for a temporary marriage, but it was probably the only one she'd ever have. And they'd ruined it!

Loreli looked to the porch, where the women stood laughing uproariously at Elvira's routing of the men. "Beatrice, go get Elvira and tie her up. If she tries to bite you, tell her you'll turn her into jerky. That seems to work."

"Yes, Loreli."

Bebe took off to retrieve the goat now chasing poor Rabbit around the yard. Hot on the goat's tail was Pal.

Trevor and Jake could fight no more. They were both lying on the ground—their swollen eyes focused on the heavens, their breathing forced and harsh.

"You throw a hell of a punch, for a hog farmer," Trevor said to Jake.

"You're not so bad yourself, for a foreigner," Jake replied.

Loreli wanted to throttle them both. After all the chaos and gossip they'd caused, they were now going to be friends? *Men!*

Jake turned his head, and upon seeing Loreli standing over him, her eyes flashing righteously, he said around his swollen jaw, "Guess we have to get married some other time."

"If I had a gun," she told him coldly, "I'd shoot you both!"

That said, she turned and left.

As they watched her angry march to the porch, Jake said to Trevor, "I think she's mad."

"I think so too," Trevor replied.

Then both men began to laugh, even though it hurt.

Later, a knock sounded on Loreli's door. She'd locked herself in over an hour ago. Although she was still too angry to want company, she called. "Who is it?"

Bebe's voice came through the door, "It's us, Loreli."

Loreli walked down the staircase and threw back the bolt on the door. Their concerned twin faces deflated her anger and Loreli was instantly contrite. She had no idea how the debacle had affected them, and she'd been so wrapped up in her own self-pity, she'd failed to consider their needs.

"Are you all right, Loreli?" Dede asked.

"No, but seeing you two makes me feel better, so come on in."

As they followed her back up the steps to her room, she asked, "Are you two okay?"

"Yes, but Mr. Barber says he's going to have Elvira arrested for biting him," Bebe answered.

"Mr. Barber deserved whatever he got. I'm sorry my friend ruined our wedding."

"We can have another one," Dede said.

Bebe added, "Miss Zora and the other ladies sent everybody home. She said she'd see you in a few days."

"Thanks, girls."

Dede asked, "Can we change clothes now, Loreli? Our dresses are pretty, but I'm hot."

She chuckled. "Sure, pumpkin. Just make sure you two hang them up."

The girls nodded their understanding, then gave Loreli a hug.

"You're the best friends a girl could have."

They grinned. She kissed them on the cheek, then they left to go and change.

Loreli finally ventured downstairs a half hour later. Art Gibson and Matt Peterson were just getting the piano back into its spot. When they looked up and saw her, both men dropped their eyes as if ashamed. "You should be ashamed," she told them. "Where are your wives? I want to thank them for the food that we didn't get to eat."

"Gone," Matt Peterson confessed.

"Took the children and told us to get home the best way we could," Art added.

Loreli thought that a very apropos punishment. "Good for them. Where are Tweedledee and Dum?"

Art pointed to the back porch.

"Thanks." She then added grudgingly, "And thanks for bringing in the piano."

Out on the porch, Jake and Trevor were being patched up by of all people, Rebecca Appleby and Millie Tate. Millie was working on Trevor's split lip, and Rebecca was stitching the jagged cut over Jake's left eyebrow. When Rebecca looked up and saw Loreli, she stopped and said defensively, "Since no one was here to help them—"

"You go right ahead. If I get that close, I may take an ax to them."

Trevor said, "Aw, lassie—"

"Don't you lassie, me, Trevor Church."

"Loreli—" Jake said.

"And I'm not speaking to you either, Jake Reed."

He grinned, then grimaced as Rebecca pulled the stitches tight.

"Are you spoken for, gentle lady?" Trevor asked Millie.

"No," Millie tittered.

Loreli rolled her eyes, then went back inside the house.

Upstairs in her room, Loreli took off her dress, then hung it in the armoire. She removed her shoes, her fancy stockings and garters, then donned a dress more suitable to the life she was leading now. It had been a while since she'd gotten all gussied up, and hanging up the dress reminded her of that. She had a hard time remembering the last time she'd danced or kicked up her heels. It was sometime before joining the wagon train in Chicago, she realized. Since then, there'd been no visits to gambling dens, no playing high-stakes poker, and no being feted and catered to for being the one and only Loreli Winters. Maybe it was because the wedding had been such a debacle, but she suddenly missed her old life. Here in Kansas, the days moved slow as molasses, and porch-sitting in the evening was what folks here did for entertainment. Of course, she'd known all this when she agreed to marry Jake Reed, but today for some reason, the prospect of spending the next twelve months here with a husband who'd never love her loomed heavily. Maybe Trevor's arrival was responsible for her sudden melancholy. He represented her old life—a life filled with good times, good food, and good money. With Trevor she'd seen the world, and could again, but she thought about the twins. No matter Loreli's melancholy, she'd made them a promise, and one did not break promises to loved ones. Shaking off her mood, she ventured back downstairs.

Rebecca was still about, as was Mule-Faced Millie Tate. Both women were out on the porch drooling over Trevor. Loreli knew it was an easy thing to do, the man could charm the robe off a nun. However, Rebecca and Millie were babes in the wood in the world of Trevor Church, but neither woman probably knew that.

When Loreli stepped onto the porch, she asked them, "Where's Jake?"

Rebecca's eyes never left Trevor. "Out back with the twins. He's cleaning up the mess."

Loreli planned to go see if he needed help, but first she had a question for Trevor. "When are you leaving town?"

"But he just got here," Millie replied with a pout.

Loreli ignored her. "When are you leaving?"

Trevor, bruised and battered but no less handsome, said, "Mildred is right, lassie. With such lovely nurses about, I may stay forever."

Loreli snorted. She knew better than to believe that. Too bad Millie and Rebecca didn't know him as well as Loreli. "Tomorrow, you go back to wherever you came from."

"Aw, Lorie, you can't be still mad."

"I am, Trevor, so don't test me. A lot of people went to a lot of trouble to make today special, but why should you care?"

"She's always been excitable," he told Millie and Rebecca, "but not even she would send an old friend back into the cold cruel world in my condition."

"If you're still here by tomorrow this time, your condition will be much worse," Loreli corrected him.

"Trevor, I have an extra room in my shop. You're welcome to recover there," Millie said, to Loreli's amazement.

He smiled at her. "What a lovely offer, Millie."

Rebecca's face soured. Apparently she didn't find the offer lovely at all. "You're an unmarried woman, Millie. What will people say?"

Millie, looking cow-eyed at Trevor, replied, "I don't care, Rebecca. It's my duty as a Christian to open my home to someone in need."

Millie's shop won't be the only thing he'll want the spinster seamstress to open, Loreli thought to herself, but that wasn't Loreli's concern. If Rebecca and Millie wanted to compete against each other for the heartbreak Trevor was sure to bring, so be it.

Loreli shook her head at their gullibility, then headed around to the back of the house.

Jake's head pounded every time he bent to pick something up. He thought he might pass out, so he stopped a moment to catch his breath. The brides had done most of the cleaning up, and he made a mental note to thank each of them personally, but there were still chairs that had to be taken back into the house, Loreli's plates to put back in the hutch—those not broken in the melee—and a beautiful woman to apologize to, he added as he looked up and saw Loreli approaching.

He waited for her to come closer. His head was ringing

like a bell. He promised himself he'd never fight again; at thirty-seven, he was far too old for such painful activity.

Dede and Bebe were helping him, and as De walked by him to put one of the old chairs back on the porch, she stopped and said, "Uncle Jake, you don't look so good. You want me and Bebe to give everybody their water tonight?"

Jake thought himself blessed to be loved so unconditionally. "Yes, but I need to talk to you two first. Girls, what I did—the fighting—was wrong."

"We know Uncle Jake," Dede said. "In Sunday school, we learned you're supposed to turn the other cheek."

Jake nodded. "That's right, but I didn't, and I was wrong not to."

Bebe protested, "But he said you smelled like a hog, Uncle Jake. One time, I socked Anthony Diggs for telling me I smelled like a hog, my sister smelled like a hog, and you smelled like a hog too, Uncle Jake."

Loreli dropped her head to hide her smile.

"The teacher made Bebe stand in the corner all day," Dede said.

Jake tried to keep a straight face. "Why didn't the teacher tell me about this?"

"Teacher doesn't like Anthony either," Bebe said.

Dede added, "Nobody likes Anthony."

Jake looked at Loreli and saw her smile. "Well, regardless, I shouldn't have been fighting. It didn't scare you two, did it?"

Bebe answered, "Nope, because me and De knew you were going to win. Didn't we, De?"

Her sister nodded. "Yep. We weren't scared."

Jake smiled. At some point, and he couldn't put his finger on exactly when, the twins had gone from being nieces to being daughters, his daughters—and he loved them as much as he loved his own life. "How about you go give the animals their water. Miss Zora left us all some ice cream. We'll dig into it as soon as you get back."

Their eyes widened with glee, and then they took off at a run for the pens.

He turned his attention to Loreli. Their eyes met and held, then he volunteered a soft, "I'm sorry."

His talk with the girls had tempered Loreli's anger—somewhat. Who can stay mad at a man big enough to confess his failings to two eight-year-olds? "Yes, you are, Jacob Reed."

He grinned a little around his swollen jaw and lips. "My head's killing me."

"It's what you deserve."

"I know, but it doesn't make me feel any better. Where's your Irishman?"

"Rebecca and Millie are fighting over him on the front porch, and he's not my Irishman."

"He was at one time."

"I don't deny that, nor that he and I had some real good times, but that was in the past. The last time we were together was three years ago in Mexico City. I was stranded there after he took all of my money and ran off with some poor gullible senorita."

"How'd you get home?"

"Playing poker. Only thing I had to bet were the diamond studs in my ears. Won those back and three hundred dollars to boot by the end of the night."

"That was the last time you saw him?" Jake asked.

"Yes, and he still owes me."

"How long is he staying?"

"Wish I knew, but I told him I want him gone by this time tomorrow. Millie wants him to move in with her."

Jake raised an eyebrow, even though it hurt. "Mildred Tate?"

"Yep, but I think Rebecca's campaigning for the position too, so who knows how it will turn out in the end."

Loreli could see Jake slowly wavering. His eyes were closed. She told him, "Why don't you go lie down for a while. And use my bed. That board you call a bed will only make you feel worse."

"Where will you sleep?"

"Don't worry about me. You just go. The girls and I will see to the rest of this."

He looked into her eyes. "I had to hit him, Loreli. A man has his pride."

"I know," she responded softly, "Go on to bed before you keel over."

He smiled and nodded, "I'll see you later."

"Okay."

When he left, Loreli headed to the pens to see if the girls needed help with the watering.

The girls did need help, and by the time the hogs, the milk cows, and the rest of the Reed menagerie were given water, Loreli's and the twins' clothes were wet from the sloshing buckets and their shoes were damp and muddy. Being a farmer's wife was neither easy nor glamorous, she thought to herself as she added fresh water to the bowls of Rabbit and Pal, but Loreli didn't have an aversion to hard work, and so finished the task without complaint.

Once the chores were done, she and the girls washed their hands under the pump, then grabbed bowls for the vanilla ice cream left by Zora in a churn on the porch. While the girls watched excitedly, Loreli filled their bowls. She was in the midst of filling her own when a slow-moving Trevor stepped onto the porch. It was apparent that the ramifications of the fight had caught up to him, just as they had Jake.

Loreli eyed his battered presence for a silent moment. "Do you want some?"

"Yes. Soft food is all I'll be able to handle for a while." He slid a hand over his tender jaw. "I think that farmer of yours loosened a couple of my teeth."

Loreli cracked, "Be glad he didn't loosen your fool head from your fool neck."

She sent him inside to fetch another bowl from the hutch. When he returned, she spooned him out a generous portion of the cream and handed him the bowl and a spoon. "Let's go to the front porch. We need to talk. Rebecca and Millie are gone, aren't they?"

"Yep."

Loreli told the girls, "Trevor and I will be out front. Will you be all right?"

Engrossed in their ice cream, they nodded.

"Well, come get me if you need anything. Your Uncle Jake's lying down, so no playing in the house until he gets up."

"Okay, Loreli," Dede said.

Satisfied, Loreli led Trevor around the house to the front porch. After they were seated, she asked, "How did you find me?"

"Olivia. I happened to be at your house when your wire arrived. I'd just gotten into town a few days before. Stopped by to say hello, and she said you weren't there.

She told me you were having a lot of items shipped, and when I asked where, she told me. She was worried about you."

"Olivia sent you?"

"Not really. I volunteered. You, married? Had to come and see for myself. Caught the train, rented a buggy after I arrived in this god-forsaken town, and here I am."

"You could have wired me so I would know you were coming."

Trevor smiled. "And miss the surprise on your face? Not a chance."

"Do you have my money?"

"Money?" he asked, eating the ice cream slowly. "What money?"

"Mexico City? My handbag? The senorita?"

"Ah, yes, the lovely Francesca. She turned out to be married, you know."

"Good. I hope her husband was nine feet tall."

"Almost. Last time I'll ever jump from a second-floor window. It made me feel almost as bad as I do now."

She shook her head. "Last I heard, you were in Cuba."

"I was for a while. Went home to see my mother for a bit. Traveled around Europe, then wound up back here."

"How is your mother?"

"Lady Jane is well. Her husband is still a bastard, though, and since I am too, my visits with her are rarely long ones."

Loreli met the Lady Jane once, many years ago, and found the Irish noblewoman quite remarkable. In spite of being ostracized by her immediate family for having an out-of-wedlock child with a Black seamen, the lands and money left to her by her grandfather made her wealthy enough not to care. "Send her my regards the next time you see her."

"I shall." He then set his bowl aside, and said, "Lorie, if you don't allow me to lie down somewhere, I'm going to pass out right here."

"I'll get you a blanket," she tossed back.

"Oh, come on, have a heart and take pity on a poor beaten fellow, will you, please? Is there an extra bed?"

Loreli sighed. "Yes, give me a moment to put on fresh sheets."

"Bless you, my child."

Loreli put Trevor in Jake's room. She'd gone up to ask Jake if he minded the arrangement but he'd been asleep, and she hadn't wanted to wake him. So, Trevor would get the opportunity to spend the night in a hog farmer's bed, probably one of the few beds in the world he'd not been in before.

By the time she got him settled in Jake's room, it was bedtime for the twins as well, so she heard their prayers and tucked them in. Giving them both a kiss, she slipped from their room and closed their door.

The house was finally quiet, and Loreli let the silence soothe her. She stepped out onto the porch, then collapsed into one of the chairs. *What a day!* The night rolled in bringing with it the familiar sounds of crickets and the unwanted assault of mosquitoes. She slapped at a few to keep them from snacking on her neck and arms, but for the most part, she simply sat.

Trevor was the last person she'd expected to make an appearance in this new life of hers. She had loved him, and loved him well. He had sheltered her, healed her, but now she was a woman full-grown, no longer the nineteen-year-old she'd been when they first met. Back then, she thought the world revolved around him; he was the funniest, boldest, and, yes, wildest man she'd ever known. Now, however, even though she knew a future with Jake would never come to be, Jake owned her heart—and no matter how many times she tried to deny the fact, or attempted to set it aside, the truth remained: Loreli Winters, gambling queen, was in love with a hog farmer named Jake Reed. She didn't know what to do with the knowledge, though. Telling him was not an option. The last thing she wanted was for him to feel obligated toward her in some way, or feel as if his plans to find a replacement for her had to be changed. He didn't love her, she knew that, but deep inside she wished he did.

Loreli yawned as the day caught up with her too. She went inside, closed the door behind her, and trudged up the stairs to her room. She could hear Jake's snores ruffling the shadowy silence. The moonlight streaming in through the open curtains gave off just enough of a glow for her to see by. Quietly, she removed her clothes, leaving on her thin chemise. She padded over to the bed and eased her way beneath the lone blanket, hoping not to disturb Jake, but he rolled over and mumbled, "Hello."

Her smile was soft. "Hello, yourself. Trevor's in your bed."

"Long as you're not in it with him, it's all right. Girls asleep?"

"Yes. How's your head?"

"Throbbing, but I think I'll live."

"Then go back to sleep."

"Come closer."

She scooted over until they were lying like nested spoons.

He draped an arm over her and said, "That's better."

Sheltered against him, she smiled. "Good night, Jake."

"Night, Loreli."

And they both slept.

The next morning, since Jake wasn't up to cook, Loreli fed the girls ice cream and cake from the wedding for breakfast. She had no intentions of attending church. Jake came down in the middle of the unconventional meal. "Ice cream?" he asked.

Bebe nodded. "Yep. Loreli says it's full of all kinds of good stuff like eggs and cream."

Jake eyed Loreli's amused face and his sore head began to throb. He really wanted to discuss why serving ice cream and cake for breakfast was not encouraged but the thought of doing so only made his head worse. "I suppose one morning is not going to harm anyone. Get me a bowl too."

Loreli grinned, then went to fetch him a bowl.

"Where's our guest?" Jake asked.

"Still asleep, as far as I know. Haven't heard a peep out of him all morning."

"Maybe he snuck away in the middle of the night," Jake said.

"I doubt it. His horse is still in the barn."

"Too bad."

Loreli eyed him. "I won't have any more fighting."

"As long as he keeps his insults to himself, I have no problem agreeing to that. Just make sure you tell him too."

"Oh, don't worry. I will."

"Why does Mr. Trevor talk funny, Loreli?" Dede asked.

"He's from Ireland."

"Where's that?"

"On the other side of the Atlantic Ocean," she replied.

"Does everybody in Ireland talk funny like him?" Bebe asked.

"Yep, they do."

Bebe said, "I'm glad we live in Kansas."

Jake drawled, "Me too."

Loreli shot him a look. If she couldn't convince Trevor to leave town, Loreli envisioned a very rocky day ahead. Having both Trevor and Jake under one roof would be like having two roosters strutting around trying to out crow each other, and she had neither the time nor inclination to play peace officer. But, she supposed, she could always bring in Elvira again if things got out of hand. Satisfied she went back to her ice cream.

Trevor didn't make an appearance until a bit after the noon hour. Like Jake, Trevor had to move slowly and carefully due to his injuries from the brawl. Jake, seated on the back porch nursing his own pains, looked up at Trevor's entrance and cracked, "Well, glad you could join us. My bed that comfortable?"

"No," Trevor tossed back, and eased himself down into a chair. "I've slept on softer logs."

Jake smiled. "You're welcome."

"Is there any food to eat, not that I can eat anything with these loose teeth."

Jake, watching Loreli and the girls jumping rope across the yard said, "You'll heal. Loreli fed the girls ice cream for breakfast."

"Ice cream?"

"Yep."

Trevor smiled. "She would, though. Never conventional, that Loreli."

Jake shook his head. "Has nothing to do with convention. Loreli just can't cook."

"Really?"

Jake turned and surveyed him. "Thought you knew her?"

"I do, but cooking has never come up. Why would I care? We always ate in restaurants or places where the food came to the table already prepared."

"Must be a nice life having folks waiting on you all the time," Jake commented.

"It is," Trevor said. "Having to look after one's self all the time can be trying."

"Never bothered me."

"Is Loreli actually jumping rope?" Trevor asked, finally noticing what Loreli and the girls were doing.

"That she is."

"Good lord. What's come over her?"

"Nothing. They're just having fun."

"Fun is playing poker or going to the London theater. Fun is not skipping rope."

"In Kansas it is."

For a moment there was silence. "She isn't going to stay here, you know," Trevor told Jake.

"I do," Jake replied.

The men's eyes met.

"She and I have already discussed it," Jake told him.

"You can't force her to stay."

"I know that too. I won't try and stop her."

Trevor peered into Jake's swollen face. "You really do love her, don't you?"

"You doubted it?"

Trevor sat back in his chair as if confused. "I'm not sure what I thought. I just knew I had to come and see what this was all about. She's never given her heart before." He looked at Jake as if seeing him for the first time. "Why you?"

Jake asked, "Why not me?"

"Because."

"Because what, I raise hogs and grow corn for a living?"

"Frankly, yes. In my world, she's known as the Ice Countess. She's turned down suits by Spanish princes, Haitian dukes . . ."

"Here, she's just Loreli. Maybe those other fellows should've had twin nieces."

"What?"

"Nothing. Never mind," Jake said.

"Well, it defies understanding."

Jake watched as Loreli took the end of the rope from Bebe so that Bebe could have a turn jumping. The happiness on Loreli's face as she and Dede recited a singsong rhyme filled his heart.

"It sure does," Jake replied.

Chapter 15

❧❦❧

While Loreli turned the rope, she could see Jake and Trevor talking on the porch. Hoping a renewed bout of fisticuffs wasn't about to break out, she kept one eye on them and one on her rope turning. Once it appeared that the men were behaving themselves, she relaxed.

When the game was over, the girls ran off to resume their never-ending jacks battles and Loreli walked over to the porch. "Afternoon, Trev."

"Where I come from, this time of day is called *morning*," he drawled.

She smiled. He was right. Before joining the wagon train, she'd never gotten out of bed before noon. Rising late was standard fare for those who lived life at night. "Well, here in Kansas, it's noon. Have you eaten?"

"Had some ice cream."

"Good." She looked at Jake. "Today would be a good day to start looking for a cook."

"We don't need a cook."

312

"Yes, we do."

"No, we don't," Jake repeated firmly.

Loreli wasn't going to argue further. "Okay, well, I'll just hire a cook for me and the girls. You want anything while I'm in town?"

"Not if it involves hiring help."

"Fine."

The stubborn set of his chin told Loreli that he was not going to change his position. Well, she had no plans to change hers either. Whether he wanted to admit it or not, he needed household help so he could be free to handle the other aspects of his life, like the organizing and his Republican party commitments. Lord knew, Loreli didn't see herself as household help, and since the girls couldn't eat ice cream every time he got injured or was unable to function as the house chef, she was going to hire someone. "Well, I'm going to change clothes and drive into town. I'll go and see if the girls wish to go with me."

And she left.

Jake watched her stride away. "She's going to hire someone anyway, isn't she?" he said to Trevor.

"Do you raise hogs?" Trevor tossed back.

Jake sighed with resignation. "I need more ice cream."

Trevor smiled. "Bring me another bowl too."

The girls decided they'd rather play with Emily's new kittens than accompany Loreli, so she drove into town alone. She had no idea if she'd be able to find someone to hire, but she had to at least ask around. She also knew that with all the gossip flying over yesterday's melee, folks might be expecting her to be too ashamed to show her face, but she planned to set that to rest right now. She wasn't ashamed because she had nothing to be ashamed of.

She parked her rig in front of the livery, then stopped inside to take out another week's lease on the vehicle. The squat gnome-like woman behind the counter looked Loreli up and down in a distasteful way, then asked, "What can I do for you?"

"I'm looking for Mr. Quaig."

"Bailey's gone. Won't be back till Sunday."

"Well, I'm—"

"I know who you are."

Loreli raised an eyebrow. "But I don't know you."

"Ruth Ann Quaig. Bailey's sister."

"Ah, well, I came to pay Mr. Quaig for another week's use of the buggy."

"It ain't for rent anymore."

Loreli paused in her search for her coin purse. "Excuse me?"

"I said, it ain't for rent. He promised it to someone else."

Loreli took a slow look around the large barnlike structure and in the corner saw the two other buggies that had been here when Loreli first came to town. "Why can't they have one of those?"

"'Cause, he promised them yours."

"Then I suppose I'll take whatever you have left."

"They're promised too."

Loreli studied the woman. Loreli understood now. "I see. Well, how about this?" Loreli began searching through her handbag. She took out a double eagle and held it up so the gnome could see the Liberty head with its coronet on one side, and the eagle on its back. The woman's eyes widened just as Loreli knew they would. A double eagle was worth twenty dollars. With the country in the midst of yet another depression, twenty dollars was a fortune in a backwater like this one. A woman of Ruth Ann's status could go her entire life and never amass twenty dollars in hand. "Do you think your brother would mind my buying that horse and buggy?"

Ruth Ann's beady eyes were fixed greedily on the coin. Loreli could sense the woman being tempted by what it could buy. Even if Ruth Ann only gave her brother half the value, she would still be farther ahead than she'd probably ever been before.

The woman stuck out her palm.

Loreli placed the coin on it, then headed for the door, tossing back, "Nice doing business with you, Ruth Ann."

There was no reply.

As Loreli headed up the walk to the sheriff's office, she thought twenty dollars a small price to pay to never have to see Ruth Ann Quaig again. It also saved Loreli the bother of having to come into town and pay the weekly livery bill. She now had her own vehicle. The buggy wasn't new, the horse either for that matter, but they would suit her just fine while she was here.

This being Sunday, there weren't that many folks out and about. Loreli guessed a good portion of the citizens were still in church having their spirits lifted by the Reverend Appleby's scorching sermons and their ears fried by Victoria Diggs's mirror-cracking voice. Most of the businesses were closed, but that didn't stop people from window shopping or shooting daggers her way as she passed by.

She entered the sheriff's office to ask if he might know of anyone to hire. He was writing down a message at the telegraph machine. He keyed a short reply, then pushed his chair back. When he noticed Loreli, he stood and greeted her with a wary smile. "Are you still mad?"

"Yes, and no."

He grinned, "Never seen so many men run so fast. Maybe the town should elect you sheriff when I retire."

Loreli's eyes showed her amusement. "Only if I can deputize Elvira."

He laughed. "You and Jake set a new date?"

"No. Maybe once he can eat solid food again, we can talk about it."

He shook his head. "So what can I do for you?"

"I'm looking to hire a cook. Do you know of anyone?"

He thought a moment. "Can't say as I do, but I'll ask around."

"Thanks, I'd appreciate it."

"Oh, by the way, wire came in for you last night."

"Really?"

"Yeah, was going to send somebody out to deliver it to you today, but since you're here—hold on, let me get it."

He returned with the paper in hand. Loreli read the words: *Hope everything I sent with Trevor arrived safe. He promised to guard paintings well. Olivia.*

Loreli found the note confusing. Trevor hadn't mentioned her paintings. Even knowing Trevor the way she did, Loreli wasn't sure if she should be alarmed by Olivia's message or not. Maybe he'd simply forgotten to tell her. In light of the fight he'd had with Jake, she found that highly possible.

Loreli put the wire in her handbag. "Thanks, sheriff. Let me know if you hear of anyone who might want the job, and I'll let you know when the next wedding date will be."

"That's a deal." Then he added, "Speaking of deals.

We're playing poker tomorrow evening at nine. You want to sit in?"

"I think I just might. If I'm not here by the time you start dealing, you'll know I'm not coming, but I will try and make it."

"Good."

She left him with a smile and a wave. Loreli could already imagine Jake's reaction when she told him she was going to play poker, but she'd deal with that when the time came.

Since her friend Fanny lived in town, Loreli walked down to her house. She wanted to thank her for her help with the wedding preparations, but no one answered Loreli's knock so she turned around and went back the way she'd come.

Her walk back to the livery took her past Millie Tate's dress shop. The shop was closed and Loreli was glad to know she wouldn't have to cross paths with Millie today. However, Millie stepped out onto the walk just as Loreli cleared the doorway, and called out, "Miss Winters? Is Trevor still in town?"

Loreli sighed and stopped. She turned back. "Hello, Miss Tate . . ."

Loreli's words trailed off as she took in the beautiful pearl-edged brooch Millie was wearing on her faded green dress. "My, what a beautiful brooch."

Millie's eyes filled with panic and she hastily placed her hand atop the brooch. "You weren't supposed to see it."

Loreli now had a better understanding of Olivia's wire. "Did Trevor give that to you?"

"Yes, last evening, and he said I wasn't to let you see it because you'd only get jealous."

"Oh, really. I don't see why I should be jealous over a brooch *I own*!"

Millie jumped a foot in the air.

"Yes, Millie, that brooch is mine," Loreli said. "Did he give you anything else?"

"Well, yes."

Angry, Loreli held out her hand. "Give me the brooch."

Millie drew back. "I most certainly will not. This was a gift."

"Give me my damn brooch, Millie."

"No, and that's that. What are you going to do, shoot me?"

Loreli reached into her handbag and pulled out her pearl-handled derringer. She pointed it at Millie and said calmly, "Yes."

Millie's eyes went moon-wide, then her fingers began fumbling with the clasp on the brooch. Her anger quite plain, she slapped the brooch into Loreli's outstretched palm.

Loreli's eyes glowed coldly. "Now, the other things he gave you. Where are they?"

With her attention glued on the gun, Millie replied weakly. "Inside."

"Show me."

Millie nervously put the key in the door lock and Loreli followed her into the shop. Millie went over to a desk and opened a drawer. She came back to Loreli bearing a pair of diamond-stud earbobs that Loreli also found very familiar. Loreli took her property and slipped it in the side pocket of her riding skirt. "He didn't give you anything else?"

Millie shook her head. "No, just the brooch and the studs."

"Good."

"You're every bit the tramp folks say you are," Millie said nastily.

"No, I'm more." And to prove it, Loreli pulled the trigger and put a bullet in a hat perched on one of the forms, sending the hat flying and Millie went into a whimpering crouch.

Loreli turned and left.

By the time Loreli got back to the Reed place, she had steam rolling out of her ears. She couldn't decide whether to shoot Trevor before or after demanding an explanation. Surely Olivia hadn't trusted him to bring Loreli's jewels to Kansas, had she? And where were the paintings? Loreli had no answers to either question right now, but as she got out of the carriage and stormed into the house, she planned on getting some. Quick.

"Trevor Church!" she bellowed.

Jake came in from the back porch. He took one look at her furious face and hoped and prayed that anger wasn't aimed at him.

"Where's Trevor?" Loreli said.

"Lying down."

Without another word, Loreli headed to Jake's room.

He was indeed lying down, but at her noisy entrance he sat up. "What's wrong?"

His eyes widened at the sight of the derringer in her hand.

"What did Olivia give you to bring to me?" Loreli asked.

"What do you mean?" he answered.

Loreli looked over at the tight-jawed Jake. "Where are the girls?"

"Outside."

"Make sure they stay there, please. Trevor and I need to talk."

Jake had no idea what the Irishman had done to earn Loreli's wrath, but Jake left the room to check on the girls, glad not to be in Trevor's shoes.

Once Loreli and Trevor were alone, she said to him, "Now, again, what did Olivia give you of mine?"

She spotted his saddlebags beside the bed. "Open your bags and dump them onto the floor."

"Loreli—"

"Dammit, Trevor. I just reclaimed a brooch of mine from Millie Tate. Do not make me waste a bullet on you."

Trevor got the message. He picked up the bags and dumped them onto the floor. Out rolled personal items such as his razor and shaving brush, but she was more interested in the black velvet pouch that lay beside them. That was very familiar as well. Still holding the derringer on him, she stooped and picked up the pouch. "Where are the paintings?"

Jake reentered the room, but Loreli paid him no mind. "The paintings, Trev?"

"Sold them."

It was her turn to stare with widened eyes, "You sold them? Which ones did you have?"

"A couple of Bannisters, and—"

She couldn't believe her ears. "You sold my Bannisters!" she fairly screeched.

Trevor shrugged, "Well, yes, lass. I figured you wouldn't

mind once you found out what dire straits I'm in."

"I don't care about your straits. You had no right!"

It had taken Loreli years to find those two paintings. Edward Bannister's Under the Oaks won first prize at the Philadelphia Centennial Exposition held in '76. When the exhibition committee learned of Bannister's race, they tried to withdraw the prize, but were forced to honor the oil painting and its creator anyway. The second painting, Sabin Point, Narragansett Bay, was also critically acclaimed. "How much of my jewelry did you sell?"

"None. I gave the brooch and the studs to the lovely Mildred for her tender assistance yesterday, but the rest is still rolled in the cloth."

Loreli asked critically, "And when were you going to tell me you had my jewelry?"

Silence.

"You weren't, were you."

He tried to explain. "Loreli, look, I ran into a string of bad luck, and the folks I owed didn't want to wait. I'm flat busted, lass. I don't have a half penny to my name."

"So you sold my paintings."

"Yes."

"To whom?"

"A fence in Philadelphia."

"And I don't stand a chance of retrieving them."

He shook his head. "No."

She wanted to shoot him right between his green eyes. "Get your things, and get out, Trevor. Now."

"But lass,"

"Now, Trevor. The only reason I'm letting you go without shooting you is because you *were* a friend, and that friendship meant something. Once."

"Lass, I still owe a thousand dollars, and they're after me. They'll kill me if I don't pay."

"Trevor. I don't care. There's no way I'm going to lend you money you have no intentions of paying back, nor will I let you use this farm as a place to hide. There are children here."

"Loreli—"

"Go now, Trevor, and I don't ever wish to see you again."

"You don't mean that, lass."

"Don't I? Our friendship obviously meant nothing to you, otherwise you'd have told me Olivia sent the jewels and paintings with you. You treated me like a rube, Trev."

"But—"

"Get your things together. I won't tell you again."

He looked over at Jake who told the Irishman, "You'll find no sympathy here, friend. I wanted you gone the moment you showed up."

Trevor began cramming his belongings back into his saddlebags. "This isn't right, lass."

"No, it isn't. I should've turned you over to the sheriff." That said, she turned and stormed from the room.

Trevor rode away from the Reed farm less than twenty-minutes later. He was angry, but Loreli was even angrier.

As she and Jake watched Trevor ride east, Jake asked, "Think that'll be the last of him?"

"I hope so." But she didn't feel convinced.

That evening, after the girls were put to bed, a storm blew in. Loreli and Jake sat on the porch awhile, but when the winds picked up and the rain began blowing in horizontal sheets, they ran inside, laughing uproariously at being so wet and windblown.

Jake closed the door firmly on the elements, then stood with his back to the door, unable to do anything but look at Loreli. Even soaking wet, she was the most beautiful woman he'd ever seen.

"I should get out of these wet things before I catch my death," she said. "Too bad the tub's still outdoors, otherwise I could take a nice hot bath." She quieted upon noticing his intense observation. "What?"

"Nothing. Just enjoying you."

She walked over until she was so close he could feel the warmth of her body mingle with his own. Looking up at his black-and-blue face, she asked, "And what do you find so enjoyable about me?"

"Fishing for compliments?"

"I am."

"Well, I enjoy you."

"Why?" she asked.

He reached out and stroked her cheek. "Because I've never met anyone like you, Loreli."

She felt the spark from his touch flow through her. "And I've never met anyone like you, Jake Reed."

"We didn't get our wedding night."

"We didn't get a wedding," she tossed back.

His mustache lifted with amusement. "You're never going to let that go, are you?"

"No. You'll probably have a real wedding some day, but I know I won't."

Jake thought he heard regret hiding beneath her sassy tone. He touched her cheek again. The dew of the rain mingled with the softness of her skin. "You could have as many weddings as you want. Just say the word and the men would come running."

Every man but the one I'd want.

Unwilling to dampen how she made him feel, Jake slowly lowered his head, then lightly touched his lips to hers, first once, and then again.

The kisses were teasing, fleeting invitations that Loreli couldn't resist returning. Passion had been simmering beneath the surface since their last time together, and now, as the kisses deepened, and the storm raged outside, a different sort of storm blossomed and spread. Hands began to explore, touch, and tempt while the sounds of their breathing rustled the darkness. He wanted her, and she wanted him. Lightning flashed, filling the room with a momentary shock of light, offering the night a brief glimpse of lovers intent upon each other.

Jake paid no attention to his aches and pains, his need for her was far more acute. The feel of her lips against his were healing, soothing. The sensations of his hands roaming over her curves in the damp dress overrode his hurts until all that remained was the vivid anticipation of the love he wanted to make. "Come upstairs with me . . ."

Loreli's desire spiraled high in response to his murmured invitation. Nothing in her well-traveled life had ever prepared her for a man like Jake, and when he took her by the hand and led her to the attic door, she went willingly, gladly.

Upstairs in her room, he undressed and she did the same. Outside, the storm filled the night with crackles of lightning and the responding booms of thunder. Inside, Jake and Loreli were as naked as Adam and Eve in the garden, and as they came together atop the softness of her bed, they were in their own paradise. Jake worshiped her with his hands and lips, then groaned as she returned the favor. It was her first time exploring him without inhibition and she reveled in it. Kneeling beside him she teased her fingers over his nipples, slowly circling and mapping until they tightened. Bending down, she nipped them with love-gentled teeth, then smiled when she heard him gasp. She lifted up, her fingers still playing, and whispered, "In some ways, a man's body is just like a woman's . . . but in other ways"—she closed her hand over the hard length of him—"men are gloriously different . . ."

Jake growled. Her warm, sensual explorations threatened to make him explode. To keep that from happening, he placed his hand over hers to stay her tantalizing movements, then gently pulled her in against his side. "I want this night to last, and it won't if you keep that up."

Her eyes glowed with amusement and desire.

He kissed her deeply, then murmured with mock warning, "Now keep your hands to yourself for a minute, and let me see if I remember my lessons . . ."

The hot words flooded Loreli's core with heat, and when he touched her there, she groaned with welcoming pleasure, and her legs parted shamelessly.

"Good . . ." he whispered.

Loreli thought it very good indeed; so good, nothing in the world mattered but the torrent building in her blood, and his bold, *bold* touch.

Still coaxing the lodestone between her thighs, Jake leaned down and touched his lips to her kiss-swollen mouth, "Is the teacher ready?" he asked.

"Oh, yes . . ."

So there, in the storm-echoing dark, Jake entered her, filling her softness with his hardness and they both gasped from the sheer bliss of the joining.

"Lord, Loreli . . ."

She purred wantonly while sliding her hands over the smooth hard surface of his back. He began to stroke and she began to rise. Words fell away. None were needed; when his body spoke, hers answered. He questioned boldly. She responded lustily. He increased the pace and she gladly matched his thrusts. She was his lightning, and he, her thunder. They were in the eye of their own storm, and as it reached gale strength, they rode it together. He played with her, teased her, letting her learn, measure, take, and she savored each lust-filled nuance, until she shattered under its force, screaming out his name. Jake, watching her climax in the flashes of lightning, gripped her hips and exploded a moment later.

The next day, Loreli was up in her room when the girls came in. "What are you doing, Loreli?" Bebe asked.

"Well, my friend Olivia sent me some of my jewelry and I'm looking at what's here."

"Can we see?" Dede asked.

"Sure."

The girls came over to where Loreli was sitting on the wood floor. They took a seat on either side of her, then stared in awe at the beautiful stones and gold she had placed in front of her. Olivia had only sent a couple pairs of ear studs, an amethyst necklace, a gold bracelet, and as Loreli reached into the bottom of the pouch, the most precious thing she owned: the small heart-shaped locket given to her by her father. It was battered and old, but the memories it brought back made Loreli study it in silence.

"What is that, Loreli?" Dede asked quietly.

"My magic locket."

"Magic?"

"Magic."

"What kind of magic?" Bebe asked.

"Well, it's the kind of magic that helps scared little girls be brave. My father gave it to me."

"Was it because you were scared of spiders?"

Loreli smiled. "Partly, but mostly so I wouldn't be scared of the dark. My father and I moved around a lot, and sometimes we had to sleep outside on the ground."

"Sometimes, Uncle Jake let's us sleep outside in his tent," Bebe said, "but we always let Pal sleep by the door. Kansas has wolves."

"That's real good thinking, but I didn't have a Pal, so I was real scared at night. There were wolves in Kentucky too, and bears, and all kinds of animals that I thought liked to eat little girls."

"How old were you?" Dede asked.

"Eight."

"Just like us!"

"Just like you."

"May I hold it?" Dede asked.

Loreli passed it over and watched Dede examine it.

Dede held it for a few more moments, then handed it back. "I wish I had a magic locket," she said a bit sadly.

Loreli asked, "Why, pumpkin?"

"So I'd be brave like you and Bebe."

Loreli gently hugged her and kissed the top of her head. "Everybody's afraid of something, De. You know how I feel about spiders."

"I don't like being scared all the time."

The plea in Dede's eyes brought tears to Loreli's heart. "Here."

Loreli put the locket around Dede's thin neck. The clasp needed repairing but Loreli managed to make it work for now. "How's that."

Dede's fingers touched the locket's face gently. Her smile told all. "Thanks, Loreli."

"You're welcome."

"Do you feel braver, De?" Bebe asked.

Dede shook her head. "No."

Loreli thought for a moment and then said, "Oh, I forgot. The locket has to be kissed every day by the person who gave it to you. Then the magic works." Loreli made that part up, of course.

Dede held the little heart up and Loreli gave it a kiss. "There."

"Do you feel braver?" Bebe said.

"A little bit."

"It hasn't been worn in a long time," Loreli said. "It probably needs a little while to really get going again, sort of like when you're building a fire."

"Well, I want to see if it works," Dede said.

Bebe asked, "How?"

"I'll ride Phoebe all by myself."

Loreli stared.

Bebe said excitedly, "Let's go."

And before Loreli could recover fast enough to stop them they were down the stairs and gone. Loreli got to her feet and hastened after them. Lord, what had she done?

Jake looked up from his reading and asked, "What's going on?"

Loreli was torn between telling him and going after the girls. The girls won out. "Just come on. I'll explain."

He got up and hurried after her.

When the adults arrived outside, they could see Bebe leading Phoebe out of the barn and into the corral. Dede brought up the rear.

As Jake and Loreli walked toward them, he asked, "What am I supposed to be looking at?"

"It's a long story, but I gave Dede a magic necklace and now she wants to ride Phoebe."

That stopped him in his tracks. "What?"

"And if she gets hurt, it will be all my fault."

Loreli ran off.

Jake, still not sure what was going on, followed.

When Loreli reached the corral, she had to jump away to keep from being bitten by Elvira. Loreli leaned down and snapped, "Jerky, Elvira! You hear me? Jerky!"

The goat-dog just looked back at her.

Snarling, Loreli turned her attention to the happenings inside the corral. Dede had joined her sister, and Loreli could see the wariness on Dede's face, so she went into the corral too.

Both girls greeted her presence with smiles, but De's eyes never left the mare.

Loreli knew that the next few moments with Dede had to be handled very carefully. The last thing she wanted to do was discourage the child, but she didn't want to see her hurt either. "De, how about you walk Phoebe around the pen for a moment, so she can get warmed up a bit?"

"What do I do?"

"I just want you to put your hand on her side and walk her real slowly. Keep your hand on her now, okay?"

"I will," Dede said.

As they all watched, Dede walked over and stood next to Phoebe. She hesitated for a moment and then slowly touched the horse's side. When Phoebe moved just a bit, Dede quickly jumped away. Dede looked over at Loreli. Loreli smiled encouragingly, but no one said a word.

Dede looked at her uncle. "Uncle Jake, Loreli gave me a magic locket."

"I heard about that."

Dede turned back and again placed her hand on the mare's side. It was plain she wasn't comfortable, but she said to Phoebe, "Come on, girl."

And the horse and the little girl with the locket began to walk slowly around the paddock. Loreli had tears in her eyes. She wiped them away.

Jake's throat was thick with emotion. No, Dede wasn't riding yet, but to see her quietly facing her fear filled his heart. A month ago, she wouldn't have gone near a horse.

An excited Bebe called out to her sister, "De! The locket's working!"

Dede's smile was as wide as Texas. "It is, Be. It is!"

Loreli could only shake her head. Lord, she loved these girls.

When the walk around the pen was completed, the audience joined the star of the show inside the pen. She was smiling. "Uncle Jake, will you boost me up?"

Jake wanted to ask her if she was sure about riding Phoebe, but he didn't. "Sure. We'll do it real slow, okay?"

"Okay."

She put her booted foot into the step he made from his hands, and slowly lifted her until she was settled on the mare's bare back. Phoebe took a step back and a panicked Dede grabbed her mane.

Jake spoke softly to Phoebe and the gentle mare calmed. "Are you okay?" he asked Dede.

For a person afraid of horses, walking on the ground beside a horse was very different from viewing the world atop their broad backs. "I think the magic's wearing off, so can we just go a little ways?"

Jake nodded. "Sure can. You just let me know, and I'll take you down."

Dede nodded.

He took a quick moment to show her how to use her knees to make Becky go forward and how to make her stop. "Are you ready?"

Dede nodded. "Yes. Just a little ways. Okay?"

"Okay. I'm going to walk beside you. How's that?"

She smiled gratefully, then Dede gritted her teeth as Phoebe took her first few steps. Loreli could see the tension in her little brown arms. The horse was moving as slow as molasses but even that was too fast a pace from the look on Dede's face. She stayed on, however, and rode a quarter of the way around the pen before asking Jake to help her down.

Bebe ran to her sister's side, yelling excitedly, "You did it, De! You rode Phoebe all by yourself!"

Dede grinned. "But not a long way."

"Loreli said the magic has to build up, remember?" Bebe said.

Dede shook her head.

Bebe had an epiphany. "Oh, De. We could ride over to Aggie's and Carrie's. . . . Uncle Jake, when De gets better, can we get another horse so she and I can race?"

Jake stared at this child with his sister's face, and told

her, "How about we get Dede out of the pen first before we start placing our bets, okay?"

Bebe nodded that she understood.

Jake, still filled with amazement, looked over at Loreli, who simply shook her head in reply. Miss Bebe was something else.

That night, as Jake and Loreli lay in bed, he told her, "You know, that magic locket hocus-pocus might actually work."

Loreli turned over so she could see his face in the dark. "It's not hocus-pocus. The locket *is* magic."

He slid his hand down her silken back. "It's just a locket. Admit it, you made the magic part up."

"I did not. It had magic in it when my daddy gave it to me, and it has magic now. How else can you explain Dede riding today."

His hand roamed over the hills of her behind, then down the backs of her thighs. "You're the magic."

He traced sensual circles over her hips and down her legs and up her back. He bent and kissed the curve of her shoulder. "I knew you were magic, the moment I set eyes on you. . . ."

Enjoying his touch, she whispered seductively, "Then how about I show you just how magical I can be?"

Jake smiled and husked out, "You're on. . . ."

And by the time all the spells were cast, they were both too sated to do anything but fall asleep.

For the next few days, Loreli divided her time between kissing the locket and kissing Jake. During the day, Dede and Phoebe rode farther and farther. At night Loreli had the wanton joys of riding something entirely different.

On Friday morning, Loreli awakened with a smile. She and Jake had shared a particularly stunning night of love-making. *A girl could get real spoiled real quick being with a man like Jake,* she told herself knowingly. In bed he was passionate, giving, and becoming more and more— skilled. Just thinking about the paces he'd put her through last night made her blood heat up again. He couldn't soothe her, though, because he was already up and off to do the morning chores. The girls wouldn't wake for an-other hour or so, so Loreli burrowed back beneath the covers and closed her eyes.

She'd almost drifted off when she heard Jake yell her name. She heard panic and anger in his tone. Hastily leav-ing the bed, she ran down the steps. "What's the matter?"

His face was tight as a drum. "The girls are gone."

"What do you mean, the girls are gone?"

His voice was deadly. "Your friend, Trevor, has them." Loreli felt sick. *"What?"*

He forced a piece of paper in her face and growled, "Read this!"

Her hand shaking, Loreli read:

Lass,

One thousand dollars or I sell them overseas. Des-perate times beget desperate measures.

TC

Chapter 16

Loreli reread the words. She felt sickened.

"Will he really do what he says there?" Jake asked.

Loreli couldn't lie. "I don't know. If he's desperate enough to do this . . ." Her words trailed off. Her worry over the girls grew with each breath she took. "We have to find them."

"I'll start with the sheriff. Maybe someone in town has seen them. He has to be holed up somewhere close."

Loreli agreed. If Trevor needed the money that desperately, he'd be nearby so he could access the ransom quickly. Had he wanted her to travel to make the exchange, she assumed he would have stated that in the letter.

Jake left the room for a moment, then returned with a rifle. "I want you to stay here."

Loreli looked at the firearm. She'd never seen him arm himself before. "I'm coming with you."

"No, you're not. What if he comes here looking for the money?"

"Then I need to go to town and get it. I will pay him whatever he wants to get the twins back. This would never have happened had I not entered your lives. I'm truly sorry for that," she told him honestly.

The mask had descended on his features. "Get dressed so we can go."

Loreli hurried up the stairs.

He rode Fox. Loreli rode Phoebe. The first stop was Matt Peterson's. When he heard the news, he put down his plow, ran and got his gun, then saddled up to help with the search.

The next two stops added Art Gibson, Brass Barber, and his son, William, to their small contingent. All of the men were armed.

The town was bustling as they rode in. Their determined faces and manner made folks on their walks pause and stare curiously, but Jake and the others paid the townspeople no mind.

Sheriff Mack's lips tightened grimly as Jake related the details. "Let me see the note."

Jake fished it out of his pocket and handed it over. The clouds in Jake's face had not lightened.

The sheriff then turned to Loreli. "Any idea where he might be?"

"If I knew sheriff, I'd already be there," Loreli snapped, more crossly than she'd intended. She was quickly contrite. "I'm sorry. I'm just upset."

He nodded. "I know you are. No hard feelings." He seemed to think a moment, then said, "I'm going to wire the marshal in Lawrence, see if he has any ideas, but in the meantime, do you know if that Trevor fella struck it up with anybody while he was here?"

Loreli didn't hesitate. "Yes, Millie Tate and Rebecca Appleby."

The sheriff raised an eyebrow. "Really?"

Loreli then told him about Trevor, Millie, and Rebecca on the porch after the fight, and then about Millie and the brooch.

Sheriff Mack grabbed his hat. "Let's go talk to Miss Tate. Jake, why don't you and Miss Loreli come with me. Brass, you and the others split up and take a stroll through town—see what you can hear or find out."

Millie's shop was closed. The sheriff tried the door, then looked in through the window. "Funny. Her shop's almost never closed."

Loreli peered through the small glass window front as well, but saw no one inside but the dress forms, fabrics, and notions.

Sheriff Mack said, "Well, let's ride out to the Appleby place and talk to Miss Rebecca. Maybe she can tell us something."

"I have to go to the bank and see if I can make the arrangements for the money," Loreli said.

"I'll meet you back at the house," Jake said.

"It will just take a minute."

"Go home, Loreli. You've done enough. The sheriff and I need to go."

Loreli's lips tightened. "Okay, Jake. Godspeed."

He turned and followed the sheriff back to the horses.

Watching him walk away, all she kept hearing was, *You've done enough*. The words hurt. He was correct, however. Satan was loose in paradise and it was entirely her fault. Trevor's perfidy had also impacted the budding relationship she and Jake had been building, but she didn't have time to worry over it now. She had to get to the bank.

Cyrus Buxton looked up when she entered. "Mornin', Miss Winters."

"Mornin', Cyrus. I need to withdraw some money."

"You can't," he told her in a sheepish voice.

Loreli searched his face for a moment. "What do you mean, I can't? I thought my money was here?"

"It is—well—was."

Loreli could feel her temper rising but she remained calm. "Cyrus, what the hell are you talking about?"

The voice of Sol Diggs came from behind her. "What he's talking about is that your deposits are under investigation."

Loreli turned. "By whom?"

He smiled wolfishly. "Me. I think some of the account numbers you gave my bank may have been in error, and since I don't want to deposit money in your account that could possibly belong to someone else, I'm waiting for further verification from your banks back East. We should have it all cleared up in, oh, a month or two."

"You picked the wrong day to play your bluff, Diggs. I need a thousand dollars of *my* money right now," she said coolly.

He chuckled patronizingly. "I'm sorry, Miss Winters, but the whole thing is out of my hands."

Loreli thought about how scared the twins must be and how much she wanted to squash Diggs beneath her heel for this pitiful little stab at revenge. "Fine. Within the hour, the sheriff is going to receive a warrant for your arrest. You're going to be charged with bank fraud, personal theft, forgery and anything else I can think of while I'm on my way to the telegraph office. When I'm done, every time you hear the word Winters, you're going to break out in hives."

His eyes were wide.

"Better tell the Queen she may lose her house too," Loreli snapped.

And she headed to the door.

Diggs hastened to stop her exit. "Uh, Miss Winters. Hold on a moment. I was only teasing. You can have all the money—"

"Save it, Diggs. If you didn't want to play the game, you shouldn't have dealt the cards." She stormed off.

Sheriff Mack and the others were gone by the time Loreli made it back to his office. His young deputy was on duty. When he read the message Loreli wrote out for him to send, his eyes widened. "You're sure about this, ma'am?"

"Yes. Send it on, please."

So he did.

Twenty minutes later, she received her answer. Arrangements had been made for the money she needed. A Pinkerton had been hired to deliver it in cash tomorrow. The Diggs matter was also under investigation. Her barrister had already begun contacting the proper banking entities. Warrants would be filed later today.

The young deputy said, "You must have some powerful friends."

"Yes, I do," Loreli said.

When Jake and the rest of the men arrived at Rebecca's she was in the yard throwing feed to the chickens. She stopped upon seeing them and walked over. "Morning, men. What brings you here?"

"When was the last time you saw Millie?" Jake asked.

"Sunday afternoon after church," Rebecca answered coolly. "She rode out here to tell me that the Winters woman pulled a gun on her and robbed her. Has something happened?"

"Yes. Trevor Church has kidnapped the twins," Jake said.

"What? When?"

"Sometime last night."

"I knew that woman would bring you nothing but trouble, Jake. Didn't I say that?" Rebecca said.

"Do you have any idea where Millie might be?" Jake snapped.

"No."

Jake turned Fox around. "Let's go, sheriff."

The men spent the rest of the afternoon searching abandoned farmhouses and talking to anyone who might know anything, but found nothing.

At one point in the search, Jake said in frustration, "They have to be somewhere."

"There's another place about a mile west of here. Let's try there before we head back to town," the sheriff said.

They all agreed, but found nothing there either.

Jake rode home filled with both anger and despair. Somewhere his girls were being held against their will, probably terrified. All he could think about was getting them back safe and sound, and then killing Church. What kind of man would use children as pawns? *Men who lived in Loreli's world,* came the answer. Jake knew that Loreli loved the girls and would forfeit her own life before letting them be harmed, but how many other dangerous people would come calling at his farm because of her? Were there other Trevors lurking about waiting to use his girls as leverage against Loreli for reasons yet to be known? Would he have to spend the next twelve months constantly on guard, and looking over his shoulder so as to keep his family safe? Jake didn't know the answers and it scared him.

Loreli returned to a silent, empty farmhouse. As the day lengthened, her worries mounted. Where was Trevor holding the twins? Were they hungry? Had he fed them? Were they well? So far there'd been no further contact from him, so she had no idea as to when and where he wanted to make the exchange. Jake hadn't returned as of yet either. She spent the day pacing and praying that he'd come home with Bebe and Dede in tow, but by five o'clock that afternoon, her prayers had yet to be answered.

An hour later, Jake returned and Loreli stepped out onto the porch. He was alone.

As he dismounted he asked anxiously, "Are they here?"

"No. Did you find out anything?"

He shook his head.

Loreli sighed. Looking at him made her heart break even more. He loved those girls like he loved his life. The worry was undoubtedly eating him up inside. "Rebecca wasn't able to help?"

"No. She hasn't seen Millie since Sunday."

"Did you go into her shop?"

"No."

"Why not?"

"We concentrated on the abandoned farms. Hoped Church was holed up in one, but searching her shop is a good idea." He remounted. "I'm going back to town." Jake knew the search might be futile, but he was at his wits' end, and he needed to stay on the move. Trying to end this nightmare fueled every breath.

"I'll saddle Phoebe and meet you there," Loreli told him.

"Stay here."

"No, Jake. Those girls are my heart. I caused this, and if you're angry at me, I can live with that, but I can't live with them being gone this way and not helping find them, so I'm going to town too. Whether you want me there or not!"

His lip tightened beneath his mustache, but she didn't care. She hurried to the barn.

When she rode back, he was mounted on Fox and waiting. It gave her hope that maybe the barriers of mistrust and anger building between them could be breached, but he acknowledged her only by saying, "Let's ride."

Sheriff Mack was still on duty when they walked in. He looked as tired and spent as Jake and Loreli. Sheriff studied Loreli for a moment, then said, "Miss Winters, I just got a wire from the state treasury people telling me to shut down Sol Diggs's bank. I got another one a little while ago from the Federal marshal in Topeka, telling me to place Sol under arrest."

"So have you?"

"No, not yet, but—" He looked at her as if he didn't quite know what to ask.

"Sheriff, can we talk about all this later?" Loreli asked. "Jake and I want to take a look inside Millie's shop. Maybe we can learn something there."

He tossed the telegrams onto his desk. "Might be a

good idea. It worries me that no one's seen her. Let's go."

Because the sheriff had keys to the doors of all the town's businesses, they had no problem getting inside. The place was dark and quiet. The sheriff found a lamp and lit it. The three of them looked around.

"Does she live here as well?" Loreli asked.

"Yes, in the back," the sheriff answered.

Lighting another lamp, the sheriff picked it up and led the way to the small room in the back. Millie's body lay sprawled across the bed. The pair of black stockings tied around her neck showed she'd been strangled.

The sheriff said sadly, "Guess we found her."

He walked closer to the bed. He shook his head. "What a waste of life," he uttered.

Loreli gasped and closed her eyes for a moment. No, she hadn't liked Millie, but no one deserved to die so violently. Had Trevor done this? The thought made her shudder.

Jake turned his eyes away from Millie's body and asked the sheriff, "Are there any other rooms here? A cellar, a crawl space? Any place where the girls could be hidden away? They're here somewhere. I can feel it."

Loreli could feel it as well, and wondered if love accounted for such strong, eerie sensations.

"There's a small storm cellar out back," Sheriff Mack said.

They quickly searched out the cellar. Large pieces of wood lay across the plywood and tar-paper roof. While Loreli held the lamp, Jake and the sheriff removed them and set them aside.

"Don't remember this wood being here before," Sheriff said.

Jake pulled up the door and called down, "Bebe! Dede! You girls down there?"

Silence.

"Loreli, bring that lamp," Jake said.

Loreli stepped to the edge of the cellar and shined the light down into the black hole. A short flight of earth-carved steps were revealed.

Jake called for the girls again, but only silence echoed.

Under Loreli's lamp Jake climbed down the steps, then took the light from Loreli so he could see the rest of the way down. Jake looked around the shadows for a moment, then his heart stopped. "I found them!"

They were lying side by side on the dirt floor in a corner. Praying they weren't dead, he hurried to them. "They're here!"

Their little bodies looked so lifeless, Jake was shaking as he knelt slowly beside them. Afraid of what he might discover, he touched Dede's cheek. It was warm. "They're alive!"

He shook their shoulders gently. "Be! De! Wake up."

They didn't move. "I think they've been drugged." He had to get them out of here. He looked up at the sheriff and Loreli. "Walt, I'm going to hand them up."

It took them a few minutes to bring the girls to the surface, but once it was accomplished, the men carried them back to the sheriff's office. They laid the girls down on the cot in the lone cell and covered them with a blanket. Their faces were dirty, their nightgowns crusted with mud, but they were alive!

While a tearfully grateful Loreli looked on, Jake examined them to make certain they had no external injuries, such as broken limbs or contusions.

"How long do you think they'll stay sleep?" Sheriff Mack asked.

"No way of knowing what he gave them," Jake said. "Their pulses are strong and they seem to be breathing well, so, we'll just have to wait and see."

Loreli walked over and ran a loving finger down each soft cheek. Paying the grim-faced Jake no mind, Loreli bent down and kissed them on their foreheads. The tears ran freely down her cheeks. Her babies were safe.

"I need to go take care of Millie's body," Sheriff Mack said. "You two going to be all right?"

Both nodded, so the sheriff hurried away.

In the silence that followed, Loreli looked to Jake, but his eyes held no forgiveness. Not that she had been expecting any. His nieces would never have been harmed had Loreli not come into their lives. "I'm sorry, Jake."

"I need to get them home."

She noticed he hadn't said "we." Loreli knew what she needed to do. "I'm—going to be leaving here, Jake. I don't want this to ever happen again."

He met her eyes. "That might be best."

Her heart broke. Deep inside she had been hoping he would say her leaving wouldn't be necessary, but she knew how unrealistic that was. Were the shoe on the other foot, he would be the last person she'd want around her girls in light of today's terrifying events. "I'll—see if I can spend the night at Fanny's."

Jake had to bury everything he felt for her deep inside. He loved her, lord knew he did, but she couldn't stay. He never ever wanted to go through an experience like this again, nor would he allow the girls to. His heart would ache every day they were apart, maybe for the rest of his life, but she had to leave. This was for the best.

Loreli looked into his familiar face and had to set aside how much she would miss him. She ran her eyes over the two precious angels sleeping side by side on the cot. Lord, how could she leave them? "You will explain to the girls?"

He nodded. "I will."

"Keep the furniture. Give away the clothes and whatever else."

"What about the jewelry?"

"Sell it. There're only a few pieces. Buy the girls some horses so they can race."

Loreli took a deep breath to keep the tears away. "Good-bye, Jake."

"Bye, Loreli."

She walked to the door and didn't look back.

In the silence that followed her leaving, it took all Jake had not to go after her, but when he glanced over at the girls, the rage he'd felt for the man who'd endangered them rekindled, making him remember why Trevor Church had come to Kansas in the first place. Jake didn't want to see Loreli Winters ever again.

Loreli spent the night with Fanny. The sheriff stopped by a few days later to let Loreli know that the twins had recovered. The news lifted her mood a bit, but it didn't fill the ache in her heart. She wanted to hold them, kiss them, tell them how sorry she was for what Trevor had done. Warrants had been issued for Trevor's arrest, but the authorities had no clues to his whereabouts.

The next day, Loreli was escorted to the train by

Fanny and the rest of the brides. They'd rallied around her, and she'd been moved by their loving support. Now, as the train whistle blew, it was time for Loreli to say good-bye.

The women shared strong hugs and plenty of tears. "We'll keep an eye on your girls, don't worry," Zora told Loreli. "And we'll all write you so you'll know how they're faring."

"Thanks."

"Do you want to know how Jake's faring?" Fanny said.

"No."

"Now, Loreli, you love that man," Ruby said.

"No, Ruby. I don't want to know and I don't want any of you stirring up trouble with him after I'm gone. If he finds himself a wife—treat her nice, for the girls' sake, okay?"

They nodded.

The conductor yelled out his last call.

Loreli looked at her friends, and the love she felt for them filled her up inside. "I have to go. I'll write soon."

She hurried to board the train. As always, she didn't look back.

Loreli decided to go to Philadelphia. As the train chugged East, she tried not to be overwhelmed by her sadness, but it was difficult. Who knew love could hurt a woman this bad? Who knew it could open up an ache inside one's heart big enough to run a train through? She certainly hadn't. She also had no idea how long it might take her to heal, or if she ever would.

Jake stepped out onto the back porch to check on the girls. Since their return he found himself unable to have them out of his sight for more than a second or two. He supposed his paranoia surrounding their safety would eventually decrease, but he didn't believe it would occur anytime soon.

They were seated on the porch just as they had been when he looked out at them two minutes ago. They'd not taken Loreli's leaving well.

"Do you girls want to ride over and see Aggie and Charlene today?"

"I don't," Bebe said quietly.

Her sister added, "Me neither."

Jake's mustache thinned. For days the house had been as solemn as a tomb. There had been no giggles, no jacks, no jump rope. It was as if Loreli's leaving had drained the life out of everything and everyone she'd touched.

"I think it may be fun. How about we go anyway?"

They nodded but they showed little enthusiasm.

Dede turned and looked up at him, and confessed softly, "We miss her, Uncle Jake."

"I know."

"Do you miss her?" Bebe asked.

Jake didn't lie. "I do, but she didn't want you girls to ever be hurt by any of her friends again. That's why she left."

Bebe asked him, "But why didn't you tell her to stay? We wouldn't have been scared."

Jake had to look away for a moment in order to corral his emotions, then explained, "Sometimes things are more complicated when you get to be an adult, Be. Loreli did what she thought was best."

He sat down between them and gently hugged them close. They put their heads on his chest and snaked their arms around him so they could hold him close as well. He kissed the tops of their heads lovingly. "This is the best way," he whispered.

"But we loved her very, very much." Dede's voice was filled with tears.

Bebe was crying softly as well.

Jake felt the water stinging at his eyes. "I know, sweetheart. We all did."

"Do you think if we told her that, she might come back?" Dede asked.

Jake didn't answer. He kissed them again instead. "How about we get ready to ride over and see Charlene and Aggie."

Both girls were searching his face intently.

"What?" he asked.

"You didn't answer."

He held their eyes and the love he had for them made him give the only answer he could. "She's not coming back, girls, so we need to go on with living."

They dropped their heads, then nodded their understanding.

"All right, Uncle Jake," Bebe finally said.

But Dede didn't reply at all.

It was raining when Loreli's train reached the station in Philadelphia. During the stop back in Chicago, Loreli had wired Olivia as to when she'd be arriving in Philadelphia, so Loreli was not surprised to see her chauffeur, Sgt. Caldwell Collins, Civil War veteran, beside the tracks when she stepped off. He was standing beneath a large open parasol.

When he saw her, he smiled and came forward so she

could quickly duck out of the rain. "Welcome home, Miss Winters."

Collins was always very formal in his dealings with her even after seven years of employment. "How are you, Sgt.?"

"Fine, ma'am. Just fine. Carriage is this way. Once I get you inside, I'll go back and get your luggage."

"There isn't any, so let's go on home."

Sgt. Collins served as both chauffeur and houseman. He knew her well. Loreli could see he had questions, but she said, "Tell you all about it later."

He nodded, then directed her toward the carriage.

After riding around in a rented buggy during the stay in Hanks, and spending the month before that on the hard seat of a Conestoga, the soft leather seats and the finely appointed interior of her own carriage made her sigh contentedly. She was home and once she arrived at the house planned to do nothing but let herself be waited upon. She would bathe in her own tub, sleep in her own bed, have strawberries and chocolate for breakfast if she desired. She wouldn't have to rise before dawn or smell the distinctive fragrance of hogs the moment she took her first waking breath. She was home, or at least the closest thing she had to one.

Olivia met her at the door and the two women shared a great big hug.

"Welcome. How are you?" Olivia said.

Loreli shrugged. "I'm here, that's all I can say."

Olivia, standing with Sgt. Collins, looked to have questions as well. "Well, the new tub I ordered arrived, so your bath's ready and you can eat afterward."

Loreli was tired. "Thanks." She then added with a

small smile, "And since I know the two of you are about to burst, I'll answer all of your questions as soon as I'm washed and have eaten."

They nodded and watched her slowly climb the grand, carved stairway to her second-floor suite.

The bath was glorious, the water hot and full of scented salts.

Olivia had come in to bring her employer some fat hot drying sheets, and set them on the small table beside the big clawfooted tub. Loreli didn't have any family, and neither did the fifty-year-old Olivia, but because the two women had been together now almost fifteen years they shared a close and personal bond. Basking in the tub, Loreli sighed. "I could spend the rest of my life, right here."

Olivia laughed. "And you'd look like a shriveled up apple."

"Well, after what I've been through that's how my heart feels," Loreli replied.

Loreli then told her all that had happened.

When she was done, Olivia was appalled. "And they never found Trevor?"

"No, good thing, though. Jake and I were going to take turns killing him. I hope I never see him again. The sheriff was pretty much convinced Trevor murdered the Tate woman."

Olivia shook her head, "Had I known what he was up to, I'd've brought the paintings myself. I'm so sorry they're gone."

"It's all right. You thought you could trust him, so it isn't your fault. He took advantage of all of us."

"I'm glad the girls were found alive, though. Those poor babies must have been scared to death."

"I'm sure they were. I was so glad Trevor hadn't hurt them."

It still pained her that she hadn't been with them when they awakened. That they'd recovered was all that mattered, however.

"By the way, Olivia, thank you for their beautiful dresses. The twins wanted to give you a kiss for sending them. Give yourself a raise in pay tomorrow."

Olivia smiled. "So, are you going to stay around here, or head off somewhere else?"

"I don't know. I may stick around. I need to lick my wounds a bit."

Olivia's eyes reflected understanding. "I wired the staff at your place in Denver that you'd be here awhile. They send their regards."

"Thanks." Loreli was thinking of letting the staffs go at the other two houses that she owned. They served no purpose really, and she was getting too old to be gallivanting around. Being in Kansas had settled her restless soul in ways she still didn't understand.

Olivia then said, "Answer this one question, and then I'll leave you alone."

"Go ahead."

"Did you love him?"

Loreli went silent for a moment. Jake's face shimmered across her memory. She confessed truthfully, softly, "Yes, I did. Hurts like hell too."

"Love can be painful," Olivia offered sympathetically. "I'll bring your dinner up whenever you're ready."

"Thanks."

"You're welcome."

*   *   *

The month of August slid into September bringing with it cooler temperatures and, in Kansas, preparations for harvest. Jake Reed woke up in the attic room and decided to go back to sleeping in his own room. He was making some progress in his quest to forget Loreli; he was only dreaming about her every other night instead of every night. He looked around the dawn-lit room. Her furniture and clothes were still in residence as if he expected her to walk in at any moment, but she wouldn't. He leaned back against the down pillows. Even though he kept telling himself that her leaving had been best for everyone concerned, he continued to reach for her in the middle of the night. The dreams he had about her were vividly erotic. He'd awakened more mornings than he could count, hard and ready, and that wasn't helping his situation either.

At breakfast he told the girls, "I'm going to move back into my old room. I don't like sleeping so far away from you."

"Can me and Dede have Loreli's room, then?" Bebe asked,

The girls were no more happy with her leaving now than they'd been at first. They were silent, moody, and continued to put Loreli in their prayers. "I don't see why not." Jake hadn't the heart to deny the request. Maybe being around her things would soothe their sadness and feelings of loss.

"Thank you, Uncle Jake," Dede said.

The girls exchanged a smile, the first ones Jake had seen since their recovery.

In mid-September, Loreli received a letter from Trevor. It read:

Dear Lass,

I'm writing you at the Philadelphia house because I know Olivia will forward this to you wherever you are. I know that you're probably still angry at me, but I must write. I'm sorry for all the pain I've caused. I lost my head when Millie refused to let me hide the girls in her shop and threatened to go to the sheriff, so I killed her. A grave mistake. I hope you found the girls in the cellar and that they are well. I am presently in a filthy jail in Brazil. I know it is presumptuous of me to ask, but if you will wire the warden here two hundred in American gold, he will let me out. Please, Loreli. I will die here if you do not answer this plea. You are my only hope.

TC

Loreli wrote down the address where Trevor wanted the money to be sent, then fed the letter to the fire in the grate in her bedroom. Tomorrow she would be turning the address over to the authorities. She'd let *them* come to his rescue.

Chapter 17

J ake fixed his tie, then looked at himself in the mirror. The items Loreli had ordered from Bloomingdale Brothers arrived about six weeks after her departure, and among the roller skates, rugs and such, had been this tie. It was plain enough to satisfy his conservative tastes yet classy enough to be worn on special occasions. He considered this night to be just that. A cousin of Denise Gibson's was visiting from St. Louis, and Art and Denise wanted Jake to come over and have Sunday supper. Jake got the sense that Denise was playing matchmaker, but he was willing to go along with it. He was still looking for a mama for the girls, and the pickings were no better now than they'd been before Loreli came along. Thinking of her name made her golden face shimmer across his mind's eye. He pushed it aside. Going to meet a woman while thinking of another was a recipe for disaster. Jake had already decided that if the cousin were even-tempered, got along with the girls, and was amenable to courting he'd pursue her with the intentions of marrying. The girls needed someone to help them get over Loreli as soon as possible, and he needed to stop putting off the search. Whatever she looked like, he'd marry her. It wouldn't be a love match, but many marriages were built on respect. This one could be too.

The cousin's name was Cordelia Dean. She was twenty-five and a seamstress. She was also a pretty little thing. As the evening progressed, Jake found he liked her wit, and her shy smile. Denise was pleased that the two of them seemed to hit it off so well, and admittedly, Jake was pleased too.

After supper, he sat on the front porch with her while Art and Denise sat out back with the girls.

"Your girls are sweet," Cordelia said. "So well mannered."

"Thanks. I think so too."

"I'll bet not many folks can tell them apart."

"You're right. Took me a few days to be able to."

She smiled. She was dressed in a plain brown dress and the shoes on her feet were buffed but worn. She appeared to be a simple woman.

She said then, "You are aware that Cousin Denise invited you to supper so you could take a look at me, and I could get a look at you?"

Jake dropped his head to hide his smile. "I am."

"Well, I—like what I see."

She turned and met his eyes.

He nodded, "I like what I see, as well."

She turned back. "Tell me about you and Loreli. Denise said she thought you loved her very much."

The question caught him by surprise. It took him a moment to recover. "What do you want to know?"

She shrugged. "Mainly, do you love her still?"

Jake drew in a deep sigh. "I could lie to you and say no, but—"

"It wouldn't be the truth."

"No."

Jake got up and slowly walked over to the edge of the porch. He looked out on the countryside. The day was ending. The sky was showing the dark purple bands of dusk. "Loreli is a very unique woman."

Cordelia added softly, "Beautiful too, from what I'm hearing."

"Yes, she is."

Silence grew between them for a bit, then she said, "I can hear the love in your voice when you speak of her."

"Sorry," Jake said.

"No, you've nothing to apologize for. Every woman wishes to have a man who speaks with such feeling."

Jake had no idea how to respond to that, so he set his attention back on the sky.

"In fact, I'm looking for that kind of man myself—one who has love in his voice when he speaks of me," Cordelia confessed. "I thought you might be him."

Jake turned back to view her. "But I'm not?"

"No. I want to be first in your heart, and right now that position is filled." She shrugged.

Jake respected her honesty, although it never crossed his mind that he would be the one turned down.

"No hard feelings?" Cordelia said.

He chuckled. "No."

"Good, then shall we go and see what everyone else is doing?"

He smiled. "After you."

* * *

In an effort to purge herself of Kansas and the memories she'd left behind, Loreli plunged head-first back into life. She began gambling with her high-powered partners again and accepting their invitations to dinners and to balls. Other gentlemen friends competed with one another to escort her to the theater, and baseball games, and she had a grand time picking the winners. Loreli was burning the candle at both ends, and moving at such a fast pace that she rarely returned home before dawn and never rose from her bed before late afternoon.

One afternoon in early October, Olivia came in with Loreli's breakfast. The tray Olivia was carrying was topped with a small bowl of sugared strawberries and a pot of hot chocolate. Seeing that Loreli was still asleep, Olivia set the tray down as loudly as she could on the small bedside table.

Beneath the sheets, Loreli jumped, then growled, "If you're trying to wake me up, you've succeeded. What time is it?"

"Four in the afternoon," Olivia said disapprovingly.

"Even with my eyes closed I can see your face. What am I in trouble for now?"

"Have you written to Jake?"

"No, and I'm not going to."

Loreli sat up, then dragged the sheets over her waist.

"He has a right to know, Loreli," Olivia told her plainly.

"No, he doesn't."

Loreli was pregnant. Had been for a good four months now, according to the doctor. She could have easily prevented the need for this argument had she used her sponges during those passionate nights, but she hadn't—because, frankly, she'd wanted his child. She wanted something to remind her of just how much she'd loved him, a piece of him that would be with her for a lifetime. Their child. Granted, at her age her body was not happy with the changes it was undergoing, but she was prepared to endure.

"It's not good for the baby if you're out until all hours of the night."

"Olivia, I'm just out playing cards, not kicking up my legs on stage. Gambling is a very sedentary life."

"And you're not drinking?"

"No."

"So when are you going to tell Jake?"

"Clean out your ears, old friend. I am not telling him. The last thing I need is him running here offering to make me an honest woman. I don't want the girls hurt again, and he doesn't love me, so I'm not marrying him."

"Shouldn't he be allowed to make that choice for himself?"

"He's a Kansas farmer, Olivia. He will walk here to give this child his name, if he finds out. He's that decent of a man."

"All the more reason to let him know."

"No." Loreli reached for the tray.

"It's his child too."

"Possession is nine-tenths of the law."

Olivia sighed. "All right, be stubborn. You could be happy, you know."

"I'm happy now."

Olivia shook her head, then exited the room, leaving Loreli alone.

In reality, Loreli was happy. She had a roof over her

head, materially she lacked for nothing, and she was carrying a life. Society may care that she didn't have a husband, but the free-thinking Loreli saw nothing wrong with raising her child alone. Yes, having Jake at her side would be the sugar on the strawberries, but life seldom gives anyone everything they desire, especially her. But all the blessings she now possessed more than made up for the bad times of the past. As always, though, her eyes were set firmly on the future, a future that held her child, Jake's child.

That evening, Loreli dressed to go out. She was having a quiet supper with a friend. His name was Madison Nance and he was one of the wealthiest men of color in the state of Pennsylvania. He'd made half of his fortune in lumber and the other half at the card table. He and Loreli had been friends for years, and whenever she was in town, they always got together. He'd sent his invite around to her house a few days before and she was looking forward to see him again.

Dressed in a beautiful dark blue gown, Loreli grabbed the matching velvet cloak and went downstairs to await Madison's driver. To her surprise, Madison arrived at the door instead.

Her eyes lit up upon seeing his handsome face, and he had the glow of welcome in his own eyes. Sgt. Collins smiled and stepped back out of the way.

Madison gave her a hug, then a kiss on the cheek, "How are you, princess?"

"I'm well."

Had Loreli ever considered taking a husband, Madison might have been a candidate. He was charming, articulate, and well mannered, but he loved money more than he could love any woman, and not even Loreli could compete with such a cold mistress.

Madison extended his arm. "Shall we go?"

Loreli took his arm. She then told Sgt. Collins, "I'll see you later."

He nodded. "You too, but make sure you get back here at a reasonable time. That baby needs rest."

Loreli was so stunned, she couldn't move.

Madison appeared stunned too. "Baby?"

Sgt. Collins nodded, then added, "See if you can't convince her to tell the father he has a child on the way. This nonsense has gone on long enough."

Loreli was speechless. Her eyes wide, she stared at the sergeant as if she'd never seen him before.

He took advantage of her stupor to add, "And if you fire me, so be it. Babies need their daddies."

Madison began chuckling. "Who is the father, Sgt.?"

"A farmer she met in Kansas. Name's Jake Reed."

Madison looked at Loreli. "A farmer? This is going to be a much more interesting dinner than I thought."

"Shut up," she snarled. "Let's go."

Still shooting daggers at Sgt. Collins, Loreli told her houseman, "I'll deal with you when I get back."

He just smiled, and said, "Yes, ma'am."

Madison was laughing.

Loreli stormed out.

Madison Nance employed one of the best chefs in the city and the evening's dinner of quail and vegetables was excellently prepared. After the maid removed the empty plates, he and Loreli retreated to his lavish study and she took a seat on the fine leather couch. He poured himself a small brandy. "Do you want one?"

"No, it isn't good for the baby."

He examined her for a moment, then picked up his snifter and sat down on a chair opposite her. The fire in the grate made the room warm, and the lit lamps added to the soft atmosphere. "So, tell me about this farmer."

"I'm going to fire that old soldier the minute I get back."

He toasted her with his glass. "No you're not. You care a lot about that old man. He's obviously deeply concerned about you."

"He had no right."

Madison shrugged. "Maybe, but the cat's out of the bag now. So, tell me."

"Nothing to tell. His name's Jake Reed, and I'm carrying his child."

"Can't say that I'm pleased. I wanted your children to be mine."

Loreli smiled. "You already have children. Their names are double eagles and treasury notes."

He toasted her again. "Touché."

Then he said, "Seriously now. I've been trying to get you to marry me for years, and now I find out that not only is Trevor Church ahead of me in the line to your heart, but I'm behind a farmer as well?"

She chuckled.

"What's he grow?" Madison asked.

"Corn, and he raises hogs."

"You're pregnant by a hog farmer?"

"Yes, I am."

"He must be some man."

"He is."

"Do you love him?"

She met Madison's eyes, then looked away. "I do, but he doesn't love me."

"Is he insane? Loreli, if you're carrying his child, that means you made a conscious decision not to take any precautions. You're too savvy for this baby to have been an accident."

She didn't respond.

"So, I guess I've answered my own question: you love him *very* much."

Loreli's mind gently sailed back to her memories of Kansas. She saw Jake on the porch, and the girls, *her girls,* ripping and running through the day. Lord, she missed them. "Like I said, he doesn't love me." She told him the story of all that had happened to her while she was in Kansas. "I never did like Church," Madison said. "Glad the twins were found safe."

"So were we."

"So why don't you want Reed to know about his child?"

"I don't want him forced into marrying me. What if I did marry him and someone else from my life shows up with bad intentions?"

Madison shook his head. "What if they don't? You'll have spent your entire life without because you're worried about a scenario that may never come to be."

"So, you think it was silly of me to leave?"

"Hell, no. Your instincts were right. What if Trevor had returned and taken the girls again? You said no one knew where he was."

"We didn't," Loreli said.

"Well, with you gone, there would have been no reason

for him to stay there, but he's no threat anymore, princess. Write to your farmer and tell him about the child. Fathers are very important. I'd not be the person I am today had my old man not been in my life. Why am I encouraging another man's suit?"

Loreli grinned. "Could it be because you're such a good friend?"

He shrugged. "Could be. I think I'm going to send you home now. I feel the need to get drunk."

She stood. "Okay."

He held her eyes, then said seriously, "Whatever you decide, know that I'll be here for you and the child, no matter what."

"I know." She walked over and kissed him on the cheek. "Good night, Madison."

"Good night, princess."

After she left, Madison poured himself a drink, then moved over to his large mahogany desk. He opened a drawer and withdrew some stationary. Taking up a pen, he began to write.

The girls were asleep, and Jake was enjoying the dark and the solitude. November nights were cold in Kansas, so he threw more wood onto the fire in his room and sat down to read the day's mail. A few pieces were from the Knights of Labor and the Republican party, but he set those aside for later. He instead picked up the fancy envelope that had been waiting for him along with the rest of his mail at the post office in town. The return address showed it had been sent by a man named Madison Nance in Philadelphia. The name wasn't familiar. A curious Jake opened it.

Dear Mr. Reed,

I hope this note finds you and the girls well. Loreli will undoubtedly boil me in oil when she learns I've written to you, but I feel it is the right and proper thing to do. Loreli is carrying your child. Those of us here who know her and love her are concerned that she intends to keep this knowledge from you. I have no idea how you will react to this surprising news, but I do know that she loves you very much. If you wish to come to Philadelphia to see about this matter, please feel free to contact me at the address above. My house and staff will be open to you and the twins for as long as may be needed.

Sincerely,
Madison Nance

Jake set the letter aside. Admittedly, he didn't know how to feel. On one level he was angry that he had to learn about the upcoming birth of his child from a complete stranger, but on another level, Jake wanted to turn cartwheels and shout with joy. A child! Their child! He could only wonder what was going through her mind. Was she ashamed, elated, angry? He would have no way of knowing until he talked with her. And talk with her, he would. Jake took out some paper so he could write back to this mysterious Madison Nance. Jake couldn't wait to see the look on Loreli's face when he showed up at her front door.

Loreli's annual holiday party was always well attended and tonight's affair was no exception. Even though she'd pared at least sixty people from this year's invitation list, the interior of her house was still packed. Among the guests were the well known, and the unknown. Captains of industry rubbed shoulders with cabbies; dowagers of all races sat together and talked because at Loreli's parties no one cared. There was dancing downstairs in the ballroom, and enough food in the solarium to feed an army. There were strolling musicians and nattily dressed waiters carrying trays topped with fine canapés and tasty appetizers.

Loreli, dressed in her signature gold gown, stood by the food table greeting guests. At her side stood Madison Nance. He'd won the privilege of being her escort tonight by being the highest bidder. Loreli had come up with the idea of auctioning off the escort position a few years ago. The money went to one of her many charities, and her gentleman friends had a ball trying to outbid each other.

As Loreli continued to smile and encourage her guests to sample the food, she told Madison, "I really enjoy throwing this party every year."

"It shows."

She grinned. "How about a dance?"

"Sure, why not?"

They made their way through the crush, and headed downstairs to the equally crowded dance floor. They arrived just in time to join in on a slow waltz. Loreli placed her hand in his and Madison led her expertly around the floor. Loreli was just about to ask Madison if he had information on a particular stock she was interested in when someone behind her tapped her on the shoulder. She turned, and as her eyes met Jake's they widened. Recognition filled her with such an overwhelming rush of emotion, she sank to the floor like a stone.

When her eyes opened again, Loreli was lying on the

rose-colored chaise in her bedroom, and Olivia was standing over her with worry lining her brown face. "Just lie still."

Loreli could now feel the damp cloth on her head. It was clammy so she took it off and handed it to Olivia. "What happened?"

"You fainted."

"I never faint."

"Well, you did."

Then Loreli remembered. Jake! She bolted upright.

Olivia stayed her gently, "Not so fast."

"Is he really here?"

Olivia smiled. "Appears that way."

"Is the party still going?"

"Yes, Madison calmed everyone."

"Good."

Olivia then asked, "Are you ready to see him now? He's very worried."

"Where is he?"

"On the other side of the door."

Loreli rose from the chaise. "I'm as ready as I'll ever be, I suppose."

Loreli didn't think it fair of him to show up this way. She'd wanted to be prepared and in control of the situation. Instead she'd fainted, something she'd never done before.

Olivia opened the door. "You may come in now, Mr. Reed."

He entered. His eyes met Loreli's. Neither of them noticed the housekeeper's soundless exit.

Jake forced himself to stay where he was. Seeing Loreli for the first time in months reaffirmed just how much he'd missed her, but there were matters and issues that had to be discussed before he and she could discuss themselves. "Are you all right? Never knew you to be the fainting type."

"I'm fine. Just more surprised than I've been in a while, I suppose. Why'd you come?"

"Talk to you about the baby."

That caught her by surprise. "How'd you find out?"

"Friend of yours wrote to me. Said telling me was the right and proper thing to do."

Loreli looked away from the emotion she could see in his eyes. "I didn't write you because I didn't want to burden you with a wife you were forced to marry."

"I appreciate that, but I'm old enough to make decisions for myself, Loreli."

She winced under his withering tone.

"I want to help raise my child, and I want his mother in bed beside me at night. I want to see her face first thing in the morning, even if I argue with her all day. I want to hold her and love her until death do us part."

Surprised again, she turned to face him.

"Marry me, Loreli Winters. Not because of the baby but because of how I feel about you."

Tears ran down Loreli's cheeks.

Jake walked over to her and pulled her into his arms.

As they held each other tight, she whispered, "Oh, Jake. I've missed you and the girls so much. . . ."

He touched his lips to the top of her hair, then raised her chin so he could look into her eyes. The kiss he gave her showed how much he'd missed her as well. It was passionate, welcoming, and brimming with love.

When the kiss ended, he looked down into her tear-bright eyes and said, "I'm still waiting for an answer."

"To what?"

He acted amazed. "I just asked you to marry me, woman!"

She grinned. "The answer is yes."

"Good."

He traced her lips with his finger. "Dreamt about this mouth many nights."

"Just my mouth?" she teased.

"Oh, other parts were there too, believe me," he teased back.

She leaned up and kissed him. "And I can't wait to show them to you."

He threw back his head and laughed. "Outrageous as ever."

She smiled. "Well, since you're so hell bent upon making me an honest woman, how about we go downstairs and get married right now?"

"How?"

"There are at least six or seven judges downstairs. We can take our pick."

Jake held her in the circle of his arms. "You're on. The sooner we become man and wife, the sooner I can sneak you off somewhere and make love to you."

Loreli moved her body softly against his and said in a sultry, playful voice, "We don't have to sneak off. We can do that right here."

Jake's blood rushed hot and hard. "To the door, Loreli. Your guests won't be happy if I have you up here for the rest of the night, so march."

She pouted.

He gave her a tender swat on the butt. "Fast woman."

* * *

Downstairs the fast woman and the hog farmer from Kansas were married under the cheering adoration of three hundred of Loreli's closest friends. Sgt. Collins gave her away, and Madison stood up with Jake.

After the congratulations tapered off a bit, Jake said to Loreli, "Do you want to see the girls now?"

She stilled. "Where are they?"

"At a friend's home nearby."

"They're here in Philadelphia?"

He grinned. "Yes, Mrs. Reed, they are. They're probably asleep, but I don't think they'll mind being awakened."

Loreli began to cry again. Her hands came to her mouth to hold in all the emotion. "Oh, Jake."

He had love in his eyes and voice as he said, "Come on. You can cry on the way."

Loreli stopped Madison on their way out. "I have to leave for a little while. Will you keep an eye on things?"

He nodded. "Sure will." He winked at Jake and walked off to attend to his hosting duties.

Outside, Loreli pulled her cloak tighter against the cold air. Conveyances of all kinds and classes lined both sides of the street for as far as the eye could see. Her neighbors once complained about all the noise and commotion that went with her annual ball, but since she'd started adding their names to the guest list, all the finger-waving and griping had stopped. "How are we getting to your friend's home?" Loreli asked, shivering a bit. The thin gold dress had not been made for winter nights.

Jake looked up the street. "Here comes the coach now."

Loreli recognized Madison's coach and coachman at once. "This is nice of Madison to lend you his coach."

"Yes, it is."

Jake wondered how long it would take her to figure out that Madison was the author of the letter that brought Jake to Philadelphia. He chuckled inwardly. She was probably going to throw a fit once she did.

The coach stopped in front of Madison's large estate. "Why are we stopping here?" Loreli asked in a puzzled voice.

Jake made his way to the door. "This is where the girls are."

Then she got it. "Madison was the one, wasn't he?"

Jake smiled. "Yes."

"That traitor."

But she couldn't be angry, not now. His actions had brought her and Jake back together. Maybe she'd reward him by naming her child after him if Jake didn't mind.

Jake stood outside in the wind. He had the doorknob in his hand. "You coming or not?" he asked gently.

"Yes," and she bounded up the steps.

The girls were asleep in an upstairs bedroom. Loreli carefully opened the door so she and Jake could tiptoe in. The sight of their sleeping faces framed in the light from the hall put tears in Loreli's eyes. She felt as if she had turned into the cryingest woman in the world, but she wiped the waterworks away and walked over to the big bed they were sharing. She gave each soft brown cheek a tender caress, then bent to kiss their foreheads lovingly. Behind her, Jake lit a lamp and turned it down very low so that there was just enough illumination to see by. Loreli knelt by the bed, and with eyes filled with awe she watched them sleep. She hadn't had the opportunity to calm their fears after Trevor's act of cowardice, but from now on, she'd be there every time anything or anybody made them afraid. She stroked Dede's cheek. Loreli could see the chain of the magic locket around her neck. Dede's eyes opened sleepily. When she saw Loreli, she smiled. "I told Uncle Jake you'd come back if he asked you to."

Loreli pulled her up into her arms and held her close against her heart.

"We missed you so," Dede whispered.

"I missed you and your sister, too, pumpkin."

Bebe awakened then, and when she saw Loreli her eyes went wide, and she yelled happily, "Loreli!"

She launched herself at Loreli like an ecstatic kitten and soon they were all rolling around on the bed, laughing and giggling. Loreli couldn't remember being this happy ever. When calm returned, Loreli listened as the girls competed to tell her all that had gone on since they'd last been together.

"I didn't win the Circle Race," Bebe said. "I came in fifth. De came in third."

Loreli turned to Dede. "You came in third!"

"Yep. Me and Sapphire."

"Who's Sapphire."

"My horse. Uncle Jake bought her for me after you left. She's a real nice horse, Loreli."

"I'll bet she is." *Dede came in third!* An amazed Loreli looked to Jake. He simply smiled. "So did Anthony Diggs win again?"

"No, he had to sell his horse," Bebe answered.

"Why?"

"Aggie said his father got behind on his mortgage," Bebe told her.

"I see." Loreli had forgotten all about the greedy Sol Diggs and how she'd brought him down.

"Anthony and his daddy worked for Carrie's daddy during harvest," Dede added.

Loreli once again swung her amazed eyes to Jake. *Sol Diggs forced to work for Matt Peterson!*

"The Lord works in mysterious ways," Jake replied.

Loreli guessed so.

Loreli let herself enjoy the company of the girls for over an hour, then she made them hop back beneath their quilts. "I'll see you two in the morning, okay?"

Both girls smiled sleepily.

Jake and Loreli gave the girls good-night kisses, then Jake doused the lamp and quietly followed Loreli out into the hall.

As the newlyweds stood in the silence just looking at each other, Loreli knew that if someone had told her she'd fall in love with, and marry, a hog farmer, she would have taken them to court for slander. But now, as he pulled her into his arms and held her against his strong chest, she wanted to proclaim her good fortune to the world. Loreli Winters had a man, a *good* man, and she didn't care who knew it!

Author's Note

A few years ago, my cousin Michelle Bivens asked if I would do a story with a twist. She wanted an experienced heroine and an inexperienced hero. I found the idea intriguing but at the time there were no heroines in my company of characters able to pull off such a role. Until Loreli. Her appearances in *Topaz* and, more recently, *Always and Forever* won the hearts of many fans. Those appearances also generated a lot of mail asking that she be given a book of her own, and as a result, the story of Jake and Loreli was born. I hope you enjoyed it.

The influence of labor unions, like the Knights of Labor, would continue to rise as the nineteenth century moved into the twentieth century. In 1925, A. Phillip Randolph, the founding president of the Brotherhood of Sleeping Car Porters, began organizing among Pullman's Black porters. The Brotherhood won its first major contract with the Pullman company in 1937, and would go on to become America's strongest and most successful Black trade union. I learned a lot researching this topic, so if I piqued your interest, here are some of the sources I consulted.

A Long Hard Journey: The Story of the Pullman Porter, Patricia and Frederick McKissack, Walker Publishing, New York, 1989.

Beyond Labor's Veil: The Culture of the Knights of Labor, Robert E. Weir, Pennsylvania State University Press, Pennsylvania, 1996.

Negro Thought in America, 1880–1915: Racial Ideologies in the Age of Booker T. Washington, August Meir, Ann Arbor, 1963.

"The Negro in the Populist Movement," Jack Abromowitz, *Journal of Negro History*, Vol. 38, 1953.

I'd like to take a moment to thank some people for their help and love. Ava and Gloria are at the top of the list for putting together another outstanding PJ party. Seventy plus participants came from as far north as Minnesota and as far west as San Diego, and we had a great time! Thanks also to the ladies from the Peters Library African American Book Club: Shirley, Petula, Charlotte and Joan for volunteering their time to help the PJ party run smoothly. Next PJ party is scheduled for Spring of 03.

I owe a big big shout-out to Shareeta, Linda, Angie, and Cheryl, of the Minga Suma Book Club in LA for sponsoring my first trip to the Left Coast, and for showing me a banging time. Thanks also to the great folks at Eso Won books for hosting the book signing.

In closing, I want to express my humblest thanks to all the book clubs across the country who've sponsored me and or my books. The African-American community is, in many ways, a word of mouth community, and you ladies and gents have been talking me up in such marvelous ways that women and men who never read romances in the past are now Beverly Jenkins fans. I appreciate the support. For those fans who've been with me since the beginning, well, you all know how much I love you, so I'll just say, thanks again. I have the greatest fans in the world. Until next time, everybody stay strong and keep reading.

BJ

The nights may be getting cooler, but Avon Romances are _____ heating things up! _____

THE BRIDE BED by Linda Needham
An Avon Romantic Treasure

The king has decreed that his loyal servant, Lord Alex de Monteneau, will rule the Lady Talia's lands and determine whom the fiery maiden will wed. But Alex is shocked to discover that there can be only one perfect husband for the tempting beauty . . . himself!

$\sim$

GETTING HER MAN by Michele Albert
An Avon Contemporary Romance

Private Investigator Diana Belmaine always gets her man—and Jack Austin is no exception. So if this clever thief thinks he can distract her with his gorgeous smile and obvious charms, not to mention deep lingering kisses . . . he may be right!

$\sim$

ALL MY DESIRE by Margaret Moore
An Avon Romance

Seeking vengeance on the lord who robbed him of his birthright, Sir Alexander DeFrouchette sets out to steal his enemy's bride . . . and carries off the wrong lady! But the fiery Lady Isabelle refuses to be any man's prisoner . . . no matter how powerfully he inflames her passion . . .

$\sim$

CHEROKEE WARRIORS: THE LOVER by Genell Dellin
An Avon Romance

Susanna Copeland needs a groom. The notorious Cherokee Eagle Jack Sixkiller agrees to pose as her husband, but the good-looking rebel is enjoying the ruse far too much. And now having this infuriatingly sexy lover at her side is starting to feel shockingly right!